$10.00

D0408497

Heart of the Storm

PATRICIA WRIGHT

Heart of the

Storm

1980

Doubleday & Company, Inc., Garden City, New York

ISBN: 0-385-14232-3
Library of Congress Catalog Card Number 78-22775
Copyright © 1979 by Patricia Wright

Heart of the Storm

Chapter One

Faye Ludlow stood by her bedroom window, thinking that there should be a law against dressing for dinner while the sun still shone. Gold haze slanted across the valley, deepening hollows and touching laced trees with light, sifting warmth into the timber and brick of Reydenham Manor. Even in stillness, Faye could smell the sea, hidden to the south by a line of hills: when winter storms roared up the English Channel the manor windows filmed with salt and afterwards old Gabriel, the gardener, had to climb over the roof cementing back fallen tiles.

You'll stand through a few storms yet though, thought Faye, leaning out and running her hands over bricks which had been fired four hundred years before. She smiled to herself and felt her depression ease; although she had come to Reydenham as a bride only the year before, already she loved it as if it were her own inheritance.

"Mr. Ludlow is asking whether you are ready, madam?"

Faye turned guiltily. "Am I late?"

"No, madam." Her maid, Susan, closed her lips tightly. She disapproved of husbands who could not wait until a lady was looking her best, and of wives who leaned out of windows when formally dressed for dinner.

Faye laughed at the censure in her voice and glanced in the mirror. "There's not even the faintest of Channel breezes to blow a hair out of place today!" For all her brave words, she regarded her image doubtfully, she was too recently entered on grandeur to feel at ease in the clinging gown which fashion decreed even for country dinner parties in the year 1938. This time last year she had made her own dresses from material bought at the local draper's. She stared a moment longer, then crinkled her nose defiantly and went to open the door herself.

"My dear sir! This is a surprise! You thought I would be late again, didn't you?" She stood on tiptoe and kissed him carefully;

ten minutes before their guests arrived was no time for smeared lipstick.

"No, I was sure you would not." His tone recalled his anger when she had kept him waiting the night before, but his eyes were smiling. "I wanted to talk to you before we went down." He nodded to Susan. "You can go now, clear up later."

"What is it?" Faye could tell her maid's outrage from the way Susan came as close as she dared to slamming the door; she would make her mistress uncomfortable for days now. "Why couldn't it wait until tomorrow?"

Rupert Ludlow went over and stood looking out of the window as his wife had done a few minutes before. The stillness was already gone; the Channel coast changed its moods almost between one breath and the next. Dry grass whispering, rooks calling, a hollow glaze spreading over sky which had been clear only minutes before. There would be a full gale before midnight, he decided. He closed the window with a snap, and turned. "It is about one of our guests. Castellan, the one coming with the Brinklows, do you remember?"

"I wrote a card for him." Faye tried not to hear her instinctive defensiveness, the fear she had unwittingly made some blunder. "I don't think I know—"

"Of course you don't know him! He's a jumped-up Jew-boy banker from the East End of London," said Rupert impatiently. "But stinking rich, they say. I've altered the cards to put him beside you, though God knows what some of our friends will think."

"Why?" Precedence at dinner was nearly sacred.

Rupert frowned. Faye's direct candor was part of the reason why he had fallen in love with a girl whom his mother did not scruple to describe as cheap; he found it a less desirable quality in his wife. "I told you, the fellow is rich, but out of a back slum. Pay him all the attention you can, flatter him, anything. I've fixed with Ralph Brinklow that he'll take the Grattans home so I can talk business with Castellan while he waits."

"Business? You mean you want me to—" Faye broke off. Rupert wanted her to fatten a guest ready for plucking; she might lack social experience, but her father was a lawyer and she had heard man's varied deceits discussed since she was a child. "What sort of business?" she said at last.

Rupert turned to the window again, to gray dusk and rising

wind. "Money, of course. Reydenham swallows it up, or didn't you know?"

"I've kept house for my father on four pounds a week. I know about money," Faye replied quietly. "I know also that at Reydenham we have enough."

"No, listen, Faye." He grasped her shoulders impatiently. "We have enough to live quietly and sell a field if we can't pay the bills. My God, farming has lost money for years and will go on that way, so long as we let half the world's produce into the country at prices we cannot match! Well, I'm not going to sell Reydenham piece by piece, chuck my inheritance away to pay household bills. It is mine, and one day will belong to Christopher." They both smiled involuntarily at the thought of tiny Christopher tucked up in his cot.

"How will borrowing help? You only lose more in fees and interest." Faye spoke with absolute certainty, she had grown up among deeds and obligations and other men's debts.

"You know how the Ludlows built up Reydenham?" She nodded, tales of bygone Ludlows who had grown rich from piracy were told all over east Kent. "Well, I wish to God I could do the same but I've hit on something almost as certain." He smiled suddenly and became again the Rupert she loved so much; eyes snapping, head thrown back, thinking of his pirate ancestors. "You know that slipway at Dover?"

Faye nodded again, mystified. Reydenham was four miles from Dover, tucked into one of the valleys hidden behind its chalk cliffs, the old slipway beside the Prince of Wales pier all that was left of generations of Ludlows who had fought and traded in the rich and dangerous waters of the English Channel.

"I haven't time to explain now, but a friend of mine has a capital idea for making money there, using the Ludlow name to sell a new kind of boat. I only need four or five thousand pounds to get started, but I might as well whistle for it unless I'm willing to sell some land." He scowled suddenly. "And that I'll not do."

"No," said Faye softly. "Not Reydenham."

He kissed her then, deep and smeary with lipstick. "Only a year, yet already it's in your bones. What do you think I would feel if after four hundred years I'm the Ludlow to lose it? This fellow Castellan could be providential if you play your cards right; he'll not be cheated, I promise. Think of it, Faye! Ludlows back at sea and making their fortune again! Give me a few years and I'll have Reydenham as well set as ever it was on the profits of privateering."

She held him tightly, marveling again how Rupert Ludlow, ten years her senior and with the charm and position to choose a wife wherever he wished, had chosen her. His hands were sliding from back to thigh, her body already softly yielding, when the sound of tires on the gravel below jerked them apart, senses spinning. As she turned, Faye caught sight of herself in the mirror and laughed shakily. "My love . . . our guests arriving and we both look like clowns with lipstick. Would that we could go down like this and shock their starchy hearts." She scrubbed hastily at her face with a towel and threw another at him. "Tell me quickly, then. What do you want me to do?"

"Talk about the slip, how we are thinking of building boats there again. Get him interested, make him feel he's getting private information about a good thing, so when I talk to him he'll feel he's lucky to be asked to invest. If you're clever enough, he may even approach me, a fellow like that fattens on inside tips. He won't expect you to know much about it, and coming from you it will seem more like—"

"More like the truth?" said Faye evenly. "Last time I saw the place, the roof was falling in and children were picnicking on the slipway." She thought now, but would not let herself think, that perhaps he had been kissing her doubts, not her. As she had learned, Rupert possessed a will of steel where Reydenham was concerned.

"Faye, you must do this for me. I'll not forgive you if you turn prude on me now. Good God, I'm not intending to cheat the man, and moneylending is his business after all." He grinned unexpectedly. "And that sounds as arrogant as hell, you don't need to tell me! It's true though, a few thousand pounds now and it will become a boatyard again with profits all round, I swear it." He put his fingers under her chin and kissed her gently. "This damned lipstick, how can you look at me so, and expect me not to kiss you?"

Faye laughed and went ahead of him down the stairs, dark oak and the odd-angled lines of the manor welcoming her as she passed. The center and front of the house were brick and stone, where prosperous Ludlows had added rooms and chimneys as the fancy took them, the back still ancient weather boarding from the farmhouse it once had been. Faye smiled to herself as she went to greet her guests, thinking that Reydenham was like the Ludlows themselves, all grace and polish, until one day you found that behind their façade neither was what you thought at all.

She had lived through miseries of awkwardness this past year, afraid of disgracing the Ludlows and hopelessly ill at ease with the kind of conversation which was instinctive to Rupert's acquaintance. With him alone she could be herself, and the binding between them had become tighter because of it; in a collection of strangers she appeared dull and stupid, imagining shaken heads and lifted eyebrows behind her back, as Rupert's friends wondered what he could have seen in such an outsider to make her mistress of Reydenham.

Tonight, she did at least know most of the people in the room, was able to weave conversation into something more than shifting faces, whose endless unfamiliarity had so daunted her during the early weeks of her marriage. Rupert knew every family of consequence in east Kent, was connected with so many people whose unexplained relationships she could not grasp, that she still lived in dread of causing offense with her ignorance. She had stayed as silent as she could while she learned what she must learn; now, people seemed to take it for granted that she had nothing of interest to say.

"Faye!" Her mother-in-law called from her seat by the fire. "Come here!"

Faye crossed the room, sensing amusement at such peremptory summons, her temper rising at the way Mrs. Ludlow still treated her as if Rupert had hired a paid dependent. She wished she had the wit to turn spite aside with laughter, and instead found herself mumbling some inquiry into her mother-in-law's health and comfort.

"No, I'm not comfortable, and if you had my health you would know better than to expect it," snapped Mrs. Ludlow. "Why is the fire not properly made up?"

"Rupert doesn't like a fire in summer, and it's been such a lovely day. Shall I put on another log for you?"

"When I am here, a proper fire is always kept burning, and September is not summer," she replied with unanswerable logic.

"Not yourself, girl, call Phipps," she added sharply as Faye instinctively turned to the hearth.

"Let me," said one of the guests hastily. "If it is too heavy for you, it must also be too heavy for your butler." He indicated frail old Phipps trying to catch her eye to indicate that dinner was ready.

She was grateful for the suggestion that it was concern which prompted her mother-in-law's censure, fingers trembling as she tried to hide confusion by sipping sherry.

"You are spilling it," said Mrs. Ludlow in a tone of goaded patience, adding, "Dear Faye has only recently joined the family."

The man turned from settling a log to his satisfaction, and bowed slightly. "I'm afraid I am here somewhat under false pretenses. John Castellan, Mrs. Ludlow. I am staying with the Brinklows and your husband kindly invited me to accompany them."

Faye stammered something in reply, confusion increased by meeting the man whose wallet she was supposed to ease open. Rupert saw nothing wrong in using whatever methods seemed most likely to save Reydenham, since he intended no dishonesty and also was a man who needed the excitement of risk if his life was to be completely enjoyable. Pirate ancestors have some disadvantages, thought Faye, smiling, but I cannot complain when his gambler's instincts led him to marry me, simply because he wanted to. Yet without Rupert to sweep doubt aside, she found the part he intended her to play intolerable, now she was faced with the intended victim.

He was dark, his features thin-boned above a long, sensitive mouth. He looked neither Jewish nor recently arrived from a back slum, and irrationally this fanned Faye's anger as she realized how much easier it had seemed to defraud him when he had been thus casually labeled. "I understand I am escorting you in to dinner," he said when she remained tongue-tied. "I wish you would tell me what this means before we go in." He drew her over to the carved Ludlow coat of arms above the stone entry: two galleons on heraldic waves, with a crest of crossed swords and the words *tiempo de empezar.*

"Time . . . it is time to begin." Faye's voice wavered, her eyes fixed on her glass, then she drank defiantly and looked up. "It is Spanish. The first Ludlow was an Elizabethan privateer, and he is meant to have said that whenever he had picked a victim to attack." She wondered whether Rupert had said it as he watched this man cross his threshold.

Castellan laughed and intercepted a decanter to refill her glass. "*Sirvase usted entrar?* Will you walk into my parlor? said the spider to the fly. It is a better motto than most of the pious hopes one sees."

"You knew what it meant all the time," said Faye accusingly. "You speak Spanish."

"It was as good a way as any of taking us both away from an uncomfortable situation," he observed blandly. "I think your butler is desperate to announce dinner if you will glance in his direction."

The dining room of Reydenham Manor was its finest room, shown to the public on Thursday afternoons, if they had the courage to pull the clanging brass bell in the porch and demand admission. The paneling was slightly waved from sixteenth-century hand tools, diamond-picked with generations of polish, the ceiling plastered in designs of corn and Kentish flowers, no foreign fancies for Ludlows. The great open fireplace was backed by a cast-iron slab showing sheep and branched beeches in craftsman's detail, set against hills still recognizable as those around Reydenham valley; as rising wind shuddered gently on the walls outside, glowing candles and starched linen heightened the feeling of comfort and well-being within.

The meal seemed interminable to Faye, laboring to talk to deaf old Colonel Grattan on her right, while convincing herself that it was impossible to introduce the subject of boatyards to Castellan on her left.

This was certainly untrue; he talked lightly on a number of subjects, willing to follow whatever lead she gave him, and plainly puzzled when her unease failed to subside. Rupert's approving glances down the table only added to her discomfort: he would never believe any excuses she offered when the task he set her had clearly been even simpler than he expected.

She found herself telling Castellan of her life in Canterbury before she married, a topic Rupert's friends always tactfully avoided. He did not seem surprised and she immediately found it easier to believe that silver and butlers were as strange to him as they were to her, although his assurance was complete, nothing betrayed by clothes or accent. He was in his middle thirties, she decided, but despite his courtesy to her, the stranger who was John Castellan told her nothing of himself. "You are encouraging me in everything I have been told I must not do!" she said at last. "Talk about myself, bore my guests, and recall habits I have left behind, like making up the fire myself."

He smiled slightly. "How others want us to behave is nearly always best forgotten, and very dull besides. Tell me, were you ever bored in Canterbury?"

"Oh, no, you see, I . . . You are doing it again!"

"You will need at least three county dinners to unlearn the bad habits I have taught you tonight," he agreed. "Speak of yourself and be damned to them all for once, why not?" He glanced down the table. "I know none of these people and neither do you, although you have learned their names and sweated over their relationships. I don't want to hear about partridge shooting or the prospects for Newmarket and you couldn't tell me if I did."

She laughed. "You are an unexpected guest, Mr. Castellan! What was that Spanish phrase you quoted?"

"*Sirvase usted entrar?*"

She nodded. "Perhaps it tells as much about you as ours does about the Ludlows. I think you are good at getting people to walk where you want them, and tell what you want to know."

"There's nothing for it but a whole succession of county gatherings, Mrs. Ludlow. If you are going to start chipping your guests' characters from behind their masks, only a course in extreme triviality will restore you to grace." He saw her face change at his words, every sense living where before he had seen only part of her kindled. Now, the whole of her was intent in hazel eyes, in curving, joyful mouth, and impatient gesture thrusting at coiled hair so it began to slip into disorder. "What have I said to hurt you?" he said gently. She was not hurt, he knew, but for an instant whole, each lack made good, and as he watched he saw life ebb again.

She shook her head, embers dying into flaked ash. "I'm sorry, but that was one door I did not want opened." She spread her hands on dark wood, supple, square-fingered, and strongly shaped. "Long after I have learned all I must learn, my hands will betray me. Before I married Rupert I was a stone carver in the cathedral at Canterbury; they don't know it, but I think everyone I ever met is chipped high into the roof where no one will ever see. To me, faces were blank stone, with the person I wanted to see hidden within. Sometimes the stone seemed to shape itself, and I dreamed that one day I would do more than just carve fluting to other men's designs."

"And you have carved nothing since your marriage?"

"No." A single word, the snap of a closed trap.

"Why not?"

"Why not?" Faye stared at him, and in spite of herself felt her lips curve, laughter a firework of release glinting upward. "I think the Ludlows might be a little shocked to find me on the roof one fine morning, chipping gargoyles into their chimneys."

"I daresay they might," he agreed gravely. "But perhaps you could prepare them for it by starting over the doors. The spark of your life should not be wasted, even if one cannot always begin with the chimneys."

"The spark . . . my father handles some of the cathedral legal work, so I have scrambled over its stones since I was a child. It worried him at first, for my mother died when I was born, but the men were very good and let me pretend to help them. Later, it was not pretense. I have handled stone as long as I can remember; until I left it behind I did not know how much a part of me it was. But I think it is not my life, or I could not have borne to let it go." She was begging for reassurance, and caught the sound of it in her own voice.

He stared at his wine, face somber. "We cannot always tell which loads we want to slip and which we would gladly carry to the day we die. Until we drop them, to see whether we feel better without their weight, and few things are improved by being dropped." He looked up and smiled. "You know well enough that carving is with you still and will not let you quit the burden of your skills, however hard you try to hide it now."

Faye was taken completely by surprise, not by his words, for their conversation had been sufficiently unusual for astonishment at his perception to be lost, but by the tightness they brought to throat and eyes. She knew; and all this long year had refused to know that she could leave all else for Rupert, but this she could not leave. She felt Castellan move beside her and then lean across to say something to Colonel Grattan, repeating it against his deafness, hiding her face with what seemed his rudeness. By the time he was finished she had herself held again, eyes dry and hands tight-gripped on her lap.

"I'm sorry," he said quietly when the Colonel's attention was diverted. "The dinner table is no place for confidences."

She shook her head. "I don't know what came over me, perhaps it is hot in here." She looked around irresolutely, as if expecting the butler to announce the temperature.

He was silent, he had done too much damage already. He had been long enough awash in malice himself for her defenselessness under humiliation to rouse his anger; the contrast between the forlorn, uncertain face beside him now and the blaze of passion when she spoke of carving was so great that he could not regret the treacherous slide of feeling his compassion had set beneath them. I wonder whether that husband of hers can kindle more than dutiful flames, he reflected wryly, whereas I would very much like to try. And that is surely another of the paths before me which is blocked by circumstance.

Faye saw him shift suddenly in his chair, expressive mouth tight, hand tense on polished wood: they had spoken only of her, but now she looked, she could see trouble clearly enough set on him too.

"I have been a selfish host, Mr. Castellan," she said abruptly. "Not just a boring one, talking only of myself."

He laughed but would not look at her. "Not at all, when we have discussed everything from Spanish mottoes to the redecoration of your chimneys."

Politely warned off, she thought, and started violently as she felt the butler touch her on the shoulder. She realized guiltily that Rupert was staring at her, conversation dying as the men eyed the port and waited hopefully for the ladies to withdraw. She had no recollection of the succession of courses, nor reckoning of how long they had been talking.

It was another hour before the guests began to send for their wraps, to remember the next day's duties and embark on the jokes of farewell. Faye thought they would never go, nerves quivering with the oppression of her throttled skills, each face around her begging afresh for her to cut them into stone.

"I'll just take the Grattans home and be back for you in a few minutes." Ralph Brinklow's voice struck through her inattention like a sculptor's mallet.

She heard Castellan offer to walk, prayed he would go, then Rupert referred to the gale and offered a last whisky. Let him go; oh God, let him go, she prayed. And heard Castellan accept, saw Brinklow nod and grin knowingly as he left.

"You must be tired, my dear." Rupert kissed her lightly. "I'll be up later." He grinned too, for her alone, warm approval in his eyes as one trickster to another.

"Good night, Mrs. Ludlow, and thank you for a most delightful evening. If ever I come this way again I shall look at the doors first, and then at the chimneys." Castellan held her fingers a moment, eyes intent; as if he really cares whether I ever pick up mallet and chisel again, thought Faye confusedly.

"Has Faye been talking to you about Reydenham, then?" Rupert came over with whisky. "My mother is the expert, if you are interested."

Castellan tilted his glass contemplatively and then set it down. "I think I will walk back after all, Brinklow can pick me up on the way. Your servant, Mrs. Ludlow."

"Don't do that," Rupert moved instinctively between him and the door, then added hastily, "it's a rotten night outside now."

Faye could not see Castellan's face, she did not need to. He might have told her nothing about himself, but she could tell his anger from the stiffness of his bearing, the way he preferred to go out into a gale in a dinner jacket rather than drink Rupert's whisky after casual words which he had seen as insulting to her. Which he would scarcely have resented so much if she had not allowed herself the weakness of resting briefly against a stranger's kindness.

"Thank you, I do not mind rain," he said after a moment.

"Or gales? You sound more like a good Channel seaman than a banker," said Rupert cheerfully. "I expect my wife has been telling you of our latest venture?" He would never see anything except his own intent where Reydenham was concerned and Faye admired the skill with which he turned the conversation, even while his words stirred alarm.

Castellan stood very still. "It is undercapitalized, I believe?"

"Well, yes." Rupert glanced at Faye in surprise, he had not expected her to talk finance with the fellow and was uncertain whether to be pleased or angry that she had done so. "But Faye doesn't know anything about that side of affairs."

Castellan shrugged. "Ventures people discuss with me usually are undercapitalized." His tone was completely impersonal, face closed, eyes watchful; it was as if the easy companion of the dinner table had never existed. This man is a true professional, thought Faye in sudden panic, from him Rupert will get nothing. It was certain, they might as well save a little pride while they could.

"But with capital it could be a real money spinner! She told you where the boatyard is? Right by the Prince of Wales pier, and what better position could there be than that?"

"Rupert, Mr. Castellan and I—" began Faye miserably, ashamed of the part she had agreed to play, a little frightened because he would discover how inadequately she had played it. How could she explain that she had not even remembered the boatyard when she and Castellan had been talking through most of dinner?

"Yes, Mrs. Ludlow told me about the boatyard and such of your plans as you have allowed her to know," Castellan interrupted. The same dry tone, but this time a slight flicker in her direction. "I fear I must decline to be a partner in it. Boatyards are not my business." Faye blinked at the effortless falsehood with which he covered her, aware again of how far both she and Rupert were out of their depth with this man.

"You wouldn't be a partner! I only want a normal business loan for a year or two." Rupert almost thrust whisky at him. "Listen. A man came to me a year ago, a designer retired from a yard down Southampton way, but his hobby is prefabrication. He has worked out how certain standard boats could be sold as kits; dinghies for beginners to start with, later simple motorboats too. He saw our slip and heard how Cinque Ports pinnaces were once built there, and reckoned a bit of history was just the way to publicize such an idea. He wants to build one splendid motor cruiser too, as advertisement, to show what we can do."

"How much are you thinking of, Mr. Ludlow?"

"Four or five thousand pounds over two years," said Rupert instantly.

"I suggest, then, that you apply to your bank for a loan. It is their business, not mine."

"Banks in a place like Dover are too busy counting pence to see opportunity when it is under their noses. They talk about depressed times for trade, but if no one ever tries to get the place moving again it will not change in ten years."

"It will change within two. No, Mr. Ludlow. I am a merchant banker, specializing in European finance, and if I were not I would still lend you nothing. Instead, for what it is worth, I will offer you my advice. You have a fine place here, concentrate your resources on what you know. Dismiss this expensive friend of yours and forget about boats."

Rupert flushed with anger. "Why should I? It is a damned good idea!"

"Possibly. The circumstances are wrong, however."

"What circumstances are wrong? You have said it could be successful, what is wrong about it?"

Castellan stared at him, and then laughed. "As a guest I would have spared your feelings, but since this was apparently a business affair I feel no such scruple. I do not lend money to men who use their wives as bait, nor do I underwrite businesses about which the proprietor knows nothing. You are no boatbuilder, Mr. Ludlow, and I am not a branch banker. And in two years the British public will not be boating on the Channel, they will be at war."

Faye watched him, astonished; his expression had not changed but she recognized the precise shaping of extreme anger in his words.

"Sold by you and your like, I suppose?" said Rupert unpleasantly. "Ralph Brinklow said it was strange to find a Jew trafficking with the Nazis as you do. My father was killed in the last war, while your snug little bank grew fat on the profits, no doubt. Well, it won't happen again. Haven't you heard of Munich? It is peace in our lifetime; you won't squeeze your . . . your specialty of European finance out of my blood and bones." He did not analyze the cause of Castellan's hostility, but responded to it instantly. He was not a man to overlook insult and the shock of having his designs so coldly torn apart tumbled words from him which the training of a lifetime would normally have kept leashed. He felt pleasure, not shame, though, when they were spoken, for this weasel moneylender had refused to save Reydenham.

Faye watched Castellan's face whiten and splinter with fury before it was still again.

He left into gale and rain without another word.

Chapter Two

After Castellan's departure, they scarcely spoke, but when Faye fed Christopher in the early hours Rupert woke beside her and watched, then lay staring at the plaster-patterned ceiling. She knew he was not asleep, and when she touched him he pulled her tight against him, still without speaking. With her instinctive search for feelings hidden behind bone and flesh, she guessed he dared not speak for fear that rage would shake his voice and make him pitiable.

The next day matched their mood, rain beating on the windows, wisteria tapping, a chill damp spreading from the cold fireplace. Rupert ate his breakfast with his usual single-minded concentration, then pushed his chair back abruptly. "I shall be out the rest of the day."

"Very well," said Faye quietly. "You remember it is the harvest supper tonight?"

"Yes, I remember. You need never fear I shall forget anything to do with Reydenham."

"I know." For Reydenham he was a man who would use his wife as bait. She went over and stood beside him.

He kissed her. "I suppose I was wrong to tackle the swine the way I did, but I'll not be put off. Somehow I'll get the money elsewhere and be damned to him."

Faye watched him with troubled eyes. "Four thousand pounds is a great sum these days."

"I'll go and see the bank again. Now Chamberlain has fixed that fellow Hitler they may be more sensible."

"Last night—" She hesitated, uncertain how to refer to Castellan without offense. "That man seemed sure it would be war. Do you think perhaps you might be wise to wait?"

"Only if you fancy his judgment above that of the Prime Minister and the Chancellor of Germany. The agreement they signed last week—it's for our lifetime. There was relief here, but my God, there were cheers enough in Germany too. They don't want war any more than we do."

Faye was silent, thinking of Castellan's certainty. He had impressed her as a man who knew his business, but with Rupert in his present mood, argument would only further inflame him. "What will you do?" she asked eventually.

"I told you, go to the bank, rob it if necessary!" He laughed. "My God, I wish I could. There are those beeches in West Wood too; it wouldn't harm the valley to have them down and I could get boatbuilding timber on favorable terms in exchange. If I could set up a private company and raise part of the money, the bank half promised me a loan last time I went. A week, and I'll have it, I promise you." His dark mood changed with the speed of the Channel coast itself and he kissed her tenderly. "In a way I'm glad about last night. It puts a stake on success beyond mere money; it seems odd, but honor as well as the future of Reydenham seems in the balance now."

Faye smiled. "There is nothing to set in the balance against the love you feel for it; you must not feel yourself put to the test for no reason. Are you going into Dover? Can I come with you?"

"If you don't mind finding your own way back. I'll be busy all day, and it will only take you an hour to look at the slipway."

"How did you know that's where I want to go?"

"I knew, just as you know that by tonight I'll have most of the money I need. We are one, or had you forgotten, Mrs. Ludlow?"

Rupert drove their rattletrap Morris like a cutter in a storm. He normally rode around Reydenham and regarded a car as an impersonal force to hurtle him wherever he wanted to go beyond the confines of the valley. Faye closed her eyes on the bends, and clutched her seat on the steep slopes leading down into Dover; she had learned to drive when she first came to Reydenham, but had little practice and still preferred low gears and her foot close to the brake in twisting Kentish lanes. Rupert had no such inhibitions, and drove every road as if he owned it, as in some cases he did.

Dover was a mixture of most of the worst styles of architecture from the past hundred years, occasional Georgian grace, soft Stuart brick, and black Elizabethan beams stranded amid a stormwrack of ugly terraces and modernized shopfronts as the town spread up the valley of the Dour in a series of utilitarian rings. But if it was slightly run-down, Dover was also brisk and friendly. Gulls shrieked and curved above tumbling rooftops, and whatever its people were doing a sliver of their senses stayed tuned to the affairs of their port. In midsentence a man would nod and say, "That's the *Canterbury* going out!" or "*The Maid of Kent*'s late in today!"—as if they spoke of children coming home from school, not the whoop of a siren as cross-Channel ferries cleared the harbor.

On either side, the town was held tight by its great cliffs. The Western Heights cast evening shadows across its streets, while Castle Hill blocked the early sun to the east, their chalk gray in rain and so sparkling white in the sun that all over the world when men spoke of England they thought first of Dover's cliffs.

Faye glanced up at the Castle as she always did, as perhaps all Dover people did without realizing it: serene, unruined, growing from close-cropped turf, a single bright spark of color where the Union Jack whipped stiffly in the wind. Dover Castle had never been set in arrogance over its people, but was a bastion of their defense since its first stone was cut and still, eight hundred years later, housed a military garrison. In the war panic earlier that year Dover had been set up as a separate naval command with its own admiral resident in the Castle, and Dover people felt the Channel more definitely theirs because of it. They never doubted the fact, but it was pleasant to feel their straits so obviously held again.

Here and there among the crowded jumble of wool shops and Woolworth's, Boots the Chemist's, and boot makers, Dover occasionally allowed a glimpse of its long past. Maison Dieu in the High Street where knights going on crusade had stayed; Ladywell Street with its pure spring renowned for spells and magic long before men named its waters for the Virgin Mary; Cannon Street, Market Place, and Biggin Street, where Roman galleys and medieval cogs had stored and armed when Dover harbor was an open estuary; Priory railway station, tunneling its lines where monks had prayed in cold cells; the houses of Snargate Street and Townwall Street, built on shingle banks which once had nearly killed the port.

The port.

Dover lived and died through its port. It was a haven, or it was nothing. It held the narrow seas or it shriveled, and Britain shriveled too.

This last day of September 1938, as Faye walked along the curving front, there were still a few holidaying children digging on the narrow beach, two destroyers anchored in the Admiralty harbor, and, beyond the black outlines of the Prince of Wales pier, a great bustle and clatter as the Southern Railway brought its passengers to and from the Continent by train and ferry. Faye stared out over the water, comforted by the peace and normality of it all. Of course she believed Rupert when he said that the war scares of the past year were over, but still . . . She measured with her eyes the miles of pier and breakwater which enclosed Dover bay: thus had encroaching silt and shingle finally been defeated and Dover kept as a haven when the rest of the medieval Cinque Ports died, their harbors grazed by sheep. So had successive governments declared their belief that wars would come, and when they came, then Dover was England's first defense.

Her glance shifted, and she smiled slightly. Huddled between the beach and the seaweed-slimed Prince of Wales pier was the Ludlow slipway: two sheds, a ramp lumped with sand, and a pile of stored timber, split with age and salt.

She could see nothing through smeared glass, and picked her way down a narrow walkway between the pier and blank shed wall, a rising tide sucking noisily in the narrow creek formed by pier and the driven piles of the slip. When she reached it, the launching ramp was equally disappointing, heaped with sand blowing in trapped eddies. Once there had been sliding doors into the building shed, now they creaked and flapped in the wind, and after a moment's hesitation, she prized them apart and squeezed inside. The shed was dark and alive with water: rain tapping on the roof and dripping through holes; the tide slapping, something trickling continuously, as if the building itself was draining slowly into the sea.

An elderly man was kneeling on the floor, and looked up at the creak of the door. "Get you out of here, missus. There be the beach for the likes of you." He returned to his work of thumping pegs into the floor.

"I was curious." Faye stared at the pegs, interest unexpectedly aroused. They formed a pattern, but she could not grasp the meaning of it.

He glanced up again, apparently recognizing the tug of craftsmanship in her voice. "'Tis a boat," he said grudgingly. "We loft the form afore putting a single edge to timber."

She looked again and could not see it, then suddenly before her eyes a shape was born: curving into shadow, spiked with driven pegs, crisscrossed by twine, chalked with a bewildering variety of lines, but without doubt the shadow of a boat. She walked the length of it on the cluttered floor, fascinated. "This is exactly how it will be?"

"Aye. When 'er lives, them'll be 'er lines."

In the maze of half-cuts and curves Faye recognized a sweeping bow, and surprising length disappearing into shadows. She was used to heights and distances from scrambling around the fearsome drops of Canterbury Cathedral: surely this shape could not be less than forty feet long, she decided.

"You like the look of her?"

She turned to an unexpected voice. A stocky, bearded man, black hair turning gray, a torn overall over shabby, cheap clothes, was standing directly behind her. "Yes, I like her." She felt quite incapable of judging chalk marks and pegs on a floor, but recognized possessive pride in the other's voice.

"There will be alterations, of course, the stem for instance . . ." He moved a pile of boards and stared at it intently. "What do you think now, Henry?"

"Same's I allus thought." The man on the floor thumped in another peg and stood, awkward with age and thick pads of carpet tied to each knee. "Too fine." He stared at it gloomily. "'Er'll be a stubborn sea boat."

They immediately launched into an acrimonious and obviously long-worn argument, which ranged from lines of sheer to angles of chine, all expressed with the deadly politeness of carefully shaped insult.

"Too fine," said Henry again, and spat. "'Er'll roll something shocking, Mr. Sisley."

"Is this one of the designs you are hoping to break down and sell in parts?" interrupted Faye.

They both stared at her. "What do you know of that?" demanded Sisley.

"I'm Mrs. Ludlow," she explained. "My husband has been telling me of his plans to sell boats in kits." This shape on the floor was surely far too big for such an undertaking.

"Prefabricated," corrected the other, and then held out his hand. "I'm Sisley, working on the designs, Mrs. Ludlow." He fingered some papers in his pocket, uncertain the moment conversation left the world of boats.

When Faye tried to shake Henry's hand too, he pulled a large purple handkerchief from behind his carpet padding and carefully draped it over his palm before he did so. "Knowing as how ladies expect things clean, ma'am." He shot a triumphant glance at Sisley before returning to his pegs.

Faye looked around the cluttered, filthy shed: whatever skills Sisley might possess as a designer, he was certainly not a tidy worker. "Do you intend to prefabricate a boat this size, Mr. Sisley?"

"Of course not. Not at once, that is. Later perhaps." He spoke jerkily, anguished by the attempt to explain his art to the uninitiated.

"Carve 'er in bits to bring 'er up, after 'er's sunk," offered Henry from the floor.

"What don't you like about her, Henry?" Faye asked.

"He knows nothing about it," said Sisley angrily. "This is a design I've been working on for years. We have to build something which will make the whole coast take notice of us; this yard has done nothing but patch rowing boats for a hundred years."

And even the rowing boats have been patched by others, thought Faye, foreboding deepening, the Ludlows haven't come near the place for generations. "I must go," she said aloud. "If you can do it, it will be good to see the place in use again."

"Aye, it will that," said Henry with unexpected warmth. "It will that, indeed."

"When . . . when do you plan to start building?"

"Next week." Sisley held the flapping doors for her, and then added in an undertone, "Really, Mrs. Ludlow, it is not helpful for your husband to make me work with that man. Not helpful at all."

Faye thought that Rupert probably had excellent reasons for placing the critical Henry at Sisley's elbow, and nodded noncommittally. "Are you engaging more men, if you hope to start building this winter?" Rupert must have been very sure he would find the money he needed.

"Two more next week, another the week after when the timber

has arrived. I suppose really we ought to repair the shed first." He looked around vaguely at rotted boards and broken glass.

Faye walked back to the town in a thoughtful mood; the car was gone from Market Square and she caught a bus which toiled up the cliffs to within a mile of the Reydenham turning. The rain had ceased, leaving a cold-washed sky behind, and she enjoyed the walk up the curling valley road, like a rabbit trail among the trees until it reached its highest point, where it ran along an exposed ridge for fifty paces before looping down through the hedgerows. The whole valley could be seen only from this one stretch of road and generations of Ludlows had stopped there to view their inheritance. Rupert seldom passed without setting his foot on the brake and Faye had quickly fallen into the same habit, thinking with love of Christopher doing the same in a few years' time.

She looked down on a small world of silence, complete in itself. A single valley set in chalk hills, with the manor grown into its further slope; folded pasture bawling with sheep, the whole framed by ancient trees dark against the skyline. There were several farms on the estate, but only hazy smoke betrayed their presence. Ludlows might prefer to be exposed to Channel storms rather than give up their view of the valley; working farmers knew better and huddled their buildings behind windbreaks and steep banks. As she watched, shadows stretched into secretive distance, ditches and coppice were lost to scuffling animals and hooting owls. Standing in stillness overlooking his domain, she felt herself closer to Rupert but in that closeness was also fear. This pattern of earth and sky and trees was the fabric of his life and for the first time she knew beyond doubt that there was very little he would not do to keep it safe. He loved her, yet until the night before, she had not realized that because she was unquestionably his, he did not see her clearly except as part of himself. Whereas he belonged to Reydenham, and therein lay a very great difference. But with knowledge came determination rather than despair, and in this too she was closer to him: if he can fight, so too can I, she thought. He for Reydenham, I for him. If either loses, then surely both are lost.

Her mind wandered, leafing through the past year, her mistakes leaping at her out of the dusk. She had been twenty-six when she married, after living all her earlier life in the confines of Canterbury, well used to managing on very little. She had been tired of the calm tranquillity of it all, and was swept away by Rupert's difference from all she knew, excited by his vigorous certainty of himself. They met casually when he stopped, seeing her beside the road with the wheel off her bicycle, and she had been different for him too. He was bored at the time and, like many men of strong will and purposes, preferred his women compliant and unexacting. His mother told him often that it was his duty to marry, and would have arranged everything for him except the proposal: instead he left her to despair of him and then chose Faye. He was not an introspective man and never thought about why she attracted him so deeply: she had no family of importance, no ties, in gratitude to him would have no opinions he could not shape, no loyalty but to him alone. She was also generous and beautiful when she came to him in her joy; he might not think about it, but he knew what he wanted and took it when chance put her beside his road.

Faye had never known a moment of doubt until she recovered her senses one morning to find herself mistress of Reydenham, hurled into a world about which she knew nothing, with carving left behind. For her, the past year had meant continuous retreat as she struggled to be the kind of wife he wanted, and she wondered now whether Rupert, too, felt disillusion at the woman he had lost when he gained a wife. For somewhere along the way, joy had been mislaid.

One evening, she mused, some bad manners all round, and everything is changed. I cannot retreat any further, for Rupert and for myself I must now stand or I shall scarcely be a person any longer. For Christopher too: on the thought came realization of her heavy breasts, the hour when she should have fed her son long past. She almost ran the rest of the way, feet rattling on the road, crunching up the drive, flying up the stairs to the worn little nursery.

Nanny had brought up both Rupert and his brother William, and then retired to a cottage on the estate to await the next generation. Three months before Christopher was born, she arrived on the doorstep surrounded by boxes and bags and announced her intention of opening up the nursery wing. "Three months it will take to get everything ready, Mr. Rupert," she said severely. "I've been waiting for you to send for me these dunamany weeks."

Rupert laughed and ordered her bags to be taken upstairs, and she had ruled the nursery ever since, the only limit to her authority Faye's insistence on feeding Christopher herself. He was now almost weaned, only morning and evening left to her of all those months when his body had been sealed to hers. It was nearly over and this was another fact she must face; she smiled to herself at the thought that a struggle against Nanny's domination would be as arduous as any she was likely to have with Rupert.

"He was hungry, Mrs. Rupert, I was just warming a bottle for him." Faye received the eager bundle of her son and ignored accusing words. This was her time and she gave it to no one but Christopher.

He was a greedy feeder, pummeling her breast and gasping for breath, not pausing until he was sated. Afterwards, he never fell asleep as Nanny said good babies should. To Faye's secret delight, he showed himself ignorant of all the rules, laughing and reaching for her, screaming indignantly if he was taken away before a full hour had gone by.

"Mr. Rupert was a good baby," said Nanny complacently. "He settled at once after feeding and slept through anything."

"Christopher isn't only a Ludlow." Faye hugged him tightly. "My father still shouts when he doesn't get what he wants."

Nanny pursed her lips. "He ought to be ashamed of himself. Mr. Rupert has never lacked fire, but covers it up decent as a gentleman should."

It was the sort of remark which would have silenced her the day before, now anger stirred. Rupert's voice of the night before came back to her, his insolence to a guest in his house the moment his wishes were balked; her father might shout but he would never have said what Rupert had said, nor would he have done what Rupert had attempted to do, for Reydenham though it was. Bait, the word remained lodged in her mind. I will not think of it, she told herself fiercely, then her lips tightened. Yes, I will: it was my fault for letting myself be bait. I will think of it and not take that path again.

Christopher was drowsy at last and she laid him back in his cot before going to change. Reydenham harvest supper was a great occasion for the valley, anticipated throughout the year. Christmas and Easter belonged to the church; summer and autumn to fetes and jam boiling and bent backs toiling in the fields; winter isolated the valley with bitter, funneling winds. But in October, the turn of the season yielded a few days for enjoyment, for contemplating stocked barns and folded sheep, for ease and the harvest supper.

Then the young men who had been strolling out during the summer decided whether to start sitting indoors with their girls, a formal arrangement families were apt to regard as binding, and the supper provided the curious with an early assessment of who would edge away from obligation by staying near their cronies and the beer. There too, the farmers eyed each other's wallets and told lies about their harvest and wool clip, about things an outsider would not have thought worth a lie, for the sheer pleasure of it. The village hall was decorated with flags from past jubilees and coronations, the children finding endless opportunities for theft as food wound its slow way from farmhouse kitchen to village trestle.

Faye heard Rupert changing gear as he came down the hill, the clatter of wheels over the cattle grid: she had never doubted for an instant that he would be punctual for the harvest supper. She clasped her fingers and stared at her reflection in the mirror: she was not so sure he would be punctual for her. The informal dress and loosely brushed hair she had chosen for the village hall suited her better than the formal tailoring of the night before, square, deep-cleft chin and direct hazel gaze arresting in plain-cut wool when they had seemed faintly out of place framed by precise grooming.

Rupert came into the room on a blast of cold air and delight. "My God, what a day I've had!" He kissed her hungrily. "Come and talk to me while I change." He began ripping off tie and jacket.

She followed him into his dressing room, laughing. "Tell me what you've done. Were you able to talk the bank into a loan?"

"Not exactly. What did you think of the slip? Did you meet Sisley?"

She nodded. "He seems a very strange man."

"But one of the best designers on the south coast. I was lucky to get him." The words were mechanical, as if he had been saying them all day. "We start building next month."

"So he told me. Were you really so sure of Castellan that you ordered timber and engaged two extra men before you had the money?"

He dragged on a clean shirt. "Sure I would get it somewhere, and I have." His face was taut and frowning again. "Let it be, Faye. I know what I'm doing."

"Do you?" She knew she should have kept silent, that this was a moment for enthusiasm and the worst possible time for a quarrel, but the words slipped out and could not be recalled.

"What the devil do you mean by that?"

"I'm sorry, I—" She broke off, remembering her resolution on the road. She kissed him. "I've been a fool, darling, to bring it up now. Let's talk about it later, we'll hold up the supper if we don't go soon."

There was a short silence, then Rupert turned and straddled a chair, arms across the back. "Tell me now." His eyes flicked over her as if criticism at once disqualified her from intimacy.

"Very well," said Faye levelly. "I distrust your Mr. Sisley and I couldn't begin to add up how much that slipway will cost to repair. He is designing a damned great motor cruiser he's been in love with for years and no one has allowed him to build before. Until he's built it, he is not interested in knock-down dinghies for holidaymakers."

Rupert crossed the space between them in a single stride and gripped her arms. "I will give you this one warning, Faye. Keep your hands out of my affairs! Others have faith in me even if you haven't; by the end of the week I'll have raised the money I need."

"I have faith in you, my darling. Faith and so much love." She kissed his stiff, angry lips and put her arms around his neck, dragging at his grip. "You asked me what I thought and I told you; it makes no difference to anything else between us."

His eyes were a bright, sharp blue, his face utterly still. "I never thought you a woman for cheap tricks, Faye."

She felt her blood chill. "Cheap tricks?"

"There is a name amongst men for women who try to win every argument by offering their bodies when it goes against them. I never thought to use it for you. You would do well to remember that you have not stone under your chisel any more, you have me, and I will never be tidily chipped out to your satisfaction."

"I wasn't—"

"Oh yes, you were. If women can't win by one means they will try another, except when I ask you to win for me of course. God knows what you said to that fellow Castellan last night to put his back up, perhaps you should have tried putting your arms round his neck, too."

Faye's heart lifted, for behind the hurtful words one thing was unmistakable. Jealousy. With time to think, Rupert had realized that in two hours Castellan had tapped something in his wife which he had never seen, and animosity had flared so sharply between them because of it. And a man of Rupert's temperament was jealous only where the full strength of his love was committed. He did not yet know it, but perhaps she ranked with Reydenham after all.

"It isn't true," she said at last. "None of it is true. I wanted to hold you and so I did. Never anyone else, my love."

"Ah well, perhaps we're going to be late for the harvest supper after all, and I'll take your way of settling our differences." Something in his voice startled her, but his expression had eased, his eyes were clear again. His hands slid from her arms to her back, to the fastenings of her dress; where his mouth had been cold against hers, now her protests were silenced. Rupert had been a passionate, demanding, and exultant lover, never before an inconsiderate one. She was completely unprepared for being taken in fury, for the agony of love when it was turned into retribution.

Chapter Three

The village hall was packed, and thick with the smells of food and mildewed cloth. More beer than usual had been consumed by the time Faye and Rupert arrived, and the uneasiness engendered by stiff collars and shiny suits had subsided. They sat down almost at once to plates piled high with beef and suet crust, trestles rocking dangerously with the weight of food and goodwill.

"Be 'ee feeling well, Mrs. Rupert?" There were too many Ludlows in and out of the manor for the name to serve.

Faye nodded, her glance slipping over Rupert at the other end of the table, "I am well," she said firmly, and was surprised to find she meant it. So much had changed, yet in a sense nothing had changed; she was herself and could not be diminished unless she allowed it. Shock and humiliation had not lessened her earlier resolve. I still intend to win, she thought, and unexpectedly there was a lift to her blood in response: she no longer avoided looking at Rupert and instead stared consideringly down the table. Perhaps women do not like their men too moral, she reflected wryly, and smiled at Rupert's expression when she lifted her glass and toasted him.

She turned to her neighbor and her smile broke loose, astonishing him with its impact. "I have been neglecting you, Mr. Dickson, you should not let me do such a shameful thing! How is your family?"

Fred Dickson was Reydenham's most substantial tenant, a brown ball of a man, so generous that every vagrant and hard-luck story in five parishes ended on his doorstep and it was hard to believe that Faye's grudging maid, Susan, was his daughter. He had been regarding Faye uneasily, her unexpected radiance nearly rolled him off his chair with surprise. "Claire and Jane be well enough, thank 'ee, Mrs. Rupert, and Susan looks fair to be settled." He nodded down the table, where Faye saw her maid holding hands with a well-polished and stridently dressed young man.

"He's the youngest boy from Stone Cross Farm, and in one o' they strange jazz bands in London, but I reckon the valley fetches 'em back for a wife."

Faye smiled. "I reckon it does. I hope they'll be very happy." She hoped also that Susan would bring more softness to marriage than she had so far done to the manor.

"Oh, aye, they'll be happy enough." Dickson plainly did not regard this as difficult: they came from the same place, and would surely be content as he himself was content. "Is Mr. William coming tonight? Be good to see him again. I brought some rope just in case." He laughed, " 'Tis lucky Mr. Rupert is squire, but the valley's mortal dull now Mr. William be gone."

The previous year, William had bullied a couple of dozen drunk villagers out of the supper to pull his car from a ditch at the head of the valley; the year before he had arrived dressed as a scarlet devil, on his way to a fancy-dress party. "Last time we heard, he was in Scotland, so I daresay he won't come tonight." Faye was fond of her scapegrace brother-in-law, always involved in the kind of schemes for which he had to be awfully and uselessly sorry afterwards; never spiteful, never dull, and never by any chance attempting to accomplish anything useful.

"Be it true, Fred Dickson, that you've given over to they Friesian cows?" Faye's other neighbor took advantage of their brief silence.

"Aye, and you'd do well to think on the same, Bert Pakenham. Double the yield, and calves good for beef."

"You reckoning to sell on the beach, then?"

"The beach?" repeated Dickson, astonished.

"Aye, nothin' but fizzy lemonade they Friesians give. Good for beach trade, though," he added encouragingly.

"Better than your pansy Jerseys, all chilblains on the udder on the first east wind," retorted Dickson instantly. "You try 'em, and you'll never buy another Jersey!"

"I might at that. Just one, then when I want a spot of warm water in the cow shed, there it'll be with no taps to run nor kettles to boil."

Faye let them enjoy themselves, her thoughts wandering. Like any small community, the valley bred dispute, the slightest controversy pursued with single-minded zest, each encounter resembling a strip cartoon marked for the next installment.

"My God, they're all going to burst like a row of balloons over a fire if they eat any more," observed William beside her. "Hullo, Faye."

"William! How lovely! Have you really managed it this year without crashing your car?"

"Now is that fair? I crashed it once and it just happened to be on your doorstep."

"Dear William, only once?"

"Only once," he said firmly. "This one at any rate. I got it yesterday."

"What happened to the other one?"

He grinned. "I crashed it."

"How disappointing of you not to have done it near here! They expected you on a broomstick at least this year."

"Well, the truth is, I thought I'd better stand well with brother Rupert," said William confidentially. "I need to borrow some money."

Faye laughed. "So does he."

"Really? My need must be greater than his. Just look at him doing his duty by the tenantry and cursing us for being Ludlows together. Come on, Faye, I've only got an hour to impress him with my devotion; you take the fat party with the snuff and I'll do the pretty with the sheepmasters."

He bore down on a group loudly defending the virtues of their respective rams and effortlessly charmed everyone until the time came for the manor party to withdraw and leave the rest to unconstrained enjoyment of the remaining beer.

His new car was a splendid Lagonda with head lamps like a dragon's eyes, and he drove Faye back to the manor in a flurry of broken twigs from the hedges, leaving Rupert to follow with his mother in their little Morris.

"William, you damned fool," he said without preamble when he came in. "What the hell made you buy a car like that?"

"I won at the races," said William carelessly. "Would you like to buy it off me cheap?"

"I suppose that means you lost at the next race meeting?"

"Something of the sort. Faye, my dear, you'd like to own a Lagonda, now wouldn't you?"

"Yes, I would," said Faye with enthusiasm. "What do you think, Rupert?"

He was looking at her with a puzzled frown, recognizing a change in her, disconcerted because it was not the change he had expected. Sensation had noosed him with pleasure through the evening, and with it had come an urge to generosity, the desire to offer his wife the reparation of tenderness. Yet the wife he saw was not asking for tenderness, and he felt the same jolt he had felt in the village hall, when he imagined he saw defiance in her toast before he satisfied himself that it was apology she offered.

"Well, Rupert?" said William. "Seeing Faye tonight, I shouldn't think you could refuse her anything. I must say old Rupert seems to suit you, m'dear, I never saw you look so fine."

"I would refuse anyone a car like that, so it is no good expecting me to back your checks. Do some work for once."

William wandered over to a tray and helped himself to whisky. "You're an ungallant devil, Rupert. There was I giving you as pretty an opening as a man could wish for and all you could do was talk about my checks."

"It is what you were talking about," said Rupert drily. "And the answer is still no."

"He's scarcely looked at her this evening. I expect they have quarreled." Old Mrs. Ludlow's voice cut into the silence. She was renowned for her habit of stating her thoughts aloud, and had once reduced a county ball to confusion with adverse comments on a royal guest's clothes.

Faye laughed, the weakness of being hurt by her mother-in-law's outspokenness something else which must be left behind. "I expect we have. But whatever you think, he has been looking at me often enough when he thought no one would notice."

"Not really *looking*," said Mrs. Ludlow serenely. "Glancing. You should know the difference, girl."

"I know," she agreed, smiling.

"For God's sake!" exclaimed Rupert. "What is this, a postmortem on my corpse?"

Mrs. Ludlow smiled sweetly. "A declaration of war, Rupert. If ever I saw a girl with her flag nailed to the mast, or wherever modern ships put them, it is Faye tonight."

"She's an old witch, you know," said William admiringly, when she had gone. "Have you and Faye really quarreled?"

"No." Rupert's face was a tight, angry mask.

"Really? Mother isn't often wrong and a Lagonda would make a splendid reconciliation present."

"Sell it to someone else. I have a better use for my money."

"Rupert is setting up as a boatbuilder," said Faye. "The Ludlow slip at Dover is to be reopened and we are going to build prefabricated boats there."

William stared at her incredulously. "You're not serious? The place fell down years ago."

"It needs repair," said Rupert. "Our family has made money there before, why not now?"

"Pirate Ludlows again? You just send me the word and I'll skipper a privateer and hold a cross-Channel ferry to ransom any day."

"I'm not joking," said Rupert sharply. "Why can't you be serious for once?"

William looked injured. "I should think the Southern Railway would pay pretty handsomely to get one of their ferries back. Damned sight quicker profit than you're likely to see building boats."

"I'll have the first one ready to launch within the year."

"To spite us all, I suppose?" said William sarcastically. "Let Reydenham go begging, because you have a notion to build boats and everyone says you can't do it?"

"It is for Reydenham I am doing it." He tumbled a sleeping dog to its feet and went out abruptly into the dark.

"He's mad," said William with conviction. "All these years he's been after me to do something useful, and he chucks the whole outfit down the drain for a boat."

"He intends to win, not lose," said Faye.

"There's going to be a war, though, isn't there, or has that fool Chamberlain got it right this time? Here am I, paying for flying lessons out of my own pocket and Rupert starts building pleasure boats." He stretched and yawned. "One of us is guessing wrong, and for once I don't think it's me. I flew to an air rally in Germany last month and they're already discussing which sauce to serve with our guts when they feel like it."

Faye thought of Castellan again. "There was a banker here for dinner last night, and he was definite enough for war." She glanced around old oak and glowing ash in the grate; the very word seemed out of place in so much tranquillity.

"There you are, then! Those money blighters with their precious exchanges are always right. Rupert never got a loan out of him?" He took it for granted that his brother would only ask a financier to Reydenham for some ulterior motive.

Faye shook her head. "He said he didn't do that kind of business." She thought painfully again of just what he had said.

"I bet he did. Oh, well, it should be amusing to watch Rupert come a cropper for once. So far it has always been me bailed out of tick at the last second." He laughed. "It's going to be me again first, though, if he really won't pay for the Lagonda. I'd better try Mother in the morning."

As autumn gave way to winter, the affairs of Reydenham became dominated by the tiny slipway in Dover, and for the first time since she had known him, Rupert's first care lay away from the valley. In some ways this suited Faye while she attempted to establish herself in Rupert's consciousness as more than just a wife set in the mold of his need; a greater relief than she would admit for him not always to be there. Before, she had suppressed thoughts she knew would not please him; now, if she was asked, she told the truth. So he asked her opinion less often and shared little of what he was doing with her, while she denied him the opportunity of refusing to answer her questions by never asking him any. She understood very well that there were strict bounds beyond which these tactics would become increasingly harmful, would kill the awareness she was attempting to arouse. She was unsure whether she wanted more than Rupert had to offer, yet no longer willing to settle for being the half-person she now realized he had wanted from his marriage.

She found some stone tumbled in a barn and started to carve. Every spare moment for a week she climbed the hill and did not notice the discomfort of blowing rain and poor light in the old building, shaping and testing, dreaming of what the stone would yield her. It was no good. Her hands still responded with automatic skill but the magic and vision had vanished. She had longed to feel stone again, to have something of worth to show the Ludlows so they would see her yearning as natural, not merely as more evidence that Rupert had brought a bricklayer's laborer to Reydenham as his wife. But she tried too hard, unable to understand why her mind was emptied of what she once had seen, and when she carved it was the image of her trouble which grew beneath her hands. Rupert's eyes watched her from pitted stone, the fearful knots of misunderstanding leered from faults and cracks.

It was no good.

At first she couldn't believe it and tried again, for the wonder of stone had never failed her before. She had made mistakes, but never carved uselessly or without excitement. And with anxiety came fear and desperate loss, even skill sliding from her grasp as her fingers shook and her mind screamed impatience at her failures. She was rescued at last by the farce of Nanny creaking up the hill to peer into the dark corners of the barn, expecting to find a man hiding there.

"For all the valley is talking, Mrs. Rupert, and with Mr. Rupert always away in Dover I thought it my duty to come."

"If all the valley is talking, then they are also looking," said Faye tightly. "And know very well that I am here alone."

"'Tis not much better," said Nanny severely. "There's been some wild Ludlows but never yet queer ones, talking to stone."

Faye began throwing her tools into a piece of sacking; she had nothing worth showing, no reason except strangeness to offer for her behavior. She might as well leave barren longing behind before she became in truth what the valley thought her. It was finished; she would never carve again.

Nanny's face softened, she had comforted too many children not to recognize despair when she saw it. "Whatever the valley is whispering, neither old Mrs. Ludlow nor Mr. Rupert have heard anything yet. That's why I came, to spare you, not interfere where I'm not wanted. If you was gentry you could be as strange as you liked and no one think twice about it," she sniffed. "Downright peculiar half of 'em. But if you think about it straight, you'll know very well you can't afford to be a single mite different from what people expect."

"No," said Faye dully, looking at dead stone. No purpose to it either: the spark of her life, the stranger Castellan had said, and it was gone.

So when she had time to spare from Christopher and the affairs of the manor, she set out to learn more of Reydenham; there was no point in tears or discouragement if there was nothing to be done, despair an enemy to unnerve the weak. If carving was lost, then it must be because Rupert was now her life; and with him she intended to win. She learned a great deal about him from her wanderings in the valley, from talking to tenants and seeing his loving care in every acre of it. He was an excellent, painstaking landlord, not easily fooled although perhaps too much open to persuasion because he could not bear anything in the valley to be out of repair or left unkempt. With him so often away, she learned too that each tenant had his own method of persuasion, from old Mrs. Parsons, who never stopped talking and visited the manor every day until she obtained whatever she wanted, to Bill Wilkins the manor shepherd and Gabriel the gardener, neither of whom ever asked for anything but allowed their needs to be discovered in the most unavoidable ways. Sheep ate her chrysanthemums and Bill announced that they would take the dahlias too unless the pastures were limed.

"I don't see what lime has to do with it," said Faye sharply. "They broke into the garden because you didn't keep the fence mended."

"Mend what you like, Mrs. Rupert, but sheep'll allus find their way out of pasture which ain't to their likin'." He met her eyes innocently. "The fence is sound enough, but they'll be through it again tomorrow if the lime ain't ordered."

"How will they know whether it is ordered or not? I might believe they won't break through once it is spread, but never just because it is ordered."

"Powerful knowing, sheep," he agreed.

She had to laugh and ordered the lime, but was less amused when Gabriel, a withered little man in serge trousers tied under the knees with string, signified his need for a new wheelbarrow by leaving the old one three days on the drive, piled high with manure and upwind from the drawing-room window.

One day in December while Christmas shopping in Dover, Faye surrendered to curiosity and walked along to look at the Ludlow slip again. From a distance she could see no sign of change and, after glancing around, she went closer.

It had not changed. The doors still flapped, the rail was unmended above the perilous drop between slip and pier, the paint peeling. She hesitated; there was no reason why she should not go inside, no reason except pride she could not explain.

"Can I be of any assistance?"

She jumped guiltily. Rupert was leaning against some stacked boards behind her, arms folded. "Rupert, you fool! You startled me!"

He nodded at a cobwebbed overhang above his head. "I was in the office and saw you scurrying and peeking like a child scrumping apples. Why not come in at the door like a normal human being? I suppose you know what's been going on in that mind of yours these past few weeks, for I'm damned if I do."

Faye felt the blood come to her face. "I don't know what you mean."

"Oh yes, you do. You've made me feel as if I was picking you up in the street each night; you've read my letters and listened at the upstairs phone rather than ask a single question about what's going on down here. D'you think I haven't watched you fairly drooling with curiosity? I wondered how long you would last out."

"What nonsense! I—" She broke off, suddenly wanting to laugh at the absurdity of it all. "Well, yes, I suppose that is about it." She went up to him and touched his face with the first gesture of tenderness between them since the night of the harvest supper. "I rather think we have both been fools."

"Perhaps we have." He kissed her, to the delight of some sailors on the pier above. "Let them catcall, since we both deserve it, don't you think?"

She nodded, trying to remember why she had held herself from him for so long, pride of a few minutes before as mysterious as code.

He hesitated. "It isn't the way I wanted it, these past weeks."

"I know, my love," she said softly. How long she had waited for him to say it.

He pulled her arm through his. "Come, I'll take you in and show you Beauty."

"Is that what you call her?"

"She's the *Ludlow Phoenix* really, but from the moment the keel was laid she's been Beauty to all of us."

She caught the note of possession in his voice; Beauty had joined Reydenham in its special compartment in his mind, and perhaps now she was there, too. "Do you remember how that man said you would never make a boatbuilder? It seems he was wrong about that as well."

"Castellan? As well as what?"

"War. Us." The time for pretense was over. "Haven't you ever felt that everything wrong between us goes back to that evening?"

He looked surprised. "The evening after, surely, when I treated you like a lout. I should know, when you've spent every night since trying to convince me that you didn't care what I did."

Bait. It was on the tip of her tongue to disclose the long hurt, the feeling of being valued only in terms of his own needs which had so chilled her, but she let the moment pass. Let dispute rest awhile, for they were one again.

He held the loose door for her while she squeezed through. "Close your eyes."

She closed her eyes obediently, wondering a little at his excitement, and heard a switch flick. "Open now."

She blinked, dazzled by naked overhead light, then saw yellow, curved timber, a living shape cresting off the cluttered floor as if land could scarcely hold it, everything even larger than she had imagined.

She hesitated, aware that whatever she said must be exactly right. "You feel she is at sea already," she said at last. "I don't wonder you call her Beauty."

Rupert laid his hand on the stem, almost as if the boat was in bed with him, thought Faye, and was immediately ashamed of herself. "You feel it too? From the first timbers it has seemed as if nothing could hold her back. Come up to the office, you can see her lines best from there." He led the way up a crumbling stairway into a tiny, floored corner of the roof, packed so tightly with paper it was impossible to move without a cascade descending from workbench to floor, from floor to the shed below. One side of the space was glazed and overhung the back of the slip, so Faye could understand how easily Rupert had seen her approach; the other was open, with a drop of twenty feet to where Beauty was building.

Faye was used to heights from her years of scrambling around cathedral walkways, but the mass of paper was so great it seemed to have a life of its own, as if it would bear her down to the floor below without her moving at all. Sisley was on his knees scrabbling for a plan, scale and dividers in hand.

"My wife has come to see Beauty," said Rupert quickly, eyes on the shape below. "I think you met before."

Sisley stood and shook hands resentfully, as if it was her fault he would have to search afresh for the papers he had been working on. "If you had waited another three weeks, Mrs. Ludlow, we would have had her planked for you to see."

"I think it is more interesting to watch each stage," said Faye carefully, catching the same note of jealous pride in his voice as in Rupert's. "I had no idea you'd done so much."

"The planking should have been finished by now. On the Solent—"

"Never mind the Solent," interrupted Rupert. "It is years since a boat this size was built here, of course there are difficulties. We're mostly using local men," he added to Faye. "One is from Deal and two from the Medway. All Kentish, though."

It was obvious that Rupert had forced Sisley to accept Kent labor against his will; it was equally obvious that because of this Sisley was able to explain every difficulty in terms of incompetent workmanship. Looking around the clutter, Faye wondered whether the man was a genius or a lunatic to design anything in such chaos.

She stood on the edge of the drop and looked down, craftsman's imagination caught by the curving length below. The hull was very narrow, the frames surprisingly light. The eye could pick out the size of bed waiting for the engines, the shaped curves for cabin timbers, precise lines of fitted transom and notched keelson. Faye turned to Rupert impulsively. "She is beautiful! I'm so glad I saw her like this, it makes it easier to understand why—"

"Why what?"

"Well, why you would risk so much for her! Why Mr. Sisley—" Why Sisley is so obsessed he is able to draw you into such risk, she wanted to say, but stopped in time. Beauty was a long way from breakdown kits for suburban families, and she looked at Sisley thoughtfully. It was disconcerting to find that she could be reconciled and content with Rupert again, yet the great vulture of criticism still sat on her shoulder.

"You may see risk"—Rupert's tone implied that he did not—"but word is getting around and there are half a dozen inquiries for her already. An unknown yard could never make its name without something spectacular to force people to take us seriously. We'll use her through the summer for advertising, and sell her in the autumn. It will be a wrench, but we'll need her profit to finance next winter's work. After that we should be in the clear, with surplus cash to spare for Reydenham."

"We'll take her down to the Solent for a week's demonstration." Sisley's eyes gleamed. "Plenty of people there I want to see her."

"Who all said you would never find a boatyard to build such a design?" asked Faye.

He colored angrily. "Who keep building hulls twenty years out of date."

She walked back into the town, upset and confused. She felt she had let Rupert down because she could only share his delight in a thing of loveliness, not his confidence in its future. He deserved success with so much achieved, the Ludlow slip alive again, its first boat part-built, and yet . . .

It is a gamble, she told herself firmly. A colossal, mad gamble with so much stacked against it that surely nothing but obstinacy drives him on. Everyone said he couldn't do it, so he is going to succeed, and he hasn't given a thought about what comes after. She was no judge of boats or profit, but even if all went well she could not see cash going spare for Reydenham next year.

She lay in Rupert's arms that night and listened to his untroubled breathing, tears wet on her cheeks. It had seemed so easy. Whatever else was wrong, she and Rupert were whole again together and could dare the world to come between them, as they had in the early days of their marriage. But the world was there, and it was a shock also to discover just how much she herself had changed over recent weeks.

She turned her head and watched his face, peaceful in frosty moonlight: Rupert never slept with the curtains pulled and only a gale persuaded him to close the windows. His mouth was slightly curved in tenderness, hair rumpled so he looked younger than his thirty-seven years. In their reconciliation they had found the greatest joy they had yet known, but Faye could not accustom herself to loving him more when this only confirmed that her unquestioning dependence on his judgment had gone.

In all his life his will had seldom been questioned, his father killed when he was a child, instinct holding him from marriage until he found a woman who would be compliant because she owed everything to him. Yet she was not like that, she had tried and failed. These last weeks she had been forced to look at herself and judge what was left with carving gone, to set value on what she still possessed, however poor it seemed in her aching loss. She could not now go back to being a mere reprint of Rupert's wishes, even supposing this would satisfy him if she succeeded.

They had not come to their contentment yet, only rediscovered its beginnings after a long and wasteful false start.

Chapter Four

They spent Christmas that year at Chillenor Hall, a famous house set in a thousand acres of parkland. Faye was still not used to staying as a matter of course at houses which formerly she had paid a shilling to visit on open days, nor to addressing people whose faces were familiar from the newspapers by their Christian names. She begged Rupert to refuse the invitation, but the Ludlows always stayed at Chillenor for Christmas, so the argument seemed pointless to him.

She tried once more, before answering the invitation. "It is Christopher's first Christmas, don't you think it would be lovely to be here together? Your mother wouldn't have the upset of going to Chillenor, either." Rupert's mother lived in a suite of rooms at the back of the manor, and was outspoken about the discomfort she was forced to endure in people's houses.

"Mother enjoys Chillenor." Rupert grinned. "They play bridge for a pound a hundred, and light a coal fire in her bedroom every night. She came down to dinner in tweeds years ago, saying it was too cold to change, and they've never forgotten it."

Faye put her arms around his neck. "Do you really want to go? I hate leaving Christopher with Nanny for Christmas."

"Yes, of course I want to go. We always go." He kissed her the way he always kissed her, warmly, completely, then immediately picking up the conversation where he had left it. "Christopher is too young to know anything about it, he's best with Nanny."

She supposed she was being unreasonable and resigned herself to going. "Promise me that next year we'll stay here. Next year at Reydenham, doesn't it sound just right to you?"

He put his hands to her wrists and pulled them apart, quite gently, but definitely. "We quarreled before over the methods you used to win an argument, remember? I don't promise any easier with your arms around my neck."

"Would you promise any easier if I argued it out across the table, then?" she said bitterly.

"Probably not," he agreed pleasantly. "Let's leave it at that, shall we?"

She made up her mind to hate Chillenor and was not disappointed. Everyone talked of people she knew nothing about; most of the guests hunted or shot, while she had never handled a gun or ridden a horse except on the beach. She went for long, solitary walks and yearned for Christopher, miserably conscious that she seemed both dull and sulky. The only interesting conversation she had was shouted down, because politics was barred over Christmas.

"We have enough talk of war, with dictators in every headline and the government sending those dreadful notices about gas and air raids through the post," Lady Chillenor said firmly. "We will let Mr. Chamberlain and Mr. Hitler manage it all without us for a few days."

"It is still going on, though, whether we bother to notice it or not," observed William. "I have an interview at the Air Ministry next month."

"Whatever for?"

"Volunteer Reserve. I have my pilot's certificate now, and if there is a war I'm damned if I'm going to slop about in the mud as an infantryman."

"Truly, William, do you think there is going to be a war?" Faye asked in an undervoice, when the conversation turned to next year's crops.

"Odds about even, I'd say. Hitler is not going to change; the odds depend on whether we let him get on with grabbing what he wants, or not. After all, he's only after queer countries in Eastern Europe no one has ever heard of according to that old woman Chamberlain. What does brother Rupert say?"

"Nothing. He won't even read those leaflets we keep getting about civil defense."

He cocked an eye at her. "Afraid an uncouth war might spoil his beautiful boat?"

"He says we can't believe anything the newspapers say," she replied quietly. She would not criticize Rupert and, although she could ask about war, like him was unable to believe the possibility of it coming. "What did you do with your Lagonda in the end?"

He pretended to think. "Now was that the one we used for tow-

ing gliders, or the one which rolled off the embankment? No, I really believe it was the one I made a profit on. How about coming
for a spin on my motorbike this afternoon, since Rupert seems to
have disappeared for the day?"

"Could we—could we go to Canterbury? I hate to think of my
father alone for Christmas."

"If you don't mind freezing if we go so far," said William obligingly. "I'll drop you off and come back later. I've got some business to settle."

"Business?"

"Business," he said firmly. "Jolly complicated business too,
you'll see. Are you going shooting tomorrow?" She shook her
head, privately considering it barbarous to go straight from church
on Christmas morning to a shoot in the afternoon, simply in
order to sharpen an appetite for dinner. William read her expression and laughed. "You should, you know. Just this once; it'll be
worth it, I promise."

She could not imagine what he intended to do, and forgot about
it in the enormous speed of their ride into Canterbury. She had
never ridden pillion on a motorbike before and William shouted
at traffic and attacked the road as if he was in the hunting field:
it was the only similarity she had discovered between the brothers,
that they both treated the highway as their private preserve.

He left her in the High Street, and she was at once wrapped in
ancient familiarity. On impulse, she walked through narrow Mercery Lane to Christ Church Gate, her lips curving into an invol-
untary smile at the sight of pleated stonework studded with color.
She had worked on the restoration of the gate, had been working
on it when she met Rupert, and loved its Tudor aggression. Sixteenth-century Englishmen had served God and established their
families; Christ Church Gate, lavishly decorated with the armorial
bearings of Kentish kindreds, left open the question of which they
thought the more important. She passed through its crouching
gloom, eyes seeking each familiar curve and ribbed vault; then out
of dimness to be overwhelmed once more by the impact of the
great cathedral beyond, hidden from sight until a traveler stood at
its feet. Thought was stilled by such splendor of tower and soaring
buttress, such harmony of stone and soft, green grass touched
honey-yellow by the sun, and her footsteps hesitated on the cob-
bles, mind tilted from its groove by wonder, the aching crafts-

man's wonder at how such immensity could touch so lightly on the ground. Fifteen hundred years of faith, eight hundred years of skill and care had gone into this building: serene, entire, and lovely, the cathedral church of Canterbury let neither believer nor unbeliever pass untouched.

She lingered awhile in the close, watching the weave of its life: wandering canons in flapping black, purposeful dean like an energetic locomotive shunting the errant to their appointed places, scampering choristers, late as usual and pursued by bells; the master librarian, thoughts lost in thirteenth-century accounts. It was the sight of the librarian which aroused her to passing time and she plunged hastily into the maze of medieval streets behind the close, until she reached the small court off Rose Lane where her father lived in a huddle of rooms over his office.

The legend *Haskell & Partners* had almost disappeared from the brass plate under constant polishing, the steep stairs so familiar their dimness did not matter. Edward Haskell could have been an able lawyer, but he was a scholar by temperament and his researches into the past held far more interest for him than conveyancing or taxation appeals. So his practice remained small and his study of twelfth-century Canterbury monks at work in Kentish marsh and forest promised to be the definitive work of its kind, if it ever reached the printing press.

Faye pushed open the sitting-room door quietly; the room was small and filled with bulky, old-fashioned furniture, firelight flickering over polished wood and docketed piles of manuscript. Her father was holding a piece of parchment to the light and did not immediately look round while she stood silently, smiling a little at his absorption. He was slightly built and rather untidy, only brilliant dark blue eyes made him at all remarkable to look at. Faye had always regretted that she had inherited her mother's undistinguished hazel, and secretly hoped that Christopher's eyes would darken from their present baby blue rather than lighten to an intolerant Ludlow stare.

He suddenly became aware of her presence and turned. "Faye! What a pleasant Christmas surprise." He came over and kissed her, although he was not a demonstrative man and Faye could remember only two or three other occasions when he had done so. "I'll call Betty for more crumpets."

Faye smiled at him, eyes unaccountably misty. "Crumpets by

the fire and Betty's cake, I feel as if I ought to have my stocking hung on the mantelpiece again."

He looked at her searchingly, but said nothing and went to shout down the stairwell. Betty had first come when he married thirty years before, and they had shouted at each other ever since: both would have thought ordinary tones an intolerably dull way of conducting their affairs.

When he returned, Faye was sitting on the hearth rug. "I haven't got long, but I hated to think of you alone at Christmas. I wanted to ask you to come to Reydenham, but we are staying away at the most enormous house, full of footmen and maids."

"I know, you wrote to me." He hesitated. "Has Rupert come with you?"

"No. I came on the back of William's motorbike." She laughed. "It is the most terrifying great brute of a thing you ever saw."

They heard Betty's heaving grunts as she climbed the stairs, and Faye went to the door. "Betty, dear, happy Christmas!"

"'Tis all the happier for seeing you, Miss Faye, and happier still if some I could name would clear the rats out of my kitchen. I've told your father and told him—"

Faye grasped crumpets and Christmas cake thrust at her. "How about Eustace? You know you would miss him if you found him stiff one morning."

"He'd be too clever to be ketched, and well you knows it." The rambling building had been a playground for mice for three hundred years and nothing they did could eradicate them. Betty called them rats and her life was filled with warfare against them, all but one of each generation which she befriended and called Eustace. One Eustace of Faye's childhood took crumbs from her hand, the current one apparently sat on the arm of Betty's chair cleaning its whiskers each evening.

Betty had brought Faye up; her father loved and understood her but Betty was the warmth lining her childhood, the smell of baking inseparable in her mind from comfort. They chattered and toasted crumpets as if the past had instantly unraveled again, Faye making them laugh with impossible tales of her new dignity. But as she talked she became aware of her father's scrutiny, and when Betty finally departed downstairs again amidst a fearful clatter of crockery, she looked up at him and smiled crookedly. "Well?"

Edward Haskell was a man of meticulous habit of mind, and did not pretend to misunderstand her. "Is there anything I can do to help?"

She shook her head, tightness in her throat. "Nothing. It is just —just that there is so much to which I must become accustomed. It is lovely to come here and find everything the same."

He watched her sadly; nothing is the same, he thought. You left all this gladly, and there is no coming back. "You have changed," he said gently at last. "It is never an easy process and for you it has been very hard. Most people change part of themselves, you have had to change everything all at once. It is nearly done, from now on is the healing and growing. Come here when you can, but don't look back; you were happy but not content here. Ahead of you lies both happiness and contentment if you will it so."

Faye would not look at him. "I think Rupert does not want much willpower in his wife." She would have said it to no one else.

He pulled her up to face him. "He does not want a wife who attacks him with her will. There is no man who does not desire a wife resolved on happiness in her heart."

Her lips trembled into a smile and she laid her cheek wordlessly to his. It was true that her father's abstracted affection and the unchanging life of Canterbury would not have satisfied her forever: she had made her choice, with love and very great happiness; now, the only way was forward. The roar of William's bicycle cut across their silence. "I must go, but there was one thing I wanted to ask you. How easy is it to form a private company?"

"What a remarkable question, my dear. I hope you aren't thinking of going into business?"

"Of course not." She heard William thumping on the door below and continued hurriedly, "Is it the sort of thing one can do in an afternoon, or a couple of days, or does it take weeks?"

"It is certainly not something which can be done in an afternoon," he said drily. "A private company must be registered and I've never yet managed to achieve that in less than a fortnight, the documents required for registration have to be carefully prepared if everything is to go without a hitch."

So Rupert could not have found the money he needed within a

matter of days by launching a private company, she reflected. Ever since she had seen Beauty, and the lavishness of everything provided for her, she had wondered afresh where so much money could have come from. A company could at least have gone bankrupt, now she began to speculate uneasily on just what the consequences of failure might be.

William came clattering up the stairs. "Hurry up, Faye, I think it's going to snow. We shall both be in trouble if we aren't well starched up and ready in our places for dinner. Hullo, sir, happy Christmas!"

Faye began to laugh. "William, where on earth have you been?"

His hands were filthy, his face smeared with black.

"Down a coal mine," he said cheerfully. "Well, dammit, Faye, we've got coal mines in Kent and I've never been down one. A fellow bet me five quid I couldn't get down three shafts inside an hour, but I managed it easily. It's a good deal more comfortable down there than it is on a bike in this weather, I can tell you!"

"Business, William?"

"Well, it was business, damned profitable business," he said, grinning. "I needed that fiver to pay some rabbit catchers I met."

"To pay some rabbit catchers?" inquired Mr. Haskell.

"That's right, sir. It's a pity you aren't coming shooting with us tomorrow. You'll come though, won't you, Faye?"

"I'm beginning to think I shall have to." Faye was scrambling into the heavy leather clothing he had brought for her.

"I only hope it doesn't snow too hard, that really would muck things up." He would not say any more and shamelessly raided Betty's mince pies on his way through the kitchen. She chased him out with floury hands to add to the coal dust, and they could hear him laughing as he started his bike in a snarl of exhaust.

"She ought to have married that one," said Betty soberly when they had gone. "He plays the fool, but he's not foolish. I've never seen anyone change so quick as she did when he came."

Edward Haskell did not reply, but in his heart he agreed with her, and returned upstairs feeling worried and helpless. He had warned Faye of the difficulties she would face if she married Rupert Ludlow; he had never admitted to himself that he could not like his grand new son-in-law, in whom he sensed a core of selfishness which Faye had never breached even in the times of her greatest happiness. And those times had surely passed, for the moment at least. He stared into the fire, feeling quite unable to judge the edge he had felt in Faye today. Defiance? Disillusion? And what the devil did she want to know about private companies for? he wondered aloud.

Faye and William arrived back at Chillenor as the gong boomed; with fifteen minutes to go before dinner there was no time to think, and without time to think Faye was relaxed and gay, able to join unselfconsciously in Christmas Eve dancing, so for the first time it was easy for their fellow guests to see why Rupert Ludlow had made such a fool of himself over a pair of hazel eyes.

Rupert was different too, responding instantly to her lighter mood, enjoying pride in his wife instead of defensiveness, refusing to let anyone else dance with her. His pleasure shamed her: all he wanted was to live at ease and give her what he thought was his to give. It was her craving for more than he reckoned was her due, her resentment that he alone should judge the measures of their life, which poisoned what he offered. They needed time, but she had grabbed in haste; with patience so much more would grow between them, and then be offered in its turn.

And in the night after, there was something more than the mastery he had shown before, laughter and generosity joining the pleasures they had already known. Their full future together was still undiscovered, but she felt the sealed gift of it in her hands at last.

A few flakes of snow were drifting down in the morning, the first white Christmas most could remember, but not enough had settled to banish a certain saintliness from William's expression.

"I thought you hated shooting," said Rupert, astonished when she decided to join the guns.

"I do," she replied serenely, "but this afternoon I thought I would come with you."

"I hope you enjoy it," he said doubtfully, wondering whether she had the slightest idea of the etiquette of shooting.

Her eyes glinted. "I hope so."

"For God's sake, Faye, don't do anything to set everyone's back up! Especially after making such a good impression last night."

She swallowed, it was not how she would have chosen to describe her feelings of the night. "Is that all it seems to you, a good impression?" Even now he never thought to offer not to shoot rather than leave her the choice of coming or staying alone.

He kissed her. "A damned good impression, with everyone seeing you as you are at last. How I enjoyed rubbing their supercilious noses in their own surprise."

She laughed, they surely meant the same in different words and today she did not feel like quibbling over meanings. Be resolved on happiness in your heart, her father had said, and she was. "I don't know how shoots are conducted, but I won't disgrace you. I may make mistakes but I am too much yours for them to matter."

He stared at her, seeing himself mirrored in her eyes. "I could say the same, since before God I often do not know what it is you want of me. But for all my mistakes, never forget that I love you still."

As he watched, her face changed with the kindling rush of light which never failed to captivate him when it came, which he could never exactly recall when it was not there. "You said it. Oh, my love, you said it."

"Said what?"

"I love you. I wondered whether you ever would."

"Good God, Faye, I've said it a dozen times!"

"No. Just this once." She smiled. "So far."

The shooting party was shifting impatiently by the time they arrived downstairs, and moved off immediately. It was bitterly cold and still snowing softly. At the end of the lawn stone steps led down into the park, guarded by wrought-iron gates to keep cattle out of the gardens. Snow was curling over tussocks and into hollows, lacing coppice and great, standing beech. The park looked chill and gray and very empty: Lord Chillenor was just suggesting where rabbits might be found when they heard a bubbling scutter, and the tussocks themselves seemed to come bounding towards them.

Dozens of rabbits came leaping from bush and bank, hurling themselves on their intending assassins. The shooting party recoiled up the steps, then took flight through the gate, pursued by a breaker of ravening, ravenous rabbits. No one thought of trigger or cartridge as the frantic animals fawned on them, slobbered over their boots, lurched and hopped and scrabbled at them. There were fat grays and silky whites with wet, pink eyes, blacks with lop-ears and strange mixtures with piercing squeals: the disappointment of questing whiskers and reaching paws was ludicrous as the gate slammed. One, bolder than the rest, scrambled on the backs of its fellows and wriggled through a gap in the ironwork. It hopped up to Lord Chillenor, covering his guests' retreat as a good host should, and begged on its hind legs, head tilted, eyes half closed. The resulting leer was straight from Leicester Square and the shooting party stared, fascinated.

"Good God, George, the lady wants to go to bed with you," observed a voice from the back. It was the end of any possibility of shooting for the day. They had only to hold game bags open for rabbits to scramble inside, to re-emerge, panting and curious into arms and around necks. It was clear that they were tame and very hungry, delighted to have rediscovered humankind.

They put them in the conservatory by the dozen, where they ate everything in sight. The servants heard the commotion and came running, abondoning the spit, which was brought clanking into action only at Christmas, until an evil smell of singeing meat filled the house and in the rush back to the kitchens the rabbits escaped again. Only the butler remained in dignified outrage, clutching the brandy decanter to his chest while the rest of the household pounded in a wild tallyho under furniture and down passages, skidding across polished floors after panic-stricken rabbits.

"Where on earth did you find them?" demanded Faye, when she encountered William in full cry.

He grinned. "Maidstone market. All tame and fattened as part of the family. I had a couple of fellows under the bushes with the whole lot in bags. They were so damned hungry they could have eaten us whole."

"You are cruel!" Faye said indignantly, laughter bubbling again. The sight of two dozen armed men put to flight by a pack of rabbits had been unforgettable.

"Not a bit of it! The poor little beggars were so overfed for Christmas they could hardly move. Thirty-six hours of fasting has made them as merry as crickets again! By Jupiter, Faye, if I'd known what it could do I'd have paid double for the one which tried its tricks on George Chillenor!" He went off whistling to help round up the last recalcitrant rabbit.

He let them all out again later, with the port and cigars.

Chapter Five

Afterwards, Faye looked back on the Christmas of 1938 as the last reach of shelter before striking out into the storm. It was the complete absence of care she remembered above all. Windows were left uncurtained, fuel heaped on fires without thought, food and drink enjoyed or left untouched as anyone pleased. Minds were delivered by ease to bounding high spirits, to uncomplicated enjoyment of the moment. There was no feeling of doom, no sense that this was to be the last Christmas of a vanished life. Just the beautiful old house, every room in use and overflowing with guests and servants, the snow drifting down on an untroubled countryside, the shouted promises to meet again next year as they all drove away.

With the New Year, change began to flow faster. It had flowed before but it had still been possible to forget the world for days on end, to pretend the flow was nothing. Faye had heard of Air Raid Precautions and flipped through government booklets on how to paste paper strips over glass and fit blackout curtains, but it had been remote, without relevance to Reydenham in its quiet valley. Rupert read the classifications for national service with his head full of boatbuilding, loans and timber, and had simply dismissed them as scaremongering. Because he could not afford to believe such fears, he did not believe them.

One by one the hammer strokes of fate fell on this complacency. Gas masks had been issued after Munich, now there were anti-gas exercises and practice alerts and dimouts. When Faye had to bundle Christopher into his baby mask she was struck by real terror, vivid and terrible because it came fresh from a clear sky. He had to be put into a mask which enveloped him completely, and if she stopped pumping air for more than a minute, he would suffocate. She sat beside him, sweat running into the stinking rubber of her own mask, pumping as if pursued, mind filled with all the catastrophes which might disable her for more than sixty seconds.

"Nanny is old, it'll have to be me!" she said in panic to Rupert. "What if the house is bombed or I feel faint with that dreadful thing over my face? I could hardly bear it another minute today. What if I have to wear it for hours?"

"Don't fuss!" said Rupert irritably. "There isn't going to be a war, and if there were, who the hell would want to bomb Reydenham?"

But the sight of Christopher screaming in his lethal mask drove Faye into a passionate interest in events. She had known what was happening before, but without any impact; now she listened to the wireless every day, puzzled over contradictory reports in the newspapers and cross-questioned anyone with an opinion to offer. Rupert became angry when she tried to talk to him, but her father shook his head and said war was coming. He was over sixty, but registered as an Air Raid Warden, spending his weekends at gas lectures and first-aid demonstrations, which made Faye feel more depressed than ever. In February, William was accepted for the RAFVR and came to Reydenham for a weekend in such tearing spirits that Susan, Faye's maid, burst into tears and gave in her notice. "I'll marry my Len this very week, if him and his band are all to be blown to pieces like Mr. William says! Fighting in the sky over London, he says there'll be, and no one can stop me being with my Len when it happens!"

Faye was delighted when she went, since she hated having a maid, and Susan's disagreeable manner and selective habits of work infuriated her. To her relief, Rupert did not suggest replacing Susan and she suspected him of being relieved at a reduction in the wages bill, however slight. Beauty would be ready for launching by April, only a month behind schedule: Faye was to perform the ceremony, to which half Dover was invited for publicity, and Rupert hoped to have the fitting out done in time for a summer cruise.

"Up the Thames and the Essex shore first," he said eagerly. "There's money on the Blackwater. Then along the south coast to the Solent; Sisley can hardly wait to show her there."

"I had a look at her yesterday," observed William. "Sorry I won't be here for the launch, but we're not given any leave for the first couple of months of flying training, and north Yorkshire's the hell of a place to get at."

"You could come if you really wanted to. I've never noticed much difficulty over you going wherever the fancy took you before," said Rupert acidly.

"This is one copybook I don't want to blot. If I kick off without leave I won't be out of the Air Force, I'll be a mechanic while everyone else is flying."

Rupert shrugged. "You're thirty-two and too old for a pilot's course anyway. You'll end up as a navigator or gunner or something."

"God help the aircraft navigated by me! I think before we're through we may need every pilot we've got to protect Susan's Len in London." He grinned at Faye. "I'm sorry the wench threw hysterics over you, but I daresay it's good riddance."

"Very good riddance," she agreed. "You think it is when, not if, don't you, William?"

"War? Yes, and have done for a year or more. So would Rupert if he'd take his nose out of the bilgewater for a moment."

Rupert flushed. "Just because I don't panic easily—"

William flicked some bread pellets idly on the table. "Sisley had some tale of missing engines when I was there today. The Admiralty has got its claws into them, I believe."

Faye watched Rupert's face, he was beside himself with anger. It was very hard for him to face defeat now, so close to success and with such great difficulties surmounted. She searched her mind for something to say which might switch his mind from fury, but there was nothing. If he was balked now, then no tenderness or understanding from her could soften his sense of having betrayed Reydenham, when he had been so sure the slip would save it. And she had few illusions: to him, betraying Reydenham was the ultimate sin and these last weeks he had thought very little of her.

"I'm going to see the makers tomorrow," said Rupert at last. "I'll show them who ordered those engines more than six months ago."

William shrugged. "You could have ordered them six years ago for all the difference it will make if the Admiralty want them. Be thankful they aren't delivered—I'd file a claim to get my money back so quick it would make your head spin."

"I don't want my money back," said Rupert coldly. "I want those engines, and I'm damned well going to get them."

He got one. As a consequence he had a savage row with Sisley, who flatly refused to alter his design to compensate for changed weight and thrust. Rupert shut himself up at Reydenham and refused to answer the telephone or pay any wages so long as the quarrel raged, and three days later Sisley tramped up the valley and stayed arguing all evening, battering Rupert with figures and specifications before finally giving way. "She'll be so underpowered she'll be unseaworthy in anything but a flat calm, and every calculation I've ever made will be wrong. But she's your boat, Mr. Ludlow, if you won't wait until we can take delivery of the other engine—"

"No, I won't wait," interrupted Rupert. "Now or ever. If Beauty doesn't cruise this summer, then she never will. I'll be out of money, you'll be out of a job, and she'll be stranded on the slip forever."

"I'd best be going then." Sisley stared out into the night. A gale was rising, throwing rain against the windows. "You may get her afloat by willpower, but you can't make her to do what she's designed to do on half the power she needs. A couple of weeks' work will give us one shaft instead of two, but it's work wasted. The whole bloody thing is no good any more." He bowed to Faye with awkward dignity and went out in search of his coat.

"Rupert, he walked here from the main road," said Faye urgently. "You must ask him to stay the night in such weather."

"I didn't tell him to come. All I want is for him to do his job and stop making difficulties, as if there weren't enough already."

"Never mind about that! If you won't have him to stay, at least take him up to the bus stop in the car."

"Mind your own business, Faye." He spoke quite pleasantly, but definitely. "If I take him, we'll have the whole damned argument again. Let him walk, and remember who pays the bills."

She went out, closing the door behind her. "If you'll just wait a minute, Mr. Sisley, I'll get the car and run you home." She remembered John Castellan leaving the house on a worse night than this: at least I have grown, she thought bitterly, since I let him go after he had done what he could for me, and will not let Sisley be turned out, who is thinking only of himself.

Rain beat on the celluloid side curtains of the little car and dripped on their knees, wind snatching as they climbed out of the valley's shelter. "I appreciate this very much, Mrs. Ludlow," said Sisley eventually. "It's a rotten night for a walk."

Faye nodded, unspeaking. It was a rotten night for everything: her buoyant optimism of Christmas at Chillenor seemed very far away.

She had intended to leave him at the bus stop, but in the end took him all the way. She might as well, since Rupert would know she had gone whether she went two miles or six. As he was about to get out, Sisley hesitated, hand on the door. "Mr. Ludlow doesn't know it, but I'm off at the end of the month. Until then I'll do as I'm told and take my money. I suppose you can't persuade him from this course?"

"No." A single monosyllable. She fitted his need, but in what had he ever listened to her?

Sisley nodded. "I thought not. Ah well, I always wanted to build this boat. It's something to know how she would have looked."

"Is she any good, Mr. Sisley?" Faye asked. "I mean, really any good, given the right conditions and the engines you wanted?"

Sisley looked out at the rain. "She's a bit short on workmanship, and now I see her built I'm not quite happy about her sheer, but yes, with a little more development, she's the very best there is." He laughed suddenly. "If any of us are alive after this war, if there is any money and anyone left who feels like boating for pleasure, then Mr. Ludlow has a winner."

"We'll search you out to come and finish your masterpiece," said Faye, smiling. "Where is your new job?"

"Admiralty; I don't know where exactly. No, Mrs. Ludlow, Beauty is all yours. I'll not work for Mr. Ludlow again." He stood bareheaded in the rain, his mackintosh flapping about his legs as she drove off.

The journey back was a nightmare of scudding, fitful moonlight, slithering turns down the valley road, rattling rain and wind. And at the end of it, Rupert. Rupert at his desk surrounded by papers and refusing to look up. Rupert unspeaking through what was left of the night when he came to bed at last, and still silent the following morning. Rupert watching her, and looking away whenever she turned. At first she had been thankful for his silence, expecting fury; then she lay all night beside him crushed by the weight of it, and when she saw him ready to go after breakfast still without a word, she could bear it no longer.

She went to the library, where he was stuffing some papers into a briefcase. "Rupert."

He did not look up. "What is it?"

Her hardly-gathered confidence ebbed. "Are—are you back for lunch?"

"Of course not."

"Do you want me to go and see the Pakenhams about their fences for you?" She could not think of anything better to say, yet hated to let him go without attempting to soften the harshness between them.

"As you wish."

"Rupert, please—" She was ashamed of the tremble in her voice, and shocked by the weakness of her will. "Rupert, I beg you not to leave me like this."

He came over and held her lightly, without passion. "Like what, my dear?"

"You know," she said miserably. "You know, and want me to grovel through every word of it."

"You go too fast for me," he said, smiling. "A moment ago it was words you wanted."

She stared at him, resolution stiffening again. "I took Sisley into Dover last night, what of it? I am sorry if I angered you, but not for taking him. Once you had time to think about it, you must have been glad we did not make him walk."

"No," he said softly. "I wish the little swine had walked. I don't want to be saved from myself, Faye. I want . . ." His hands tightened on her shoulders. "I want to be left alone to go my own way, and I want you beside me as I go." He smiled and held her to him. "There! That's a confession! I was angry because I needed you and your support was gone."

"I am always there, my love. Always." She kissed him fiercely. It was futile to regret, superfluous to condemn what he could not help. It was terrifying that love should hold so much pain, but this was the love she had, there was no escape. With it, she was alive; without it, she was lost.

Next day, Hitler walked into Czechoslovakia: Munich and the Sudetenland had not satisfied him after all. A tremor ran through the country, and after it the old patterns did not reform. War had moved close enough to be touched. Gabriel looked up from his roses the following morning and remarked, quite casually, "Be fighting by autumn, Mrs. Rupert. Be you willin' for me to grub up they herbaceous and plant potatoes? In the last one we dug up the lawns as well."

Faye agreed with a heavy heart, and when she went for her daily visit to her mother-in-law, found her equally fatalistic. "Poor Neville is very upset," she said mournfully. "I'm sure he can't *concentrate* properly with all this talk of war."

Since Mrs. Ludlow possessed a tortoiseshell cat of that name which she credited with all kinds of supernatural powers, Faye did not immediately grasp whom she meant. "Have you wormed him recently?"

"Neville Chamberlain! Really, Faye, the things you say!"

"Oh, Chamberlain." Faye wondered fleetingly whether the Prime Minister would be improved by worm powders, and decided he would not. "I should think he is upset, risking war with little more than his umbrella to protect us all. I hear William is flying biplanes still: he says they go ninety miles an hour with the wind behind them."

"We'll manage somehow," said Mrs. Ludlow vaguely. "I wouldn't trust William flying faster than ninety miles an hour. His father was just the same; he volunteered for tanks, you know, just because he was bored in the cavalry."

And it killed him, thought Faye fearfully. Please God, not William. Not William with his uncomplicated warmth; not William, please.

Mrs. Ludlow, however, was not following the same train of thought. "Remember, Faye dear, knicker elastic and hairpins. Hot-water bottles and silk stockings."

Faye accepted this unlikely list without a blink: she was becoming accustomed to her mother-in-law. "What for?"

"Shortages, my dear. I remember from last time exactly the things you couldn't get. Vintage port for a packet of hairpins! It was ridiculous."

"You exchanged port for hairpins?"

"I wish the girl would listen. Yes, dear, and really, by 1918, I felt everything slipping whenever I went out." She put her hand on Faye's arm and repeated, "Everything," in a meaning whisper, so she would not think only hairpins were in question.

"I had better stock up on food," said Faye thoughtfully. "Sugar perhaps and tins of things. Baby food for Christopher."

But Mrs. Ludlow dismissed food shortages summarily. "There was always plenty at Reydenham, although you might have to go to London for delicacies. Whatever happened in the towns, we never went short."

Faye took her advice over elastic and hairpins, she also followed her own instincts and began to stock up with food, too. She thought perhaps life had changed enough for Reydenham no longer to be able to stand aside in its plenty while others starved.

As each day passed, there was a fresh toll of bad news; the pattern of days shifted, yet remained disconcertingly the same, and the country was far from geared to war. Britain and France guaranteed the integrity of Poland and the engine was delivered for Beauty; Italy invaded Albania and Christopher stood for the first time; the National Service Act conscripted all young men of twenty, and invitations went out for Beauty's launching ceremony.

Susan arrived on the doorstep in a gust of angry tears, demanding to return as lady's maid: Len had received his papers and was to report to the Buffs* depot at Canterbury the following day.

"I'm afraid I couldn't have you back," said Faye apologetically. "We're cutting down on staff everywhere." It was not just that the coming of war was sucking young men from the valley; their money also was disappearing at a frightening rate into the insatiable needs of the slipway. Rupert's determination increased with each obstacle, and extra payments were often needed to obtain the deliveries he needed.

Susan looked sulky. "It's not fair. Married ten weeks and then my Len's took just because his birthday isn't until July. Why him? There's lots as could be spared and never missed."

"Someone has to be first." Faye thought of newspaper pictures showing Germany's armed power. "Soon it will be everyone."

" 'Tis all very well for you, with a babe and a man too old to fight," muttered Susan. "What do I care for they Germans and Poles if my Len has to go?" She left at last, but with a strong sense of grievance. Her man had been taken from well-paid work and thrust into khaki at a few shillings a week, and all the Lud-

* Nickname for the East Kent Regiment.

lows could do was sit in their manor and say she couldn't have her job back. Len would surely be out in July, when he was twenty-one, and then she would show them all; quite how, she wasn't sure.

As a child, Susan had liked her parents' farm, clamoring to feed the ducks and ride on jolting plow horses. Now, after the excitement of London, where she had helped behind the bar in a West End restaurant while Len's band played, she found it dirty, wet, and unutterably dull. At the end of a week she announced she was off. "I'll get a job in Canterbury near Len, Pa. Now the Ludlows done the dirty on me, I'll not stay to be a burden on you."

Fred Dickson took off his spectacles and laid them on the scrubbed kitchen table. "You're no burden, daughter. Your ma is getting old for all the work there is here."

"I've been thinking, though, Pa. I was wrong to leave Len and come here. He'll be out in a couple of months; I ought to stay by him." She knew she could always catch her father on the score of duty.

"I'll not stop you if you be set on it. Though I reckon there's no chance of Len being out in July, nor any other time, neither. In for the duration he is, like I was in the last one."

Susan tossed her head disbelievingly and packed her bag the next day, but her father's judgment was accurate. More groups were called up during May and June, none were released. She drifted back to London when Len's company was sent to Wales for training, and was soon serving behind her bar again.

"Waiting for Len to come home, she says." Dickson fixed large, mournful eyes on Faye when she encountered him in Dover. "But I dunno, the first thing out of hand in war is women, an' I reckon my Susie's the same as the rest."

"She'll be back." Faye reflected that she almost certainly would scuttle out of London if war came, since everyone agreed that the capital would be devastated by bombing within days of its outbreak. She looked around her at shoppers strolling down Biggin Street, at the calm permanence of castle and white cliffs, and felt the same quiver in her heart as when she saw Christopher in his gas mask. Then she took a deep breath: there was nothing to be done. Nothing but live these last strange weeks of peace and pray for a miracle, knowing the time for miracles was past.

The naval headquarters in the Castle was sprouting wireless antennas, a dozen half-inflated barrage balloons crouched like drowsing elephants by the harbor, which was slowly filling with navy ships. But even in Dover harbor, peace and war were still evenly balanced: Southern Railway boat trains clacked in and out, the Lord Warden Hotel was filled with the rich on passage, Channel ferries as busy as ever, setting naval launches bobbing as they churned in and out. The beach was packed with holidaying families, stop-me-and-buy-one men in striped jackets selling water ices for a penny from tricycle barrows, tin buckets clattering in the wind under the awnings of roadside stores.

In the third week of July, Beauty completed her engine trials in the harbor and met open sea for the first time. Faye stood on the end of the Prince of Wales pier and watched: she had wanted to be on board but Rupert refused. "We'll have one of the engine fitters with us; Henry must go and myself of course, as well as two crewmen, so I'm afraid this time there isn't room for you."

So she stood and watched them go by and thought how small Beauty looked after months of seeming enormous on the stocks. She felt forlorn after the excitement of preparation, and privately believed that Rupert could have found space for her if he had wished. Ever since she yielded to him after taking Sisley to Dover, the aching difficulty of her marriage had increased, until she sometimes felt she was two different persons, astonished to find her face unchanged. She was the Faye Ludlow whom Rupert saw; quiet, sheltered Faye, who supported him in whatever he chose to do and seldom offered opinions of her own. Yet all the while she was growing fast, driven by strength she found within herself: strength to be restrained when Rupert was not; to show understanding and see his obstinate insistence on risking so much on Beauty for the tragedy it was, rooted in fear of failure and trapped with adverse circumstances deserving pity, which also she must not show. And most difficult of all, strength to take it lightly and not forget the saving grace of laughter.

Her hazel eyes had always changed subtly with the flow of her thoughts: nearly green one moment, flecked with light the next. She had learned to hold her expression still under stress, but when she forgot, it changed too with each shift of feeling. She plucked her eyebrows into a delicate curve, left alone they grew thick and uncompromisingly straight; men were intrigued by the deep cleft in her chin and missed its long, firm shape and the tight determination which could come to her mouth if her spirit was aroused. It was a face full of the same contradictions she felt within herself and no one had yet understood more than a trifling part of her, although perhaps John Castellan had seen more than most. But since that evening she had changed again, and nothing said then still mattered now with carving gone. Bait. That alone she could not forget. Rupert certainly had not yet grasped the self she tried to show him, and with him she now needed all her defenses, all the shelter she could find.

As she discovered more about him, and did not like all she found, she was surprised that knowledge made no difference to her love: sometimes she wished it would. Perhaps it would not hurt so dreadfully to find herself unknown to him if she did not love him so much; standing on the Prince of Wales pier to watch Beauty put to sea, she could feel tears in her throat when he did not even look up as he passed.

Almost at once, she could see that all was not well. Although there was a heavy swell, it was by no means rough, yet Beauty wallowed the moment she met the open sea. She was designed for the fast and economical use of power, chine and sheer precisely balanced to thrust and weight. At speed she would be tough and durable, timbers keyed to stresses speed would create. Without speed she was frail and awkward, calculations misplaced, weight and gravity wrong: if she could not poise herself on the step of power, her light construction was a deadly danger.

Faye watched as she swung and wallowed, leaped a moment in grace and then was trapped again by a sequence of water she could not surmount. At first she thought Rupert must be continuing the half-speed trials he had been engaged on in the harbor, then she saw the stem turn, the sickening lurch as it could not swing in time. The painful crawl back to the shelter of the breakwaters seemed endless, hull leaden with shipped water, and Faye thought she held her breath the whole time. Rupert did not look at her this time either as he passed, his face expressionless, hands grasping the brass coaming, and she walked all the uphill miles back to Reydenham alone.

Chapter Six

Faye thought that the most terrible part of Beauty's failure was Rupert's silence. He never referred to it at all, as if the months of striving, of dreams and hopes, had never existed. He did not come home until early the following morning, and when she went downstairs she found him asleep in an armchair, face stubbled and hands hanging loose.

She covered him with a rug, chased the housemaid away from her clattering brooms, and took Christopher out to play in the garden. When she brought him back to the nursery at lunchtime, Nanny looked up from her knitting. "Mr. Rupert has gone out again."

"Gone? Where?"

Nanny put Christopher in his high chair, where he immediately began to bang his spoon on the table. He was a child who either bounded with activity or was asleep. "Just out, he said."

"Didn't you tell him I was in the garden?"

"He knew, but said he was in a hurry."

Faye could understand that Rupert found it difficult to face the world after such failure; it was still bitter to discover that to him she was no different from the rest.

She spent the day fidgeting about the house and garden, every sound turned into Rupert's return.

"Shall I lay dinner for two, madam?" In her imagination Phipps looked contemptuous of a wife who did not know her husband's whereabouts.

"Oh yes, please. I am sure Mr. Rupert will be home soon," she said hastily, as if he was already after an appointed hour.

But still he did not come. She ate a few mouthfuls without any idea what she was eating, the house silent and creaking around her, ears straining for the sound of a car down the valley road.

Afterwards, she went into the library, where neat files, marine catalogues, and well-handled plans of Beauty stared at her in silent accusation. She wondered whether to clear them away, whether Rupert would be thankful to find everything gone when he returned. She decided that he would and started to shuffle them together, then stopped, painfully aware that he might also be glad of an excuse to turn his disappointment into anger against her.

She drifted back to the drawing room to hear the news. A British military mission was to go to Moscow, but it was not clear whether an alliance with Russia was to be expected. There had been reports the week before that Winston Churchill had advocated such a move and Rupert exclaimed angrily that he was thankful Churchill was out of office, since so far he had been wrong on every issue of policy that anyone could remember. For himself, he would prefer Hitler to a pack of Soviets. Faye sighed and switched off the set: council workmen were clearing out the caves under Dover's chalk cliffs for use as air-raid shelters, and it seemed to her that the menace was Hitler now, not Russians in the distant future.

At that moment she heard the car. Gears grinding, wheels rattling on the grid. Although it was late, the long summer twilight was as soft as a silk painting, the first stars glinting through trees still reflecting crimson from the sun. Faye went out and put her arms around Rupert as he climbed from the car. "You must be tired, my love." She had wondered what to say to him, but the sight of his face swept everything but instinct aside.

He kissed her, but did not hold her as he usually did, as if he feared it might seem like weakness. "You mustn't worry about me, I can last more than one night without sleep." He stretched and breathed deeply, looking around him. "Thank God to be back in the valley anyway. I feel better already."

And that was all.

He went to bed and slept for fifteen hours; when he woke he slipped into his old habits as if they had never been broken. He walked the valley, gun under his arm, he called on tenants and reckoned up repairs and timber for felling; he began exercising his hunter and remarked that cub hunting would soon begin. He never once went down into Dover or climbed beyond the southern edge of the valley, from where the Channel could be seen.

He seldom touched her during the day but was more loving than he had ever been at night, tenderness mixed with passion as he wordlessly accepted all the comfort she could give. It was as if he felt ashamed to admit his need when others might be there to feel contempt. The news continued to worsen, and in mid-August came the bombshell of a treaty between Germany and Soviet Russia. Britain and France had missed any chance which might have existed for alliance with Russia, and now Poland was encircled by enemies, the last span of peace measured by days. After the news they heard Parliament being recalled, which had never before been done by radio; the next day an Emergency Powers Act was passed in a single hectic sitting, under which almost anything could be done to prepare the country for war.

Anything except produce the men and arms needed in the short time left.

Faye went down to Dover two days later, feeling it might be the last time she would ever do so. No one knew what to expect when war came, everyone was speaking more quietly than usual, the sun shone brilliantly, and when she returned to the car with her purchases she saw another marching crisis line on the news posters: "Britain affirms guarantee to Poland. Treaty signed."

"Thank God," said a young man who shared his paper with her. "I'm tired of belonging to a nation of funks. There's no escaping this one, and it's time we stopped trying."

Faye looked at him curiously. "You're glad?"

"Of course, aren't you?"

And then she realized that beneath the dread, she was glad. The long scramble for safety was over, the unreal life they had been living nearly finished and pride regained. They might die, but no longer could men say that in their time Britain had lost her heritage. "Yes, I'm glad," she answered simply, and smiled.

He gave her his newspaper. "You keep this, I must be off. I expect my papers will have arrived at home, I volunteered for the Navy three weeks ago."

"Good luck." It was all she could say, and when he had gone she went in search of the ARP office. An hour later she had signed up for ambulance duties; not many women likely to be exempted from the services could drive, so she was welcome enough, even if there was a distinct air of reproach that she had left it so late to volunteer.

"Most of our members have done a great deal of training during the summer," said an elderly man, shuffling her forms together impatiently. "It is a very different matter driving a two-ton lorry to driving an Austin seven. What do you know about first aid?"

Faye had to admit that she knew nothing and was immediately given a list of lectures to attend, driving instruction she must undergo, and issued with a map of Dover. "Learn every street and how to get there. Imagine whole areas too ruined to drive through, and work out routes to reach wherever you are sent just the same." He also issued her with an armlet and tin helmet, and she gathered she was lucky to get them. His satisfaction was obvious when he told her that Folkestone and Deal had neither.

Afterwards, she walked down to the harbor and stood a long while looking out over the water, at ferries fretting in and out, at white ensigns flying from a strange mixture of trawlers, tugs, destroyers, and patrol boats, more gathering even while she watched. The white cliffs took on fresh meaning, the Castle with its flag, the sweep of blue sky above. There were few children on the beach any more, instead soldiers were filling sandbags and along the Prince of Wales pier some more were unhitching a solitary antiaircraft gun. She walked as far as the Ludlow slip: it was closed and deserted, a padlock on the doors.

Henry was leaning on a railing nearby and looked up at her approach. "Come to say goodbye to Beauty, Mrs. Ludlow?"

"For the moment. After the war we'll get that other engine and make sure she lives up to her name."

"Aye, after the war. That Solent chap knew how to build a grand boat, I reckon, if she were properly done."

"One day she will be." It seemed to be a day for making pledges. "Was she damaged at all?"

He shook his head. "As trim as you could wish, once we'd 'auled 'er up. 'Twere a sad business, but Beauty were naught to blame. Before Mr. Sisley went, 'Henry' 'e says, 'with one engine, she'll be a trippers' boat in a flat calm if 'er's lucky; with two, she'll carve the Channel apart.' I reckon 'e were right. All wrong as she were, she still 'andled sweet."

"Even Solent-designed?" Faye said, smiling.

His grunt might have been amusement. "Dover-built. There be things about 'er I don't 'old with, and that there Sisley too, but one day she'll go right noble, you see if she don't."

Faye wondered how to break it to Rupert that from now on her days would be spent ambulance training in Dover, but she need not have worried. She was late returning and ran upstairs to change for dinner, to find his case open, the bed piled with clothes.

"I'm off," he said the moment she entered the room. "The post came with my papers after you left."

"Off? Where?" She stared at him in astonishment. Rupert, who had always laughed at William for volunteering.

He shrugged. "I don't know. I've got to report in London. I wanted the Navy, but it looks as if it'll be the Army after all."

She sat on the bed, heart hammering at the thought of him going. "Why didn't you tell me? When did you—"

"The day after Beauty failed, I went to London. I wanted to go right away, start again, not think any more. I signed up there, since everyone is set on their war."

"Couldn't you have told me?" she cried bitterly. "At least told me afterwards what you had done?"

"These last days at Reydenham . . . it has been just as it always was. As if nothing had ever changed or ever could." He stared out at steep slopes, hard with chalk and soft with the labor of generations. "I wanted to savor everything, live a lifetime in the short span left. It's finished now, I suppose, but I didn't want to think of it."

Reproach died on her tongue; there was a long silence. She felt very empty. He had lived the last span of the life he knew as he wished to live it, and it had hardly included her at all. Except for need and comfort in the night.

"When are you going?" she said at last.

He looked at his watch. "Half an hour. Will you come down to Dover with me? I've rung the solicitors and told them to draw up a power of attorney so you can deal with everything here while I'm away. I'll call in and sign it on the way. I've written to the bank, too."

"Shouldn't your mother—"

"No. I've paid everything for her for years. My father left the property in trust to me, he didn't hold with women meddling with money."

"And you?"

He laughed. "I've no choice. No solicitor would care for Reydenham like one of the family, and you'll guard it for Christopher better than most."

"And for you, my darling."

He strapped his case in silence, then came over and pulled her down on the bed beside him. "Half an hour. It's little enough, God knows." They kissed, and delight came fresh and new in the urgency of half an hour left, of no time left at all for anything but themselves together.

If only it could always be like this, thought Faye, lovely and precious and uncomplicated; like this, only not with very much less than half an hour left before he goes.

"Do you love me?" she asked like a child, watching while he dressed swiftly. Five minutes now.

"A lot," he said, and laughed. "Or hadn't you noticed, Mrs. Ludlow?"

So they drove up the valley in contentment and stopped where Ludlows always stopped to look back. Back at paths he had walked the day before and might not walk again, at the manor growing from its hill, where Christopher slept unstirring from his father's touch before he went. They stood awhile, his arm about her shoulders, and then got back in the car. "I'm glad to go," he said suddenly. "Except for leaving you. This war . . . it's madness to have stumbled into it, but it's good to have things simple again."

"It seems a high price to pay for simplicity," said Faye drily, and saw his face darken. Let's keep it simple and hold contentment tight, she thought. She still could not grasp that he would have left for war, surely soon for war, before the day had passed.

They called at the solicitors to sign papers. "Remember," said Rupert. "Hold what you can for Christopher."

"And you," she repeated obstinately. He was thirty-nine and with no experience of soldiering: the war would surely be fought with him safely behind the lines.

"Promise me."

"I promise," she said obediently, and they kissed lightly, softly on the lips at Dover Priory Station, the platform full of steam and kissing couples.

"Until sometime, my love."

"Until somewhere, very soon," she said. "Call me, if you can."

And so they parted; tears did not come until she lay alone that night and listened to the rising wind outside.

Chapter Seven

Less than a week later, Hitler invaded Poland. Faye never forgot the agonizing wait afterwards, while still the government hesitated. People avoided each other's eyes and no longer feared war, but fresh betrayal and Britain crawling from her plighted word. Generations of high-nosed Ludlows looked down in painted scorn each time Faye passed them on the stairs, as if they wondered what manner of sheep England had bred since their day: when Chamberlain's tired old voice brought the nation to war at last, there were no cheers, only a deep sense of rightness.

Rupert was in Cambridge, taking a signals course. He was not allowed to tell her, but had no difficulty in dropping enough hints for her to guess at once where he must be. He knew nothing of signals and found the theory difficult, but Faye gathered he still had hopes of transferring to the Navy if he passed his course.

She wrote to him each day, increasingly anxious letters in which the war had little part. Indeed, the war seemed to fade out of existence almost as soon as it had come. Dover bustled with ships, with thousands of soldiers being ferried to France, with guns and tanks and stores piled into Channel ferries conscripted like the men; otherwise the war might have been imagined. Mines were laid and exploded unexpectedly in the Channel, a U-boat cornered and sunk off the Goodwin Sands, but that was almost all; resolution drained away into uncertainty again, until men shrugged and began to look to their own interests. Goods were short, but the government hesitated to impose rationing, so resentment spread as prices rose, the families of men already conscripted suffering real hardship as they were paid a fraction of booming civilian wages.

It seemed absurd to worry about money when everyone had expected a holocaust within hours of the outbreak of war, but as the strange winter of 1939 dragged on this became Faye's overriding worry. It started quietly enough, with a bill from the solicitors for drawing up her power of attorney, a small amount, but she decided to wait to pay it until she received a balance sheet from the bank: when she did, she could not believe the figures she saw. She knew, of course, that Rupert had overspent on Beauty but assumed that most of this was covered by lower expenditure at Reydenham and by backing he had received from elsewhere. Now she saw precise columns of red-inked figures amounting to nearly four thousand pounds overdrawn: the manager would be grateful to have the matter adjusted without delay.

She wrote to Rupert at his army address of mysterious figures, and his reply contained no reference to money. She wrote again, more urgently, and then again in panic, for bills were flooding in. Installments were due on Beauty's engine, the builders who always carried out repairs on the estate had not been paid for a year; then the War Agricultural Committee wrote, laying down plans for increased production at Reydenham, offering grants and subsidies to speed the work, but veiled threats also if it was not done.

Rupert wrote again, at last. His course was cut short and he was under orders for France; Faye's hopes rose and she turned the pages of his letter hastily, but there was no mention of leave before he went. Surely soldiers always had leave before they went abroad? She wrote again and on Christmas Eve, at last, he rang up.

She was overjoyed to hear his voice and for a moment could not scramble her thoughts together, the four months he had been gone a gulf of loneliness and anxiety she could not cross.

He sounded cheerful, delighted to be going to France. "I was thankful to be in the group pulled out of the course, you never saw such stuff as we were meant to be learning! In France at least it will be the real thing."

"Not fighting? You aren't going to the front?"

"I don't know. I have to report at Abbeville, I've sent you a temporary address."

"Have you any leave first? Can I meet you in London? Will you be coming through Dover?"

He laughed. "Steady on. I don't know whether I'll come through Dover or not. I'm still you-know-where at the moment."

"Surely you must have embarkation leave?"

"I don't know," he repeated. It seemed strange to Faye that he should know so little when he was off within days, and she suggested again that she should meet him in London.

"For heaven's sake, Faye," he said impatiently. "I can't just go off to London now! How is Christopher?"

"Oh, Rupert, do you know, he's beginning to speak? He follows me everywhere and hardly falls over at all."

He demanded to hear more, and they forgot time until the operator interrupted. "Rupert," said Faye desperately. "Could you ring again? I must talk to you about all the money we owe. What should I do about all the bills coming in?"

"I can't ring again today, I'll try tomorrow. You'll manage, love. Tell the bank I'm in France, and then they'll have to leave the overdraft until I'm back."

"Sorry, you time is up, caller," the operator interrupted.

"I love you, Faye. God bless." His voice was relieved, delighted to have got off so lightly; crisis no longer existed when he was not connected with it.

Faye replaced the receiver carefully, hands clammy. He would not ring again tomorrow. She remembered all those months when he had concentrated everything on Beauty and ignored the coming of war: now he was immersed in war and the ruin threatening Reydenham had no meaning for him. No, that was not true; love of Reydenham was the force which had driven him into greater and greater risk, and finally to disaster. Hold what you can for Christopher, he had said. He knew, she thought, he knew what he had done and said his farewell to the valley those last few days before he left. Certainly, he must have leave but would not come, unable to bear the reality of his inheritance packaged for the auctioneer's hammer. She stopped on her way upstairs, and stared at the Ludlow portraits. How could she hold anything at all for Christopher in the storm now building over Reydenham?

It was the strangest Christmas she had ever spent; she thought of the gay party at Chillenor the year before and smiled wryly to herself, remembering how she had not wanted to go. Christopher at least enjoyed the day, staring wide-eyed at the Christmas tree with its spun-glass balls, and shouting with joy when Father Christmas trudged past the windows with his bag. Gabriel had offered to dress up and go around the village, where so many men away meant a dreary Christmas for everyone. He was filled with beer at every stop and ever afterwards a whole generation of Reydenham children thought Christmas incomplete without a hiccuping Father Christmas bellowing off-key carols into the darkness.

Otherwise, they were alone, only Nanny and Cook left of all the Reydenham staff, her father on ARP duty in Canterbury. She had had some idea of discussing her problems with him, but was glad she could not. He would strip himself of means to help her, and scarcely touch the pile of debts she was facing.

Faye sat by the fire after Christopher had gone to bed, and stared into the flames. She must think. No, not think, she had done enough of that. She must decide what to do, and do it. The bank was the least of her worries; while Rupert was in France they would not insist on repayment, although she would find no further credit there. Reydenham rents were due on January 1 and these would provide enough to live on and start reducing their debt, but in wartime it seemed unpatriotic to ask for increases. There were government grants to boost production, and if she could last through to next harvest, then profits should grow and the worst of her worries might be over. If she could last until harvest. She bit her lip, for this was the reef of impossibility on which she must founder. There was no way to last until harvest, for the most disastrous of her problems was only just beginning to surface, like rocks at low tide. The mystery of where Rupert had obtained his money was solved. As the chances of agricultural profit increased, one by one the callers came to Reydenham wanting their money back. He had borrowed from almost every friend he had, sometimes quite small sums, but the total was terrifying and certainly not yet complete. Faye had been puzzled when the first hints were dropped, the first apologetic letter received; now she faced almost daily humiliation as increasingly explicit demands for repayment were made.

Some showed her Rupert's scrawled promises to pay, others had trusted his word and felt it dishonorable to ask for anything in writing: most disliked pressing her, a few were disagreeable or insulting, but she did not doubt the sums they mentioned. When added to the unpaid bills and overdraft at the bank, she needed over ten thousand pounds to clear Reydenham of debt and start setting it in prosperity again.

Ten thousand. It was as remote as peace itself. Even time was lacking, time to pay, and time to think about paying. Faye had qualified as an ambulance driver and did a four-hour shift three times a week, meeting the ferries from France. There was little fighting, but always some men sick from wet and cold, others who fell from bridges or tanks, or blew off their hands with faulty ammunition. Every ship brought a few stretcher cases and often she did far more than her four hours, driving them to hospitals all over Kent, since the main Dover hospital had been evacuated.

A great banging on the front door distracted her, long before her confused reflections had reached any decision. "Faye! It's William, let me in!"

He lifted her off her feet and hugged her. "Happy Christmas. I had a thirty-six-hour pass and thought I'd come and see you."

Nanny came out of the back and was hugged in her turn. "Mr. William, really, you'll get us all killed with the door open for every German to see!"

"The blackout!" said Faye guiltily, seeing light spilling out over the gravel.

William slammed the door. "The Jerries will all be flat on their backs in a pool of beer tonight, not stalking Reydenham through the trees. Nanny darling, find me something to eat, will you, I'm starving. I walked all the way from Dover."

"And you'll walk all the way back, Mr. William. You can't stay here with Mr. Rupert away."

"Oh, rubbish! You're chaperone enough for a parcel of Thames bargees. You don't mind, do you, Faye?"

"Of course not. Oh, William, I'm so glad to see you!" She was unexpectedly close to tears; William could not help but at least she could talk to him, lift anxiety a trifle by sharing it.

He gave her another hug. "It's a different Christmas to last year, isn't it? I could do with some of those damned rabbits to eat right now. D'you know, I tripped over old Gabriel with his toes turned up in the lane, dressed as Father Christmas. Drunk as an owl, I give you my word."

"Oh dear, I should have made sure he got back home safely." She explained hastily, and William laughed.

"I threw him in the barn at Stone Cross. He'll have the devil of a head tomorrow, but he'll be all right." He ate ravenously, telling her with his mouth full that he had been posted to Northern Ireland. "Northern Ireland! I know what that means, flying second pilot in some damned great crate the size of Dover Castle, looking for submarines. They say I'm too old for fighters."

"I'm glad," said Faye simply. "Submarines can't shoot back so easily."

"Well, I'm not! Although I suppose I'm lucky to be flying, not plowed out of my course like poor old Rupert."

Haltingly, she began to tell him just how disastrously his brother had left affairs at Reydenham, and William whistled thoughtfully when she had finished. He was sprawled by the fire, air force jacket with new white wings undone, looking completely unchanged by his months of training. He had the same bright blue Ludlow eyes and high-crested hair as Rupert, otherwise there was no likeness. William's eyes laughed even in repose, where Rupert's often sharpened with temper, and although younger, William's face was more lined than his brother's since he used it all the time, in mimicry, gaiety or for emphasis. Lined from drink, too, thought Faye critically, as she topped up his glass: even in adversity Rupert had been abstemious.

"You'll have to mortgage the place," said William after some thought. "Even in wartime, it must be worth more than ten thousand."

Faye went over to the desk without speaking and placed a document in his hands. "It already is. Interest is due on the first of January."

William fingered the paper. "You had no idea?"

"I knew he was spending too much, but no, I had no idea. I think as time began to run out, he lost count too . . . he would not let anything stand in his way . . ." She hesitated. "I think perhaps he came to know he would fail, but instead of admitting it, he doubled his stakes."

William dropped the deed on the floor. "I wish I could help you, but I've got a fiver in my pocket, a bust-up old car at my billet, and not much else besides. You'll have to sell; there's no entail and you have power of attorney."

"Rupert would never forgive me. I'm not sure I'd forgive myself. Four hundred years of Ludlows here, and jumped-up Faye Haskell sells it all while her husband is away fighting for his country."

"Fighting for his country be damned!" said William brutally. "Rupert was pulled out of his course because they knew he'd never pass it. He'll be sorting bumph in some base headquarters for the rest of the war. What the hell else can you do except sell?"

"I don't know," said Faye unhappily, her thoughts on Rupert, just the wrong age for the kind of war he would enjoy. How he would loathe clerking while others fought. She felt desperately sorry for him, perhaps above all because he would hate her pity.

Ten thousand pounds. In wartime, even furniture would sell for a fraction of its value.

"My mother," said William suddenly. "She hasn't spent anything for years, and there's a pocketful of family jewelry. I'll see her in the morning for you."

"Rupert told me once that he paid everything for her. I don't think she can have much."

William looked skeptical, but said nothing. His mother was housed at Reydenham free, but he had borrowed from her too often himself to think her poor.

He returned in triumph from his visit the following morning, hands full of jewelry. "It's ugly stuff," he said disparagingly, dropping it on the table. "Ludlows have had a taste for gold by the ounce ever since they grew rich robbing Spaniards."

"There . . . there wasn't any money, was there, William? I hate to sell your mother's jewelry. Whatever did she say?"

"Precious little money, she's another of Rupert's victims. He owes her God knows how much, and promised her a half share in that damned boat of his in exchange. She said it might be better for us to pretend the jewelry was stolen and claim the insurance."

Faye laughed, she could imagine Mrs. Ludlow saying and meaning it. "How dreadful of Rupert to owe her too, she never said a word to me."

"Dirty linen. She'd stick pins in a wax image of him, but keep quiet to a stranger."

Stranger. My God, thought Faye, staring at brooches and rings, what more must I do to become a Ludlow? "How much do you think it will fetch? I've no idea how to set about selling it, have you?"

"I'll do it on my way through London if you like. Plenty of people with funk holes lined up, I daresay, and anxious to turn cash into things like this." He shoveled them into his pocket, even while the ignoble thought crossed Faye's mind that, fond as she was of William, he might not be quite reliable with money.

She went to thank Mrs. Ludlow before driving William to Dover, the relief of an easier mind making her feel wonderfully optimistic. She had never possessed jewelry apart from her engagement ring, and had no idea of its value, but the pile of gold and stones was reassuring. For no particular reason, she thought it might be worth as much as four thousand pounds, so she could start repayments and restore confidence with Reydenham's creditors; if only she could hold on awhile, she was confident that the war and careful husbandry would bring prosperity back to Reydenham.

She was embarrassed to think of her mother-in-law stripped of possessions which must be precious to her, and kissed her impulsively. "I don't know how to thank you, or what I would have done if you hadn't come to the rescue."

Mrs. Ludlow looked surprised. "I kept the things Max gave me, the rest belongs to Reydenham. I always thought it sadly vulgar, although it does seem a pity not even to *try* for the insurance."

"I think the insurance company would do a great deal of investigating if we did," said Faye, smiling.

"I should think of a very good story, and so I told William," said Mrs. Ludlow with dignity. "I should *enjoy* to think of a good story."

"I bet she would," said William feelingly as they drove to Dover. "I might be tempted if I thought for a moment they were insured, but I expect that's another bill Rupert hasn't paid. Sorry," he added as he had to swerve violently on a steep bend. "I ought to know this road well enough to drive it in the dark."

Driving had become a nightmare, with headlights blacked out except for a minute slit of light, no streetlights, and obstructions in the form of roadblocks and air-raid shelters looming out of the dark without warning. Faye had only six gallons of petrol a month for all her needs, so in daylight she nearly always cycled or walked, Reydenham's isolation becoming a real problem, like so much of ordinary living which everyone had taken for granted before. It was scarcely possible to travel the fifteen miles to Canterbury, and back again, in a day without the car and so she seldom saw her father; with military priority on all lines there were often hours of delay before a telephone connection could be made, and while the government hesitated over introducing rationing, half the day could easily be wasted in searching for the most simple of purchases.

She said goodbye to William at Dover Priory, a place she was coming to hate, and he promised to ring her as soon as possible, in the middle of the night if a line was not free before.

She sat and waited for his call. When it came she could hardly bear to lift the receiver. "Faye?" His voice was distant, the line bad. "There's a flap on, so I'm back at base. I didn't have much time in London."

Her heart sank. "Did you sell them?"

"Lord, yes. I started in Regent Street and ended in some greasy den down the Strand. All in an hour with a taxi clicking up the minutes. I've put the check in the post to you tonight, it'll take a day or two from here, so don't worry."

"How much?"

"Fifteen hundred quid."

She thought perhaps she hadn't heard right. "Fifteen hundred for all your mother's jewelry?"

She heard his chuckle distinctly enough. "D'you know, Faye, you sound quite suspicious? Cross my heart, it was the best I could do. The fellow in Regent Street quite turned his nose up and said what rotten taste our ancestors had, and the next one I went to nearly had me apologizing because the stones were cut on the cross or something."

"I'm not suspicious," said Faye hastily, and she wasn't any more. William at least had struggled halfway across the country to see her for a few hours and done what he could to help; it was just that he was so well used to selling today and being flush tomorrow. It was an everyday matter to him, to be dispatched with the least amount of fuss. Whatever her inexperience, she would have managed better herself. I'm on my own now until Rupert is back, she thought fiercely when William had rung off, there's no one to rely on but me.

Fifteen hundred pounds. Set against Reydenham's debts it was not much, but it was something, and she sat scheming how to use it to the best advantage. The bank must wait. I'll see the manager and fix up something to keep him quiet, she reflected, deciding to pass William's check through her own small account in Canterbury. It was two in the morning before she went to bed, and by then she had decided on her course of action. Half the money must go to settling the most pressing debts, towards paying those friends whom she knew were seriously worried by the amounts Rupert owed them. An installment must be paid to the most ag-

gressive of Beauty's suppliers since they could insist on bankruptcy
proceedings; the mortgage interest too—the list was endless. And
from it all she must save as much as she could for expanding production at Reydenham. From this would come salvation, if any
was to be found, and it must not be neglected in the morass of
present debt.

She lay the rest of the night, tossing in the cold spaces of her
bed, thinking of the avalanche of things she must do. She knew
that farmers were delighted by the return of prosperity after two
generations of agricultural depression, that the opportunity for
profit was there, but she herself knew nothing of farming. Rupert
had lived all his life in the valley, he would know whether her
hoarded pounds should go on more sheep, on cattle, or plowing
up pasture as the Committee wanted. The valley farmers shook
their heads and muttered of poor land for the plow, but she simply could not judge. She turned over again and thumped the pillow flat. Rupert had charmed thousands out of the bank manager;
if only she could ask him how it was done. If only she could hold
on, surely Rupert would be home on leave in the spring. She
turned on the light and read his last letter again. He sounded
pleased with everything and said he was with good fellows in the
mess; she thought of William's comments and sought for any hint
that he might feel chafed by whatever position he held, but there
was none. To be in France was still a novelty; army life was
strange, but its strangeness was interesting and companionable.
He had found his simplicity and was enjoying it. He wrote
warmly, but she could hardly avoid a pang of envy: if only events
would allow her the luxury of living to orders set by other people's
contriving.

She felt tired and jaded in the morning and had to cycle to
Dover for her ambulance shift through raw, gray scud blowing up-
Channel. She shared her duty with a girl called Beryl Meek and
seldom was anyone more misnamed. Beryl was square and lowering from her heavy, capable shoulders to the straight fringe ruled
above her eyes. Before the war, she had wheeled trolleys and
heaved sacks of dressings in the local hospital, so was expected to
be unaffected by the sight of horrors and given to Faye as crew,
since everyone assumed she would be more sensitive. Faye
thought she might be, too, and dreaded failing in some way if she
was faced with an emergency. So far there had only been routine

to endure: the few cases they handled decently swathed in bandages before they left France.

"I dunno more'n you do, about first aid an' that," confided Beryl. "But at least I'll not faint. You'd be surprised what I found in them sacks in the 'ospital in my time."

They were waiting on the Prince of Wales pier for a leave ship. The harbor was peaceful in meager winter light, everything dim and gray: the Castle hidden in murk, cliffs dingy below. No light showed and it was bitterly cold waiting on the exposed pier. After a while, Faye climbed out of the ambulance to get away from Beryl's hospital reminiscences, shuddering as wind slashed through layered clothes. It was going to be a rough night, and she tried not to think of the long bicycle ride back to Reydenham when she had finished her duty. At least their remoteness saved them from having evacuees, who had flooded into Dover in the early days of the war, and were now drifting back to London as nothing happened. At least that's one list I'm not on yet, she reflected with satisfaction.

She walked across and looked at the Ludlow slip. To her surprise she saw a chink of light showing, and went down to investigate. The doors were still loose, and she was stirred by strange nostalgia as she encountered the smells of boatbuilding again. The sound of sea and wind was all around, and she felt Rupert as almost a physical presence, as if he knew she was there and had stopped in his tracks in France, smiling, head turned towards home.

Henry was there, a pot of varnish in his hands, and turned in surprise when he heard her step. "A rough night, Mrs. Ludlow."

"I'm waiting for a ferry with my ambulance," explained Faye. "I saw some light and came down. You'll be in trouble with the ARP if you leave it like that."

He put down his pot and methodically filled the chinks she pointed out. "I'm powerful glad to see 'ee, Mrs. Ludlow. I'm not a writing man nor I'd've written afore. They navy men be pokin' about the slip these many days since."

"Doing what?"

He scratched his head. "They've got a lot of gear to shelter. I reckon this old slip'd be handy for cable and suchlike."

Faye thought swiftly, hand instinctively on Beauty's polished planking. "You think they'd just take it?"

He nodded. "Aye. T'harbor's all navy now. 'Tis natural. You'll be paid summat, I reckon, but precious little."

"Where would Beauty go?"

"Out under canvas on the beach. I been varnishin' all week. We'll bed 'er down snug, don't you fret."

Faye thought about it as she sat freezing in the ambulance, waiting, waiting endlessly. "Why the 'ell they don't run 'em punctual-like, I dunno," grumbled Beryl. "Fair fit to give you glass tits tonight."

Faye grinned; with Beryl added to Canterbury stonemasons, she ought to have a vocabulary fit to shock even the Navy if necessary.

Faint lights flicked on at the eastern harbor entrance, swiftly blotted out again by a passing shape. The western entry was blocked and out of use to ease guard-ship problems, the eastern unlit except for an instant as a ship entered.

"*King Orry*," read Beryl as cursing sailors stumbled over berthing ropes in the darkness. "As daft as racehorses the names they give ships. What kind of king would that be then?"

Faye was sufficiently intrigued by the crew's unfamiliar, lilting speech to ask while soldiers stumbled down the gangway, crushed under huge packs.

"The last *King Orry* led the whole bloody German High Seas Fleet in to surrender at Scapa in '18," came the instant response. "The Isle of Man Steam Packet Company delivers the goods: pongos to Dover, Jerries to Scapa, you on a day trip to Douglas, come the peace, love."

Faye recalled her school atlas with an effort and the little island in the Irish Sea from which Manxmen came, and retorted gaily, "Come the peace, and I'll be there on all three legs!"

He glanced at the Manx three-leg sign on his jersey and laughed, before turning back to ropes and bundled soldiers. It was pleasant to find the whole United Kingdom in Dover harbor. After that she noticed several Manx boats with strange Celtic names; some Scots trawlers with perpetually hungry crews as food was sold off to pay for drink; paddle steamers from Brighton, Weymouth, and the Thames thrashing slowly after mines with only a single machine gun to defend themselves; east coast drifters crewed by elderly trawlermen who had fished the Arctic before she was born; a few destroyers, too few to stay in harbor longer than the minimum time to refuel. She reflected that in some ways the war brought the nation together, in others it isolated people to an extraordinary degree. Reydenham and Dover became the limits of her world, even the vital rail link to Folkestone symbolically closed by a massive chalk slip, relays of men working to clear it while the traffic piled up.

An idea had been hardening in her mind through the long wretchedness of the night, and on her return from delivering their stretcher cases to the military hospital ten miles out of town, she went in search of her section ambulance officer.

Mr. Jewell was a man of massive proportions, with a very large, very red face and eyes like flattened rivets. Faye disliked him for no reason she could name, but could not help her unreason, only hide it. She no longer carved stone, but she lived by perception and impression, leaped into feeling whether she willed it or not.

He was contemplating a damaged ambulance with gloom when she found him, and immediately launched into a fierce condemnation of the Army and its habit of digging unlighted holes.

"I wanted to have a word with you about that, Mr. Jewell," said Faye carefully. "You know I've been all night waiting for the leave boat?"

He swelled up alarmingly. "Don't tell me you've damaged another of my ambulances."

"It was lucky I didn't. Without any lights and my hands so cold—"

"I've told them and told them my ambulance drivers is young ladies and not a load of navvies! The boat was due at nine o'clock."

"It arrived at two in the morning." Faye disliked the label of a lady unfit for heavy duty, but persevered in her purposes. "It occurred to me that if we could put the ambulances under cover nearby and just go on the pier when we were needed—"

"Nowhere under cover, young lady, that the Navy aren't already using. I had a look myself."

"There's an old boathouse just below the pier, big enough to take at least two ambulances. It belongs to my husband, I know he wouldn't mind lending it."

"It's empty?" She could see he was drawn by the idea of a forward post under his command.

"It has a boat in it, but we could lay her up on the beach if I could borrow some men for an afternoon. I was in there last night and decided it was our duty to lend it for the ambulances." Faye gazed at him innocently. Once the Navy took the slip and paid the few pounds it was worth, her judgment told her that they would never get it back: an unofficial loan to the ambulance service might well protect their ownership. Without realizing it, Reydenham had become her first care as it had been Rupert's, and she was possessed by an obstinate determination not to fail in her stewardship: Beauty was part of it, the slip was part of it, and this war without fighting had not the power to turn her aside. She missed Rupert, groped for him when she woke before recollection came flooding back, but there was a spark of her mind which wanted the war to last long enough for her to restore his inheritance, and she dreamed sometimes of Reydenham reborn, her gift awaiting his return.

Within a week, Beauty was snugly lashed under canvas in an angle of pier and seafront and the ambulances installed, their drivers loud in Faye's praise. She had the grace to feel shamed by their thanks, but her strongest emotions were triumph and a growing zest for the struggle she faced.

Now for the bank, she thought.

Chapter Eight

Faye muttered to herself and began adding a column of figures for the third time.

"Mummy come in garden, Mummy come in garden!" Christopher came running into the library and she lost her place again. She had an instinctive money sense, but could not easily force it into order on paper.

She swept the little boy into her arms and kissed him. "In a minute, darling, we'll go and see the lambs. Run along and find Nanny until I'm ready."

"Nanny sleeping." He wrinkled his nose and made a great snoring noise. "Lambs now."

Well, why not? thought Faye, glancing out of the window at spring sun and spraying blossom. She was so very tired of figures, of doling hoarded pounds into bottomless holes of debt; tired of waiting for leave boats in freezing darkness; tired of sleeping alone, reading and rereading Rupert's letters to conjure his presence into the empty spaces of her heart. He had been away for seven months, while the war floated like scum on the fret and boil of more urgent affairs, seven months when nothing happened except endless toil and anxiety. Yet her careful figures were beginning to show where profit might one day lie if only she could stay sane and solvent long enough. She needed Rupert back in six months, the war to last another year, she decided: we will not be safe by then, but at least we should be clear of disaster. Sometimes she almost dreaded turning on the wireless and learning the war had fizzled to a finish, the grants for plowing and contracted grain withdrawn.

Christopher tugged her out of the door and they ran together, tumbling and laughing up the steep slope behind the house and into sheep-strewn parkland beyond. Christopher would soon be two years old and she thought of another child with longing, smiling as she watched him scampering after lambs. Later, later, everything was later. Soon, surely, Rupert would be home again and there would be time for life.

They tiptoed back to the house, pretending to be pirates raiding Dover. It was Christopher's favorite game, and ended on their stomachs, crawling down the passage to the larder to seize treasure trove. Rationing had come, and Christopher stalked tidbits as his mother did pounds in the bank.

They were met by Cook with a rolling pin and Christopher darted squealing down the passage to grab whatever she had left there when she saw them coming.

"You've heard the news, madam?" Cook folded down her sleeves, breathing heavily. She was old and fat, even laughing made her gasp.

"What news?"

"That Hitler. He's jumped at last." She sniffed, "Get this old war done quicker now, we will."

Hitler jumped both fast and far. Denmark fell in less than a day, Norway was lost within a week, although a month passed before a scraped-up British force was there and back, the Navy losing heavily in the process. But leave boats still came into Dover from France as if Norway was another world, and sometimes Faye heard sailors gibing at the soldiers that BEF no longer described a British Expeditionary Force, but meant Back Every Friday.

Chamberlain was thrown out of office by a House of Commons driven to fury by halfhearted, bungling incompetence, but the new names which began to filter through to a doubting nation only increased their confusion.

"First they say 'tis Halifax, now 'tis Churchill for Prime Minister, but I dunno, I'm sure." Mr. Jewell usually came to share cocoa with the morning shift. "Mad as a hatter that Churchill, my father always said. He lost a packet of mates at the Dardenelles and Churchill thought that one up."

"Seems to me we're wasting our time," muttered Beryl. "We've lost this bloody war. In 'ospital the patients died on the days the surgeon 'ad 'is mind on 'is garden instead of the operating table."

"Of course we won't lose it," said another girl sharply. Anne Simpson, remembered Faye, her father was a colonel in France. "You shouldn't even think such things."

"It's 'cos ole Chamberlain ain't thought such things we're in the mess we are," retorted Beryl. "In 'ospital—"

"Yes, yes, but war isn't like hospital," intervened Mr. Jewell hastily.

"I don't see why not. You dies in both, and loses bits of yourself, too. In some of them sacks I've 'andled—"

Mr. Jewell turned a deeper shade of red, and Faye turned on their wireless more to drown dispute than because she expected any news of interest. The announcer's voice was telling of German troops pouring into Holland, Belgium, and Luxembourg at dawn that morning. British forces were leaving their positions in France and advancing to their assistance. It was May 10, 1940, and Christopher's second birthday.

The effect on Dover was immediate. Four destroyers left harbor almost at once; the paddle steamers went next, minesweeping gear cleared and ready, then the trawlers vanished into sunlit haze. Next day the traffic was the other way, with fresh ships arriving, refueling, and leaving again, sometimes within the hour. A sailor jerked his head at a newly arrived destroyer as Faye stood on the Prince of Wales pier, watching. "The *Codrington*. Twenty-three hours out of Rosyth, she set up a record and no mistake."

Faye nodded, the scene deeply impressive, a terrible and splendid moment in which to be entangled. She was kept frantically busy as the ships came in and out. Many were too small for medical personnel and the inevitable accidents of haste came ashore: in between there were moments to stand and stare, to sense time quickening under the stresses of unseen battle beneath a brilliant, sunlit sky.

The same ships began to come in again, crawling through the eastern entrance with decks awash and superstructure ripped, towed by trawlers and packed with survivors retching oil, whispers spreading of ships which would never return. Faye had not been home for a week, and all telephone lines out of Dover were jammed with official traffic, so a friendly army dispatch rider promised to go past Reydenham to give them word that she was well.

Yet things had scarcely begun.

In the harbor they knew everything and nothing. They seldom had time to listen to news broadcasts, but rumor spread under the full sail of naval conjecture, as shore-party sailors saw ships they knew come and go. "Blockships," the buzz went round, "that means the Jerries have reached the coast and the bloody pongos can't hold 'em."

"Gor' blimey! Look at the *Codrington*, in and out again! Any more for the Skylark, mate!" And Faye knew the unspoken thought was how the hell can the destroyers keep going much longer without sleep and maintenance.

Destroyers were tying up directly alongside the harbor moles and each side of the Prince of Wales pier; she wondered dimly whether their wash would sweep the Ludlow slip away altogether and was too tired to care. The wish that peace might wait for one more uneventful year already belonged to another life. Stretchers began to be double-banked in the ambulances, off-shift drivers snatched rest where they could, then went back to help as wounded off incoming ships swamped their few vehicles. There was plenty of hot, sweet tea on the pier, and very little else, as the available food, medical equipment, and doctors were concentrated in hospitals and first-aid centers where they could do most good.

Faye felt helpless, imprisoned by inexperience. She feared driving in such congestion, the inevitable jolting which brought agonized screams from her load, but as time went on she came to dread relief from driving even more. Then she had to stand and decide who went next, who would die whether they went or not, who would still live if they waited another hour in shock and glare and pain.

"There's six more below." An exhausted-looking lieutenant was checking stretchers up a destroyer's gangplank. "We've orders to embark a civilian, so they'd best stay where they are for the moment, they're better below than waiting in the open. I hope to God he's on time, I don't fancy Belgium in daylight tomorrow." He laughed. "I sailed in a regatta off Ostend last summer."

"You're going back tonight?"

"To the Scheldt, I think. Antwerp hasn't fallen yet, although there's hell's own fires burning in the port. That looks like our passenger now," he added. "I'll get the rest of the wounded sent up."

Faye glanced round curiously; a man out of uniform on the Prince of Wales pier that day was a rarity indeed. It was John Castellan.

She watched, completely astonished, as he spoke to the lieutenant and showed him some papers. He was hatless and dark-suited, attaché case in hand as if he had come straight from behind a desk to catch a suburban train, and looked singularly out of place in the ordered turmoil of Dover harbor. He turned abruptly, attention caught by her stare, then smiled with instant, unguarded pleasure. "Mrs. Ludlow. Our encounters seem destined to have a flavor of the unusual."

She flushed, silenced by an absurd desire to ask whether he had got very wet after he left Reydenham in fury twenty months before. Of course he did, she thought, and said like a child, "Hullo, Mr. Castellan."

He took in her stained ambulance uniform, overbright eyes and shadowed face. "You have found yourself one of the hardest jobs in the country by the look of you. Might I suggest you go home and rest awhile? You may not believe me, but I think this battle has hardly begun."

She experienced the same jolt as when she sat beside him at dinner: she had become so very unused to care or interest in her affairs. She looked away from him, at the last, most serious stretcher cases being carried off the destroyer. "I can't, not yet. Surely the worst must be over?"

"No." His certainty recalled the harsh exactness with which he had judged Rupert's boatbuilding long ago, and with it came memory also of one insult which could be redeemed.

A civilian would need the highest priority to be in Dover harbor today. "It does not look as if you are on your way to deal in European finance with the Nazis, Mr. Castellan."

He glanced at the waiting destroyer. "It would suggest a flair for trickery quite out of the common run," he agreed, smiling again, aware of the apology she intended.

"Shouldn't you go on board?" asked Faye anxiously. "You need the darkness tonight . . . the lieutenant said you were bound for the Scheldt."

"I wonder why the Navy is called the silent service? I understand they are not ready to leave for another fifteen minutes, although your friend the lieutenant will undoubtedly contrive to make it appear that they are waiting for me, and not the other way around."

She laughed, feeling enormously better for the touch of normality he brought with him. She longed to ask what was taking him to Belgium at such a time, but was certain he would not tell her if she did. Instead, she turned aside to heave a water container out of the way of a returning ambulance. "I wish you a dark night and a late dawn for your journey."

He took the container from her one-handed, and she noticed for the first time the handcuff and chain which secured his left wrist to his attaché case. "Where do you want this?"

"Over there." The case looked heavy and her mind suddenly pictured its weight spinning him helplessly into the muddy darkness of the Scheldt. Ships sank every day now. She touched his wrist lightly. "I hope you have the key handy." Her throat was unaccountably tight.

He stood very still, an expression she could not read in his eyes. Then the long mouth twitched into self-mockery. "I hope so too, if the need arises. Remember to get some rest soon, Mrs. Ludlow."

"Faye. If our meetings are so unusual, we ought at least feel properly introduced." Without reasoning clearly, she wanted very much for him to take some warmth from England with him where he was going.

He nodded, neither accepting nor rejecting what she offered, and went up the gangplank as the destroyer whooped its farewell. She watched it out of the harbor, feeling weighted with sadness: the lieutenant waved when he thought his men were not looking; John Castellan stood by the rail, unmoving, perhaps watching her, perhaps the receding shore. She could not tell which.

That night Faye heard of a naval lorry which would pass the turning for Reydenham on its way, and on impulse begged a lift. There was a slight reduction in activity in the harbor and she was worn out; she would not admit to superstition, as if by taking Castellan's advice she might in some way help to keep him safe.

She walked down the valley road on legs which seemed to lack any stiffening of bone, and in all the length of it there was no glimmer of light, the moon cold above, bathing the earth with peaceful, mocking whiteness. She found herself praying for clouds and rain, for fog in the Scheldt, and stumbled heavily on the rough road. The crunch of stones underfoot at last, a rattle of blackout curtain, then flooding light. The hall rushed in on her with its smells of wood smoke and polish, ticking grandfather clock, and solidity of oak wavering in front of her eyes.

She heard the flutter of voices, felt something in her hand, and drank warm, sweet tea. It steadied her slithering senses and made her giggle, thinking of the whole British nation fighting its war on warm, sweet tea.

A moment later, she was asleep.

Chapter Nine

She woke slowly, turning and burying her face again in soft linen. The room was muffled in blackout but all around were the sounds of full daylight. Feet crunched on gravel, a farm horse clopped slowly by, birds were calling with the soft persistence of day rather than the urgency of dawn.

Only the house was still, and she smiled sleepily as she pictured Nanny chasing Christopher out of earshot. It was good to be back, away from blood and men as loose as jelly on stretchers, away from twisted steel and ships fit only for scrap. She was surprised to find herself in bed, her last memory being of the hall, and supposed they must have induced her to climb the stairs somehow; with recollection came crowding images of Dover, a driving urgency to return, and she leaped out of bed, ripped open the curtains, and began to dress. As she did so, she kept glancing out of the window as if she expected to hear the roar of battle: there was nothing, only a gentle wind and the smell of drying earth.

She ran downstairs and through the empty house, doors set wide to sun and warm air. She found Cook in the kitchen, clucking and motherly over her long sleep. "Proper tired out you were and no mistake, Mrs. Rupert. Sit you down and have some tea."

Tea again, thought Faye; she looked at the clock, half past three. Half past *three?* "Is that really the time?"

Cook laughed. "You slept the day round. Master Christopher's been picnicking in the orchard to keep it quiet for you."

Faye ate rapidly, tasting nothing. "What news is there?"

" 'Tis bad and more than bad. Them Dutch have given up. There's a letter for you from Mr. Rupert."

Faye read it as she finished her meal. He was fine, the Army was fine, everything was fine. They were shooting rabbits and thinking of organizing a fishing expedition if it wasn't too sunny. He loved her very much. The letter was ten days out of date.

She went into the library and searched anxiously around the wireless dial, finding only music. Surely there would be news soon. She wandered about the room, running her hands over leather bindings, fingering last year's diary with Rupert's writing sprawled over its pages, picking up his pen. Was he in Belgium, too, by now?

News, at last. It seemed days since she had heard it ungarbled by haste and rumor. She jotted down the places the announcer mentioned, and searched for an atlas. Holland was gone, the Belgian government had moved to Ostend, a heavy German attack was developing against the French along the Sambre and Somme rivers, the RAF was bombing Germany.

It took her awhile to find the Sambre and Somme, far to the west of where she expected: when she did, her finger paused a moment, then she shut the atlas with a snap. I think this battle has hardly begun, Castellan had said: it looked as if he would be proved right yet again.

Christopher came bounding towards her when she went out, chicken feathers stuck in his hair, yelling Indian war cries. They rolled together on prairie grass, then hid in the cucumber frames from Nanny, pretending to be Peter Rabbit.

"Gabriel will catch us and drop us in his watering can," Faye whispered as they tiptoed to the parsley bed; Peter Rabbit always felt sick after too many carrots.

Christopher crammed his mouth with parsley before spitting it privately behind some rhubarb. "Parsley good for sick."

"Parsley very good for sick rabbits." She nibbled a stem and wiped her whiskers delicately.

"Gabriel not catch us."

"Mr. McGregor nearly caught Peter."

"Gabriel gone."

"Gabriel gone!"

Faye forgot to whiffle her whiskers in her surprise, and he jumped around her shouting, "Mummy whiffle! Mummy whiffle!"

She whiffled him all the way back to Nanny. "Nanny, Christopher says Gabriel's gone?" She could not remember when she had last seen him, when she had last seen Nanny, for that matter.

"They're asking for men to go and shoot parachutists if they come here next, and Gabriel's gone with the rest. He were too old for the last one and fair delighted he's good enough with a shotgun for this. I tried a shotgun once," she added, gentle old hands closing on a broom handle.

"He must be over seventy," said Faye blankly.

"He's good with a shotgun." Nanny's tone was the same she used with children attempting to argue. "They're practicing over on Colonel Druitt's land and some of them are using their hunters as a mounted patrol. The Germans'll not come here."

Faye had never for an instant considered that they might, and did not now. If they had any sense they would run like hell from Gabriel with his shotgun and Nanny on her broomstick, she reflected. I wonder what people would make of that, a hundred years hence, if I carved it high in the shadows of Canterbury Cathedral roof. It never occurred to her that it was strange she should be thinking of carving again in such a crisis, when before it had seemed lost forever.

She drove back to Dover in the evening, car stuttering on its last dregs of petrol as she coasted down the Western Heights. Below her, the harbor stretched almost empty in gathering haze, some trawlers berthed where the destroyers had been, a Manx and a Railway ferry loading against the mole—quite what, she couldn't see.

The Ludlow slip was still there, bodies sprawled in sleep all over the floor, Mr. Jewell flat on his back and snoring fiercely. Faye left them and picked her way along the pier through a jumble of fuel lines, guns, drums of ammunition, and sleeping men. It was one of those freak moments in a battle, when a series of chances brings an instant of silence in a bombardment, although the bombardment continues, when everything is in passage and men can only hold their breath and wait.

Across the Channel the storm had grown and twisted and fed on itself, probing weakness, swirling through cracks of irresolution, pounding anything in its path to ruin. Now it was poised and ready, changing shape, direction, and force with bewildering speed as only killer storms can, the ones men see only in the instant they are swept to destruction.

In Belgium, Louvain had fallen after fierce defense, Brussels was abandoned, the British Army heavily engaged in unfortified positions occupied only hours or even minutes before. Rupert, thought Faye. How is it possible to hear names and places and I cannot tell whether he is there, whether he is alive or dead? She thought of Castellan too, when Antwerp was lost and returning sailors told of towering oil fires and blazing ships in the Scheldt.

St. Quentin, Péronne, Cambrai. It took a while to realize that the names they were hearing were no longer Belgian but French. Laon, Arras, Abbeville. *Abbeville*. Dover people knew the Channel coast, and when Abbeville was first mentioned they stared at each other in disbelief. Abbeville was a scant ten miles up the Somme estuary, far to the south and nowhere near Belgium.

The harbor was suddenly full of troops and guns as well as ships, guardsmen and riflemen of Britain's last reserve being taken by ferries on their familiar run to Calais and Boulogne. Only it was not familiar any more, with the sounds of battle heard clearly now and smoke drifting across the Channel.

Faye was frantically busy again, the wounded overflowing into Marine Station, into Priory Street and Snargate Street, where once she had shopped for fish. At night they could see gun flashes closing on Boulogne, sparkling in the streets, then in the harbor; with the dawn three days after they had gone, the troops were coming home again. Dirty, exhausted, and bandaged, the Guards formed up and marched smartly through Dover as if on parade, and camped in the hills beyond. All that day gunfire rolled across the water and every snatched minute was spent staring across the shining Channel: twenty-five miles away their men were trapped and fighting for their lives in what was left of Calais and Boulogne.

Mr. Jewell ordered half his girls off duty as dusk fell that night. It was two weeks since the Germans had struck, and only the white cliffs and the bright, defiant flag on the Castle seemed unchanged. Faye slept instantly on the concrete floor of the slip, and it seemed only minutes before she was shaken awake to let others rest. When she went out she found the harbor urgent with activity, water slapping against the pier as ships with unfamiliar numbers on the bows arrived throughout the night. Their funnels were blistered with haste, dark Atlantic paintwork mingling with the lighter gray they had grown used to: the Navy was gathering to salvage a nation from defeat.

Along the Prince of Wales pier a destroyer was just leaving. "The V*imiera*," said a sailor, coiling rope. "I sailed in her back in '36. She's the one to save them poor bloody pongos."

"She's going to Boulogne again? I thought it had fallen." Faye stared at the darkened shape moving silently across the harbor.

"So it 'as, apart from the mole. Two thousand men piled up there with the Jerries 'olding the town. The admiral's told the *Vimiera* to see what she can do." He grinned. "She'll get them out."

The minutes dragged by. An hour and a quarter to Boulogne at half speed, and slip in on the dark of the night. An hour to load? No time at all if the Germans saw her. Faye stacked stretchers and filled buckets in readiness for another dreadful day, every sense tuned across the Channel. She noticed that the sailors on the mole were abstracted too, faces lifted to the south at every turn in their work. The Navy knew what its own were doing.

The sounds of battle were around Calais now and further south and east, from Boulogne all was silent. The silence held throughout the night, men swearing quietly if the wind shifted and made the cauldron boiling around Calais seem to come from Boulogne. And in the dawn *Vimiera* came home with a foot of freeboard, guns useless because men were crammed so tight they could not be worked. It was the first small triumph snatched from a hell's brew of disaster.

From Calais there was to be nothing saved but pride. They saw the huge pall of smoke as the town was consumed, as men fought and died within sight of home and no orders came to take them off. By then the scale of disaster was terrifying: half a million men were encircled, backs to the sea, driven ever inward by German attack, including almost the whole of the British Expeditionary Force, shattered remnants of the Belgian Army, and no one knew how many French. Calais was one end of the trap, the sands south of Ostend the other, a distance at first of some fifty miles; Calais could not hold but hours might be gained there, so in Dover they looked across their strait at the town which was part of themselves, and saw flames and smoke and four days gained, and very few come home.

Faye felt a personal pang when the *Vimiera* was smashed to wreckage with bombs, some slight solace when she did not sink. "The Belgians have surrendered! The bloody Belges have buggered off!" The words leaped from lip to lip: Calais gone to the south, now the northern end of the pocket was ripped open as the

Belgian Army laid down its arms, and in all the remaining stretch of sand and dune there was only one port left. Dunkirk.

Faye went on mechanically bandaging, lifting, checking, gulping gallons of tea, feeling hideously sick. Not only Rupert but the whole Army was lost. Gabriel with his shotgun, she thought stupidly. He's going to need it after all.

The ferries went first.

She stood, back aching, and watched them go: three with the legs of Man blowing stiffly from the peak, jack at the stern, two familiar Dover boats with Dover crews, then three more, including a Channel Islands ferry, then two ugly, unmaneuverable train carriers. It was May 26. Their journey was far longer than it should have been because of minefields, and as the Germans crept up the coast opposite, it became longer and longer to keep out of range of their guns.

One of the Manx boats was first back in the morning, carrying nearly double the passengers allowed by her Board of Trade Certificate, upperworks pitted with bomb fragments and even machine-gun bullets from Germans in the dunes.

"I'd like to watch the harbor master in Douglas counting this lot," said one of the deckhands, grinning. "We'd be piled up in Athol Street before we stopped." He was helping Faye carry stretchers down the side, surely even one more exhausted soldier would break her back with his weight.

She found herself scanning filthy, stubbled faces for Rupert. She asked men their regiments but it did not help much since he had been attached to a headquarters and she had no idea of the units around him.

"The Buffs are out there somewhere," said Mr. Jewell angrily, face mottling to a personal insult. "They sent the last lot out a month ago with only two weeks' training. They'll never see Kent again."

"The whole bloody Army is out there somewhere," said Faye furiously, only stonecutter's language suiting the moment. "My husband is out there, and Beryl's boy friend, and Anne's father. We'll not get them back by wringing our hands and doing nothing."

Mr. Jewell's jowls flapped like herring in a net. "Well, really . . . I was only saying—"

"And she was only saying summat as needed saying," interrupted Beryl. "'Tis you should be carrying these 'ere stretchers, you ole rat, not scribblin' on your pieces of paper. I never saw what good paper did no one in trouble, an' my Billy's in bad trouble over in Belgy-yum."

"Organization," said Mr. Jewell, salvaging pride. "There's a lot of organization needed in an operation like this."

Beryl rubbed her palms on her skirt before lifting another stretcher with a grunt. "I believe you, and the admiral and 'is staff and the 'ole bleeding Navy got their heads down doing it, not you."

"Wow!" said the sailor appreciatively, watching Mr. Jewell's departure. "Give me a boatful of Glasgow drunks on the Saturday-night run, rather than you girls under full sail."

Beryl snorted. "In 'ospital we 'ad a short way with the likes of 'im. We'd allus ask their 'elp, see, and bring 'em everything in a puzzle. In them sacks we found things to bring 'em, I can tell you."

Destroyers had joined the ferries now, some arriving direct from convoy duty, others still scarred from the Norwegian campaign. Next came tugs with strings of Dutch schuyts escaped only days before from the collapse of Holland, and Thames oyster catchers which had never left the shelter of their estuary before. Then the pleasure boats began arriving, launches and yachts and elderly paddle steamers, bright paint and scrubbed teak decks making men pause in unending labor and remember picnics on the Isle of Wight or saxophone dances off Margate. They were painfully slow, quite unarmed, and unseaworthy out of the sheltered waters from which they came, but if they lived could carry two thousand men a trip.

Each morning the same words were on every lip as the thousands now working at Dover looked at the sky: "No wind today." Thank God, another day without wind for the paddlers, and for men wading into surf off open beaches. It was May 29, and seventy thousand had come home. Four hundred thousand to go. One destroyer was sunk that day and six too badly damaged to continue. The first of the Railway ferries was lost, and then during the morning the fearful word spread that the *Canterbury* was gone. Dover-crewed and in and out of the harbor daily, everyone knew the note of her siren, the rake of her bow, the way her captain had the best record for timekeeping along the coast. And she was gone.

Driving an empty ambulance back to the pier, halfway through the fearful afternoon, Faye glanced at the strip of beach by the slip and saw two figures folding canvas back from Beauty.

She leaped from the cab and shouted at them. One was Henry and he lifted an arm in salute, but did not stop what he was doing. She ran back to her ambulance and pulled it out of line, then let herself down through railings and dropped into soft sand. "What do you think you are doing?"

"Taking Beauty across, Mrs. Ludlow. I'm hearin' they're short of boats to ferry the boys from the beaches. The destroyers have to stand off like."

"You just put that canvas back! You know Beauty can't go! Don't you remember how she was when you took her out of the harbor before?"

"'Tis flat calm, Mrs. Ludlow. Flat as in harbor, she'll do well enough."

"She has only one engine! It's been calm for a week, when did the Channel ever stay like this for more than a few days?"

He did not stop unlacing canvas. "As to that, I'll not say. 'Tis in other hands than mine, I reckon. I know Beauty, though, and in this sea she's well enough."

"D'you realize it is nearly two years since her engine has been run?" Faye could hear her voice rising. Beauty belonged to Rupert and to Reydenham, and both had paid heavily enough for her. She was perfect and lovely, and lacked only another engine to make her complete; she at least was not going to be thrown heedlessly into the maelstrom of war. "You're not taking her, and that's that."

Henry's mouth tightened obstinately. He gave no other sign he had heard. "Give over, Alf," he said briefly, and the other threw his side of canvas across before scrambling up on Beauty's deck.

Faye tried again. "How many men do you think you'll bring back in her? Five? What are you going to use for fuel?"

"I reckon us'll manage." He turned to her, almost with compassion. "'Tis no manner of use, Mrs. Ludlow. Them's our own boys trapped over there, and I'll be where I'm needed." He ran his hand gently over varnished planks, almost a woman's caress. "Five men is five men, and I'm thinking we'll make it eight."

"All right," said Faye dully. She had thought herself exhausted before, beyond worry or thought or horror; she had not understood that after exhaustion comes another, darker road of stripped nerves and tilting mind. "I can't stop you, but if you go, I go."

Henry took off his cap and scratched his head, white hair flicked by the smallest of breezes beginning to blow from the east. "'Tis up to you, Mrs. Ludlow. We needs three and I'm not able to stop thee, neither."

Faye backed her ambulance into lined-up traffic again, and returned to the pier in a daze. She must be mad. She tried to think how to stop Henry, laid her head on the steering wheel, and immediately swooped down the slope of dissolving balance.

It was simply less trouble to go than to stay.

She handed her ambulance over to Anne Simpson, and went.

Chapter Ten

In the east the sky was paling. Luminous gray changed to green and then brilliant red-gold, curling mist off the surface of the sea. Beauty was rolling slightly, single engine throttled back and driving her steadily over a smooth water. She was not powered out of the water as her design intended, but safe and stable enough in such conditions.

Faye slept the whole night through and woke feeling fresh and excited. She knew she ought to be afraid, and was sure fear would come; for the moment she was content to lie looking at the sky and think only of strain removed. She remembered very little of their departure from Dover, made simple by the calm efficiency of improvised organization. Fuel, a mechanic to check their engine, a hastily copied chart, stores: the Navy might have been sending pleasure boats into battle as part of a long-rehearsed drill.

It was going to be another windless, sunny day. All around them were boats heading east into the dawn and Dunkirk, or back to England, loaded beyond all reason. They were used to crammed ships tying up at pier and moles, but at sea the sight was far stranger, stark peril inescapable as twenty-foot yachts heeled within an inch of their gunwales, a destroyer limped by, stern blasted but soldiers packed on her decks like bale goods in a warehouse.

At least navigation was no problem, which was fortunate, since Henry knew only the inshore waters around Dover and Faye and Alf had never been to sea before. Alf was a maintenance mechanic with East Kent buses, and before that had worked in a cable factory on the Thames: he seldom spoke about anything except engines, and it was hard to avoid the impression that he had come solely to gloat over a piece of machinery hitherto unknown to him.

"Look yonder!" said Henry suddenly.

"What is it?" Faye felt disinclined to move before it became absolutely essential.

" 'Tis the *Canterbury* coming 'ome."

At first she could see nothing in blowing mist, then outline hardened and she saw the flared bow and obstinately civilian lines of Dover's own *Canterbury*: bombed, part-burned, listing, and scarcely making steerage way, she still had troops on board, her crew shouting good luck when they saw Dover as Beauty's port of registration. After that the signs of war began to multiply. Wreckage sloshed lazily on the swell, oil streaking the surface of the sea. Silently they stood and watched a huge black cloud of smoke lift over the horizon and spread to meet them, until the sun disappeared and the sounds of battle sounded clearly over the water from the shambles which was all that remained of Dunkirk. From where they were the harbor looked blocked with wrecked and burning ships.

"Gawd!" Even Alf came up to look. "We ain't going in there?"

"If others can, we can." Henry tightened his hands on the wheel.

Their doubts were settled by an officer shouting through a megaphone from a naval launch. "Small craft, ahoy! Close in to the beach five, six miles north of here, fill your boats and ferry men out to the larger craft standing off. Good luck!" A wave and he was off.

Their immediate relief at being turned away from Dunkirk was short-lived. The smoke helped hide them from aircraft; as they cleared its shadow the drone of engines overhead became more menacing, seemed directed straight at them.

"See here now, missus," said Henry, eyes on the beach about half a mile to their right. "You take the boat 'ook and go for'ard. When I sees a likely spot, I'll be looking for summat to berth 'er to." He jerked his head at the beach. "There's plenty of rubbish lying about. You fend us off and shout out real loud if you sees anything fouling us. Right?"

Faye nodded. She was frightened now and wiped sweating hands on her skirt. She was still wearing her ambulance uniform and a sweater borrowed from Henry.

She gripped her boathook and stared at the beach. Black columns and groupings of men. Junked, burned-out vehicles. Individual black dots and splotches wading through the surf, swimming and splashing to boats lying just offshore, watching silently the ships beyond their reach. To steady herself, Faye looked seaward, to waiting destroyers and ferries about a mile offshore; she was ashamed to find herself calculating that any bomber pilot in his senses would go for them rather than a tiny motorboat. She jumped as the nearest destroyer opened up with its guns and watched, fascinated, as a smear of German aircraft came in low over the water. At the last moment they changed course straight for a ferry, stopped and loading soldiers dead ahead.

"No! Oh God, no!" She spoke aloud, and as she spoke saw the aircraft jerk as they released their bombs. One hit the ferry well forward and for an instant there was just a shower of sparks, then the ship shuddered, slewed, and took a whole stick of bombs stitched down its length.

They were among survivors almost at once, thrashing, shocked, frightened men; men scarcely sane with fury as they shook their fists at the bombers; silent, suffering men dying as they were hauled aboard.

Faye did what she could. Appalled by the cries of the drowning, hands clammy on the boathook, her strength slithered away from her. She sobbed aloud with the effort of heaving bodies over the side, with the horror of grasping an arm and feeling it tear in her grasp. The destroyer's boats joined them and in the end it was done, and her terror also. She was still terrified, but there was no time any more.

An unhurt sailor stayed to help her, and once their eyes met and both smiled, struck by the same extraordinary sense of unreality of life under a summer sun, half a day's journey from England's hills and fields.

"Hold it, girl," he said quietly once. "You're doing well."

"I haven't started. Oh God, I've hardly started yet." She had not meant to speak aloud and passed her hand over her eyes, unable to bear the thought of hardly starting yet.

"Starting's the worst," he said insistently. "Later, giving up would be harder."

She saw the familiar legs of Man on his torn jersey. "What ship was that?"

He stared at the listing, burning hulk, still obstinately afloat. "*King Orry*. The last one led the German fleet in to surrender, did you know? In '18, at Scapa. We were thinking she'd do the same."

"I know." Faye remembered the proud boast from the winter before. "This time one of the others will have to do it for you."

He laughed. "Aye, they'll do that, there's five more of us here today. It'll not be *Mona's Queen* or *Fenella* though, they've gone too."

Three gone out of eight, and they had hardly started yet.

As the day wore on, the sea as well as the harbor filled with burning and sinking ships. They were kept busy without going near the beach and only darkness brought relief as the bombers turned for home. Then it became possible to think again and realize that more ships were carrying men safely home than were lost to mines and bombs.

In the dusk, the lines left on the beach looked thicker than ever. No panic, just lines and lines of men who had fought twenty days without rest before reaching the sea they knew that Britain ruled.

"We've fuel for a run ashore and then Dover in the dark," Henry said at last. He had clenched an empty pipe in his teeth all day, now he filled it, match flaring. No blackout here, thought Faye grimly. Crimson light reflected off low oil clouds, and inland it was possible to see the rippling flash of German artillery as they closed in for the kill.

"Dover'll do for me," said Alf fervently. "And don't you go calling for no hard astern at the last minute, tain't fair on a man nor 'is engines, an' this one ain't been greased proper for months. Fair wicked, I call it, the way some people treat engines."

Henry winked at Faye. "You come down every Saturday night and grease her, mate, and I'll stand you a beer. But if I wants hard astern, I wants it bloody fast, see? It's you as'll 'it a mine first, not me."

Alf departed below, muttering. "Like a kid on the pond at Folkestone," said Henry scornfully. "What I say is, engines is made to go astern, so why shouldn't they bloody well do it when I wants 'em to?" He turned to Faye. "You see them lorries?"

Faye looked toward indistinct darkness of beach and dune, flicked with phosphorescence. Some soldiers, more enterprising than the rest, had pushed half a dozen wrecked lorries into the surf and were standing on their improvised jetty, waiting. "Yes."

"I'm going in, very slow and careful-like. You 'ook on if you can, or throw 'em a rope. Stop us striking if you can while they come aboard."

Faye thought of Beauty's thin planking and nodded. "How many? You remember we said eight at a pinch?"

Henry laughed. "Twenty-five, I daresay. We've 'ad that and more today."

Slowly, they edged shoreward. Faye leaned over the bow, straining her eyes into darkness, the glare elsewhere making clear sight extraordinarily difficult. She saw a patch she thought was seaweed, then another, and shouted.

A hail, loud and confident, came back; the soldiers were up to their waists as the tide came in.

She cupped her hands. "Are you British?" She quailed at the thought of ropes and men drowning in a confusion of French or Flemish.

"Not 'alf we ain't," came the instant Cockney response. "Take us 'ome, will yer, ducks?"

"I'm going to throw a rope." Faye found herself lowering her voice as if the Germans were already on the beach. "Can you make it fast and get aboard while I try to fend us off?"

They came over the side, teeth chattering, slipping and heaving each other up with deadened, water-puffed hands, while the boat bumped and banged against unseen metal, Faye leaning further and further out in an attempt to hold her clear.

She tried to keep count, but it was impossible. A soldier barged into her, nearly knocking her into the water, and she clutched his sleeve. "Can you see how many are on board?"

"'Alf a mo." He scrambled on the rail, wet khaki pouring water down her legs. "Arsenal and Spurs together, includin' the ref and 'alf a dozen linesmen."

Her tired brain fumbled with his meaning; an only child with a studious father, she had not the slightest idea how many made up a soccer team. "How many?"

"Pushin' thirty, I reckon."

Thirty. "You must stop them," she stammered. "We can't take so many. We've only just fuel enough to get to Dover, we can't—"

"Leave it ter me, miss." He leaned over the rail and bellowed at faces in the water below. "'Snuff, lads. Be back in the Skylark ter-morrer."

Faye had a glimpse of white faces set with desperate disappointment, dead-beat, shuddering with cold. They turned back without a word, no jostling, a hand for the last man back on the swamped lorries. He looked about seventeen, shrunk into sodden cloth.

Faye could not take her eyes off him. "Tell them we can take one more."

The boy thrashed across the narrow gully of water and was heaved up the side somehow. "Good luck, good luck, see yer in the Ole Kent Road!" There was no resentment, only envy at his good fortune, and Faye felt her eyes prick. Tomorrow the bombers would be back, tomorrow the wind might rise and it would all be over.

She could not easily move from the bow, and there was no purpose in trying as Henry cautiously worked Beauty clear. Their journey back to Dover was uneventful apart from the great volume of traffic around them in the dark, and the fear of mines. Faye dozed uneasily but was too wet and cold to rest properly. Sometime in the interminable night a breeze came cutting across the sea, icy to exhausted bodies in sodden clothes. The sea began to chop dangerously for the overladen Beauty, occasional waves slopping water over her bow.

At last discomfort overcame exhaustion and Faye stood up, bone-stiff, a trembling deep inside her. The bows dipped again, more heavily, and a sliced wave licked briefly at her feet. That bow should be twenty feet above the sea; loaded like this, she would sink if half a dozen men sneezed at the same time. Very carefully, she began to pick her way aft, treading on fingers and stumbling over huddled bodies: she could feel collective shuddering as she went.

Very faintly, dawn was lighting the east again. Only one day had passed.

Henry was at the wheel still, face stubbled, skin sagging. " 'Tis roughening up."

Faye nodded. "How much further?"

"Two, three hours perhaps. The wind'll drop with the sun."

"I hope so." It would be too late for them, but for men still waiting on the beaches she prayed for another windless day. One more, please. Two, perhaps. She thought of the black lines of soldiers and the sinking ships: how many men, how many days were left?

Very carefully, she began to shake men awake, packing them into the stern. She could tell that Henry disapproved, since Beauty was no higher in the water there, but she reasoned that if Sisley designed her to ride high at the bows, then she should meet the seas easier angled nearer his intention.

The men were so stiff and exhausted she had difficulty in shaking them into understanding; when she had, they were willing and good-humored, crowding upright with linked arms to prevent those outboard from falling in the sea.

"Well?" She wriggled back to Henry at last.

He nodded slowly. "Aye. 'Tis better." He glanced behind him, where water was lapping the deck planking. "I never thought to bring two ton of live Cockney home in place of me fish."

And so, with the morning, they came back to Dover.

Chapter Eleven

They left again in the evening. It was Friday, May 31.

Less than a week ago the most optimistic estimate had been that forty thousand might be saved from all the defeated armies: already more than two hundred thousand were home, ships shuttling, trains clanking out of Dover, Folkestone, Ramsgate, and Margate without a minute's pause. A million sandwiches cut at Paddock Wood for men passing through who had not eaten for a week, a hundred and twenty trains a day out of Dover alone.

"I reckon Kent, the Navy, and the Southern Railway are winning this war," observed Henry as they passed under the cliffs and set course eastward again. "Leave it to us, and if the weather holds, we'll have the lot of them." They were not winning, but they were not losing any more.

"Kent first," said Faye, smiling. One day I will carve him like that, she thought; deep-creased with weariness into stone, pipe, three days' beard and all. High on the west roof of Canterbury looking out over Kentish oasts all the way to Dover. After this war I will carve again and nothing will stop me. In the midst of death and destruction, the lost vision was back, and she knew it. She did not feel tired, but very strange, mind swooping almost out of reach.

She slept after making Alf promise to wake her at midnight; when he did, she was so stiff she could scarcely stand. She understood now how men ceased to be frightened in battle; in the end fear is worn down by the sheer discomfort and toiling effort of war. She brushed aside Henry's protests and relieved him at the wheel. No skill was needed to motor across a calm, moonlit sea, and without rest he could not last another day.

The night was still and very beautiful. A silver path stretched behind them as if the moon itself gave promise of safe return, crimson glow slowly lifting over the horizon ahead, the deep booming thunder of guns robbed of menace by stillness of air and mind. She moved the wheel slightly and felt Beauty stir beneath her feet; she had come fresh and unknowing to the sea and already the spell of it was in her heart.

It was thirty hours since they had been on the beaches and during that time much had changed. The Belgians had gone; but French and British troops were still fighting fiercely to hold the perimeter of their trap as the German grip tightened. The beach where they had loaded troops two days before was under machine-gun fire, further north a five-mile stretch had had to be abandoned. There were more wrecks: burning, bombed, mined, and shelled.

Towards midday they noticed for the first time that there were fewer men, too. The long lines were dwindling, and drifting west toward the harbor as more of the beach was swept with fire.

"Just as well," grunted Henry. "That bow'll not take much more."

"Nor the engine, neither," said Alf belligerently. "'Ard astern, full ahead, stop, start. Tain't fair on no engine."

Faye leaned out as far as she could, craning to see the bow. They had been ferrying troops from the beach to a destroyer most of the morning, and although the sea was still calm, there was enough surf on the beach to crunch Beauty's delicate bow each time. She could see splinter marks and Alf was baling below; they were headed empty back to the beach and she felt overwhelming relief in the certainty that this must be their last trip.

She heard a shout and turned to see a fighter low over the water, guns firing, torn water racing toward them, bullets slamming through Beauty's fragile planking, an enormous roar, and it was gone again. It happened so fast she was still lying sprawled over the bow as Beauty shuddered once and water gulped through great splintered tears, its weight wrenching split timbers further apart. Before her eyes the stern broke away, throwing Henry into the sea, Alf trapped and screaming as they rolled, then she was swirling dizzily downward into cold darkness.

She touched something once and kicked herself away in panic, terrified of being trapped in wreckage. Chained by the wrist in the mud of the Scheldt until I am dead; tilting senses flung confused images together in her mind, so she had scarcely consciousness enough to retch her lungs free of water when she surfaced.

She felt hands, an edge of wood against her ribs, light swinging across her sight. She was fearfully sick.

She had been picked up by a whaler from the destroyer they had been filling all morning; as they went alongside she opened her eyes and saw Henry sprawled beside her on the planks, sodden and gasping as she was, but alive. Not Alf, she remembered. Not Beauty any more.

Willing hands helped her to scramble up the side of the destroyer. The need to move, not to get in the way, to remember that every foot of space belowdecks was filled with wounded, was itself a restorative. She stayed on deck and they left her thankfully, for they had fifteen hundred on board already, lifted from the beach, saved from the water, sick, wounded, and starving; the remnants of a gallant rear guard, half of them French. She was not even the only woman; there were three nurses and a Belgian nun, no one could summon up the energy to ask how she had come to the beaches.

"Here, miss." One of the soldiers stripped off his tunic. "Put this on, it's dry. Not clean, though," he added with a grin.

She was trembling and could not undo the buttons of her ambulance tunic, so the men around her did it for her, offering French Army greatcoats, British battle dress, anything dry they still possessed. One of the Frenchmen had brandy in a flask. Vive la France, she thought hazily, the British would have weak, sweet tea. The spirit nearly made her sick again, then formed a puffball of warmth in her stomach, feet and fingers seeming a great distance from her eyes.

"Christ, we're off at last! About bloody time, too!" The men stirred and called to each other as they felt the deck throb. While Beauty had been busy all morning, they had been sitting, huddled in their hundreds on an open deck, stopped a mile offshore.

Faye looked up and saw the Frenchmen silent, one or two in tears. She held the hand of the nearest, without thought of strangeness. "You'll come back." She felt tears on her own face, too. She pushed to the rail and looked where Beauty had been, but there was nothing to mark it any more. The Frenchman took a long swig at his flask and passed it to her again. "Finish."

"No!" Her grip on his hand tightened urgently. "Not finish. We'll all be back."

His teeth showed white against stubble and dirt. "Finish cognac, not war. Now is time for cognac, later war again."

She drank deeply. It was a time for cognac. You'll see, Henry had said long ago, one day she'll go right nobly, and she had.

On an empty stomach and an endless stretch of time without rest, Faye Ludlow came home drunk to Dover.

Chapter Twelve

Faye opened her eyes and stared stupidly at a stained, cracked ceiling. The cracks resembled mountain ranges seen in contour and flies were toiling up their slopes, falling off, trekking obstinately along swooping lines again. When she moved, the room swam unpleasantly around her, and she closed her eyes, willing herself back to sleep.

Everything was still and quiet. She had been so long in haste and noise, on shifting decks and bumping ambulances, that silence nagged at her. She opened her eyes again and this time was assailed by familiarity. She was lying on a stretcher in a classroom pinned with drawings of scarecrows and horses, men sprawled in every attitude of sleep and exhaustion around her. She knew where she was now: when she had driven ambulances those unhurt but too exhausted to leave Dover with their units had been piled hastily into halls and schools to recover.

The stretcher was horribly hard. She rolled over with a groan and stood up, room swimming again. Her eyes were gummy, she was filthy, and her head ached. She remembered the cognac and croaked a laugh, then held her head again. What a time to have the first hangover of her life.

In the school hall she discovered the WVS dispensing sandwiches and tea, and drank cup after cup, sugar pumping fresh life into her veins. She could not face the journey back to Reydenham or think where she might find petrol for her car, so from habit she went to the harbor, walking slowly, gratefully absorbing warmth. She guessed it must be early evening, she had slept nearly a full day through.

Still no wind.

The harbor had changed again. There were the same scenes of disembarkation, of masses of men trudging away to Marine and Priory stations, of naval berthing and dispatching parties purposeful with hawsers and stores and spares, of wrecked ships fighting to stay afloat. But the little ships were tied up out of the way, their moment over, it all must be nearly over.

"The Navy and ferries are going in tonight to take the rear guard off," said a fisherman she accosted. "They've lost four destroyers, a minesweeper, and a couple of ferries today. It's too dangerous in daylight now."

"How many still to come?"

He shrugged. "They say we got over sixty thousand today and the beach is nearly clear, but there's some in Dunkirk itself and the rear guard is still holding. The Navy won't desert them at the last."

As the sun set, Faye watched the destroyers and ferries slip into the dusk once more. Eleven destroyers and thirteen ferries left, and nearly as many sunk. All night the harbor was at work and by dawn the moles and pier were clear of troops for the first time in more than a week. Exhausted men and women stood about, drinking tea, or huddled in sleep where their tasks ended. Faye waited with the rest, no one felt able simply to leave, not knowing what had happened. From railwayman to admiral, Dover had set heart and sinew to a task whose magnitude they had not at first realized, and anything less than complete success would be a bitter disappointment. This was personal, this was their battle and they wanted very much to win.

Slowly the sky lightened again, and out of the sun the ships returned.

First some destroyers full of French, then the faster ferries, then the rest, shepherded by the remaining destroyers. As the troops poured off, everyone was trying to count the ships, and suddenly the word went round, "None lost!" In darkness, out of a wreck-littered harbor, the town under fire, they had lifted every man without a hitch. Most of the ships looked lightly loaded to eyes accustomed to crammed decks, but the task was done. No one who could disengage from battle and reach the harbor was left behind.

Faye went to the slip, not looking at Beauty's empty canvas thrown on the beach, and slept another whole day through. I will feel able to walk back to Reydenham tomorrow, she thought, and her heart lifted on the hope that a message from Rupert might be waiting for her there.

It was dark again when she awoke. She went out into stillness and leaned on the rail beyond the slip, thinking. Water was lapping at the pier behind her, flaked moonlight lay across the harbor, somewhere a train clanked over points. Already Dunkirk's beaches seemed like a tale she had been told, not lived; the lifetime crammed into the past few days set aside by her mind until memory healed.

After a while she became conscious of tobacco and went down without surprise to find Henry sitting smoking where Beauty once had been. "You all right, missus?" he asked gruffly. "I'd'a thought they'd keep 'ee in bed awhile."

"You, too." Faye looked at his exhausted face, underlit by the glow of his pipe.

"They did. I walked out, I'm too old to be kept on they hard stretchers."

"Me, too." They both laughed, eyes on the place where Beauty had been, score marks from her keel still deep in the sand.

"Alf," said Faye at last. "Have you told anyone? Was he married?"

"I told the navy fellow yonder with 'is lists. I dunno about no family, wedded to 'is engines, Alf were."

"I must find out," Faye spoke half to herself. "No one may have known he came with us."

Henry nodded at the harbor. "They thought last night was the end, but the Navy's gone to try for the French again."

"Oh God." Faye felt her stomach chill. "They came back half empty last night."

"Still men there," said Henry simply. "The Navy'll not leave any to be taken so long as there's a chance of getting 'em out."

Another wait and another dawn, and again the ships returning, this time laden with men. Part of the rear guard which had made the whole extraordinary salvage possible had been snatched from Dunkirk mole as German guns entered the town. Officially the evacuation was over, but a few more British and fifty-two thousand French were saved that night.

Then, last of all, in the full light of day a single destroyer passed the eastern entrance: H.M.S. *Shikari* coming home after staying for the stragglers and, as a last act of defiance, demolitions blown behind her and Dunkirk harbor blocked. Three hundred and fifty thousand had been taken off, their ransom paid by 228 ships and countless small craft like Beauty who would return no more. There was sadness in Dover as it all ended, and in harbors as far away as the Clyde and Tees, yet the mood was not sad, rather fiercely proud. So often men die in vain, but this time there was no doubt of their achievement, for together they had saved a nation. Although weaponless, Britain had an army again and after long wandering in the dark a clear, untroubled spirit also, fresh-kindled from the ashes of defeat.

Faye went back to Reydenham in comfort, the car filled with navy petrol stolen by Henry. Six days had passed since she left and it was extraordinary to realize that for others the passage of time had followed its normal course. The hay was still uncut, the same broken branch lay beside the road, Christopher came shouting out of the house demanding another game of Peter Rabbit.

"Later, sweetheart, later!" She hugged him tightly, until he fought away from her.

"Why Mummy crying?"

"Mummy's tired, that's why." Nanny shooed him away. "She'll play with you later."

Faye felt her lips shaking. "Any news of Mr. Rupert?"

Nanny shook her head, tears in her eyes.

Faye stood very still, she had been sure there would be a message. "I would know if he was dead," she said aloud. "Surely I would know."

Nanny wiped her hands slowly on her apron, hands which had tended Rupert from birth. "There's a mort of women all over the country saying the same at this moment."

"Then the least the rest can do is hold their tongues!" Faye pushed past her and ran up the stairs to her bedroom, slamming the door. She was too tired, too overwrought to understand that Nanny, too, was only speaking bewildered thoughts aloud.

The luxury of lying in warm water was unbelievable, eyes closed and thought stilled; of brushing her hair and breathing the scent of roses through the open window. By the time Faye came downstairs again she felt marvelously restored, tiredness set aside for the moment. She wondered whether she should apologize to Nanny but decided against it: it was impossible to visualize what the future held for them all, but if they were to survive it was toughness, not resignation, they would need.

Disaster piled on disaster in the following days as German armies plunged ever deeper into France, as Paris fell without a shot fired. Paris gone. Faye clenched her hands involuntarily; ah, Ru-

pert, where are you now? I must not think of it, she told herself
fiercely, he is safe or I would know; there is more to France than
Paris. On Monday, June 17, Faye, Cook, Nanny, and Gabriel sat
around the kitchen table waiting for the one o'clock news, Christopher turning somersaults at their feet. Gabriel had his shotgun
leaning against the wall, he was off to Colonel Druitt's again after
lunch. " 'E's a fair beggar an' no mistake," he observed to Cook
with satisfaction. "You should'a heard 'im swear while we was
stickin' the carving knife into an ole straw dummy." He paused to
select a word suitable for women's ears and failed, adding simply,
"I never heard no swearin' like it in all my years."

"I don't see what good no swearing will do," said Cook tartly.
"And you tell him I want my carving knife back in time for Sunday."

"Jerries might come, Sunday."

"All the more reason for me to be needing my carving knife
myself," she retorted. "No Jerry comes into my kitchen, Sunday or
no Sunday."

"Oh, hush," said Faye impatiently, ear to the crackle of the set.
". . . one o'clock news and this is Frank Phillips reading
it . . ."

"I like him," said Nanny unexpectedly; now the announcers
gave their names to guard against false news, they had become
part of the drawing together of the nation. As they all had become part of it, sitting together around the kitchen table.

They stared at each other aghast as the voice quietly recounted
the unbelievable. France had asked for an armistice, French armies everywhere were ceasing to fight; France . . . France was
gone, too.

Faye switched off the wireless, nobody spoke.

At last Gabriel stood, the scrape of wood loud on the flagged
floor. "I reckon we'll be bloody well gettin' on with it ourselves,
then." He picked up his shotgun and walked out.

Cook gave a shriek. "The language he's picking up from that
colonel! At his age too, he ought to be ashamed!"

Nanny heaved to her feet with a sigh. "I'll be getting Christopher's lunch. He won't think much of Hitler keeping him from
that."

Faye wandered into the library as she often did these days. She
felt closest to Rupert there, but today she eyed the telephone in

anger. Ring, damn you. Men were still being evacuated from western France, another perilous ferrying operation running over far greater distances, but now time had stopped short, the Germans motoring for the Atlantic over undefended roads. Christopher came in and started to run around her, chanting, and she snapped at him savagely, ridden by urgency for Rupert. For the first time she began to think he might be lost and laid her head on the desk, tears slippery on polished wood.

The telephone rang.

She jerked upright and stared at it, as if longing alone had tripped the bell. It rang again and she snatched at it with trembling fingers. It's probably only someone from the valley, she told herself firmly. "Hullo?" There was a long-distance crackle to the line. "Hullo? Who's there?" She was shouting, voice jumping and shrill.

"Faye! Hold your hair on, its me." Rupert, maddeningly self-possessed. Rupert. *Rupert*. She wanted to box his ears for being so calm and instead felt tears again, pouring now. "Faye, are you there?"

"Oh, Rupert," she said very quietly. "My love, you're home and safe."

"Well, I'm in Weymouth, so not quite home, but safe enough." He sounded boundingly cheerful. She forgot her own ridiculous optimism on entering harbor again after long peril, and felt obscurely that he should be . . . she did not know how he should be, but certainly not so plainly enjoying days she had lived through in such desperate fear for him. "I got out of St. Nazaire on one of the last boats," he continued gaily. "You never saw such a picnic. I've hitchhiked half across France, first to Paris and then to Bordeaux, then north again. It was quite a lark I can tell you, you'd have laughed—"

"No," she said quietly, "I haven't been laughing. Are you all right?"

"Fit as a fiddle! Plenty of navy rum on the trip back, too, since we got devilish wet coming aboard. I was lucky to be on a destroyer, not one of the passenger ships."

"I'm glad, my darling, I'm so glad." She felt absurdly numb, so it was a real effort to infuse enthusiasm into her voice. She wanted him to ring off so she could finish weeping; no, she did not want that. "Will you be coming home?"

"I don't think so, not at once. We're being sent all over the place for re-forming, I'll ring again when I know. All well and peaceful at Reydenham, I hope?"

She nodded, then said, "Yes." She had not the heart to spoil his homecoming with news of Beauty.

"Look, there's a terrific line of chaps waiting to ring, I must stop. Love to you, darling. Kiss Chris for me. See you soon!" The line went dead.

She replaced the receiver carefully and looked up to see Nanny in the doorway. "He's safe."

Nanny nodded. "I heard, I couldn't help it. You've much to thank God for, Mrs. Rupert, and as I always say, for each blessing there's a stone to trip over. Now's the time to look at the blessing, not the stone."

Faye stared at her in incomprehension. "Whatever do you mean?"

"If you don't know, I'm not telling you." She went out again, closing the door softly behind her.

Faye slept that night in a restful ocean of care set aside, and woke happy in the dawn. She lay quietly, and could not think how she had let Rupert's return be soured by resentment. She rolled over to the cold side of the bed, taking the bedclothes with her, laughing aloud with the pleasure of Rupert alive and beside her in the night again. I have another self, she reflected, a greedy, disagreeable self who wants too much, niggling and chipping away at grievance like a discontented mason at stone unsuited to carving. She grinned at her fancy and leaped out of bed; who wanted more when Rupert was coming home again?

She went through the house that day like an armor-piercing bullet. Furniture was stacked and polished, flowers picked, Christopher shouting with laughter as they whirled from room to room with dusters and mops. Of all the Reydenham household only Nanny and Cook remained, and now she looked at the manor with Rupert's eyes, Faye saw how unkempt it had become.

"I'll have to go back to Dover tomorrow," she said in the evening. "I must be posted as a deserter by now, or whatever they do with runaway ambulance drivers."

"What if Mr. Rupert comes home while you're away?" Nanny pursed her lips disapprovingly. In her heart, she still thought that proper ladies did not drive trucks.

"He'll understand. I expect I'll just be away for shifts, there can't be much doing in the harbor now." If Mr. Jewell could get her shot for desertion, he probably would, she reflected wryly, and before she went she really must spend some time with her mother-in-law.

"I've heard from William," she said as soon as Faye entered her rooms. "Poor William, he says the planes he is flying are so large he can't stunt them at all. It does seem a waste, when anyone can see that he is made for something exciting. First of all those upsets in France, and now such a silly posting for William, it does make you wonder how intelligent our generals are, doesn't it?"

"I seem to remember you thinking the RAF had been exceptionally bright to keep William out of exciting flying." Faye smiled to herself at her mother-in-law's sense of proportion.

"Faye dear, I wish you would not pick on everything I say in such a caviling spirit! I do not wish to be unkind, but really it is a most undesirable fault."

"But then I have so many undesirable faults, I should never open my mouth if I had to watch them all." She heard the sharpness in her tone but could not regret it.

"Yes, you have," agreed Mrs. Ludlow cordially. "But I'm so glad that at least you aren't stupid, Faye. Rupert assured me you were not, and I see now from the way you have managed here without him that he was quite right."

Faye burst out laughing. "Although you doubted it before?"

"Well, of course, dear. Rupert really only understands Reyden-ham, so is easily taken in. It will be nice to have him home again soon."

Faye stood and kissed her unlovingly. "Very soon, I hope."

They all gathered around the wireless before she left for Dover, this time to hear Mr. Churchill speak. The others had heard him before but for Faye it was the first time, and the extraordinary effect of his voice and words took her by the throat. Took Gabriel and Cook and Nanny too, she noticed, glancing around. Alchemist's magic fused a mood into words, banished uncertainty and gave expression to thoughts each held yet lacked the power to speak.

"*What has happened in France makes no difference to British faith and purpose. We have become the sole champions now in arms to defend the world cause. We shall do our best to be worthy of that high honor . . . and fight on unconquerable until the curse of Hitler is lifted from the brows of men. Let us therefore brace ourselves to our duties and so bear ourselves that if the British Empire and Commonwealth last for a thousand years, men will still say, 'This was their finest hour.'"*

I wonder whether it will seem as splendid in a thousand years, Faye mused, or whether this is us, our time and place, and no one else will ever quite understand. She felt enormously, completely happy.

Everything suddenly became very simple and very difficult. Simple because all they had to do was win, and beside it everything else was insignificant; people spoke more gently, behaved more considerately, completely forgot barriers which before had ruled their lives. Very difficult because in Dover, with the enemy only twenty miles away, Gabriel's shotgun was one of the more sophisticated weapons available to repel invasion. All the brass bed knobs in the valley had already vanished for use as practice grenades by the newly formed Home Guard.

Faye went back to her ambulance duty again, but spent most of her time shoveling sand into bags. Each day the number of gun emplacements in the harbor grew and she no longer noticed the strangeness of Market Square and Biggin Street buttressed by sandbags and trapped with slit trenches.

"They've got guns along Wellington Dock at last!" Faye was as excited as the rest when the holes they dug slowly acquired weapons. "There's more men due in tonight, too." Rupert was somewhere in the Midlands, frantically busy, he said.

"About bloody time." Beryl rested on her shovel, face sweaty from the heat. "Them Jerries'll just love playing sand castles with us on the beach. What do they think we're going to chuck at 'em, bleeding seawater?"

"A month. It'll take a month to get the men sorted out and armed again." Nothing had been heard of Anne Simpson's father, but his rank made her their military expert. "It'll take the Germans time too, they can't just swim over."

Beryl snorted. "Don't see why not. Nice weather, and nothing to stop 'em barring my shovel."

The mention of swimming set Faye's mind nagging again at an anxiety she had tried to ignore. She wanted very much to know whether John Castellan had returned safely from wherever he had been. Well, why shouldn't I simply ask? she thought, exasperated. When she returned to Reydenham she leafed through a London telephone directory in the library, reflecting that it was fortunate he had such an unusual name. . . . Castellan, John H., Castellan, Joseph H., Castellan J. & Son, Merchants and Bankers . . . She looked at the entries doubtfully, then grasped the telephone without allowing time for second thoughts.

The usual wait for the operator, then long, unanswered ringing from his private number. What on earth will I say if I get on to a wife? she wondered suddenly. She gripped the instrument, willing him to answer, snapping at the operator when she tried to cut her off.

"There's no reply, madam, and ringing an hour won't change it." She sounded as if people had been making unreasonable demands of her all day.

Faye swallowed, it was absurd to feel so upset about someone she scarcely knew. "Please could you try just once more?"

"If you say so." She sounded rather more friendly, as if aware of her distress. It made no difference, and on impulse Faye decided to try the office number, the unknown Joseph more than she could contemplate.

"Castellan's, can I help you?" A girl's voice.

Faye hesitated. "Could I speak to Mr. John Castellan?"

"I'm sorry, Mr. John is not in the office. Who is calling, please?"

"When are you . . . is he expected back?"

"I don't think so. Who is calling? Shall I put you on to Mr. Joseph?"

"No . . . no." She nearly rang off, then obstinacy came to her aid. "My name is Ludlow, Faye Ludlow. I happened to see Mr. Castellan about three weeks ago in—" She wondered suddenly just how much his office knew of Mr. John jauntering off on destroyers and ended lamely, "He was in a great hurry, and I wondered whether he—" She floundered again. "Whether he was available for a moment in the office today."

"I'm sorry, Mrs. Ludlow," the girl repeated. "I'll leave a message for him. He's not often here at the moment."

"But he does come in? When was he there last?"

"I think I'd better put you through to Mr. Joseph." She sounded wary and uncertain, as if she were fobbing off a dunning mistress, thought Faye with a choke of laughter.

"I don't want to bother Mr. Joseph. Just tell me whether he has been in since—since the end of May."

There was a mumble in the background and then a man's voice. "Can I help you, madam?"

Faye set her teeth and said slowly and distinctly, "Are you a commercial establishment or not? Will you kindly tell me approximately when Mr. John Castellan was last in his office, or when he is next expected in?"

"Mr. John was here a week last Monday, madam. I'm afraid I couldn't say when he will be in again."

"Thank you very much," she rang off, swamped with unreasoning delight. He made it, she said aloud. He damned well made it. I bet they're all scuttling off to Joseph H. to tell him about John's loose women ringing up, but I don't care. She thought of his thin, clever face and devastatingly swift judgment: she had been the one to swim for her life, not him. She laughed at herself and did not know why; she ought surely to have known that he would make it.

Chapter Thirteen

Everyone became tearingly busy as time sped inexorably by.

Smoke rose over Calais and Boulogne again as the German invasion fleet grew, was bombed, and grew faster still. If there was a moment spare, goofers could stand on the Western Heights and watch ships jinking wildly to avoid bombs as they passed the dangerous narrows. Most went by night, but urgency forced some to risk it in daylight and Dover again received damaged and burning ships.

Soldiers came to the valley, digging trenches and emplacements ready for weapons if any could be spared, showing the farmers how to make tank traps out of scrap iron and old carts, constructing runnels in places where hedgerows sloped steeply to the road. Faye stopped one day and asked what they were doing.

"Blimey, missus! We ain't got more'n rifles, so we're aimin' to drown the buggers in oil."

"Oil?"

The sergeant in charge winked. "That's right. As the Jerries pass by, Bill here'll stand up straight an' thump out the bung, an' I'll lie flat and try to get the whole bloody lot alight with paper and matches."

"While the Germans stand around laughing?" She was unable to decide whether they were serious.

"Aye, it's dead easy. They'll be so bloody 'ysterical the rest of us can pick them off like canaries in a cage. That Gabriel, he's got his pad picked out in a tree already, Gawd 'elp the Jerry as gets 'is shotgun up the arse."

The men laughed and went back to digging. In Dover it was possible to see change setting in, with new antiaircraft guns by the harbor and on the Heights, fresh troops arriving daily, and the Navy going quietly about its business; in the valley and all the other valleys further inland it was still pitchforks, shotguns, and oil drums. Another month, thought Faye, six weeks perhaps, and then I hope they do come. It's time they, too, learned about defeat.

She left the car in the drive and went indoors, surprised not to see Christopher. He always raced out the moment he heard her engine, bubbling with what he had done all day and demanding rides on the running board.

In the hall she stopped abruptly, blood pulsing under thinned skin as she saw an army cap on the chest. It was probably only an officer from one of the units which came and went in the valley: none had been billeted on the manor as fighting positions were manned continuously, but there were constant requests for water, old implements, and timber.

She called but the house seemed empty, sun flowing over polished oak and faded carpets; windows and doors open as they had been for weeks in this lovely summer, checkered green beyond.

Voices, shouts of delight from Christopher and . . .

She ran and shouted too. "Rupert!" Then she was in his arms kissing blindly, and knew nothing except him against her, face tight to his.

He held her away from him. "You feel as if you thought I was still in France until this moment."

"You seemed as far away as France."

"Let me look at you, see how beautiful you are after all those Frenchwomen."

She held him tightly. "Not yet. I need to feel you first, looking is for later."

Then Christopher came, holding their legs and jumping up and down, shouting. Rupert released her and swooped him up on his shoulders. "How he's grown! Almost a man to take my place in the valley and set the Jerries running, eh, Chris?" He rolled him on the grass while Faye watched, eyes misted.

Later they sat on the terrace, lights off because of the blackout, the night soft around them.

"How long, Rupert?"

"Tomorrow."

"Tomorrow! Surely when you haven't been home since getting out of France—"

"Precious little time for leave these days. I'm meant to be in London picking up equipment, but the CO said he'd blink at an overnight stop if I could hitch a lift. I was lucky, nearly door to door in a navy lorry."

"Then what?"

"Hampshire, I think. Portsmouth, somewhere like that. It's a buzz, mind, no orders yet. I'll have proper leave in the winter when the Jerries have come and gone."

He had asked nothing about her, as if he assumed that life in Dover and the valley had gone on undisturbed since he left, as if invasion three miles away as the sea gull flew would leave them untouched for his homecoming in the winter. He had not inquired how Reydenham still existed under its weight of debt, or where she had found money to plant the crop now ripening. As if he rejected the knowledge that it must be her strength, not his, which now sustained the place of his heart.

He looked fit, bronzed from long hours in the open, absorbed in his new life, excited by his escape from France. "We must have walked at least a hundred miles by the end," he explained eagerly. "Then Phil found this truck . . . you would have laughed to see us drive into St. Nazaire in a vegetable trailer, although the Frogs were pretty hostile by then, I can tell you."

He talked more than she could remember him doing before, and looked more like William enjoying some unusually splendid joke. In his signals HQ he had seen no actual fighting and the mad scramble through France made him feel part of the war at last.

Faye discovered that he had changed in another way, too. His joke about Frenchwomen had been no joke, but unease bringing the wrong words to his lips. His lovemaking was different, more skilled, and brought with it an unpleasant taste of derisive teaching. Afterwards, she lay in his arms and listened to his even breathing. She felt shamed, not so much by the image of unknown women held as he held her now, as by instinct which told her how very little she had been missed.

He had been ten months away; sometimes she had thought of him unfaithful and told herself she would not know. The war would be to blame, not Rupert, and she herself too, if she failed to understand. In her heart, she had neither believed nor faced it; now she did and the reality stunned her. It was not a case of forgiving or understanding: all the intimate joys were dead, her responses shriveled when he handled her as whores had taught him, when she sensed comparison in his mind.

She had come to him with delight, ten months' longing in beating blood and yielding body. Now she lay in desperate unhappiness, knowing that wherever the fault lay, if fault there was, she had failed him. He slept undisturbed, but she knew him too well to think she had given him much pleasure. Sometimes revulsion had not been far off, and if he had been a more sensitive man he would have known it: as it was, she thought she probably merely seemed cold and dull. He was disappointed, for he cherished happier memories of her, but supposed she must be tired and slept when he became bored.

He slipped out of bed very early the next morning, for he must leave soon and did not want to waste dawn in the valley. Faye stood by the window and watched him climb the steep sheep paths to the woods, pausing sometimes to touch a familiar tree or rub grain between thumb and forefinger. Once he stooped and laid his hand on the earth, then stood quietly looking at his valley, and she felt close to him again. She went to run herself a bath, scrubbing fiercely as if to scour herself clear of the night. So war is like that, she said aloud; I knew it before, now I have to live it. She wanted more children but hoped very much there would be none from the night which had just passed.

When Rupert returned for breakfast he was full of questions about the different farming on the estate, about the Agricultural Committee's demands for grain, about unrepaired roofs and patched fences. "There hasn't been any money for repairs," said Faye irritably. "Every penny has gone into seed and fertilizer and more stock. We get grants, but only for part of the work. The Committee will do it themselves and take the profit if we can't manage."

"All the same, old Dickson's roof won't last the winter gales out. I wish you would see to it, Faye; Reydenham has always looked after its tenants properly."

"I daresay it has, but Reydenham was always solvent before."

"No one is going to be dunning for debt at the moment, and there's nothing they could do if they tried. You mustn't let it bother you."

"Well, it does bother me!" Faye snapped. Yesterday she had not wanted to spoil his homecoming with harsh facts, today she felt no such compunction. After all, she had spent the night coming to terms with reality. "Especially when I get bills with every post which I haven't the least idea how to pay." She flicked a couple across the table which had come that morning. "Your mother sold her jewelry to keep us going this year."

"What?" he demanded incredulously. "D'you mean you talked my mother into pawning her jewelry?"

"Selling it. And you may think this isn't the time for collecting debts, but not everyone feels the same. Most people have been very kind but some of your creditors want to leave an invasion area and take their money with them. Nearly every day someone rings up or writes. Last week an old woman waited a whole day to beg for her fifty pounds back. What could I say? Why shouldn't she have it if she needs it?"

"Because it's wartime and for the moment we're all in this together. If the Germans come—"

"Yes, if they come, then none of us will be worrying about money. What if they don't and the war goes on for years?"

He grinned. "Then debts will have to wait. With another engine, one day Beauty will beat anything in the Channel and then—"

"Beauty's gone, Rupert. Sunk at Dunkirk."

"Sunk? What the hell was she doing at Dunkirk? She wasn't even seaworthy."

"Oh yes, she was." Faye looked at silver teapot and damask tablecloth, seeing Beauty bringing thirty-one men into Dover. "She was as seaworthy as the rest of them. What about the *Medway Queen*, a flat-bottomed paddler who held the record of seven thousand saved by her alone?"

"Damn the *Medway Queen!* Why the hell didn't you tell me about Beauty?"

"You never asked," she said simply. "At first there seemed no point upsetting you when it was done, then—"

"Then you didn't dare," he finished grimly. "My God, Faye, you fling debt in my face as if I'd brought ruin on Reydenham, but what about you? No wonder people are dunning you with their security gone."

"It's done," she repeated, "and I wouldn't change it if I could. I tried to stop Henry taking her, now I'm glad I failed."

Rupert shrugged and said nothing, moodily buttering toast.

Faye took a deep breath. "There's another thing. What should I do about Christopher?"

"What about him?"

"This is an evacuation area now. I must stay, with the estate and my duty in Dover, but he and Nanny could go away somewhere. I'd send them to my father but Canterbury is not much safer than here. You must have dozens of friends with large houses who would have him."

"Chris stays here. Ludlows don't run away and leave their people behind."

"I would be here," said Faye evenly. "Haskells don't run away either."

"Chris stays here." He came round the table and kissed her. "Don't let's spend our time quarreling when I must be off so soon. I daresay you couldn't help Beauty, it was just the shock of it caught me." He pulled her to her feet, sliding his hands up her arms to hold her face cupped in his palms. "Don't change, Faye. Don't ever change. The girl I married in the teeth of everyone—I want to keep her forever. I know it is sometimes difficult for you here alone, but one day I will be back, hoping to find the same Faye I left behind."

She looked at him, eyes very clear and direct. "But then we are none of us the same, are we?" She watched the blood rise in his face, his lips tighten. "You didn't ask, but I was with Beauty when she sank; I had never seen more than a cut hand before and I have carried men almost torn apart in my ambulance. I ran my father's house, but now I am responsible for Reydenham and everyone on it, for debts and enough for us to eat with rations getting shorter every week. You've just eaten three days' worth of Cook's butter on your toast. We can't go back, my love, we go forward, or we die."

"I don't want you to change," he said, almost sullenly. "Everything else, not you."

"In the greatest thing of all, my love, I have not changed, if only you would look."

The sullen look faded and he smiled slightly. "That's my girl." He kissed her lightly, undemandingly, as if he feared to rouse passion again, which had burned with such joyless fire the night before. Then he went to see his mother, leaving the sweetness she had offered him drying on her lips.

Rupert drove when they went into Dover, the car skidding under his touch in a way Faye had almost forgotten. At his suggestion, Christopher came too, easing the difficult minutes with his chatter; neither of them wanted to think of heartache or misunderstanding, only to part in affection so that next time they might build afresh.

How far they had come in a day and a night to find parting in affection had become the sum of ambition, reflected Faye sadly. Next time . . . next time they would outrun their ghosts and be themselves again. Pray God there would be a next time, and not Germans rolling down the valley.

"Why you shiv'ring, Mummy?" Christopher demanded. "I'se not cold."

"No, darling, I'm not cold either." She rumpled his hair. "Goose on my grave." She shivered because she loved her husband, yet could scarcely bear his body near her until time helped blur the print others had set there.

And time came to her rescue now, too, sliding past faster and faster, bearing Rupert away with only trivialities spoken.

When she returned to Reydenham she found Gabriel waiting for her beside a thin, leathery individual with bulging, plate-glass eyes.

"Mrs. Ludlow? Druitt's my name, Timothy Druitt." He chewed and spat words at his feet. "Understand you're in the ambulance service?"

"T'Colonel asked me to bring un over to see 'ee, when I told un 'ee drove like," interrupted Gabriel anxiously.

Faye looked at the Colonel inquiringly. "I do drive as you see, when I have the petrol. At the moment I rather think I will be walking until the end of the month."

"No! No! Your ambulance! You'll be driving an ambulance soon?"

"Of course." She looked from one to the other in quick suspicion. "What is it you want?"

Gabriel shuffled his feet. " 'Tis like this, missus. There be guns in Canterbury—"

"The Yanks have sent over crates of sporting rifles for the Home Guard, Mrs. Ludlow. I intend to see we have some here but those useless . . ." He cleared his throat while Gabriel waited hopefully. "Those useless fellows in Canterbury won't give us priority transport. By the time we get there, the best will be gone."

"I can't use an ambulance for transporting guns."

"You come back empty from the military hospital, don't you? Well then, it's only a mile out of your way."

"I'm sorry, Colonel, there's no way I could do it," said Faye definitely. "Or next time the Germans bomb the Red Cross, who are we to complain?"

"Good God, woman, they do it anyway! Beat 'em and string 'em up, that's the only way, not complaining to some . . . some committee in Geneva!"

Faye looked at him thoughtfully, a few good guns in the valley seemed a comforting idea. "I'm getting a lift in a navy lorry on Friday to see my father in Canterbury. If you care to come, we could drop off a couple of crates at the crossroads."

So it was settled, Gabriel and two cronies meeting them with wheelbarrows and trundling oblong wood cases triumphantly down the valley road to Reydenham, where the Colonel broke them open. "Good God Almighty," he said, hands gloating on thick yellow grease. "Who'd have thought Yanks would have the sense to send us ammunition as well?" Wedged between guns of a dozen different calibers were as many clips as could be fitted into the space.

Faye lifted a rifle gingerly, grease sticky on her hands. Attached was a label: "From Mr. & Mrs. Larry D. Richardson, Hartford, Conn. May God bless you and bring you to victory. It throws slightly right, but good hunting!"

The Colonel shrugged. "They're three thousand miles off."

"Still . . ." She picked up another, a note pasted to the stock this time. "Would you want to be three thousand miles off now?"

"Good God, no!" He paled with horror. "Or fifty. Dover's the place to be."

"Well then," she said, smiling. "You're where you want to be, you've got a rifle at last, and a nice scented note from a lady signing herself Sadie-Veronica. What more do you want?"

The Colonel snorted and went in search of cleaning rags, but she noticed him reading the notes, and by the time the rifles were cleaned and laid on the grass, the simple goodwill and heartfelt prayers of unknown Americans had touched them all. What a strange chance, reflected Faye, had brought sporting guns from Hartford, Conn., by air and lorry and wheelbarrow to Reydenham valley, from shooting game in peaceful American woods to killing Germans in beleaguered Kent.

"My God," said the Colonel, impressed. "I didn't know they still had Indians in New York." He showed Faye a label from Ike Busenburger of New York. " 'The notches on the stock is Injuns— go add some Germans, fella!' "

"It looks quite old," suggested Faye.

"Them Yanks is allus bloody boastful," muttered Gabriel. "They'd not like to think on us baggin' Jerries without they'd got summat else."

The men left soon after, climbing directly up the hill into the next valley, festooned with weapons, six precious rifles left behind as Reydenham's share.

"Anything you want, my dear." Colonel Druitt turned quite pink with gallantry. "You can always call on me."

Faye had a brilliant idea. "You have so many more men left in your village than we have here, why don't you take two more of our rifles? Then perhaps one of your people could come over and fix Dickson's roof for him." She looked at him limpidly.

He chewed and champed, then picked up two extra guns. "I'll send a fellow with tiles and timber tomorrow. Reydenham can count on us when the Huns come."

"Reydenham can look after isself," said Gabriel indignantly.

"Too small, my man, too small! You need large formations for war!" He shook Faye's hand heartily, well pleased with their bargain. "D'you know, after the war I might go to New York? I mean, Indians, by God!"

Chapter Fourteen

Because of the distance she lived from Dover, Faye was usually on duty in daylight, sunny hours on the beach filling sandbags welcome relief after the anxieties of Reydenham. Occasionally ships berthed with dead and wounded, mostly there was nothing to do but shovel sand. Access to the sea was cut off by barbed wire, mines, and builders' scaffolding, its beckoning coolness out of reach to diggers laboring in punishing heat.

The slip was covered with barbed wire, too, but the ambulance crews found a way of sliding between pier and rotting rails while others held coiled wire clear. It was delicious to sluice clear of sand and sweat during stand-easy, to swim away from the others on tired muscles and float, eyes closed, like a child again.

They were used to sounds of battle in the Channel and, floating idly in July heat, Faye at first took no notice when noise grew in her ears. Then, without further warning, there were aircraft overhead, steep-climbing bursts in the harbor, shock waves hammering through water into her bones. With an enormous roar the harbor guns opened up, the beat of machine guns directly overhead from the pier. She spluttered with water swallowed in the suddenness of it all, her clumsy breaststroke seeming to make no progress back to the slip. Another string of explosions, waves chopping across the harbor, the sound of engines coming closer; the slip, oh God help me, the wire. She was swamped with panic, nearly drowning on shock and inadequate swimming, when she saw barbed wire sprung across her only exit from the water. Unless someone held it from above, there was no way out.

She shouted, voice lost in stunning noise. She was not going to get out. She was going to drown within touch of slip and pier and no one would know. She was not a strong swimmer and waves beating against the pier were bringing her dangerously close to stonework and submerged wire, so she stroked tiredly away. Ahead, she saw a German bomber blow up with streaking orange fire, and forgot exhaustion while she willed the crew to jump, gasped with relief when a parachute opened, and only afterwards remembered he was German. She felt closer to him than to the gunners on the pier above, the two of them in pawn to death while the rest of the world ignored them to fight its war. A shrieking roar as dive bombers ripped overhead, flattening water as they leveled off within feet of the surface, jinking to avoid almost horizontal fire off the pier. Faye was enveloped in smoke, blotted out by noise as they dropped their bombs, body cringing into its seawater burrow and refusing the simple movements needed to keep it afloat. She struck out blindly, not expecting to reach anywhere, and almost at once her feet touched sand, floundered, felt it again.

"Mind . . . wire!" A faint, tinny squeak.

She blinked, shapes solidifying again. She was on the beach. The beach? Through thick stuffing in her head she could hear indistinct shouts and lay thankfully, then spluttered, drowning in three feet of water.

I'm going to live, she thought, surprised. I'm not going to drown in a bucketful of water, I bloody well won't. She retched on a laugh and stood on legs of straw. They had to cut their way out to her through torn wire and all the while she stood, teeth chattering, in yellow, churned water. The bombs had fallen so close that their explosion would have killed her in the sea, instead they had landed in the shallows and driven deep into sand, saving her life by blasting wire clear for her to find safe foothold. She laughed again; fancy Hitler wasting a whole stick of bombs to stop me from drowning.

She was still laughing when two soldiers reached her, and carried her back over planks springing precariously on part-cut wire. "The general will love this," said one. "Tearing up his lovely wire for a woman paddling on the beach."

"Blame it on Jerry, who's to know?"

"You haven't met this general, then; he'll know the difference between wire cutters and bombs."

Faye felt the other shrug. "Then he'll know the difference between a live woman and a dead one. What did you think of doing, leaving her there?"

They put her by the sea wall, and after a while an ambulance came. "My Gawd," said Beryl. "You was still in the 'arbor?"

Faye nodded.

"Teach you to go swimmin' 'alfway to France on your own. Gaw lumme, them Stukas, my Bill told me about them. Fair make you piddle, don't they?"

Faye began to feel resentful at receiving so little sympathy. "At least the Stukas put their bombs in the right place. I'd have drowned for all the rest of you cared."

Beryl stared. "Drowned? You was only in the water five minutes."

"Five minutes! I couldn't have been!" Hours, days had passed.

"Quick in, quick out, them Jerries was. They didn't 'it nothing neither, barrin' your beach." She heaved Faye into the back of the ambulance and rattled her triumphantly back to the slip, only a few yards away. No one could visualize the eternity of time she had lived, or thought she might need more than a blanket and, of course, a cup of tea. She dressed with fumbling fingers, cold to the spine in noonday heat.

The other girls left her alone, thinking to be kind, but she wanted to talk about what had happened: she ought to go home but lacked the will to move.

"Listen." Beryl cocked her head and a moment later they all heard it, the breathing whine as sirens gathered strength for the up-and-down yowl of warning. There was a concerted rush, duty crew to the ambulance, the others to sandbagged dugouts in what had once been a flower bed at the end of the pier.

Faye stood stupefied, unable to remember whether she was on duty or not, thinking only how monstrous it was of the Germans to send another raid against her when she was still paralyzed by the first.

"Go on!" Anne Simpson gave her a push. "No point having more of us here than we must."

She stumbled into a slit trench and lay there panting, feeling as she had in the sea; a desire only to sink and be done with it all. The ground under her cheek was shaking from the guns, the noise tremendous: slowly, inconvenient will uncurled again, restlessly questing, annoyed with her body for lying in fear while urgency was all around. I wonder how many more are killed by curiosity than courage in war, she thought wryly, and stood without further reflection, her mind lacking reason after successive shocks.

She was jerked back by Beryl. "You aimin' to get in one of them sacks in 'ospital?"

"I wanted to see." Faye knelt beside her and looked out over the harbor, at high-leaping water and puffball smoke, specked aircraft above: high and steady, wheeling into the sun's glare and then sliding down faster and faster until it seemed impossible they could avoid smashing straight into the water, black dot of bomb released, then the extraordinary flick and twist along the surface to safety. Every gun was firing, ships in the harbor, from the two moles, the pier, all along the promenade: Faye realized that a great many weapons had come into Dover these past few days.

"We're no longer a pushover," she said aloud.

Beryl nodded and grinned, thumbs jerked at the sky. "Cost 'em a bit to drop scrap iron in the 'arbor."

Away on the cliffs, Faye could see the speck of color flying above the Castle, aircraft flashing past battlement and gray stone, for the moment intent on the ships below. Despite herself, her imagination was caught by the strangeness of it all. This was Dover, where she had shopped a hundred times, where the bank was demanding payment on Reydenham's overdraft; these were the white cliffs of England, not distant places read about in the newspaper. It was difficult to think of the diving aircraft and lazily lifting water as real, which would come again tomorrow and the day after, and would not rest until all this dear familiarity lay in ruins.

Or they do, she thought grimly.

Suddenly the aircraft were gone again and in their place intertwined trails of white in the sky. "Ours!" Beryl thumped her shoulder and climbed out of the trench. "We've caught 'em this time!"

A brilliant flash in the sky, moments later a flat report and pieces falling, black against blue. They looked at each other and shook their heads; it was impossible to tell whether it was friend or enemy.

The Germans came again half an hour later, exactly timed for the British squadron's withdrawal, then again, and five times the next day. The few, vital weeks of reprieve were over.

Each night Faye listened to the news, birds singing outside the window, and each night the day before seemed unreal, as during each day the twilight peace was unimaginable. "Heavy enemy formations attacked Dover . . . Dover and Folkestone . . . Dover and Ramsgate . . . the Channel ports . . ." Each time it was

Dover the announcer mentioned and soon the press fastened on a nickname, Hellfire Corner, and sent reporters to sit on the Western Heights and watch. So far the battle was evenly poised, advantage one day to the Germans with a ship sunk, a dozen barrage balloons flaming over the harbor, the next to Dover—for so at first they thought of it—when the fighters were ready waiting or the guns broke up an attack before it was launched.

Only the balloons were fun, like fat women on dirty seaside postcards, dripping flaming grease.

At first the town escaped lightly, until the Germans discovered just how much water there was in the harbor in which to lose their bombs. Then they began to concentrate on the moles and port, and the misses went into the streets.

It was late in July when Faye, cycling to her morning shift, saw great clouds of heavy smoke towering above the Western Heights, even before the harbor came into view. Oil. After Dunkirk she could not fail to recognize an oil fire, and began to pedal faster.

When the harbor came into view she dismounted, and stared at the scene below her: gray-blue water, gray clustering town, and gray-spread Castle above, but where the white cliffs should be there was nothing but blackness, curling on its own heat. The eastern arm of the harbor with its stocks of coal was well alight but the power within the inferno came from blazing fuel oil within the Camber, an enclosed naval harbor at the angle of eastern mole and cliff below the Castle. She could see ships alight there, the water itself crackling fire. A slight breeze flicked the smoke away for an instant and she was able to glimpse a sunken destroyer, other burning ships, one of them pouring more oil.

She swooped down perilous cliff bends in minutes, wind whistling, eyes blurred with speed, the old bicycle jarring. The slip was deserted, so she pedaled slowly along the harbor, searching for their ambulances; even in the main harbor water was iridescent with spilled oil, the stench suffocating, while ahead blackness blotted out everything but orange fire below.

She found an ambulance just short of the Camber, Anne at the wheel. She nodded to Faye. "The *Codrington* has sunk. The Stukas came in with first light and broke her back, the Prince of Wales's yacht too; they're trying to save a storeship now, they say she's got ammunition aboard."

"Ammunition? Half Dover'll be flat if ammunition blows up here!"

"Why do you think firemen are still on board in that?" They fell silent, trying to see through smoke strangely shafted with sun. Twice they had to take men overcome by heat and fumes to a dressing station, each time when they returned it seemed the fire was less, before they realized it was only the smoke which grew thicker. The firemen were mostly Dover's own: shopkeepers, ex-policemen, and car-park attendants who had never before faced fire fighting on board ship, or blazing oil, or fifty thousand tons of coal white-hot on the staithe.

"It's less," said Faye suddenly. "Surely it's less this time."

They waited tensely for wind to drive smoke aside, and thought it would never come. When it did, the glow was there but some of the anger had drained from it, *Codrington* and coal abandoned as beyond hope while every effort was concentrated on the store-ship and blazing oil. Anne sighed. "It's less, thank God. I'll go home now and leave you to your shift. Shall I ride your bike back to the slip and leave it there?"

"I wish you would—" Words dried on her lips as clear above the roar of the fire they heard the warning sirens again. Whistles sounded, pounding feet in the murk, shouts to take cover. Faye's throat dried; the flimsy slip was no protection, but here on the open harbor road with its vast smoke marker, she felt completely naked.

She and Anne ran for an angle of wall and crouched in dust and rubbish while the guns broke into their hell of noise, yet strangely the attack never developed. She supposed there must be fighters above the smoke and stood, astonished to be untouched. She looked across the harbor: the fire was worse, the coal staithe shimmering with heat. The raid had given it time to bite again even if no damage had been done. She put her face on the ambulance bonnet as she saw men going into the flames again, unable to watch. A hand shook her, a policeman saying something she could not hear through the noise of the fire. His gestures were unmistakable though, he wanted her to take the ambulance to the Camber. I can't, she thought despairingly; my God, this war has only just begun and already I can't remember a world not made up of fear. Her legs were like posts, the steering wheel slippery under her hands, the heavy ambulance skittering on rubble and hoses as heat grew on their faces, darkness closing in the sun. Clothes, faces, harbor wall and water, everything was blackly greasy and reflecting an oven glow. Soon, they began to pick up casualties: retching, smoke-sodden men, white eyes and pink mouths agape. Faye could feel her face stiffening with heat from the monstrous hearth of coal, hands trembling when she thought of explosives on the burning ship.

"That's the lot!" A naval petty officer thumped the side of the ambulance. "Bring us some tea back with you!"

Faye nodded and stared into the murk. Was the glow less again? "You'll manage it?"

"Lor' love you, miss, it's nearly done. 'Cept for the old *Codrington* of course." He scowled, "Artificer on her I was, three years back."

"The Navy seems to spend its life sailing each other's ships," observed Anne, a certain Army superiority in her tone. "They might have birthed half of them themselves."

Faye laughed, she too had noticed the extraordinary intimacy of the Navy. "There's no news of your father yet?"

Anne shook her head. "My mother heard from one of the other officers. I think he's dead, but she still hopes for a miracle."

When they returned to the harbor half an hour later, there was no doubt about it: smoke towered as high as ever, but the vicious twist had gone. Faye sat through the day in smoke and smuts ferrying exhausted men into clear air, and in the evening Mr. Jewell came in search of her.

He climbed into the cab, gasping and fanning himself as if he had been fighting the fire single-handed. "What a shambles! I've been looking for you everywhere."

"I took the ambulance over from Anne at the end of her shift." Faye's dislike of the man had grown over the weeks, as he always seemed to turn up at the end of a job. If she had known more of the strains of war, she would have recognized her feelings as the resentment of one who had consistently been caught in the wrong place at the wrong time for someone who had not. He might easily have been bombed in his office while she remained safe on the harbor wall: it had not worked out like that and she hated him for it.

"You ought to have checked in at base as soon as you could, wherever you took over. You know that perfectly well." He mopped his face. "You own that slipway we've been using, don't you?"

"My husband does. Why?"

"We've orders to pull back into the main depot; they say we don't need ambulances down on the pier now most casualties are likely to be in the town. Just as we had it nicely organized too!"

"What will happen to the slip?"

"How do I know? Only navy personnel are to be allowed into the harbor."

Oh, well, thought Faye, with Beauty gone, I suppose it doesn't matter. She stopped her ambulance as she drove back for the last time from the fire, and leaned on the promenade railings, gazing over the harbor. Already it seemed that a fresh retreat was beginning: the harbor part-blocked, the pier deserted, and as she watched, a tight line of ships slipped out of the eastern entrance and disappeared into haze. The destroyers were leaving Dover.

She could never remember seeing the Admiralty harbor empty before: always it was a shifting weft of ships and now there was nothing but a tug and a few trawlers. Abandoned, empty, Dover had had its moment as the haven of the nation, and the cloud staining the sky was like the shadow of the enemy already on its beaches.

She sighed and went back to the ambulance, then stopped, foot poised on the step, head tipped to an unfamiliar, snarling roar. Oh no, she thought, not again. They've won, they've got us out of the harbor, what more do they want? Another raid now seemed more than she could bear. This noise was different though, deep-throated and louder all the time, yet no air-raid warning had sounded. Then she saw bow waves, low shapes and specks of color coming out of the dusk, to disappear behind the pier and into Wellington Dock.

"MTBs and MGBs," said a naval stoker coiling hose pipe along the front. "There's been a few in there a while now, I reckon they'll be sending several flotillas now the destroyers have gone. There'll be good pickings along the French coast with all the barges Jerry'll be bringing across." He grinned. "Good fun to fight in, torpedo boats, I might have a crack at getting in them myself."

Faye checked in and scrubbed her ambulance, a hateful chore. The disinfectant stung her hands, the water was never hot enough, and on this occasion everything was covered with smuts and grease. She had felt uplifted by the torpedo boats, as if the harbor had been lost and won again while she watched, but pride and excitement did not outlast sheer, bleak discomfort. Her back ached, and however hard she scrubbed, the oil seemed immovable; when Mr. Jewell came over with one of his pieces of paper in his hand she nearly threw her bucket at him.

"Now we are all one unit again, I must reorganize the duty rota. I've put you down for Mondays and Thursdays, Mrs. Ludlow, is that all right?"

She shrugged. "It'll have to be, won't it?"

"I thought it might suit you, living so far out, to do your duties together." He blinked at her anxiously, "I don't want to make things more difficult for my young ladies than I must."

"Thank you." Faye heard the grudging note in her voice and looked at the paper; perhaps he was trying to be helpful after all. He had written her down for two double shifts of sixteen hours each, and after her initial dismay she realized that it would make life much easier. In the main depot there was room to sleep, and short of invasion they were unlikely to be actually on the move for that length of time. The long journeys from the valley were bad enough in the summer; in winter it would be a blessing to have to do them only twice a week. She thanked him again, with rather more warmth, and watched him trot over to the next group like a dog trailing its lead in the hope of a walk.

With some difficulty she discovered it was Friday, everyone having lost count of time, and the weary climb back to the valley was lightened by the thought of three days' grace, three days' freedom from raids, three days to touch the threads of normal life again.

Reydenham was not quite the haven of normality she thought it, but compared to Dover it was peace itself. There were troops in the woods, guns arriving for the pits dug by the road, and challenges in the dark as she cycled down the winding lane to the manor. Christopher was in bed when she arrived, Cook exclaiming at her shrimp-pink face and scolding her like a child for unwise sunbathing. "It's not sun." Faye stopped, overwhelmed by the effort of explanation; the great oil fire of the day had already slipped with the rest to another existence. "Have you anything to eat?"

" 'Tis Friday, and no one's been to get the rations. Unless you brought them with you, Mrs. Rupert?"

"No, I didn't have the books." She felt numb at the thought of rations and cycling the hills again to find them. "You must have some cheese or soup or something."

"Cheese is rationed," said Cook unanswerably. " 'Tis the end of the week, like I was saying. I've some soup, for all that the vegetables are so high in weeds you wouldn't believe. We don't often see Gabriel nowadays."

"We'll weed them ourselves tomorrow." Faye could hear her voice trembling. "It's no good waiting for others to do things any more. I'll have soup and bread, and anything else you can find." She sank into a chair in the library, filthy as she was. Damn Cook, damn Gabriel for enjoying himself with Colonel Druitt instead of weeding vegetables. Tomorrow . . . tomorrow she must chase after them all, and walk the valley too, with harvest almost on them. She blinked in the dim light and stared at a pile of letters on the desk; tomorrow she must also face debts and begging and threats again. She was asleep before Cook returned with the soup.

Chapter Fifteen

Afterwards, Faye thought that the strangest thing about the summer of 1940 was the way it never settled into any pattern. Everything was different, yet there was no framework of difference for the mind to grasp. Dunkirk, the raids on Dover, then harvest at Reydenham with the great air battles of August overhead: events crowded on each other while the complication of life increased from day to day. There was no time to adjust to one crisis before the next arrived, until she found it difficult to concentrate on anything at all. She snapped at everyone and heard herself doing so, then felt resentful when her apologies were coldly received. Christopher eyed her doubtfully and no longer demanded games and stories, tagging after Nanny instead; she slept badly and woke sweating with terror, longing to find Rupert beside her in the empty bed.

In the valley, they worked fifteen hours a day, short of fuel for their few tractors, above all short of men. The sun was relentless, glorious day succeeding glorious day, while above them vapor trails and the rattle of guns became so familiar that they had to come very close before they looked up. There was one relief: as the fighting spread inland, first to the airfields of Kent, then to Sussex and Surrey, Dover was left aside, merged into the greater struggle. There was the odd raid or chased aircraft sweeping the streets with fire as it scurried for safety, but with the harbor nearly empty it was no longer the main target. Faye began to look forward to her spells of duty, when she could sleep in the back of her ambulance; if they were called out she no longer suffered with the shocked and mangled bodies they carried, and afterwards felt guilty because her main thought was of disturbed rest. The hotels and houses along the front were battered and pitted with bomb fragments, the rest of the town still relatively untouched: occasionally they would be called down to the inner harbor if the

MTBs had suffered badly in the night sweeps; mostly the Navy took care of their own.

The town and hills around were full of men, exercising, digging in, practicing with new weapons: instead of looking with dread at the Channel each day, they began to curse the Germans for not coming. All that wire, and waiting, and now hoping; it seemed ridiculous of them not to come. Then they could be beaten and it would all end tidily.

Overhead the sun flashed on climbing, twisting aircraft, spent bullets rattling in the streets, once a German fighter crashing above Stone Cross Farm in a gout of flame, the pilot buried in Reydenham churchyard. Dover harbor became busier again as air-sea rescue launches searched for shot-down crews, and the urgency of the moment forced more convoys to brave the straits by daylight under fire from long-range guns at Calais and Boulogne.

Each night the nation gathered around the wireless, in ambulance station or kitchen, in factory and farm, listening to the announcer's unemotional voice give the day's tally of downed aircraft like a cricket score. As it mounted steadily, suddenly a sense of splendor banished weariness, and made each one feel his full worth for the first time, and the worth of his neighbor, too. Few can ever believe that their lives have changed one jot of history's tale; now for a brief span the whole nation believed it and grew to meet their own vision.

Faye was tired but it did not matter, nor did she dream at night any longer. She slept completely and woke in the morning with each sense ready-strung, each tree and field traced separately on eye and mind because it was still unconquered. Rupert was camped in the Hampshire downs and wrote of raids on radar stations and airfields; he telephoned sometimes too, and then Faye was able to feel his presence more clearly, even through crackling wires and cut connections. He was enjoying himself, she could tell, his drive harnessed to a task he could master; he was an uncomplicated man and relished the stark simplicities of life stripped down for a struggle to the death.

One night in late August, Faye had just switched off the wireless, when they heard a series of distant explosions.

"The sireens haven't gone, have they?" demanded Cook. "I didn't hear no airplanes, neither."

"We don't always hear them from here." Faye turned off the

light and went out on the step. On a still night like this they usually did hear the siren. Everything was quiet, a few birds calling drowsily, the sky clear and faintly orange in the west. "It must be the Army exercising." She hoped the Home Guard were not included in their maneuvers, for she had plans to lure Gabriel back into the garden soon, and a night exercise would keep him obstinately up a tree with his shotgun for at least another week.

She crossed the stable yard and walked over shadowed grass, breathing the scents of night. Suddenly there was another pattern of explosions, much nearer, a flash of light over the brow of the hill, a slight shudder beneath her feet. No engines, nothing. It could not be the Army, though; those explosions had been enough to knock down half a dozen houses.

"Is it them dratted Germans coming?" Nanny loomed out of darkness, breath wheezing. "Shall I get Christopher into the trench?"

"Surely there would be more noise if it was invasion?" Then they both heard sound above, a rush of air and another precise pattern of explosions. "Shells! They can reach us with their batteries at Calais!" She remembered white plumes reaching out for convoys in the straits and felt herself chill. Dover was not a ship with an hour's bombardment to endure on its way, but tied down to map and grid reference for the guns' dissection. "Best leave Christopher where he is, they're aiming at the town, not us, and plotting the flashes in the dark." Now they knew what to look for, it was obvious. For two hours the Germans fired slowly and methodically, pacing their shots down the hillsides, away from Reydenham, closer and closer to harbor and town. When they stopped at last, they could hear a different sound in the distance, a single Royal Marine battery beyond the Castle replying to the challenge. Britain was no longer an island.

Faye bicycled into Dover the next day, fearing what she would see, and at first saw nothing, before realizing that what she had taken for heat haze was dust hanging in still air. The ambulances were smothered in dust too, although she saw little actual damage in the streets. "The Catholic church and some houses," said Anne, on her knees scrubbing. "The road to Canterbury and the far end of the town are a mess, they were firing too long for the center here. This time," she added grimly.

"They landed some in the woods above Reydenham. We didn't know what on earth was happening."

"Nor did we, until some of the wardens who'd been in the last war told us." She flung her cloth back in the bucket. "It was worse than bombs, and this time they were only playing with us, doing their sums and counting flashes."

Faye nodded. The shells had been a good two miles from Reydenham, but the feeling of helplessness as gunners flicked switches twenty-five miles away, sapped at will itself. "I must get Christopher away," she said aloud. "They've only to give their dials one twist too many to send a whole salvo into the valley."

"I'm surprised you haven't sent him away before," said Anne frankly. "Kent is no place for children these days."

"Rupert wouldn't hear of it, but—" She broke off, she was not a woman who enjoyed discussing her husband with others, and she foresaw endless arguments over the telephone if she was to get Christopher away. Increasingly bitter arguments, she thought with a sinking heart. "The only trouble is, I don't know where to send him. All my friends live near Canterbury, and it's not much safer there than here."

"I'll write to my mother if you like, she's alone now and a child in the house would do her good."

"Would you? Where does she live?"

Anne smiled. "On the edge of a moor in Yorkshire. If he is to be safe anywhere, he'll be safe there."

Faye found herself looking at her watch every few minutes as the hours of her duty crept by, praying she would be out of the town before the German gunners decided on more sport. Hardly anyone spoke, the usual jokes stilled, every ear stretched for torn air, which was all the warning they would get. Above them the air battle raged, the attention of the world focused on its ebb and flow; in Dover that day they scarcely thought of it.

By late afternoon they were beginning to relax, to pity the night crews and speculate whether the Germans would only fire in darkness. Then it happened. A single explosion, and while they stared at each other, the same dread pattern of five more, very close, the ground leaping, dust falling.

"Get over into the shelter, I'll call you if you're needed." Mr. Jewell's cheeks wobbled, sweat pouring down his face.

They hesitated, wanting to go, ashamed of how much they had disliked him. "I reckon I'll stay," said Beryl at last.

"I said, get over the road! All of you into the shelter, quick!" His voice squeaked uncertainly; they went, and he would not look at them as they left.

"Who'd'a thought it of ole Jewell?" muttered Beryl in Faye's ear. "I won't be able to 'ate the bastard now, proper spoiled my war, 'e 'as."

The shelter was crowded and reminded Faye of photographs she had seen of the Spanish Civil War. The same faces filled with staring eyes, the same dirt and weeping children, even two nuns in a corner, comforting a tearful woman who had been knocked off her bicycle by the blast. She put her head in her hands and began to count—how long did it take to reload a battery of guns, how many seconds for shells to travel twenty-five miles? She was answered by another shattering roar, so close the lights went out.

They had not time to start counting again before they heard Mr. Jewell's squawk at the entrance. "Duty crew! Up to Prior's Terrace, quick! There's been a hit on cottages there."

Beryl and Faye hesitated, the shelter which had seemed so unpleasant only minutes before a refuge they dared not leave. "C'mon," said Beryl at last. "If that ole woman Jewell can do it, we can."

Shells had fallen neatly at each end of Prior's Terrace, the stench of cordite nauseating, earth, tiles, and rubble scattered everywhere. Rescue workers were already digging frantically into collapsed houses, three bodies laid on the pavement. "Leave them," said a dust-caked policeman when they would have put them in the ambulance. "There's one at least trapped alive. You can come back for the dead later."

Prior's Terrace sloped up the hill to the west of the town, and waiting beside the bodies they stared across the Channel, the coast of France clearly visible. "There!" said Faye suddenly, hands tightening. One, two, three, four, five, six flashes along the coast between Calais and Boulogne: they glanced at each other fearfully, thinking of shells already hurtling toward them over the sea. They landed with a shattering crash along the seafront, a white-plastered building sliding quite slowly to the ground in a shower of masonry.

"If you can see 'em, you're alive," said Beryl shakily. "Let's go and 'elp them diggers, surely shells won't never land twice in the same place. Gawd, think of doin' this every day until the war ends!"

Faye thought of it that night, back in Reydenham with only the sound of wind in the trees outside. She had opened one of Rupert's bottles of whisky and was on her second glass. Courage was like whisky, she decided hazily, once tipped out it was not replenished. She did not know how much of hers had run into the sea off Dunkirk and over the rubble of Dover, but she did not think she had too much left. And when it was gone, it was gone.

The telephone rang. "Oh, damn!" she said aloud; she did not think she could face Rupert tonight, to wrangle about Christopher, and stamp down resentment at his cheerful incomprehension over the life she was leading. Tonight also to hide whisky in her voice. She lifted the receiver carefully. "Hullo?"

"It is my turn to inquire about your safe return from the war. I am happy to hear you are well, Mrs. Ludlow."

"Who—" She stared at the instrument blankly, mind shuttling among the whisky fumes, then she knew who it must be. "Mr. Castellan."

"Formality is with us again." She heard amusement in his voice, then he added, "I really am relieved you are safe, Faye. I nearly rang several times these last weeks, hearing so many reports of bombing in Dover, then tonight with news of shelling too, I felt as you did, I daresay, when you rang my office. If I don't ask I will never know."

She laughed involuntarily. "Did they run off to your partner complaining about strange women disturbing the calm of British banking?"

"To my father, yes, they did. I was grateful for your concern and discretion though, and told them to mind their own business."

"And thank . . . thank you for ringing, too. I was feeling rather depresh . . ." She took a deep breath, head spinning, whisky loosening her tongue. "I hated the shelling today."

There was a long silence, so she wondered whether the connection was cut. "You would be very foolish if you did not," he said at last. "Drink won't make it any easier."

"I haven't—" she began indignantly.

"Yes, you have, and don't feel you've committed one of the

seven deadly sins. Alone and frightened, it is the easiest thing in the world to do. I know, having done it myself. Tip the damned stuff out of the window and go to bed."

Tears were pricking her eyes, tears of shame that he should know she had been drinking, of shock the whisky had hidden and now could hide no more. "It is thinking of tomorrow, and tomorrow. No end to it. Mondays and Thursdays, I hate Mondays and Thursdays."

"Why those days particularly?"

His voice was perfectly detached, as if he was used to dealing with drunks on the telephone every night of the year, she thought, infuriated. "Because they are my duty days," she snapped. "I'm sorry to sound such an idiot. Good night."

He laughed. "You'll have a hell of a head in the morning. Good luck, my dear." He rang off.

Just in time to make sure I didn't hang up on him, she thought indignantly, dropping the receiver back on its rest with a clatter. Do him good if I had. Her glance shifted to the whisky bottle and she hesitated, more than half minded to have another drink just to spite him, then with a sudden gesture she thumped the cork into place, turned out the light, and opened the window.

Night air flicked gratefully over her face, steadying her senses. She leaned her forehead against cold glass and stood, staring into the dark. It is going to be a long war, she thought drearily. No shortcuts, no quick answers out of the whisky bottle. Endless processions of Mondays and Thursdays, of tasteless food and shabby clothes and no money. If I'm going to last, I've got to realize just how long it is all going to take.

All the same, there was no point wasting good whisky.

She groped her way to the desk, locked the bottle into the pedestal cupboard and came back to the window, key in hand. She hesitated, metal hard against her palm, then threw it as hard as she could into the dark.

She climbed the stairs with heavy, shuffling steps and threw herself on her bed, fully dressed, swooping dizzily down a slope of insensibility. Her last conscious thought was that she would indeed have a hell of a head in the morning.

Chapter Sixteen

Slowly, slowly the weeks slipped by. The battle overhead drew to its peak and then, with victory scarcely grasped, changed into a savagely different gear. What they had thought of as triumph was only reprieve; the enemy could not come this year by sea, instead he reached out directly for the towns and cities, railways, ports, and factories of Britain. As the hours of darkness lengthened to favor the raiders, people slept night after night under tables and in dank shelters, struggling to work in the morning through littered streets by disorganized, intermittent transport. And then faced the next night again. Queues in shops grew, rations shrank; children counted the number of raisins in a bag and mothers wondered wearily what they could cook which might taste a little different. If china cups or dishcloths came in, word traveled across a town in minutes and an hour's wait might yield a few irreplaceable items; girls with their first dates carefully boiled blackout material to remove the dye and made themselves purple blouses until sewing cotton ran out too.

Faye was grateful for Mrs. Ludlow's advice in the matter of elastic and hairpins; both were unobtainable and could be exchanged for items which other prudent souls had hoarded. Once, she helped dig an old lady from under her wrecked staircase and found her unwilling to be rescued, insisting on staying until daylight to look for precious kirby grips in the rubble. "Hairpins are all very well in their way," said Mrs. Ludlow complacently, "but elastic will see you through the war in comfort, you mark my words." She had reels of every type and thickness in her cupboard.

"I keep thinking what a fool I was not to buy more of everything while I had the chance." Faye thought wistfully of loaded shelves at the grocer's, the eager enthusiasm of butcher and fishmonger with their beautifully arranged slabs, the piles of fruit which had always stood on the sideboard at Reydenham.

Now she was lucky to find a few apples and their five rations together provided a joint six inches square one week, a few chops the next. "Have you any medicinal paraffin?"

"My dear Faye, what a thing to ask!"

"There was a recipe on the wireless this morning," she explained. "How to make fruitcake with grated carrots and medicinal paraffin. William will be home on leave soon, and Christopher—" She swallowed. In ten days' time Christopher was to go to stay with Anne's mother in Yorkshire. She had argued fiercely with Rupert every time he rang, but he had not altered in his conviction that it would be a betrayal of the Ludlows to send Christopher away. In the end, Faye had decided that he must go whatever Rupert said, and ever since had lived in a turmoil of guilt and recrimination. Within a day of her decision the German guns had stopped their bombardment and scarcely a shell or bomb had fallen in Dover since.

"I think you are very much at fault in sending Christopher away," said Mrs. Ludlow severely. "I suppose one cannot expect you to have the same feelings as Ludlows bred at Reydenham, but you might at least accept what you are told."

Faye shrugged, too tired and uncertain in her mind to argue. She got the paraffin, though, and then had to soothe Cook's outrage at the idea of baking a cake made of medicine, carrots, cold tea, and powdered egg. Christopher was thrilled by the thought of real cake, no longer remembering anything larger than a rock bun, and frayed at her nerves with demands to hear about Yorkshire, going into peals of laughter at her attempts to mimic a Yorkshire accent.

"You're going up with him?" asked Anne when they shared a duty the following Thursday. "You'll have a terrible journey across London with all the raids and everything."

"I know. I'd better ask old Jewell to change my duty in case I'm not back in time. I wish I was sure I was doing the right thing," she added. "It's dreadful, but I almost wish there would be a few more shells in the valley just to be certain. They're all against me in this. Nanny has never left Kent before and considers Yorkshire barely out of the Stone Age; Rupert and his mother think I'm teaching Chris to behave like a cowardly shopkeeper. Like me," she added bitterly.

Anne glanced at her and then away again. She was an army daughter, and although she sympathized with Faye, could not help being shocked by such open defiance of her husband. Only Beryl had no doubts. "You put your little tacker somewhere safe an' be thankful. If you see rollers going round, you don't shove your kid's fingers in 'em, now do you? If we was sensible, we wouldn't be puttin' our own tits in 'em, neither," she added feelingly.

They were back by the Prince of Wales pier, the first time they had been in the harbor since the oil fire of the summer. There had been an early-morning raid which left several gunners killed and wounded, and the MTBs had also run into trouble overnight. Faye thought she had become hardened; instead she discovered in herself a deep loathing for more pain and suffering, for filth and blood and agonized, clutching hands. Several of the sailors were terribly burned, their plywood MTBs having petrol engines and very little armor plate; the dreadful smell of roasted meat clung to the inside of the ambulance, so they had to drive with windows wide to the raw winter air.

Afterward, they parked the ambulance and stood on the deserted seafront, sky gray and hollow, a sharp wind kicking up edged sea even in harbor. The slip was still there, wooden slats clattering in the wind, a half-burned torpedo boat tangled in wire and shallows alongside. They went to look at it, wondering which of the tormented bodies they had carried had fried in flames fierce enough to burst open part of the deck, bubble varnish, and melt metal fittings.

"I wonder they don't pull it up on the slip," said Faye suddenly. "It'll sink if it's left much longer in this wind."

"Good thing if it did. No much left worth pulling anywhere." Beryl wrinkled her nose at the acrid stench of charred timber.

Faye climbed onto the pier and stared down at it, excitement stirring. She did not know much about boats, but watching Beauty grow had taught her something and she did not think she was looking at a total wreck. About half the ply skin and most of the deck planking needed renewing, no doubt some of the framing as well. The engines—well, there was nothing she could do about engines. She pulled herself sharply from the drift of her thoughts, then was swirled away by the tumult of them again. Henry and half a dozen like him could repair this, she was certain.

"Looks a hell of a mess, doesn't she?" A young naval lieutenant was standing beside her, peering gloomily into the wreckage.

Faye started, heart thumping. "Surely she looks worse than she is?"

"Try telling that to the fitters. We had half a dozen boats shot up last night. Poor old 20017 will be on the bottom before they get around to her."

"She's yours?"

He nodded. "We ran into a gaggle of E-boats. I thought we'd had it when the fuel tank blew up but we filled with water so quickly the fire went out." He had bandaged hands and a bright pink, singed face, strangely naked without eyebrows. "Another boat towed us in but the rope parted in the chop at the entry, or she'd be snug in Wellington Dock. She'd sink just the same there, I daresay," he added bitterly.

"My husband owns that slipway." Faye spoke unconcernedly, not looking at him.

He grinned. "It looks just about ready to join 20017 on the bottom."

"One day, perhaps; not this winter, though. If you rounded up some of your friends we could probably get your boat out of the water before it's too late."

"And then what? They're working flat out on the others; they'd never send fitters over here and she'd sink on a tow."

"I've got some carpenters." Faye tried to sound indifferent. "If we could patch her up enough for a tow—"

"Could you? Could you really, by God? It does seem wicked just to leave her to sink!" He pawed at his crisped face. "Give me an hour to roust out the lads and some cable . . . Have you got a winch in that shed of yours?"

"No," said Faye regretfully. "I've got plenty of ply and planking, though, laid up and seasoning since before the war."

He frowned. "We'll need a winch. She may not look much half submerged, but she displaces over fifty tons. We might get her lodged on the slip at high tide, though, and give ourselves time to scrounge a winch." Their eyes met and both laughed. "God, you've made me feel better already. I came here like a mourner at a funeral."

She touched his bandages. "It's not surprising. I'll go and find Henry, our foreman, and meet you back here as soon as I can." She reflected that it was fortunate she was crewing with Beryl, who would think it natural to use an ambulance about her own affairs, rather than Anne, who certainly would not.

She ran Henry to earth in a bar, somewhat the worse for beer. He looked frail and old and she had a moment of doubt, but when she broached her project to him he reached for his coat at once, brightening at the thought of a boat and timber under his hands again. "Aimin' to get the slip back at work then, missus?"

She nodded, unable to say why a battered MTB seemed so important to her. It was a strange feeling: one part of her mind was assembling all the many things she must do if this madness was ever to be more than fantasy, the rest of her scampering further and further from reality, like a horse let into a sunlit field after a long winter in its stable. Repairing MTBs was war work; she could resign from the ambulance service with a clear conscience. She would be making something again, not shoveling up the pieces of other men's destruction.

Henry downed the last of his beer. "Cash paid on the nail, if you get an Admiralty contract. You'll have a nice little business there by the end of the war, if you can swing it. You'll need a winch, though."

"The lieutenant said so, too. He thought he might scrounge one from somewhere."

"You'll be lucky. Small stuff perhaps, but the Navy's not stupid. He'll never be able to walk off with a winch."

On due consideration, Lieutenant Alan Wyllie agreed with him. He returned to the slip with nearly thirty naval friends, drums of rope, and fenders, and they spent the rest of the afternoon sweating and splashing in icy water, maneuvering the waterlogged torpedo boat onto the slip. It was done at last, but only just. The bow was well out of the water, the remains of the stern still submerged, although as the tide dropped they opened the engine-room vents and drained off enough water to heave it a few feet higher.

"An easterly gale will break her up." Henry laid his hand on the battered hull and stared across gray sea. "Protected against everything else, but a mile and a half of open harbor'll kick up enough of a sea from the east to grind her to pieces. We need a winch to get her inside, quick."

"I know." The lieutenant looked ready to drop, his bandages sodden. "Big things, winches."

"Cement, bolts, and hawsers, too," said Henry inexorably.

"For heaven's sake," said Faye impatiently. "Leave him alone. He has done everything he can tonight, and we all need a night's sleep before we do any more."

Henry shrugged. "You've got till the next easterly."

"All right, so we've got till the next easterly," she snapped. "Beryl said she'd come round this way with the ambulance, we'll drop you off in the town. Can we take you anywhere, Lieutenant?"

"Alan. Back to my billet, I suppose. I'll walk, though, they'll not let a civilian vehicle into the base."

"I'll walk, too," said Henry huffily. "Not worth waitin' for no ambulance."

"I'm sorry." Faye put her hand on his arm; whatever happened, Henry must not be antagonized. "We're all tired and cold. Truly, there's nothing more we can do tonight."

"There's nothing more we can do tomorrow neither, without we get that there boat out of the water and an Admiralty contract signed." He stumped off into the dark.

"Admiralty contract? Once the heat is off the base workshops, they'll send their own men over to repair her." Alan Wyllie looked bewildered. "We just have to keep her safe a few days."

Faye looked at the dim bulk of 20017, flared bow high over her head, the slip shaking under its burden at each slop of the tide. "If we don't get her out soon, she'll take the slip with her." It was too early to divulge any far-reaching plans to Lieutenant Wyllie. "Alan, would you like to come home with me tonight? Just to stay a few days while you recover? You look as if some home comfort would do you good." She did not want him running off to base workshops yet awhile.

Fortunately she had the car, petrol hoarded through the fine weather against just such January days as this, and he needed little persuading. Over dinner he told her he came from Birmingham and had been a stunt cyclist before the war; Faye asked Mrs. Ludlow through to share the meal with them, so no disapproving letters would find their way to Rupert, and had to explain rather more than she wanted to in the process.

"Well, my dear, you know your own business best, but if I was an admiral, I wouldn't give a girl like you a contract to repair a warship," she said at once, without looking up from her tapestry.

"Tell me, do you think I have the delphinium shades quite right?"

"Yes," replied Faye unhesitatingly. "You know you always get them right. I don't think the Admiralty will be anxious to give repair work to the Ludlow slip either, so do you think you could entertain Lieutenant Wyllie here for a couple of days while I get things fixed up before approaching the Navy?"

She selected some fresh wool. "I understood you were taking Christopher north in a few days' time."

"I was, but he'll have to wait. Everything seems quiet enough now," she added defiantly. "I'll ring Anne's mother and apologize."

"I seem to remember you accusing Rupert of selfishness when he wanted to keep Christopher here; how would you describe yourself now?"

Faye flushed. "Practical. The shelling hasn't come near us in weeks, and with invasion forgotten at least until next spring, it is time everyone remembered that we're bankrupt, without a tenth of the money we need to plant next year's crop and last until harvest. Shall I lay a bet with you? If I bring up tomorrow's post unopened, you will find three quarters of it is bills we cannot pay."

"I never gamble, and you should not either. It is a very bad habit," said Mrs. Ludlow severely. "You will not mend warships on an overdraft."

She had put her finger precisely on the difficulty, reflected Faye ruefully. Somewhere there must be a winch, but she could not pay for it, nor for repairs to the slip and the other equipment they would need. Unless they were obviously able to do the job, there was no point approaching the Navy; if they were not going to get a contract, then she must not follow Rupert's example and plunge further into debt for nothing.

She lay in bed later, staring into darkness, every muscle tense. This she wanted very much to do, and not for the money as everyone thought. Well, not only for the money, she amended in a moment of honesty, but could not probe further into the great desire which had sprung on her out of nowhere as she stared down at 20017, the stink of burned flesh still on her clothes. All the same . . . an Admiralty contract on favorable terms would cut through their worst difficulties in a matter of months.

She rose very early, and let herself quietly out of the house. Alan Wyllie had been almost comatose the night before, and before he roused she had a great deal to do. It was another raw day, rain scudding on typical Channel murk: a westerly, thank heaven, but strong, very strong and driven by more to come behind. She bicycled into Dover, for surely there were emergencies ahead when petrol would be vital, and arrived with her clothes plastered like wet paper to her shivering body. She had her ambulance pass and knew most of the sentries, so there was no difficulty in reaching the slip, and she found Henry already there, rigging extra ropes and fenders.

Even so, the grinding shift of so much dead weight was shaking the timber under their feet. "We've got to get her out of the water, or let her go," Henry shouted above the wind. "The slip'll not stand much more of this."

"Do you have any idea where I might find a winch?" Faye could feel grating lurches right through her body.

"I bin thinking." Henry paused deliberately. "The coal staithe. It's in too much of a mess to use at the moment, but there used to be several winches there. You remember that overhead wire?"

She nodded. Coal came direct by cableway from mines seven miles away.

"There were all kinds of engines and pulleys to do with that, if you can get your hands on 'em. When I was a boy, they 'ad an old steamroller with a winch mounted on the back for loading direct into barges."

"When you were a boy?" Henry must be seventy; on the other hand, a mobile winch was beyond her wildest hopes. "How long since you saw it last?"

"Close on twenty year. The coal company has all its spare stuff stacked in they cliff caves behind the Camber."

"We need to know whether it is still there," said Faye thoughtfully. "No good stirring up the Harbor Board and heaven knows who else unless we know what we want. If it isn't, then we need to look at the staithe." The Camber and everything it contained was Navy property, well guarded and inaccessible to civilians. She thought of Alan Wyllie, and discarded him regretfully; he would jump at the chance of getting his boat out of the water, and approach the Navy directly. This she needed to do, and have tools and timber and men ready before the Navy knew anything about it.

Yet surely, if it was there, it could not be extracted without official formalities. She thought of the feeling every sailor had for the ships of his service, and made up her mind suddenly. "Do you know anyone who could drive a steamroller, supposing we could get it?"

Henry shrugged. "Drive it meself, I daresay. I did a spell on the roads once. What are you planning, missus?"

She told him briefly, adding, "I know some of the men in the Camber from the big fire last summer, I expect they'll listen to me if they're still there." The great oil fire was folklore already; with the institution of the George Cross for civilian gallantry, three Dover firemen had been the first recipients for their deeds that day.

She cycled along the exposed length of promenade, mind tussling with unfamiliar problems. The wind was still freshening, harbor flecked white, her face stung by icy rain. She was stopped at the entry to the eastern base, a young and confused seaman waving aside her ambulance pass and peering behind her as if he expected to see a formation of Germans in support. His petty officer came out of the guard hut when she would not leave, and she recognized him with delight.

"Mr. Doggett! Do you remember me? We shared the shelter of a coal truck last summer when the oil was burning."

"That I do, ma'am," he said warmly. "But you've no business here now, worrying young Ted, playing soldiers." He brushed the boy's rifle aside and took her into the guard hut, tropically hot from an iron stove. Coal from the staithe, Faye thought enviously. "What can I do for you, since I don't suppose you're here for the fun of it in this weather?"

Faye smiled at him. "I want a steamroller." She had decided that direct assault to arouse interest was the best tactic, and was not disappointed when he burst out laughing.

"A steamroller? Thinking of mowing your lawn or something?" Two other sailors in the hut regarded her with dropped jaws.

"It's the wrong time of year," she replied, straight-faced.

He handed her a chipped mug. "Just tell us slowly, all right? You really want a steamroller?"

She sipped gratefully at metallically strong liquid, not particularly recognizable as tea. "That's it. You know the caves at the back of the Camber? Somewhere in there is an old steamroller. I want to borrow it."

"Just the sort of thing I always wanted to borrow meself," observed one of the men.

"Go on," said the petty officer. "You got as far as you borrowing a steamroller. Why?"

Faye hesitated; she certainly had their attention, if nothing else. So she explained about 20017 precariously balanced on the slip, artistically depicting Lieutenant Wyllie in a fever from his wounds at her home after his efforts to save his boat the day before, how they would have to cut the cables and let her sink if the wind increased further. "Henry remembered the steamroller here had a winch, and sent me to ask your help," she added untruthfully. "To the MTB base she's a write-off, but if we could only get her out of the water—"

"I know where the roller is," offered one of the men. "I'm interested in old things like that, and had a look at her one day."

Petty Officer Doggett pulled his lip reflectively. "Seems a pity just to let her sink, like. You're sure the MTB base has nothing suitable?"

"Lieutenant Wyllie begged them to do something yesterday, but they wouldn't. Now he's too ill to try again, and I don't know who to approach." She looked at them helplessly, "They told him it wasn't worth salvaging, but surely any boat is worth trying to save?"

"They always was idle buggers over on Wellington Dock," observed one of the sailors dispassionately. "You want me to get some of the lads to dig out that there roller, 'Swain?"

Doggett was watching her, not quite convinced that he had heard the truth, but he was bored and his professional pride easily aroused. He nodded at last, and Faye only just stopped herself laughing aloud: a battle she had expected to be overwhelmingly difficult won almost without effort.

The Camber naval base was working well below its full capacity during the dirty weather of February 1941, and before long they had a couple of dozen men heaving at stacked rubbish to clear a space around the old steamroller at the back of one of the caves.

A sailor climbed up and rubbed at a brass plate. "Roaring

Tom," he read. "Don't look as if she'd roar very easy now, does she?"

"He," said Faye firmly. "You can't go calling an ugly brute like that female. Or something called Tom, either."

"Thomasina," said Doggett, grinning. "Be female this one, all right. Full of temperament afore we get her moving, if I knows anything about it."

"Perhaps she'll take a fancy to you, Mr. Doggett," said Faye. "You know, follow you around and whistle under your window at night."

It did not seem likely. They had cleared a space around her by midafternoon, and half the base seemed to be greasing and polishing energetically, arguing over ways to fire her boiler and trundling coal from the staithe. An officer turned up and started to protest about theft of coal company property, but Doggett took him aside and eventually he departed, looking worried, in search of the commanding officer.

Doggett winked at Faye. "Old MTB man, the captain, shot up off the east coast. He'll take care to keep well away once he knows what we're doing."

It became increasingly doubtful just what they were doing, as light drained from the afternoon. The engine was greased and gleaming, solid Victorian brass and iron scarcely pitted by twenty years' disuse, but no amount of cajoling could raise sufficient steam for movement. They lit a small firebox, piled in coal, waited until every dial swung, then clanked in gears as gently as they knew how. Usually there was a despairing whistle and a cloud of smoke, then the fire went out; when they tied down the safety vent in desperation, nearly everything became red-hot, the whole contraption shook, clanked forward one pace to cheers, then swung open the fire door and emitted a stream of burning coal.

"I told you she was female!" said Doggett, wiping a blackened face. "Have a bit of explaining to do in the morning if we set the base on fire."

"Henry," said Faye. "He said he could drive it. Let me go and get him, just in case he can remember what they used to do."

He shrugged. "She certainly hasn't taken a fancy to me."

Henry said nothing when he was admitted, walking around the sweating sailors and chuckling to himself when he saw signs of their struggle all around. Then he swung himself onto the steering platform and ran his hands lovingly over brass knobs and levers. "Fire 'er up, then," he said at last. He looked at their blackened clothes and chuckled again. "Sweet and gentle-like, or she 'as 'er ways of gettin' back at you, as you'll 'ave noticed."

Female again, thought Faye, smiling. And I just think, being female, that I might respond to Henry's gentling if I was a steamroller. He almost certainly did not know what he was doing, she decided, but he eased and stroked, swore when the roller began to shake, spoke approvingly as the dials swung.

"Watch out for that there fire door when you puts in the ratchet," shouted someone.

"When I puts in the ratchet, I puts in the ratchet," said Henry with dignity. "When she's ready, an' not before." Thomasina began to vibrate and emit puffs of steam, funnel glowing in the dusk.

"My God, she'll burst," muttered Doggett. "Put it in, man."

With a fearful clank, Henry put it in; there was a pause, a lurch, and squeal of metal as the roller slowly began to move, then picked up speed. Giant flywheel revolving, rollers striking sparks, rusty joints screaming like an elephant in rut, Thomasina lurched out of the Camber, flattening the wire barrier as she went. There was a liquid crunch as an oil drum was minced, the roller slithering on black stickiness as Henry wound the steering wheel frantically, then Thomasina straightened with an angry cough and disappeared into the dark, trailing sparks.

They all stood paralyzed, then chased off after her, stumbling over flattened wire, slipping on oil, laughing like children at a party. Faye found her bicycle undamaged and pedaled furiously after them, the cherry-red of the roller's funnel her only guide in the dark. Henry circled the open area at the end of the Prince of Wales pier five times before he finally found the right valve release; when he did, the indigestive roars as Thomasina settled to rest brought soldiers running from their emplacements, too.

Faye arrived first on her bicycle, to find Henry smugly uncoiling hawser from the winch. "The likes of 'er responds to a gentleman's touch. Henry, my ma used to say, allus remember that women like their little courtesies, an' you'll be surprised how easy the rest comes."

"Just so long as she stays in his bed, not mine," said Doggett when the rest arrived, panting. "Come on, lads, let's get the bugger to work while she's in the mood."

The mood had passed, a wicked blink of light all that remained of as fine a head of steam as ever Dover harbor had witnessed, but at last it was done. As midnight struck, 20017 jerked slowly up filched rollers and into the shed above, water and wreckage pouring out of her shattered stern, Thomasina digging her iron anchorage deep into the road above and most of Dover's defenders gathered to watch.

"Lucky the Jerries didn't know what they were missing," observed one of the sailors. "Fair pushover this place'd be tonight, with all them bloody pongos goggle-eyed over the pier."

Somehow they all had the feeling that the war was shelved for a few hours and felt better for it, even if it was waiting for them again in the morning. Before she started the weary trip back to Reydenham, Faye gave Henry precise instructions: their exploits would be all over Dover within hours, and they must expect callers from the MTB base in the morning.

She was exhausted, cycling back to Reydenham almost more than she could contemplate, and she would have bedded down in the cluttered little office at the slip, except that she felt she might need Alan Wyllie by her side in the morning. She intended to think out her next moves on the way home, but her mind was blank: no sense of triumph, no surviving flicker of amusement for the ridiculous farce with the steamroller; just wind and rain roaring out of the dark, and how very long the journey took.

Chapter Seventeen

She drove the car down to Dover the next day, towing a trailer of ply and timber; Alan came with her, excited by the thought of his boat safely out of the water. His hands were oozing yellow through their bandages, so she had to drop him off at his base for attention, and only just avoided the thought that with rather more resolution he might have started healing so he would be of some use.

A naval truck was drawn up outside the slip and Henry met her at the entry. "They've come, a damned nosy lieutenant, name of Beatty."

"Good." She put confidence she did not feel into her voice. "Start unloading the ply I've brought and make sure you carry every piece right past him." She discovered a morose-looking officer in grease-stained overalls, gloomily contemplating 20017's wrecked stern. "Hullo, what do you think of our piece of salvage?"

He fumbled a cigarette out of a crumpled packet and offered her one; his eyes were pouched with weariness, his skin gray and unhealthy, as if he had not been in fresh air for a long time. "You know Alan Wyllie?"

"I met him the day before yesterday, when we first tried to get his boat up the slip," said Faye, taken aback.

"I wondered why the hell you worried about such a wreck. Both engines gone, after fifteen feet gone, everything else in a god-awful mess. Alan too," he added, glancing at her again. "Proper circus you had down here last night, I understand. You never heard such a fuss as is going on in the Camber this morning. A little matter of flattened wire, missing coal, and crushed oil drums if I heard aright."

Faye laughed. "You heard right."

" 'Scuse me, missus, sir." Henry pushed past with a sheet of ply, followed by two more men carrying framing timber.

"How about going up to the office?" suggested Faye. "You're going to repair her, surely, after all our efforts?"

Up in the office, Beauty's plans were carefully arranged with dividers and slide rules well in evidence. Beatty looked around him with interest. "In the boatbuilding business yourself, Mrs. Ludlow?"

Faye nodded and picked up a photograph of Beauty, sheer and lovely on the stocks before launching. "This one was not quite complete when the war came. She sank at Dunkirk." She had considered carefully how to give the impression of long experience without actually telling lies. "If you are too busy we could patch the hull of your torpedo boat for you, so she's fit to tow to Wellington Dock. Most of our workmen are overage, so are still around, and I've plenty of good timber."

"So I see," he said noncommittally. His cigarette was a sodden mess, fingers twisting with overstretched nerves. Maintaining cardboard thin, petrol-engined MTBs with inadequate spares, when they were in constant battle with the sea and the enemy, had obviously brought him to the edge of a breakdown.

"What were you before the war?" asked Faye, drawn out of self-absorption by sympathy.

"Garage foreman in Durham. And you?"

Well, what was I? thought Faye. "I helped my husband in this slip," she said at last. "Henry was our foreman, there isn't much he doesn't know about boatbuilding."

"All right," he said suddenly. "We can't handle a job like this at the moment, and there's plenty of time, since she'll need new engines. You get on with it on a progress-payment basis, but we'll need to see the quality of your work before the first payment is made. I'll discuss it with your foreman, so I can get an idea whether it'll be a botch-up to get her round to the dock, or something more."

She'd done it.

As soon as Beatty went down to talk to Henry she saw the men in the shed exchange glances and grin, the atmosphere change in a moment. They had a purpose they understood again; no more laboring at unskilled jobs or waiting in queues to help irritable wives.

Only when she had picked Alan up and was rattling home did worries crowd in. She had no money, and Beatty would not sanction payment or a firm contract until he saw what they could do. If she pressed him she might get something, but she wanted to seem reliable, give the impression of a prosperous yard closed down only by the war; she wanted a contract for the full job, not just a botch-up as he called it. Then they might get more work and the fearful financial specters stalking the Ludlows would be banished, and Reydenham would keep the benefits of wartime prosperity.

"Let's stop and have a drink," said Alan suddenly. "You've been marvelous, we must celebrate." She had an overwhelming desire for her bed, but felt secretly apologetic for her lack of sympathy in the morning, and followed him into a crowded bar.

She looked around her with interest. Rupert belonged to clubs but had never taken her to ordinary pubs; her father certainly would be shocked by his daughter in a common bar. The Five Bells was musty and encased in oak beams which looked as if they would withstand anything short of a direct hit. There was an alert in progress and inland a good deal of firing, here only an occasional thump or tinkle of glass penetrated the calm. The landlord produced two weak gins from beneath the bar at the sight of Alan's bandaged hands, anything stronger than diluted beer already a luxury.

"Cheers," he toasted her over his glass. "D'you know, I think what you have done is the most incredible thing I've ever heard."

She laughed and drank, gin bouncing at once to her head. She couldn't remember when she had last eaten. "With the help of half Dover and most of the Navy, we got your boat up the slip."

"She would have sunk without you." He held her hand in his bandaged ones, pink singed face making him look absurdly young. "When I woke up yesterday in your house and they told me you'd gone down to Dover again, I—" Mugs on the shelf above began to jump and clatter, thuds coming closer, so everyone stopped talking and looked at the ceiling.

"Oh God." Faye shivered. "Why do they always have to come back this way?"

"Don't worry about them! It's London again, only the odd one in trouble will pull the plug over Kent. Listen, I'm going home on two weeks' leave, my mother is alone and I must go, or I'd sooner stay here with you. Will you come up to London and spend a day with me? It'd make all the difference if I had you to look forward to."

Faye pulled her hands loose. "I'm married, Alan."

"Well, of course I know that! I wasn't suggesting—I mean, I just wanted to take you out and do a show, see a bit of life. A thank-you from 20017 if you like. Surely there's no harm in one day for ourselves and forget the war?"

A harsh, crackling thud shook the dingy bar and clattered a mug off the shelf above. Well, why not? thought Faye. It is long enough since I did anything except scrub ambulances and scrape for money. I might be dead tomorrow, and Alan—Alan probably will not see the war through. She looked at his pleading face, shyly uncovering admiration for her: it was over a week since Rupert had telephoned and sometimes she wondered uneasily whether they would manage any better together on his next leave. She made up her mind suddenly. "I'd like to. We'll have to fix it up now, though. You can't telephone."

He looked taken aback at such a businesslike approach and cleared his throat nervously. "Next Tuesday? I'll meet you—I'll meet you—" He paused, both of them disconcerted afresh by the thought that anywhere he named might be shut or destroyed. "Under the big clock at Victoria? Twelve o'clock?"

"If the trains run." She stood up, wishing she had refused to go. I must be crazy, she thought, he seems almost as young as Christopher, and I have enough to keep me busy twenty-four hours a day without going up to London for days out.

When the time came, she nearly did not go. She knew almost nothing about boatbuilding but was kept frantically busy scrounging fittings and tools Henry wanted, knocking up long-shut boatyards, lying in wait for Lieutenant Beatty when he came off duty, searching for scores of items it had never occurred to her that they would need. At Reydenham there was a new season's seed and fertilizer to obtain, dozens of ministry forms to fill in, visits to tenants and the Agricultural Committee, endless difficulties over obtaining more than the barest essentials. The bank manager to see again. Money, money, money. There were grants for plowing and sheep and reclamation, checks for goods delivered, rents due in March, but inexorably more flowed out than in. Now, wages must be paid at the slip as well until the first Admiralty payment was agreed; the men must be content and working well or it might never be more than a few pounds for work done, and then polite dismissal.

Rupert was delighted when she told him the slip was back at work, and cheerfully told her to order whatever she needed since within a year Reydenham's credit would be good again. She hung up on him in a fury, the first time she had ever done so, her weakening resolve to meet Alan in London setting instantly into obstinacy.

At least William was due home on leave at the end of the month: who would have thought that scapegrace William would ever become a last hope in a financial whirlwind?

The London train was crammed to the racks with soldiers and sailors, bulky kit bags filling every available space. It was raining and the smell of cheap tobacco and wet cloth overwhelming; the windows pasted over and the heating broken. Faye had been looking forward to a peaceful two hours and instead found herself fortunate to be wedged on a gaping suitcase, cold hands clutched on her bag. She had told Mrs. Ludlow she was going to try to raise a loan in London since the Dover bank was uncooperative, and to her surprise, had been given some more jewelry to sell.

"Take it," Mrs. Ludlow had said. "I want to live at Reydenham free from debt again, and if anyone can do it, you can. I was angry with Rupert for marrying you but I am happy to find myself mistaken. Of course, I could not anticipate a war," she added in self-extenuation.

Faye now regarded her mother-in-law as she might a stuffed and strange creature under glass, and felt no more than mild annoyance, accepting that she intended modest praise. Instead, she sat in the train and thought of all the things she must do tomorrow, after a day wasted with Alan.

Then, it did not seem a day wasted. Alan's delight that she had come, his simple admiration, lifted her gloom and brought the wonderful relief of forgetting everything except his pleasure in her.

He was waiting anxiously under the clock, his face lightening when he saw her. He twirled her around and exclaimed at her careful choice of prewar fur jacket and soft wool dress. "Let me look at you! What a sight for a sailor, by Jove!"

She bobbed him a mock curtsy. "Thank you, sir. You look rather splendid yourself."

He laughed and tucked her hand under his arm, taking her bag. "I feel it now I don't crackle like tissue paper every time I sneeze." He was wearing a new uniform, and the boiled look had gone from his face, flaking skin all that was left of his scorching. His hands were only lightly bandaged, too, and with recovery he seemed older and more confident.

Unexpectedly, she found herself enjoying the day very much. London was strange with its sandbagged entrances and scanty traffic, and she felt happily irresponsible in its anonymity, Alan's hand around her waist and his lips brushing her cheek when he bent to tell her a joke. They went to a run-down pub for beer and a sandwich filled with what he called bear's breath, a fuggy smear of tasteless paste, then strolled in St. James's Park, throwing twigs at the ducks and laughing at their comical disappointment when they found they were not edible. They walked up Bond Street and chanted rude rhymes about the junk on display, anything of worth being safely in the cellars, and ended holding hands on a bench in Hyde Park, admiring the first daffodils to struggle into flower.

Faye sighed and laid her head on his shoulder. "It's been a lovely afternoon, Alan. Do you realize we haven't talked about the war once? Or nuts or clenches or forming pieces; I thought I'd forgotten how to talk about anything else."

"Or dung and the best time for sowing wheat," he said, grinning. "I had that all the way down to Dover when you drove me back to base."

A sudden, dreadful vision of fertilizer and piled bills filled her mind, before she pushed it away. I won't think of it today, she thought firmly. Tomorrow it will all be waiting for me again. "I'm starving," she said aloud. "Can one eat in a restaurant nowadays, or do you have to have a ration book?"

"Do you mean you haven't eaten out since the war began?" he demanded incredulously.

She shook her head. "Eighteen months of grocery queues and smoothing down Cook every time she has to prepare stuff the cat would have refused before the war. At least she cooks it, not me."

"You get cat's food in restaurants too, but at least you can just order and not think about it." He pulled her to her feet. "Come on, I'll race you to that bank there."

He was hampered by her bag, so Faye won, laughing and ridiculously flushed with triumph. "You forgot all that shoveling and cycling I've been doing these last months! You're the one who is used to going everywhere on twelve hundred horsepower!"

"Oh, Faye, I do love you so." He kissed her inexpertly, then with increasing assurance. "Honestly, Faye, ever since I saw you on the pier caring about 20017 when everyone else had written her off, I haven't been able to think of anything but you."

She struggled free of him. "Alan, please! You mustn't!" The dreadful clichés of how they must just be friends rose to her lips, only to be discarded. "I'm dreadfully sorry," she said miserably. "I never thought—"

"I suppose you thought it was just a boy's puppy love? Well, it isn't. Darling, darling Faye, you've got to listen to me. Truly, this last week I haven't been able to think of anything but you, I even boiled milk instead of water for tea!"

Faye suppressed a choke of laughter, touched and flattered by his earnestness. "Alan, you must listen to me. We've had a lovely day together, I'll never forget it. But I shouldn't have come, although I can't be sorry I did. You—"

But Alan Wyllie was not to be checked. His devotion tumbled out words; he adored her, he could think of nothing but her, he was counting the days to the end of his leave. He swept aside Faye's protests about her marriage as if it was nothing. "What does it matter? I *love* you."

"Well, I don't love you," she said, exasperated, wanting to laugh at the spectacle they were making among the daffodils of Hyde Park. "If I did, it might be different, but I don't."

"Of course I know you couldn't love me as much as I love you, but you must at least like me a little." He looked at her hopefully.

"Don't be absurd, Alan. Of course I like you, but—"

"Well, then! And it is no good telling me about your husband either. I stayed at your house, remember? I'd be a fool not to realize that he doesn't treat you as he ought."

She stared at him, stricken. Could this brash boy really have sensed in a few short hours something folded from sight within herself? Had all the splendid dreams become such a crumbling façade that the first stranger through the door could see it for what it was? For what she would not admit it had become? "I don't think you have any right to say that," she said eventually, voice stiff in her throat.

"No, I haven't any rights at all," he replied savagely. "I apologize. Naturally, you wouldn't taken me seriously, why should you?"

He looked hurt and sulky and defenseless, so she wanted to box his ears and comfort his distress at the same time. She did neither, having caused harm enough by her heedlessness.

They left the park in silence. Faye thought of Rupert and wanted to weep; at that moment there would have been pleasure in unfaithfulness if she had felt anything more than affection for Alan, or if she had felt less. She could not take his devotion, however fleeting it was likely to be, and use it to assuage her heartache for Rupert.

"I must go," she said. "There's something I've got to do before the shops shut." She realized with compunction that he would have theater tickets for the evening, but the thought of more time with him was unendurable, the fresh hopes of the night she would arouse. Of course she had been a naïve fool to think she could have a casual day with a boy like Alan and it would mean nothing. With a girl his own age, perhaps; with an older married woman, never.

"Yes, I suppose so." He stood indecisively at the curb and then handed over her bag. "Can't I come with you?"

"No." There was no way to soften it. "Thank you again for a lovely day."

He snorted drearily. "Don't forget your bread-and-butter letter."

She left him; there was no more to say.

Chapter Eighteen

She was worried and unsettled by her parting from Alan, and wandered a long time without any clear idea of where she could sell Mrs. Ludlow's jewelry. Eventually the rattle of shutters made her aware of how early shops closed in wartime, and brought also the familiar lurch to her stomach at the thought of bombs which darkness would probably bring. She found herself in the Strand, and remembered William had sold the earlier, better-quality jewelry there, but the first three shops she went into disclaimed any interest in the pieces she showed them. The fourth was more accommodating, the assistant adopting a familiar manner which immediately suggested that he thought they were stolen, and then offering thirty pounds for the lot.

She snatched them up and went out into bleak grayness, recalling how she had despised the price William had obtained, which now seemed enormous. Everywhere, shops were shutting and she hesitated, uncertain whether to try for a train back to Dover before it was too late or search for a hotel when she could not afford to stay at the few she knew by name. Money. If only she could get a reasonable price for the jewelry, then she would be able to use a few pounds to stay somewhere respectable. She walked on, feet echoing as the streets emptied. She looked longingly at the Strand Palace Hotel and the Savoy, walking with increasing urgency as the dark reached over her shoulder.

It was hopeless.

Few shops were still open, and when a helpful assistant did suggest one which bought jewelry, he added, "Be shut by the time you get there, madam. People leave work in daylight nowadays. We've had raids most nights this month, so far."

She could not return to Reydenham empty-handed, she would have to stay the night and try again in the morning. But when she asked the assistant whether he could recommend a cheap hotel, he ran his eyes over her and shrugged. "Not in this part of London for the likes of you, madam. Most of the smaller ones are taken over for the homeless, anyway. Best go to the Strand Palace."

She wandered back down the Strand, footsore and hungry; she had eaten nothing except the bear's breath sandwich since the night before. The great hall of the Strand Palace was intimidating and noisy, the only room available would take nearly every penny in her purse. She signed the book before she had a chance for second thoughts, then sat in the luxury of her room close to tears; in wartime you went to a restaurant or did not eat, and she certainly could not afford a meal in a place like this. She supposed hazily that she could go to Charing Cross, at a main-line station there was bound to be a buffet still, but London was unfamiliar and the effort of it seemed overwhelming. She took out the trinkets Mrs. Ludlow had given her and looked at them carefully: they were not particularly elegant but solidly made, and several stones looked expensive to her inexperience. She slipped them back in her bag, determination stiffening again, she was not beaten yet.

With resolve, an idea slid into her mind. John Castellan. She pushed it aside guiltily, today was surely lesson enough in unwanted complication; as she brushed her hair, it returned. He was rich. Very rich, if Rupert was to be believed. She stared at her reflection in the mirror, hairbrush stilled; he had taken the trouble to telephone her.

No. She brushed again, hit her head and exclaimed aloud. Well, why not? He had been angry with Rupert for duplicity, not the request for money; she would tell him exactly what she wanted, and why. He was a banker, after all, and not in the services like everyone else; it was his duty to help the war effort. She was startled by her own reflection, and stared, astonished by narrowed, calculating eyes and uncompromising mouth. She scarcely recognized herself, until the absurdity of it stirred amusement, and familiarity returned.

She went over to the telephone without giving herself time for thought; if he was not in his office she would take it as an omen and not try again. Odds against, she thought; it's a fair gamble. The telephone rang a long time and she realized that City offices probably shut early, too. A man's voice answered at last, aggrieved and breathy. " 'Ullo?"

She was stricken by fresh doubt. "Is that Castellan's?"

"Yes, madam, but they've nearly all gone 'ome. I'm the fire-guard, see, and 'alfway up the stairs wiv me buckets."

She blinked, the suave image of banking halls dissolved. "Is Mr. Castellan—Mr. John Castellan still there?"

"Mr. Joseph. Mr. John's not often in nowadays."

"Oh." She felt ridiculously deflated. In an arid blankness without plan, Castellan had come to seem a gilt-edged bolt-hole. Damn Joseph, why was he always there?

She heard clatterings and a flurry of imprecation from the other end of the line; the voice when it came again was somewhat chastened. "Beg pardon, madam, someone tripped over me buckets. The caretaker, 'e says Mr. John is expected in later. Shall I ask 'im to pass on a message?"

She caught the avid curiosity of a family retainer, but did not care. John Castellan was perfectly capable of making any explanation he chose. She gave him her number and name, chuckling at the disapproval in his tone when he realized she was a married woman in a hotel room; she had won her bet with the fates. She had a bath while she waited, blithely ignoring instructions to use five inches of water only, scarcely noticing when an air-raid warning sounded, guns thumping far over to the east. He was hardly ever in, yet he was coming tonight; surely after such a stroke of luck she must also get the money she needed so desperately?

The telephone rang at last, his voice guarded and lacking the warmth she had felt in him before. "Faye? It is a surprise to hear you are in London."

"Just for a night. I wondered—I wondered whether you would have time to call in here on your way home for a few minutes?"

"Why?"

She was jarred by his brusqueness, brought abruptly from confidence back to uncertainty. "It would be nice to see you again, I mean—" She heard the false ring in her words and sensed refusal at the end of the wire. She took a deep breath. "I want to borrow some money from you."

"The banking business is certainly going to be revolutionized when women take over," he commented. "I should be with you in about an hour." The line went dead.

Her hands were shaking when she hung up. He was coming, but there could be no doubt about the difficulty of the interview which lay ahead.

It was nearly two hours before he arrived, pushing through
heavy blackout curtains in front of the swing doors, and by then
her courage had contracted to a hollow in the pit of her stomach,
indistinguishable from hunger. He saw her at once and came over
while she was still struggling out of the depths of a worn leather
chair. "I'm sorry to be late, there's a raid on the docks and the
roads from the City are blocked with hosepipes. Drink?"

"No, thank you." She flushed uncomfortably, recalling how un-
erringly he had diagnosed drink in her voice before.

His expression relaxed slightly, although above dark cloth his
face looked tight and watchful, an echo of his voice earlier. "They
serve a good apple joice in the bar here."

"I bet they don't, "said Faye indignantly. "You've just made it
up."

He laughed. "You're probably right. Let's go and see."

She was adamant in her refusal, so hungry she was fearful of al-
cohol's effects on her. She hoped for nuts or biscuits on the bar,
but the war had swept away all such luxuries even from the
Strand Palace; she watched the chattering throng instead, miserably ill at ease now she was faced with the incalculable entity
which was John Castellan. He seemed content to sit in silence,
too, after a successful difference of opinion with the barman when
he refused to accept that all ice-making activities had ceased for
the duration, and she wondered whether he intended to put her at
a further disadvantage or was merely tired. It must be exhausting
to work hard, as she guessed he did, with snatched rest interrupted
by the constant bombing London had suffered through the winter. "You wanted to borrow money from me," he said at last.
"You had better set about doing it." He glanced at his watch.

Faye bit her lip. "I'm sorry to keep you from your home so late.
I wouldn't want your . . . your family to be worried."

"I have no wife, Mrs. Ludlow, which is what I imagine you are
endeavoring to find out. I probably should not be here if I had."

She felt blood beat in her face, eyes darkened and ears drum-
ming before confusion cleared, leaving her ice-cold and angry.
"You delight in putting me in the wrong, Mr. Castellan. I have
been attempting to sell my mother-in-law's jewelry this afternoon,
you may have that in security for a loan if you wish, nothing else."

"You and your husband certainly have the damnedest idea of
my profession," he observed, standing up. "We'd better go and

eat, or they will be telling us the war has seized up all the tin openers, too."

She was so relieved by the thought of a free meal that she went with him without a word; the raid was coming closer, lights blinking, some of the diners leaving for the cellars, but she was too ravenous to care. She thought of Alan once, and hoped he had found a companion for the evening, the day already strangely hazy in her mind. Dover and Reydenham too, as Castellan steered the conversation away from controversy, choosing food and wine, commenting acidly on breaking glass and noisy drunkenness from a group of officers in the corner. She wondered whether he felt awkward in civilian clothes when most men his age were in uniform; one day when she did not need his money she would ask, and pay back some of the embarrassment he had caused her. He always spoke directly, and she was too preoccupied with her own affairs to wonder why his attitude was so uncompromising, when it was his kindness she remembered from before.

The food was good, better than any she had tasted in more than a year; soup, unrationed hare, and splendidly crisp rolls. After watching her awhile, Castellan intercepted a waiter and kept a bread basket on the table. "You could put a few in your bag in case you are hungry in the night," he suggested, his manner easing for the first time.

"If there are any left, I will!" Life was flowing, circumstance tightly held again. She helped herself lavishly to vegetables. "Do you know, I look across the Channel sometimes and fancy I can hear the Dover sole having the time of their lives?"

"Warmongers," he replied gravely. "Think how fat and luscious they will be in five years' time."

"Five years! Not another five, surely?"

"What do you see ending it? Or am I missing some secret weapon at Dover?"

She thought of the harbor, bare of everything except minesweepers and MTBs, the shabby town and battered streets. Another five years, it was unimaginable. "Surely by then there will be nothing left," she said slowly. "No food, no men, no hope."

He poured more wine. "There is always something left. You, for one. I shall be surprised if the Ludlows under your stewardship are not more prosperous by the end of this war than they were at the beginning."

Her fingers tightened on the stem of her glass. "Does that mean you will recommend a loan from your bank?"

"No, it does not. As I explained once before, Castellan's is a private merchant bank specializing in foreign exchange. I hope I have sufficient professional scruples not to lend their money to chance acquaintances over dinner, however charming."

She stared at the tablecloth, locked in a kind of violent despair. She saw everything starkly clear, as she had not since she became too overwhelmed to consider more than the individual crises crowding in on her. Without money, she and Reydenham could not last long enough for the profits of war to flow. She looked up at last and saw him watching her, and from somewhere pride came to her rescue. "Thank you for the dinner, Mr. Castellan." She pushed back her chair. "Perhaps you had better go before the raid comes any closer."

He glanced at the ceiling. "Methodical devils, the Germans, dusk-to-dawn service from east to west. I am willing to lend you my own money, on certain conditions."

He spoke without any alteration of tone and she stared at him, mind scuttering. "You don't even know how much I want!"

"I feel reasonably certain that even in your most optimistic moments you cannot have expected Castellan's to finance a major development scheme," he replied drily. "I am more interested in what you want it for."

She made a wretched muddle of explanation; Reydenham and its needs were straightforward but she found it difficult enough to understand her own involvement with the slip, without having to explain it.

He listened without interruption, frowning slightly. "I suppose it all sounds ridiculous to you," she said resentfully at last.

"No. I am not quite clear about what happened to the previous boat, however, which you say has sunk."

She thought of Beauty; of course he had immediately seen part of the force which drove her, the loss which could only be wiped out by another keel from the Ludlow slip. Words came easier as she explained about Beauty's end off Dunkirk, unaware of skillful questioning which drew the tale of the months since from her, the bomb when she was swimming in the harbor, the wreckage and misery of ambulance driving, even the story of the steamroller. She did not mention the scorch of loneliness, the unconcern with which such great burdens had been piled on her, but he had understood things she left unsaid before.

She had not known how drained and happy she would be at telling it all at last, when no one else had bothered to ask or felt more than censure for her failures; she did not even notice bombs coming closer. As she finished, awareness rolled in again, driven by the mounting toll of terror before: the sharp bark of guns down by the river, uneven engines overhead, the shudder of explosions jolting into bone.

Castellan stood abruptly and came round the table, his hands on hers, pulling her to her feet. "It is a mistake, you know, Faye, to think you are the only one who is frightened. It is more than time we joined everyone else in the cellar anyway."

She stumbled through kitchens and down steps, unaware of his touch, mind shrinking from noise and deep, heavy punching through the entrails of the earth, and also from shameful knowledge at last of why the slip was so important to her.

The Strand Palace had fitted up its cellar quite comfortably, but it was crowded and, coming late, she and Castellan had to sit on the steps. He kept her hand in his and she looked at it as if from a great distance, thinking how unromantic it was being bombed. It was just a miserable, terrifying mess and human contact the only defense against it. She pulled away at last, fumbling at her hair and pretending to laugh. "Who ever would have thought we would sit on drafty cellar steps together, Mr. Castellan?"

He smiled. "Wine-cellar steps. I always aim for a touch of class in my dealings."

They had a split second of warning, a sliding, slithering tear, then an enormous roar from nearby; the lights went out, concrete shuddered and groaned around them. Faye felt herself clamped against Castellan's waistcoat, the bite of steps in her back, a high singing in her ears. For a moment she was too dazed to breathe; when she did, her lungs filled with dust and she choked painfully.

She felt Castellan move, then a torch beam flicked over the crowded cellar and she heard his voice asking whether anyone was hurt. Miraculously, no one was, beyond cuts and bruises. On the steps they had felt more blast than most, and the small space was swept with a bubble of relief, as if its occupants realized they were unlikely to come so close to destruction again and survive. He was still holding her. "All right, Faye?"

She nodded; now it was over she felt quite calm, unsurprised when he kissed her, grit on their lips, an avowal of life, no more, under the shadow of death.

Like a thunderstorm which has muttered and growled all evening and at last passed overhead, the raid faded away soon after and they were able to emerge from the cellar, to faint candlelight and no more damage than glass and plaster crunching underfoot. Castellan kept his hand on her elbow, steering her around upended tables and potted palms. "Which is your room?"

She thought a moment. "Three thirty."

He went behind the reception desk with his torch and came back holding her key. "I think we'll go up by the stairs, I never fancy lifts directly after a raid, even if they happen to be working. Stay here a moment."

He disappeared in the direction of the bar and came back carrying a siphon of soda water, the sight so ridiculous she could not help laughing. "If you had any sense of occasion it would be whisky."

He looked at his dusty suit and grinned, "Hollywood does everything so much better than real life. I think you might dislike washing in whisky." He came up to her room with her, his torch vital in dark, littered passages; it was somehow typical that he should have one when it was needed.

He was right about the water too; neither tap was working, soda water as welcome for rinsing off dust as for drinking. With refreshment her senses returned, stripped and trembling, where the fact of survival had set her apart from shock before. She began to shiver and noticed pink-tinged soda water from a cut she had not felt.

Castellan looked unfamiliar too, hair rumpled from toweling, the side of his face discolored, one eye closed and bleeding. She exclaimed when she saw him. "You're hurt!"

He touched his face gingerly. "I hope not. I'm flying out of England tomorrow. It was lucky you caught me clearing things up at the office."

"You will think twice about the consequences of taking me to dinner again." She bit her lip on the light retort, Rupert and

Reydenham and the strangeness of John Castellan in her bedroom rushing in on her.

He came over and held her, not to give comfort as before, but with love. "It would always be worth it, Faye. Would to God—" He broke off abruptly and released her, going over to the window, jerking at curtains and flinging them wide, the room at once faintly orange from a flame-smeared sky.

After a moment she went over and stood beside him, not touching, staring out into the wasteland. She had known, she had surely always known that he had not been angered by Rupert's duplicity but because she was his wife. And because of it, she had forced him here tonight, to take and not to give. "Be careful where you are going," she said at last; he understood her too well to attempt pretense, when Rupert held all she had to offer.

He fumbled in his pocket and leaned on the windowsill, writing in the strange light. "Five thousand, I remember, was what you—" His voice stumbled, then he caught himself. "Was what your husband wanted originally. Will that be enough?"

She nodded, staggered by anyone casually writing a check for five thousand pounds on a windowsill.

He closed her fingers on the paper. "One condition. When this is over, you try stone carving again whatever the Ludlows say. That at least I can give you."

"I will pay interest—" she began, then words dried as the sense of what he had said penetrated. "Why?" He had recognized her longing when she spoke to him of carving long ago, but knew nothing of how she had tried and failed, nor of desire reborn after Dunkirk.

She could not see his face properly in the gloom but sensed he was smiling. "Because the knowledge that you were doing what you were surely made to do, would give me more pleasure than any amount of interest. In some ways, I am not a banker by instinct. Meanwhile, a boat is certainly better than driving an ambulance under shellfire."

"It is a quittance with some kind of honor," said Faye frankly. "I realized just now in the cellar, even before the bomb fell, that the slip was my funk hole away from blood and rubble. I am not proud of it."

"I don't think the seafront at Dover is a well-chosen funk hole." He touched her lips lightly. "And in my reckoning, you have earned any quittance you may find a dozen times over. Goodbye, my dear."

She stumbled after him. "Will you let me know when you return? I couldn't bear—I can't keep ringing your office!"

His mouth twisted, faintly underlit by the torch. "For both our sakes, I think it is best to be done with each other before it is too late."

"Tell me where you are going then!"

"No. I'm sorry, but I can't."

"You see," she said miserably. "I knew you wouldn't. Don't you understand? Whatever we ought to do, I can't live the rest of my life not knowing whether you are alive or dead, whether—"

"Given luck, I should return alive," he said gently. "Don't imagine things, Faye. I am attached to the Treasury now, but still a banker about his business, not the spy who stole German plans single-handed."

"Please, John." She stared into darkness where he was. "I must know." When she had seen him last he had been on his way to Belgium when everyone in his senses was leaving it, and she did not think him quite the staid banker his words suggested.

"I am often in and out of the country these days, I think there would be no end to such a commitment. You are not a fool, and after this evening you understand well enough that while you feel some concern for me, I feel a great deal more for you. I would not have come tonight, except I could tell you were in serious trouble."

She swallowed, his words and what she sensed in him so much at variance with his detached manner that they were difficult to grasp. "And you think that now you've paid me off, I will go on my way rejoicing, hoping for your death perhaps, with nothing to say I owe you five thousand pounds?"

The torch jerked in his hands; his eye was still oozing blood and she thought irrelevantly that he must have a fearsome headache from the blow he had taken while he held her safe. "Listen, Faye. If you cared for me at all, I wouldn't be making a fool of myself talking, I promise you." He glanced around the darkened bedroom and laughed abruptly. "I'll never have a better chance, that's certain. But when you rang my office this evening you thought of nothing but my bank balance. I am not blaming you, just stating a truth the rich must become accustomed to. Because we came within a hundred yards of death together, at the moment you are seeing rather more than my wallet, but it means nothing. Tomorrow you will wonder what the hell we were doing, talking like this. It is not like that with me; do you know that for weeks after I rang you at Reydenham I could scarcely sleep for thinking of you needing drink to keep sane, alone under shellfire? I nearly came down a dozen times, and would have if I'd thought I could do more than make everything harder for you. One bomb together changes nothing and I do not intend to let you split me apart every time you choose to recall my existence and wonder whether I am still alive."

Faye was appalled by the bitterness of his tone, although she knew he would not have revealed so much had the bomb not jolted his reserve as well as his senses; and, however light he made of it, he was also under the strain of wherever he was going on the morrow. Then, he too would be wondering what the hell he had been doing, talking like this.

"I could not care for you," she said at last, "since before tonight I scarcely knew you." And you made no attempt to let me find out more, she thought but did not say. She was still shocked and trembling from the bomb, her head aching too. She was very conscious of the edge of bed against her knees and craved the comfort John Castellan could give her if he would. Rupert . . . Rupert had found pleasure when he wanted it in France, so why not she? She pushed aside thought of the poison which had seeped into her marriage since; she had nearly died an hour before and John surely needed her as much as she needed him, the night before he went. She would make it up to Rupert afterwards.

Castellan was watching her, and she did not know how clearly her face betrayed her: the same narrowed mouth and calculating eyes as in her mirror earlier, when she schemed how she might use him for her purposes. "You wouldn't know me any better if I became guilt to be forgotten rather than a check to be cashed," he said drily, answering her thought rather than her words. "Our lives lie apart, and you have no wish for it to be otherwise."

"At least I need to know you are safe," she repeated obstinately, not really listening, unable to believe he meant to leave without even kissing her again.

He shook his head, unspeaking.

She was angry then, with the sharp, unreasonable anger which comes after fear. If he was waiting for her to beg for what he must know she wanted, then he was much mistaken. Yet with rage, her own will stiffened again and she no longer needed him. He was the one who could be hurt because she did not love him, not she, and it was for his own sake he intended to keep from her, not hers. I have no wife, he had said earlier, and although she understood very little about him, she knew now that once he must have been married to a woman who thought of him only as a bank balance. Her anger ebbed as quickly as it had come, this cruelty at least she could not leave to fester. "We may never meet again, then," she said slowly, "but I want you to believe that it was not only your wallet I saw when I thought of you. As you said, our lives lie apart, but if they did not I should want very much to be waiting for your return, your check torn up in the wastebasket. I will tear it up anyway if you do not promise to let me know each six months of your safety, in as impersonal a way as you choose." It was scarcely a risk, now she had grasped how much he wanted her to have his money. "Send that strange man I spoke to on the phone with his buckets, if you like."

He gave a gasp of laughter. "Beecham. Castellan's would collapse without him. Oh God, Faye, you win. You know I can't leave you to face bankruptcy alone."

"I would do it, John, without your promise." She wondered whether he believed her, or simply needed to believe something, keep some thread of concern to tie him to the future, going tomorrow, surely now today.

He flicked out the torch and put it in her hand. "You'd better keep this." He held her a moment in the dark, then she heard his footsteps crunching away down the passage.

He had not kissed her again.

Chapter Nineteen

She traveled back to Dover in a compartment full of drunken sailors, aching with tiredness, thoughts as confused by relief from financial disaster as they had been the day before by its imminence. She had sold Mrs. Ludlow's jewelry for an absurdly small sum and paid Castellan's check into her own account: she intended to use it surreptitiously and as sparingly as she could, determined to pay him back as soon as possible. She pushed her way into the corridor after a while and stood with her hair swept by soft Kentish air, watching lambs jinking over fresh-springing grass, unopened blossoms knobbed black against clear blue sky.

It was a bad day for flying through hostile skies.

She had bought a newspaper at the station and tried to imagine where he might be going, but grasped only that the war was spreading further every day. The Italians were retreating in Ethiopia, the Germans advancing in North Africa, their agents busy in Iraq and Syria. Ships were sinking in their dozens in the Atlantic, the previous night's raid on London had been light compared to the one on Hull. She shuffled the few pages together in a rage and wished the reporter had been with them in their cellar. What do you see ending it? John had said; she looked at the paper and saw nothing. Eighteen months of war and everything was infinitely worse than it had been at the beginning, the excitement and challenge of the previous year gone, endless years of destruction and effort stretching ahead.

There was shelling at Dover and the train waited two hours in the tunnel just short of the town for it to stop: the long bicycle ride back to Reydenham had never seemed so tedious, even five thousand pounds in the bank no longer lifting her spirits as it had.

Triumph returned when she reached the head of the valley and looked down the mellow length of it. She could plow up the rough pasture behind Stone Cross now, and buy the extra sheep they needed. She leaned against a gate and planned with her eyes all the things she would do to bring Reydenham back to full and lovely plenty, and was singing as she coasted the last easy mile to the manor.

Its windows were open and welcoming, to her and to the spring, generosity of line and setting making penny-pinching effort irrelevant. She forgot John Castellan and went into the comfort of polish and dark paneling, her mood so heightened that moments passed before she found the stillness strange. The manor was the center of all around it and was seldom completely quiet: voices, feet crunching on gravel, activity in the kitchen, all these were normal. Today there was nothing.

She called once and then pushed through baize doors to the kitchen. Stillness again; a kettle simmered on the hob, Tigger the cat licking methodically by its warmth. The garden was empty too, no Christopher calling and searching her handbag for the gift she had brought; in sudden panic she ran up the stairs and pushed open the door to her mother-in-law's rooms.

"Ah, Faye." Mrs. Ludlow turned from where she was standing by a window. "Did you wonder what had happened to us all?" She seemed distant and gentle, face textured as if made from harsher material than it had been before.

Faye looked at her sharply, and then away again. "What's wrong? Where's Christopher?"

"Nanny took him over the hill to play with the Druitt boys. Ridiculous, isn't it? She thought I'd want to be alone, I thought I'd want to be alone, but I don't."

Faye was touched by the appeal in her voice, the first softness she had ever detected in her. "Come downstairs then, and we'll make an excuse to have a glass of Rupert's sherry. I sold your jewelry for more than I dared hope." In the train she had mentally doubled the price she would tell Mrs. Ludlow she had obtained, now she trebled it, feeling pleasantly benign as the giver for once.

"William is dead." Mrs. Ludlow sat down abruptly, she looked like an old photograph of herself, smudged and out of focus. "There was a telegram after you left, then a letter this morning." She fumbled in the pocket of her dress and handed over a crumpled envelope. "Read it; you were fond of him, I believe."

Even in grief, she had the power to infuriate. Faye took the letter over to the window, wanting to shout that she was more than just fond of William, her mind totally closed to any idea of his death. The letter from his commanding officer tore disbelief apart: ". . . attacked a submarine shadowing a convoy. The U-boat was probably destroyed, but Flight Lieutenant Ludlow's aircraft was hit and he attempted to ditch alongside a naval escort. Unfortunately the sea was too rough, and his aircraft sank immediately, without survivors . . . I am sure you know your son well enough to understand that I am not just trying to ease your grief when I say that William was one of the best-liked officers on the station . . . it may also be some comfort to you that he was well content in Coastal Command after some initial resentment at being passed over for fighters. He told me once that living near Dover gave a man a taste for watching over ships . . ."

William, dead. Faye felt part of herself break off and fall, crushing hope, striking sparks of fury and hatred, until finally it came to rest in sadness. William was dead.

She turned at last and gave the letter back to Mrs. Ludlow, unspeaking. She wanted very much to be alone. Instead, she had to stay, and make tea and talk about anything but William.

At last there was the sound of Christopher below, shouting excitedly for her to see the shaggy pony he had been lent for the journey home. "Mummy, can we keep him, *please*? Mrs. Droot says I can if you say yes. They've got heaps of ponies and the 'Cultural's cross 'cos they say they must have sheep."

Faye hugged him. "The committee want us to have more sheep, too."

"P'raps they wouldn't notice the difference," he said hopefully. "He 'most looks like a sheep."

"He most about does," Faye agreed, laughing. "I'll tell you what, you hide him among the sheep and I'll plow up twice as much rough grazing as the committee expect."

"I'll show him to Daddy," he said eagerly. "Daddy's coming home soon."

She found the message from Rupert on the desk: he hoped to be home on leave any day now, he could not say quite when.

He came late at night three weeks later, when they had almost given up expecting him. Christopher heard his feet on the stones and came racing downstairs in his pajamas, then they all crowded to the door forgetting the blackout, forgetting for a moment that

William would not follow him, laughing perhaps about wrapping his car around a gatepost in some inaccessible spot.

Any awkwardness Faye felt with Rupert was lost in the unexpectedness of his return, the sheer pleasure of having him in the house again. Boots thumping on the floor upstairs, wet towels screwed up on the floor, shouts for Nanny when he could not find his shirts, squeals from Christopher galloping around the passages in the dark. Later, they ate by candlelight, fire crinkling into ash, old timber snapping in the house around them as it always did at night.

"God, it's good to be back." Rupert stretched, yawning. "Come here, Faye." He gathered her onto his knees and sighed. "Poor old William, I never thought there'd be a crash he wouldn't walk away from. I still don't quite believe it."

"Read the letter your mother has tomorrow," Faye said shortly. "You'll believe it then." It was ridiculous, but she could not rid herself of a feeling of shame, as if she were being seduced by a total stranger. She had hugged and kissed him unselfconsciously when he arrived; now with his hands idly exploring her body, she felt frozen, unable to respond. It had been so long, and without much warmth or understanding from him in the time between, he had become an idea in her mind and ceased to be a physical presence.

She understood his mounting anger, yet could do little to assuage it. She tried, and her trying was not enough. He gave her no time, used to such unstinted giving from her in the past that he was infuriated by anything less: he had been looking forward to his homecoming with such keen anticipation that he had forgotten any awkwardness there had been in their parting. Now, he felt cheated to find his return so unremarkable.

He came down with her to the slip next day and was delighted by the progress there, with five men working full-time. He prowled around stacked timber and drums of varnish, fingered new tools and solidly repaired walls. "All this must have cost a stack of money," he said at last. "I thought you told me there would be something to spare for Reydenham this year."

"So there will be." Faye ran her hand over fresh timber at 20017's stern. Framing was finished, now it was the slow, skilled work of double-skinned ply-planking. "We're doing this on Admiralty progress payments, and they've sanctioned all the timberwork now. We can't do the engines or fittings, of course." Just under three thousand pounds of John Castellan's money remained, and this was one month when she did not want Rupert examining his accounts too closely. Later, the amounts would be too scattered to pick out easily, and so long as he had sufficient, Rupert was not a man to worry over columns of figures.

"Need some more work soon," broke in Henry. "Three, four weeks an' we'll be done on her." He jerked his head at 20017, the note of pride unmistakable.

"I spoke to Lieutenant Beatty, he might let us have some planking work if they go on smashing boats up at the present rate." She had also buried shame and seen Alan Wyllie again, since she needed all the influence she could find at the base.

Henry scratched his head. "Seems wicked to want 'em to get smashed up."

"It makes no difference whether we want it or not. It happens just the same, so we might as well have some benefit from it." Faye heard the harshness in her voice when it was too late to recall. "This war owes the Ludlows something."

"Beauty," said Rupert. "William, too. It certainly does." He climbed up to have a look inside the torpedo boat.

Faye went out and stood on the open slip, feeling very desolate in the bleak wind ruffling across the harbor; presently Rupert joined her. "You've done marvels, Faye. I don't know how the hell you've managed it, but one more big job like this and we must be nearly in the clear."

I did it on another man's money, she thought, and cheated both of you. "Don't you think you could have thought of William before Beauty?" she said aloud. William, William. The wound left by his death simply refused to heal.

He looked surprised, unable to think back over his words. "What do you mean?"

She shrugged. "If you don't know, I can't tell you."

His face darkened. "Look, Faye. You've done a bloody good job here, and not so badly at Reydenham either, but there's not much else to be said for it. Precious little comfort I've had of my homecoming so far; it seems to me old Nanny is better pleased to see me than you are."

Faye tightened her grip on a weatherworn rail. "I'm pleased to see you, God knows I'm pleased to see you; it's been so long, my love. It's just—it's just that it has *been* so long, I—we—I seem to need a little time to be used—"

"To get used to your husband again? That's splendid! My God, it's the most outrageous thing I've ever heard; what the hell have you been doing while I've been away that you find it so difficult to feel easy with me?"

"I didn't mean—" She broke off helplessly. Was he so very wrong after all? Tomorrow, you will wonder what the hell we are doing, talking like this, John had said. How much worse would she feel with Rupert if John had taken what her need offered in the aftermath of shock? Or was it memory of her wanting which stood between them now?

Rupert grasped her arm and almost forced her up the slip. "We'll thrash this out before any more of my leave is wasted! I've no mind to find you taking most of it to become accustomed to me again." He pushed her into the front seat of the car and slammed the door, letting in the gears with a jerk.

He drove out of the town, worn tires murmuring, stabbing angrily at the brake on every corner, until they reached the Western Heights. Then he pulled off the road, the wind drafty through torn canvas. "Right, we'll not leave here until we've got everything straight and no more nonsense."

"There's nothing to get straight," said Faye, irritated. "For heaven's sake stop behaving like a villain in an old film."

"I shall hit you in a minute," said Rupert quietly, "and it would probably do you a great deal of good. You've been running around thinking yourself God for too long; repairing boats, sitting on the knee of half Kent I shouldn't wonder, looking sweet and thinking about contracts. It is time you pulled yourself together and remembered there are some things the war does not excuse."

Faye choked, reaction physical at so unexpected an attack; she could not have answered if she had wished. Then throat and mind cleared, images reeling past her of how she had contrived to encounter Alan Wyllie again, when common decency should have kept her from him forever after their disastrous parting in London; of the way she had used John Castellan, a check to be cashed, in his own words, when she knew him vulnerable to her demands; there was even Colonel Druitt, flattered into below-cost repairs on the estate. I wouldn't have done any differently, she reflected; those who survive can't afford too many scruples, but at least I need not feel outraged when I am found out. What a relief that in Rupert she had a man who would not let himself be used, who was master of his domain and intended to remain so. She looked up, smiling. "Rupert, don't let's quarrel, we have so little time. You know there is no one else but you, and because of it I have perhaps grown heedless of others. Never heedless of you, my love, but you are not here and somehow I have to manage on my own."

He grunted, fiddling with ignition keys. "I want you to give up the idea of taking on more work at the slip. Reydenham is enough for you to manage."

Her mood disintegrated abruptly with the slam of his indifference on the great toil of all she had achieved. "Then I suppose we could sit around Reydenham drawing room going elegantly bankrupt! What makes you think I enjoy contriving and begging and cycling twelve miles a day to hammer a boat? But while I can save it for him, Chris is not going to be the first Ludlow without his inheritance!"

"Even if I am the first Ludlow to lose his wife to a bank overdraft? My God, I'd sooner it was—"

"To another man? No, Rupert. It will always be you for me."

He stared at her, glimpsing what she was trying to offer; a different self from the one he had married, but refined in the fires of adversity and given in love. He saw a direct gaze, taut body, clear eyes which would not weep; in all their marriage he had never known her to weep and rather wished she would. He kissed her then and drove home thinking that plenty of whisky before they went to bed would complete a cure his words had started.

She wanted him still, and he was disconcerted to discover just how much he wanted her, anger sharpening whenever he found her full attention not focused on him. He was baffled by new reserves he discovered in her, alarmed when she did not instantly respond to him as he expected. Delighted and relieved as he was to find Reydenham and the slip flourishing, he also found himself unable to fight clear of resentment once he realized she was succeeding where he had failed. Even Christopher seemed to have more place in his wife's life than he did; he had been so long away that his son was a stranger to him. Rupert would not admit to jealousy, but thought it intolerable if Christopher's needs intruded between Faye and himself when his leave was so short. So he slipped into a habit of criticizing whatever Christopher did, since it would also be deeply hurtful if Faye should manage to bring up his son, sole heir to all the Ludlows, as successfully alone as if his father had been there.

Reydenham, Faye and his son, all uniquely his and from each he felt himself excluded.

He knew he was being unfair but could not apologize or explain although he tried, words ready-framed for use; in all his life he had seldom needed excuses and could not now begin. Instead, he relied on his body to express for him all he wanted to speak, and thought that there at least he would not fail. Ten days' leave; he looked at her pensive beside him in the car, and smiled. No, there he would not fail.

He called through to her after dinner while she sat gazing into the fire. "Where's the key to my pedestal cupboard, Faye?"

She started guiltily, then decided on honesty. She knew he regretted his harshness of the afternoon, and if their love was to survive, then they must banish any pretense between them. "I threw it out of the window."

"For God's sake, why?" He appeared in the doorway, hands full of keys.

"I was afraid of drinking too much, alone with shelling and debts." She went over and put her arms around his neck. "I have been very long alone, my love."

He held her, tightly, urgently then, and forgot the need for whisky, both finding at last the pleasure they had lost since before he went to France.

The next few days of his leave passed swiftly, in many small joys. They picnicked in the woods and played hide-and-seek with Christopher; Rupert found his fishing rod and they drove to a mere behind Sandwich, where he taught her how to cast; he borrowed two horses and they all went riding together, Christopher's pony like a large squirrel squirting among the beeches. Then, unexpectedly, Faye began to find the days long. Rupert insisted on her staying close to whatever he did, as if he was retraining a disobedient gun dog, she thought resentfully. He refused to let her go to the slip and took all decisions on the estate, without telling her what he was doing. When she expostulated that he would soon be gone again, leaving her with unknown undertakings, he simply said she needed a complete change. In this he was certainly right, but it was a change she could not yet afford and she became increasingly impatient when he refused to accept telephone calls and locked the post out of reach.

Physically, their relationship was better than it had ever been. He was loving and more skillful than before, she had put the fact of his unfaithfulness behind her, although she knew it was not ended. It was the war, they were so long apart, and she had herself discovered the cravings which loneliness and fear inflamed. She accepted without question the excuses she made for him, but found it difficult to sleep after his lovemaking, her body aroused and mind worrying over all the things which must be going wrong without her care. The hours of darkness lengthened interminably, black, haunted and anxious, Rupert breathing easily beside her.

At least they went to Canterbury one day, and she was able to think of her father crossed off the list of all the endless things she must do when Rupert was gone. She turned over restlessly when she thought of it in the night, now infinitely preferable to save up hours and minutes and spend them prodigally in a visit of love. She decided then to go again, cycling each way because she wanted to go, and wipe out the grudging sourness of going simply to save a day. She smiled wryly into darkness: she would certainly cycle; after this leave there would not be a drop of petrol left for weeks.

But they went a long way together in the few days of his leave, with nothing to remember but themselves. When he had gone it was as if another piece of her was chipped off and falling to the ground.

Chapter Twenty

The war trudged on.

In summer it was bearable, with warmth and extra food from valley and woods, the beginning of clothes rationing preferable to empty shelves. As the days began to shorten again, the endless defeats seemed blacker, the few victories trifling by comparison. Yugoslavia, Greece, Crete, and Libya were lost, only the siege of Tobruk a matter for pride; Ethiopia was gained, but then no one expected the Italians to do anything else except run away and the battle for Keren was unexpectedly bloody. The battle cruiser *Hood* blew up, leaving three survivors out of thirteen hundred crew and only the sinking of the *Bismarck* soon after could wipe out the shock of it; Hitler invaded Russia and people started talking of Napoleon and reading *War and Peace*, then it appeared that the armies of a people's Soviet were as vulnerable as everyone else's, and gossips remembered instead the collapse of Russia in the previous war. Raids on London almost ceased through the summer; instead the Germans began working their way methodically through the provinces: Bristol, Liverpool, Coventry, Plymouth, Southampton; destruction spread to every corner of the nation. In Kent, two land mines expunged the village of Sturry as if it had never been.

Little changed in Dover. Shelling continued, the occasional clutch of raiders came in low over the sea and were gone again in minutes, leaving a dozen killed behind them, occasionally an unlucky hit on shop or bus garage buried three times that number under rubble. At the end of May they came for the balloons again and everyone indulged in forbidden goofing, like castaways starved of entertainment; in June they were able to cheer the RAF bombing Boulogne in full sight of spectators on the cliffs; in July, Syria was gained and the first murmurs of unease about the Far East were heard, as the Japanese walked into Indochina with the permission of the Vichy French government.

To Faye, the battle of the Atlantic was personal, since it had killed William, the rest a massive cliff of scarcely grasped disaster overhanging her frantically busy days. Reydenham was thriving under the urgent need to produce every grain of wheat and lamb chop possible, fueled at last by the capital it needed: soon more money would be flowing in than out. The slip was more anxious; 20017 had been towed round to Wellington Dock and for some weeks Faye had to pay men to do loss-making odd jobs scrounged from the base through Lieutenant Beatty. Then he was transferred, and the prospect looked bleak until she started searching out Alan Wyllie, and using his invitations to make friends among the dockyard engineers.

Alan. Faye cupped her chin in her fists and stared down at the working floor of the slip from the office above: it was daylight outside but all windows had long since been boarded up and they worked by artificial light, emerging pasty and blinking in the evening. Alan had another MTB now, since he was passed fit long before 20017 was ready, and when he went on patrol he always passed close, slowing his engines and waiting for her to wave. He had introduced her to Beatty's successor, and after they had gone out a few times together, work started coming in again. It grew rapidly with a series of hard-fought patrols in late summer and the Ludlow slip at last became established as particularly suitable for patching splintered plywood skins. It was slow, craftsman's work and the overworked MTB base thankful to subcontract the worst of it.

In gratitude alone, it seemed impossible to refuse Alan's next invitation to a services' dance held at the Maison Dieu in the center of town, and nearly three years since her last party, Faye enjoyed it too well to refuse when he asked her again the following month. Alan was an amusing companion, he admired what she was doing and had a seaman's respect for work on which his life depended. He was lonely and overstrained as she was; he wanted to go to bed with her and vaguely thought her strange behavior in London must have been due to shyness. He was very young. He surrounded his idealized vision of her with romantic fancies and found them strangely satisfying to think about on long patrols. He was in no hurry, would indeed have been shocked by haste, but reckoned he would have her one day, her growing poise and maturity exactly the haven he sought in an uncertain world.

At first, Faye held herself very much apart from him, then she came to the conclusion that he felt no more than a boy's infatuation for her, and relaxed. It was pleasant to go out occasionally, to be sought after as a partner at the Maison Dieu, and there was also a certain revenge to be taken on Rupert. She had found it very hard to adjust again to him not being there, her body charged by his intensity, and only when he had gone did she realize that tenderness and understanding had been so completely absent from their relationship, that without his presence there was nothing left. He continued to be an erratic correspondent, sometimes ringing up three nights running and then leaving her several weeks with only a scribbled note. She was uncertain whether he wanted to catch her lacking in some way, or whether he simply forgot her at intervals.

Alan borrowed a truck to drive her home after the third dance he took her to, chancing service police, who were especially alert on Saturday nights. The chill of winter was in the air and Faye shivered in the unheated cab, wrapping her coat tightly around her.

"Cold?" He looked at her sideways, hands busy on knobs.

"A little. It's chiefly the thought of winter again, the third of the war, just think of it."

"You mustn't think of it," he said cheerfully. "More and more of the bastards are disappearing into Russia; we'll have them on the run any day now." He skirted cautiously around the side streets of the town, reversing when he thought he saw a checkpoint. "Probably get drafted out of MTBs if I'm caught with a truck," he observed once. "Convoy duty in the Arctic is about the worst posting they could think of in winter, I expect."

"Drop me off here," said Faye hastily. "How do you think I'd feel if you were sent to the Arctic because of me?"

He did not reply, grinding the ancient vehicle up the steep hills flanking Dover until they were safe from casual patrolling, then he pulled into a lay-by and switched off the engine. "Would you care if I was posted away? I mean, really care?"

Faye eyed the dark lay-by with suspicion, but there was so much simple longing in his voice, she replied lightly. "Yes, of course I should, why else do you suppose I come out with you?"

"No, but, Faye—" He seized her hand and began kissing it, then her face, nuzzling at her neck. "No, you must listen to me this time! You can't keep holding me off like this, you said you liked me!"

"Well, so I do." She felt cross and ridiculous, attempting to brush him off like a troublesome puppy. "That's no reason to make a nuisance of yourself."

She could not see him clearly but felt him stiffen. "A nuisance? Is that how you think of me? We'll see about that." He began to fumble at her clothes, muttering. It occurred to her that he had had a great deal to drink.

"Listen, Alan." She could not take him seriously, and guilt anyway was never far below the surface of her reactions to him. She had treated him so badly, using his devotion for her purposes, feeling only exasperation when he wanted more than her passing attention. "I like you, but I have no intention of sleeping with you. Grow up, or stay with girls your own age." She spoke more fiercely than she intended, for his hands were waking her body, six months since Rupert had gone again; she felt herself gentling in his hold, the tide of long-held passion flowing like combers on un-trodden sand.

She wanted to give herself to this boy who needed her so badly, to hold him and calm his fears. She owed it to him in reparation for her selfishness and he deserved it for his courage, night after night in his frail craft loaded with explosives and petrol. In a world filled with such infinitely great wickedness there could be no wrong in giving him the little comfort he could find from her; and Rupert did not know her well enough to recognize the part of her which would be lost to him. It was this last thought which tore her from Alan's arms and seeking body, forced her hand into her pocket and brought the hardness of her torch against his head.

He cried out, sliding half to the floor, hands to his face while she sat trembling at what she had done.

After a while she held him gently and eased him back against the seat. "I'm sorry, Alan."

He stirred, then turned and half fell out of the cab, to vomit in a ditch. It was some time before he returned, and all the while she sat and shivered, deep inside herself.

"I think you'd better explain." He climbed back at last. "It is no good playing the innocent wife to me. You were willing enough."

I've done him good, she reflected wryly. One day, his wife

should thank me for this night's work. "I was willing," she agreed, "but I love my husband, and it was my willingness I couldn't bear."

Half-truth? Quarter-truth? No truth at all, she decided with rare self-knowledge. She had no sense of rightness because she had kept faith with Rupert, only a further weight of wrong to bear from the injury she had done Alan. It had been the burn of injured pride, of knowing Rupert would not notice a piece missing from their marriage. Another piece; in that same flash she had glimpsed the tale of missing pieces, and pieces wrongly placed, had seen herself ready to riffle through what was left, not from compassion for Alan as she had thought, but in resentment toward Rupert, who surely could have been home more often if he had wished.

Alan sighed and ground at the self-starter. "You could have fooled me. What is it, a year since we met? In all that time I don't think you once mentioned the fellow." He let in the gears with a jerk. "Sorry."

"Sorry for the gears?"

He grinned reluctantly. "Sorry for everything. I'm a tick, and you're a damned, deceiving woman." He dabbed at streaked blood on his cheekbone. "What the hell did you hit me with?"

She showed him her torch in the faint light of the dash, and then stared at it, mouth drying. It was the one John Castellan had given her nine months before.

Next day she swept through Reydenham like a torrent in spate, criticizing, checking, sending Cook to the cooking sherry for solace, and bringing Nanny heavy-footed from the nursery when she heard that Christopher had been sent to deliver rent notices to the nearer tenants.

"He is nearly four years old," said Faye coldly, "and wants to do what he can to help. Reydenham will be his one day, and the sooner he realizes the effort of keeping it, the better."

"'Tis a nasty, wet December day, and not the time for a child to be out in the half-dark. Unlike some others I could name," she added, having appeared in an enormous flannel nightgown the night before to greet Faye's late return with outspoken condemnation.

Faye laughed, she never resented justified criticism. "I won't do it again, I promise. Perhaps Rupert will be home for Christmas, and we could have some kind of party here."

Nanny pulled at her lip reflectively. "We've still got most of that American parcel, and Mr. Dickson was saying he might have some bacon to spare."

Faye returned to her figures, determination redoubled. She had woken resolved to return to an undivided mind, whatever the cost. She would not see Alan again; she must also repay Castellan and be rid of him, too. Her lips moved as she added and subtracted, wrote more notices for rent due at the end of the year, estimated expenses. By the summer wool clip she could surely do it; in fact, the bank might lend her the extra she needed, now the overdraft was being paid off, the slip and estate both profitable. She stared out of the window, at wet leaves and soggy, depressing day: she ought to write to John and release him from a promise he had not wanted to make. "The American parcel" was his, a gift from a Mrs. John Castleman in Washington. It had taken a moment to realize who it must be from and invent an aunt to satisfy the household's curiosity. Then she had felt a lurch of relief, for she had begun to worry, more than six months having gone by since he had promised.

She squared her shoulders and returned to her ledgers. No. She would pay him back as soon as possible, and he had taken her at her word and used impersonal means to keep their agreement. For the rest, she still needed to know he was safe.

The next day would be a Sunday, and she decided to have everyone together, planning for Christmas. An upheaval in routine would make a celebration in itself: she was becoming worried about Christopher, alone in a valley of few children. She wondered again whether she had done right to keep him at Reydenham when she did not feel justified in taking him even to the stores at the crossroads; the valley had not been hit by any more shells but few days went by without Dover and the roads into it receiving anything from a single salvo to four or five hours' barrage. One of the men at the slip told her that he had counted nearly a thousand shells into the harbor alone: everyone hated their distinctive, flat whoof far more than bombs, the lack of warning and helplessness against guns twenty-five miles away almost paralyzing in its effects. Fortunately, the harbor was large, the slip minute by comparison, and shells continued to fall in the water with comforting regularity, but the town was filled with crumbled masonry and makeshift tarpaulin roofs.

Christopher burst into her room while it was still dark next morning. "I've been up for hours and hours, cutting paper! Can I have a little flour for paste? Can I, Mummy, just a very little?"

She yawned and kissed him, it was fun to be absorbed in her own home for once, to forget everything but streamers for Christmas. Tomorrow she would be sweating at the slip again, steaming curves into new framing timber. "We'll all mix paste like mad this afternoon. You'll have to search the woods for holly and a Christmas tree, too." She jumped out of bed and swung him round. "Daddy will be home and we'll have the gayest Christmas for years." Since the last Christmas of peace, she thought suddenly, with William and his rabbits, and danced Christopher down the passage to outpace memory.

Nanny met them at the top of the stairs. "Them Americans have come in."

"What's the matter with it?" Faye's thoughts leaped with alarm to Castellan's parcel, full of precious dried fruit and fats.

"They're all bombed and sinking," said Nanny with a certain relish. "Proper mess they be in, by all accounts."

Faye stared at her in astonishment. "Bombed? I put everything on the top larder shelf myself, out of your reach, mister," she added, tickling Christopher until he squealed.

"Bombed," repeated Nanny. "Over in some place the other side of the world. On the wireless they were saying they'd certain sure be with us now."

"You mean the Americans are in the war?" demanded Faye, abandoning thoughts of sultanas. "Who have they been bombed by?"

Of this Nanny was not too sure, the tale of Pearl Harbor unfolding while they painted newspaper and Christopher smeared paste all over the kitchen. With the Russians mounting a massive counterattack before Moscow, their own Eighth Army rolling the Germans back again in Africa, and now America in the war, it was possible at last to imagine an end to it all. Not soon, though. She cycled to Canterbury on a bitter December day and found her father unexpectedly opposed to a festive family Christmas.

"I just don't feel like it," he said apologetically. "It seems wrong somehow, men dying while we forget there's a war on."

"Who could forget it?" said Faye bitterly. She glanced around the littered room. "Do you remember the war every moment you are working on your charters? Surely we deserve a little forgetfulness sometimes?"

"I go fire watching in the cathedral three times a week, and last winter we went to help at Gravesend," he said defensively.

She saw she had hurt him, for Canterbury had only been hit by a few scattered bombs, and surely was likely to remain quiet, consisting of little except the dominating bulk of the cathedral. She put her hand on his arm persuasively, "Please, Dad. I'd like you to come to Reydenham this year. Christopher has never had a normal, happy Christmas and everyone is so weary of bleakness. We need to have the carol singers in and not count how many lumps of coal we put on the fire; he has to have one day different in all his year."

"Is Rupert coming home?" he asked, weakening.

"I hope so, he's trying to get to Africa but they keep sending him on fresh courses instead." She remembered William's strictures on Rupert's signals technique and felt renewed sympathy for him. He wanted so much to take an active part in the war, and so far had been posted from one headquarters to another.

"I should think he would want to have you to himself, then, and how am I to get to Reydenham these days?"

"You're going to drive," said Faye triumphantly. "I've saved the petrol and I'm going to bring Christopher to the carol service in the cathedral, it must be safe on Christmas Eve. We'll take you home with us and hope Rupert can think of some way of getting you back again." Even if it means stealing a little service petrol, she added privately to herself. Military petrol was dyed to prevent precisely this, but Faye had long since learned from her naval friends that the dye could be removed by the simple expedient of pouring the petrol through a gas-mask filter. She never forgot William's death over the convoys and was normally scrupulous over the use of petrol, but this she felt was an exception.

He gave in, and presented her with a jar of mincemeat as his contribution: she gathered that most of the cathedral staff had pooled a week's rations and manufactured an undisclosed quantity in a twelfth-century ewer, all modern vessels having gone for scrap.

By such means, her Christmas store grew steadily. Rabbits and pigeons were becoming scarce, but Dickson gave her half a pig, which, he said, "the ministry had seen burned, being diseased-like."

"A diplomatic illness?" inquired Faye. "Spots only on the side facing the inspector?"

He roared with laughter. "Some paper-pushing clerk, 'olding his nose fifty yards from the sty. 'E worn't worried what the pig 'ad, so long as 'e wor sure we wasn't eating 'im. Nice moss-lined 'ole we 'ad awaiting, poured in quicklime and all."

"I'll give it a good scrub before I cook it," promised Faye, wondering about the effects of quicklime on their digestions.

He chuckled. "Don't you be a-worriting, Mrs. Rupert. Good flour that were, done up in a quicklime bag. My boy made the switch while I helped that there clerk out of the mire."

Faye did not ask what kind of mire had awaited the ministry clerk, the Dicksons of this world having been bred to outwit authority, and hung the bacon triumphantly up the chimney. With mincemeat already in her store cupboard, they saved their rations for Christmas pudding, each in turn stirring and wishing.

"What did you wish, Mummy? I wished for a stocking so big"— Christopher held his arms wide—"and for Mrs. Jellybag to play the organ faster'n she did for Easter!" Nanny spared Faye a reply by hauling him off instantly to the nursery as punishment for using a forbidden name for the vicar's imposing wife, who was addicted to playing chants at a brisk gallop. Like Christopher, she had cheated and wished more than once, for Rupert home, and Alan and John safe.

Mrs. Ludlow made crackers from scraps of material tied with elastic, and refused to tell anyone what she put in them ("More elastic, I expect," said Cook darkly). Faye pedaled furiously up and down to Dover, saving petrol coupons for Rupert's leave and the trip to Canterbury, bargaining shamelessly for a bottle of whisky from naval stores, having regretfully discarded the notion of running across Alan accidentally again.

A handsome cut off her bacon clinched a deal for the whisky, and on her return with it she went in search of Gabriel.

She found him disconsolately riddling potatoes, his age now excluding him from the Home Guard. He had never regained more than passing satisfaction in his old routine since the excitements of

1940, but his eyes brightened at the sight of the whisky. "'Tis a long while since I've seen a full bottle, Mrs. Rupert."

Faye thought of the half-empty bottle still locked in the desk cupboard. Before Christmas she would have to find someone who could pick locks. "You know we're expecting Mr. Rupert home for Christmas? We're going to be quite a big party and of course beef or turkey is impossible, but I did just wonder—"

Gabriel scraped mud off his boots with a flower label. "You offrin' the whisky, Mrs. Rupert?"

"It depends," said Faye cautiously. "Not for casualty mutton or a tough chicken." She held the bottle so he could see the navy label, far better than the underproof variety occasionally obtainable by civilians.

He ruminated, eyes on the bottle. "I did 'ear there was some deer still, up over Channock. You like venison, Mrs. Rupert?"

Channock Park; she remembered making a stately visit there with Rupert soon after they were married. Conscience stirred briefly and was easily repressed. She nodded. "It would be just right for a homegrown Christmas."

No more was said, and the next day Cook came to her complaining that Gabriel was missing. Faye spent a rather uneasy day, thinking at intervals of Gabriel's bravado with his shotgun: she did not know much about shooting deer, but surely it was an inadequate weapon for such an enterprise?

Gabriel returned two days later; she discovered him placidly picking brussels sprouts, a certain complacence of expression suggesting success. She decided to play this particular sequence his way, country good manners always favoring an indirect approach. Accordingly, she complimented him on the sprouts and solicited his opinion on the war in Africa.

"Got 'em on the run again," he said at once with satisfaction. "'Tis they Americans' turn to be caught with their panzers down. Last summer now, I was worried about that there Sewage."

Faye was familiar with his description of the Suez Canal, as he had long ago confessed himself baffled by two armies locked in combat to gain control of a canal full of effluent. "I hope none of the Channock gamekeepers were caught in the same way?"

"Not many gamekeepers these days," he said regretfully. "I need a mite o' bacon for the tractor driver though, I didn't tell 'im nothing about no whisky. Mrs. Dickson be skinning and 'anging un for 'ee, I told 'er Mr. Rupert'd be needing both 'aunches."

Faye handed over the whisky, reflecting that the whole valley now knew her as a poacher; at least if everyone enjoyed part of the bounty she could be sure that no whisper of their common activities would reach beyond Reydenham.

Rupert came home three days before Christmas, so would be able to accompany them to Canterbury, Christopher chattering with anticipation days before, having no recollection of ever previously leaving the valley.

Rupert continued the habits of his previous leave and kept Faye always with him, but she was so determined that everything should be right and so pleased to see him, she did not mind. The slip was running smoothly, winter an easy time in the valley, so she simply abandoned herself to the pleasure of being close to him.

The morning of Christmas Eve passed in a whirl of holly and streamers and pounding herbs on the kitchen table. In his excitement, Christopher upset a bowl of paste on the drawing-room carpet, and then disgraced himself by attempting to remove the sticky mess with one of Rupert's shirts.

Faye heard the commotion from the kitchen and ran through to find Christopher sobbing and Rupert pale with anger. "Well," she said when the matter had been explained to her, "it is not surprising he thought it a rag, when you throw your clothes all over the place! Chris, love, stop howling and ask Cook for the floor cloth and a bucket."

"Leave him, Faye. I'll deal with this, he's been in a household of women too long. If the boy hasn't the sense to recognize a shirt when he sees one, then he'd better stay at home this afternoon until he can."

Christopher's sobs ceased abruptly and he stared at his father, mouth agape. "I'se going to Canterbury."

"Oh no, you're not," said Rupert grimly. "You'll stay here and clean up the mess you've made."

"Go and get a bucket and a proper cloth, Chris, and clean it up now. You've plenty of time before we go," said Faye quietly.

But Christopher had no luck. Mystified and unsettled by his disgrace, appalled by the prospect of missing a treat anticipated for so long, he stumbled into a table, upsetting a bowl of fruit and sending their few hoarded oranges plopping into his discarded pastepot.

"Well, pick them up." Rupert was dangerously quiet. "No, for God's sake, don't put them back on the dish! Although I suppose I might have expected you would be growing up with the manners of a yokel."

Christopher held the oranges desperately, paste dripping down his front and onto the carpet, without any idea of what to do next. Finally he dropped them back in the pastepot, needing his hands to wipe a tear-smeared face, glutinous whiteness promptly transferring itself to his hair, eyes, and the seat of his shorts.

"You had better take your son to the bathroom, hadn't you, Faye?" Rupert spoke with the deliberate, pretended sweetness of extreme exasperation, and strode out of the house.

Christopher was stiffly silent while Faye sponged him clean. At the end of it she took his hand. "Now we'll go down together and clear everything up, so no one will even think about paste again, then we'll surprise Daddy by finishing all the decorating before he gets back."

"Then can I come to Canterbury?"

"Yes, darling, of course you can. Daddy was only angry for a minute, he's not very used to little boys." She knew this was the trouble. He felt no sense of possession with Christopher, growing up with a Haskell temperament and her father's dark blue eyes; and Rupert was a man who found fault where he did not possess completely.

"I'm glad he isn't," muttered Christopher. "When's he going 'way again?"

Faye did not answer, her heart heavy.

The paste was difficult to clean, having sunk into the carpet, and it was nearly an hour before she set out in search of Rupert. She found him in the vegetable garden, his temper further ruffled by Gabriel's dawdling pace of work. "I've told him that if he doesn't mend his ways, he can waste someone else's time! Here we are at Christmas and not half the garden dug. He needn't think that just because there is a war on, he can sleep in his tool shed whenever it pleases him."

"He must be well over seventy," said Faye defensively, not wanting another argument if she was to redeem her promise to Christopher. Of course, Gabriel was often infuriating, but she could not imagine Reydenham without him. "Rupert, I wish you would come in, we must have an early lunch if we're to reach Canterbury in good time."

He stared at her, without moving. "The boy is not going."

"He has cleaned the carpet very well, and will apologize when he sees you. There's no cause to punish him any more."

He shrugged. "You must trust my judgment in this. Chris is spoiled enough without weakening over punishment he richly deserved. It is bad for any boy to live in a household of women."

She could sense how pleased he was to find a lack in his son's life which he alone could fill, and her anger cooled. If she could only persuade him to generosity it might give him the sense of belonging which he so much lacked with Christopher. "Rupert, please. It was to have been such a happy time together."

"Was it, Faye? Or are you missing the gaiety of your naval friends with an inconvenient husband home?"

"Nanny. Or was it your mother?" she said immediately, without rancor. "I have been to three dances at the Maison Dieu and came back late once in a naval lorry, as there was no other transport. I know it was silly and people gossiped, so I haven't done it again. There was no harm in it, my love." She put her hands on his shoulders, deeply thankful now that there had been no harm in it. Except, of course, to Alan. "I do a lot of work for the Navy, Rupert; it was difficult to refuse to go, but since then I have refused."

He shook her off at once; she had forgotten how much he resented any attempt to erase grievance with tenderness. "Just as well if you have refused. Small wonder Christopher is growing up as he is, with his mother—" He checked himself but some demon of jealousy made him add: "Don't try my patience too far, Faye, although I suppose I should be thankful you are not carrying a child I shall look at and wonder whether it is mine."

She gasped, then from somewhere came the vision of herself with Alan: it had very nearly happened. She ought to be happy he cared enough to feel suspicious. She had never felt more miserable in her life.

"I'm sorry, I shouldn't have said that." The apology was jerked out by shock at hearing words he had not even thought before. "Tell Christopher he may come if he wishes." He walked away hastily, and only reappeared when they were gathered by the car, silent and too nervous to shout for him, in case they provoked another explosion.

"Always awkward-tempered, Mr. Rupert," observed Nanny, not without pride, while they waited. "As I said to Cook, he's never been a gentleman to take liberties with."

Faye felt Christopher shiver against her side, and hugged him tightly, unspeaking.

The cathedral was both gratefully familiar and very strange. Soaring stonework and arches curving into darkness comforted Faye's unhappiness, and made Christopher forget everything except wonder, the candle he held just one among hundreds sparkling in the dark. To him, there was nothing unexpected in massive scaffolding holding blackout screens instead of stained glass, or about earth piled in the aisles to protect the slabbed floor: it simply made vastness more splendidly exciting. Faye knelt and stood and sang, thoughts so jumbled she made no sense of anything. She had never been conventionally religious but, brought up with this great building woven into her life, a fraction of its stone the work of her hands, she could not avoid the sense of eternity which was inescapable in Canterbury She did not pray now, beyond the incoherent appeals of her heart, yet found some solace where so many had come before her, seeking easement in distress.

She looked around at leaping arch and fluted shafts flowing triumphantly upward, drawing the eye into shadowed space. Imagination and memory filled in carved flowers and ribs of stone, the massive vaults and procession of pillars, and for an instant her spirit rested on its way.

She felt her father watching her and shifted position so her face was hidden from him. He understood her well enough to know there was something wrong, to sense change since her eager insistence that he should spend Christmas at Reydenham. She glanced at Christopher and smiled: head thrown back, he was bawling carols learned by heart at the top of his voice. He at least had left unhappiness behind.

Afterward, she retained only hazed impressions of their celebration Christmas, like shell bursts on a beach.

There was Christmas Eve, when most of the valley crowded into the hall to sing carols, Dickson confiding that his Susan was back and pregnant, her husband overseas for more than a year past; there was Rupert wrenching open the pedestal cupboard because she had forgotten to have the lock picked, freshly annoyed by splintered wood. Rupert coming to bed later, not drunk, but not sober either.

She lay awake waiting for him, trying to work out exactly what had gone wrong. It was not a time for tears, but rather for generosity. For realizing he had been long away, had been fed stories by Nanny which might easily have been true, and perhaps found himself irritated by the prosperity of the valley, when he had left it bankrupt. She turned over again on the reflection that John Castellan's money was something else she could not explain: Rupert had more, not less, cause for resentment than he knew.

When the door opened, she sat up and switched on the bedside light.

He stared at her. "You ought to be asleep."

"As if I would sleep before you came! My love, I'm sorry things went wrong between us today, and over a pot of paste, too!" She saw Christopher's woebegone face again; it had not quite been over a pot of paste. She would not think of what he had said to her in the garden, either.

"For heaven's sake, Faye, leave it, can't you! It's beyond me why you must make such a fuss about nothing, and turn the house upside down for Christmas in the middle of a war!" He sat heavily on the bed, hands hanging between his knees. "I'll be overseas soon, then you can have everything your own way as usual, only easier."

"There is no way I want, except for us to be—easy—together again." For the first time her tongue stuck on the word love.

Her too obvious effort to be conciliatory only rasped further at his dissatisfaction, and the vision of Susan was suddenly cold in his mind; she was carrying another man's child with her husband overseas. When Faye came to him in the garden he had wanted only to punish her for standing by Christopher against him, and spoke the first accusation which came to his lips. He had not meant it, and tried to make amends with apology he had choked on before; now he could not forget his own words. He suspected the unfamiliar, and each time he came home he recognized less of a life he had previously accepted as completely his. He stared at Faye, unappeased, and saw falseness in the curve of her smile: it was not only Christopher who needed authority restored if the war was not to destroy his home as surely as if it had been flattened by shells.

He got into bed, turning away from her deliberately, and within minutes was heavily asleep.

The fact of Christmas saved them. Everyone had their place in the traditions of the day, there was no time to brood, they were never alone.

Rupert began the day by staring into the space where Faye was, and ended by laughing over the story of the venison. In the afternoon he took Christopher for a ride to try out his pony in the bridle which was their Christmas gift to him, and when they returned Faye produced the last of her surprises, a bowl of nuts and sultanas flaming with brandy, for each to snatch as many as they could, little fingers only allowed, the winner to be presented with the last orange.

Christopher was afraid of the flames at first, but soon realized that their blue thinness posed no danger if he was quick, shouting and shaking the dish in spectacular cheats with the rest. "Six! I've got six! How many have you got, Grandpa?"

Faye watched her father count slowly, lips pursed. "Five, and a nut I ate."

"It doesn't count if you ate it, Grandpa! I've got another, look! How many have you got, Nanny?"

Faye saw Rupert begin to frown as they let Christopher get the most, then he leaned forward and began to flick out sultanas with steady concentration. When the flames died at last, he was an easy winner and took the orange, saying casually, "Bad luck, Chris. You can't win 'em all."

Christopher stared at the orange; if she was fortunate, Faye was able to obtain two a month on his child's ration book, adults rarely saw them at all. "I like proper oranges much better than the horrid stuff in bottles."

"Don't be a bad loser, Chris," said Rupert, quite pleasantly, putting the orange in his pocket. "It's something we all have to learn and the sooner you start, the better." He glanced at Faye, as if to make sure everyone in the room understood that she was to blame for Christopher's failure to behave as a Ludlow should.

Christopher mumbled something and began to eat his sultanas.

"What did you say?" He went on eating, head bent, until Rupert closed his hand over his pile of fruit. "What did you say?"

"Tell Daddy what you said," Faye interposed, hoping it was not anything too dreadful, fearing more punishments on Christmas evening.

Christopher emptied his mouth. "I said his hands were bigger 'n mine, and he didn't *deserve* to win."

There was a frightful silence while they avoided each other's eyes, then Rupert scooped all Christopher's fruit back into the bowl and handed it to Faye. "I expect you could do with these for cooking, when they keep telling us in the Army how short civilian rations are."

"Yes, we saved up a long time for today, thinking it was worth it for the pleasure we would have," said Faye evenly, feeling the first sour satisfaction of deliberate deceit with John Castellan's providing in her hands.

Chapter Twenty-one

February 12, 1942.

A bleak, rough day, a harsh westerly blowing up-Channel. It was the sort of day when the German batteries left Dover alone, the fall of their shells too difficult to mark, and at the slip work was proceeding with the kind of unhurried absorption which suited the men best. They enjoyed the rush and skill of improvisation when they felt it was really necessary, but usually regarded any urging to speed as a deep-laid plot to confound their craft and hide shortcomings of organization. Faye tried to break through this attitude but had eventually become used to it since she encountered it every day in the valley too. She insisted on time sheets and they filled in what they were doing on Monday and dotted in ditto marks for each subsequent day; she introduced bonuses for faster working and upset all the existing rates of pay, so everyone seethed with discontent for weeks. On the other hand, when a minelaying MTB had to be refitted in a single night, it was done with hours to spare. In the end, she gave up and contentment grew again. Whatever was said of bankruptcy, crisis, or the need for change, they had heard it all before, generation by generation, and took no particular notice unless their interest was stirred; steadiness in disaster imperceptibly becoming stolidity of endeavor.

"Summat's going on." Henry straightened up and cocked his head, listening. Little by little, hammering and sawing ceased and they all listened, startled, to the coughing roar of MTBs starting up.

Someone heaved back the doors to the outside slip, and as they stood shivering, five boats appeared round the end of the pier and roared across the harbor, far faster than the usual speed permitted. One weaved slightly and they saw a flash of white from the bridge. "Mr. Wyllie," grunted one of the men. Alan was well liked at the slip and there had been one or two pointed questions as to why he came no more. "Why the hell are they going out in daylight?"

They stood in the wind, still listening, after the boats had gone: above the cloud they could hear aircraft, a few minutes later heavy gunfire and the rattle of machine guns in the Channel. Two more MTBs went streaking across the harbor, like children anxious to join a promising party. Faye felt the coldness of disaster fastening about her. Rescue launches for ditched pilots, the odd trawler or minesweeper sailed in daylight, nothing else.

They went back inside the slip, hammering strangely broken as one, then another paused to listen to continuing explosions out at sea. Faye left early, pushing her bicycle in cold drizzle up the hatefully known gradients of the Western Heights. Light was draining from sullen gray overcast but the sounds of war were all around, drawing away eastward. Aircraft, bursts of automatic fire, then the hollow rip of MTBs at speed again. Eyes straining, she counted them back across the harbor: four, then a pause and one more. She waited, shivering, willing the other two to appear and at very long last, they did. On the wireless that night they heard how the German battleships *Scharnhorst* and *Gniesenau* had steamed through their straits undamaged, how all the Navy could find to throw against them was a few MTBs too frail to penetrate their destroyer screen, and a flight of elderly Swordfish biplanes with a top speed of ninety miles an hour. The MTBs returned safely, every one of the Swordfishes was lost.

Not Alan, this time; instead a different handful blown apart in flimsy, outdated machines. The tally of disaster was still running, faster and faster as the third year of war unfolded. Three days later, Singapore fell and British power in the Far East was lynched. In March, the Japanese landed in Java and Australia was bombed for the first time; during the summer, as bombing became mercifully lighter in Britain, the hard-won gains in Africa, the bitter recovery in Russia, were lost again.

Afterward, Faye remembered 1942 as the worst year of the war. It had already gone on so long, it still had so unimaginably far to go. Everything was known, no one felt there were any surprises left. The shape of the winning alliance was set; grief and drab shortages hatefully familiar. Only the ultimate price in blood and ruin was incalculable, and growing larger every day. Yet there was no turning back, and in all the long years Faye never heard anyone suggest it; there was just the weariness of how long it took.

The slip was frantically busy, and the Navy were already suggesting expansion, with plans to double the covered area and rebuild the ramp itself, complete with winch and deepened entry. More MTBs and MGB flotillas were coming into Dover and they felt the tide of victory turn the day the minelayer *Welshman* steamed into harbor and became the first naval ship of size to anchor there since the destroyers were withdrawn after Dunkirk. The German batteries at once stepped up their fire but they all felt it was worth any bombardment and stood on the cliffs, watching her with open delight.

Faye was singing as she coasted the last mile to the slip in early April; spring was here again, profit flowing from the slip at last, the only anxiety whether the Navy would insist on taking it over as it grew in size. But if they did, I might find time to carve again, she thought; I ought to go back to the ambulances, but I couldn't bear it. She saw Beryl occasionally, but Anne crossed the street if they met: her mother had been disappointed when Christopher did not go to Yorkshire and she felt an army daughter's incomprehension for someone who patched boats when there was real work to be done.

Faye let herself into the slip, still humming under her breath, even the sight of the men brushing on more varnish than their contract allowed leaving her cheerful mood untouched. No amount of restriction stopped them putting the finish of pride to their work. Up the ladder to the office where she flicked over the post; what luxury to open bills and know they could be paid. She thought of stone again but shook her head; for the moment she was gripped by excitement at the slip's success: this was her own and she did not intend to let the Navy take it over if she could help it.

She opened a small packet marked private, expecting naval fittings, and found torch batteries instead. She fingered them, surprised but grateful; batteries were almost unobtainable and her torch often the only pinpoint of light on the long journey back to Reydenham. She stiffened suddenly, eyes on the calendar, remembering John putting his torch into her hands after their brush with death in the cellar. Wine cellar, she remembered, smiling. Another six months had passed.

She smoothed out the wrapping paper and stared at the label. Upright, black, rather hurried writing, the postmark EC4. Yes.

"Mrs. Ludlow?" She tore herself from her thoughts and greeted one of the navy engineers, expecting queries about the MTB they were repairing, already a week late. And they are putting on extra varnish, she thought, irritated now. But after perfunctory inquiries about the boat, he stood, fingering his cap, awkwardly ill at ease. "Mrs. Ludlow, I—that is, the boys at the dock thought you ought to know—" His voice trailed away unhappily.

"You are thinking of taking over here? I've seen it coming, don't worry, Lieutenant." He would not decide such matters, and meanwhile she wanted him to sanction a new roof for the whole building when the extension was built: at Admiralty expense of course. So she smiled at him and added, "I'm not a boatbuilder by choice." In some ways I am not a banker by instinct, John had once said. Before the next six months were up, she would have repaid him.

"No, that is, yes, I expect by the end of the year we will be doing all our own repairs. The thing is—" His eyes dropped and then he blurted out, "Alan Wyllie was killed last week in the raid on St. Nazaire; 20017 was shot up and sank, too. We . . . we thought you'd want to know, having . . . having been close to them both, as you might say." He blushed furiously at his clumsiness in linking man and MTB in the same death, yet it was fitting. Alan, looking down at his waterlogged boat by the slip, hands bandaged, face frizzled pink. Alan inventing rude rhymes in Bond Street and kissing her in Hyde Park. Alan craving for comfort she had denied him.

She thanked him, or supposed she did, and when he had gone, she walked along the cratered harbor promenade haunted by a terrible lack in herself. The lack of loss, of sorrow for a boy whose wife would never now thank her for maturity she had helped give him. Instead, she had taken.

Who could say that if she had given more, he might not have lived? Might have had more will to live, been luckier, a little less brave? She leaned on twisted, pitted railing and gazed across the harbor: gulls were screaming, the air sharp-edged and cloudless.

It might have been peace, and was not.

She had denied Alan out of pride, not faithfulness, because she hated to think that Rupert would not notice what he had lost.

Would that she had given Alan all she had to give and did not now feel such terrible remorse. Then at least she would deserve Rupert's condemnation, surely find it easier to recompense him for wrongs she understood than endure the bitterness of appeasing injustice.

For Rupert's leaves had continued in the same disastrous pattern: he insisted that she stay close by him and then found fault with what she did, accused her of nothing but behaved as if trust no longer existed between them. Worst of all, his lethal gibes reduced Christopher to paralysis, so he seemed in truth the cosseted booby his father called him. This had finally provoked a ferocious quarrel, in which each felt the other irremediably in the wrong, and in its aftermath Christopher disappeared for a whole day, hiding himself from harshness he did not understand. Once he was found, Rupert had walked out, two days before the end of his leave, and was now in Scotland, on yet another course, with no sign of a posting overseas. He would be home again before the end of the summer and already Faye dreaded the thought of it. If only he could come home for good and let suspicion rest . . . run affairs himself so she could resign authority into his hands again . . . she shook her head, frowning. Perhaps.

The summer passed very slowly. Shelling intensified, the post office shattered, Market Square no more than thrown-back rubble, the Folkestone Road blasted. The center of Folkestone itself was blown out by a land mine, and for the first time notices were pasted up warning that the penalty for looting was death. The slip was safer than the town, shells hurtling overhead with a terrifying, tearing rip, the ground leaping as more streets were torn into dust. There was no certainty about it though, the next sparkle on the French coast could mean the gunners had lowered their sights a single notch and they would be blown apart.

Faye found herself shaking with nerves again, the need for control undermining her last reserves. Control in front of the men at the slip, control before the inhabitants of the Ludlows' valley, above all control with Christopher, who did not understand the strain she was under and needed constant attention when she was home. He was bored by his confinement in the valley, increasingly restless as he was penned in day after day with the limitations of Cook and Nanny, the only relief a stately visit to Mrs. Ludlow on her sofa.

The precious time of day was after supper, the ritual of the news over, windows wide to the last of the sun. Then she would read books of another age where no one thought of war, or laboriously unravel socks for unobtainable darning wool, and feel briefly eased by stillness. Even at night she often heard the uneven thump of German bombers, the distant shake of antiaircraft guns firing far inland, destruction spreading still further with the so-called Baedeker vengeance raids, methodical attacks on England's lovely heritage: York, Bath, Exeter, Norwich, one by one they were joining the industrial cities in their ruins.

Dover was bombed again, too, mostly by night, and Faye was thankful for the serenity of Reydenham folded away in its valley, even if she did not sleep easily any more. She was woken by the telephone after a particularly noisy night at the end of May and at first her only reaction was outrage, minutes after she had fallen into restless sleep. She turned over and buried her face in the pillow, but it rang on and on and at last she fumbled reluctantly for the receiver.

"Faye? It's Beryl, you know, Beryl of the ambulance."

"Beryl? Why on earth—"

"Faye, listen. We just bin called to Canterbury, every ambulance in Kent's going just about. They've copped it terrible; cathedral, the lot gone. I know your dad lives there, so I thought—"

Faye felt her heart shrivel, one by one everything she held precious was being taken.

"D'you hear me, Faye? I'll come by the end of your road in ten minutes if you want to 'op a lift. Wear your uniform."

"I'll be there," said Faye dully. "Thanks, Beryl."

She scrambled into her old uniform, fingers clumsy, body icecold. Her father probably dead, the ageless, eternal cathedral gone. Its ribs and vaults and flowers of stone, a heap of dust. There was no way for the mind to grasp it.

The ambulance was waiting by the time she reached the crossroads, the old Morris gasping on a drain of petrol she kept for emergencies. "The messages started coming in about midnight," said Beryl. "Standin' on the roof you could see the 'ole sky lit up. Gawd, it must be a mess up there, tain't as if it's a big town."

"No," said Faye. "It's not a big town." Her heart shifted its beat; long, heavy hammer strokes jolting her ribs as the rising sun threw light on a towering cloud of smoke ahead.

Ropersole, Denne Hill, Barham Down: the old Roman road from Dover to Canterbury ran straight as a drawn line toward the dark stain rising into the dawn. Iledon, Bishopsbourne, Bridge, Patrixbourne: still they could see nothing, no dominating bulk of the cathedral, no gray-etched beckoning tower; the sun had disappeared, lost in monstrous clouds of dust and smoke.

Then, as they dropped down the last hill to the city, there was a touch of wind, thickness wavered and broke, and for an instant they saw it. Darker than dust, more solid than smoke, the cathedral still stood, pinnacles of Bell Harry tower touched yellow from sun and flame. Then it was gone again, and only darkness remained.

"It was there, Beryl, it—"

"It was there, chum. Gaw' blimey, if they can miss that, no wonder they've bin tipping five 'undred shells a year into the 'arbor."

Then they came to the streets. Hosepipes; heavy rescue; men sweating over rubble with no breath left for words. Blocked streets, throat-grasping dust, the roar of blazing gas mains.

Faye lost her way immediately in a city where every lane was familiar, and helped Beryl load the ambulance with crushed, dust-masked bodies, peering at each one expecting it to be her father or Betty.

The Canterbury hospitals were already overflowing, so a policeman told them to drive to Maidstone. "Will you manage all right if I stay?" Faye looked around at an earthquake world: sky, streets, and color lost. Only rubble, everywhere.

"Sure. There'll be plenty of 'elp in Maidstone." Beryl hesitated. "Good luck."

Faye nodded. Surely good luck had ended long ago.

The most difficult thing was finding where she was. Smoke blotted out any sense of direction, shattered glass and torn-up roads turned narrow lanes into thoroughfares, shopping streets into a chaos of tumbled brick. At length she stumbled on Mercery Lane leading to the cathedral, crunching with glass and spilled plaster, but otherwise untouched, and realized she had crossed the main street without noticing it. Friar's Court, where her father lived, was somewhere in the wilderness of masonry she had climbed with such great difficulty, seeing nothing she knew. She turned back, running now, hands torn from scrambling over brick, coughing with dust and smoke. She had gone too far, she must have gone too far. She stopped, helpless; in this part of the city there was nothing left.

An ARP man found her sitting and gave her tea. "It's worst here, the rest is not so bad, but this whole quarter's completely gone."

"My father—" Faye gulped cold tea and stood again. "My father lived here somewhere. Friar's Court."

They looked about them silently. "You won't find it," the warden said at last. "They're posting up names at the police station as fast as they get them, you'd best go there."

"I'll come back." There was so much to be done, but first she must know. "I'll come back and help."

A frond of wind wavered gently again, bringing an instant of freshness, and they saw the cathedral standing clear and untouched, surrounded by ruins. "The library, cloister, and Chapter House t'other side have gone," observed the warden, flipping a thumb. "And the whole bloody section this side. How the hell they missed, I don't know; they were aiming for it, all right." He turned away, back to the heartbreaking task of searching the ruins.

Faye dug and bandaged and served tea and carried shattered bodies throughout the day. There was no end to it, would not be an end to it for days and weeks to come. She went to the police station several times, where a great crowd was reading hastily written lists, then turning away in silence or in hope. Late in the evening she went again and Betty's name was there, dead.

Betty, the only cuddling warmth of her childhood. Betty with her smells of flour and soap, shouting about mice up the stairwell. The trail of Eustaces taking crumbs from her fingers, the latest no doubt buried with her under five stories of ruptured brick. Betty grunting up the stairs to hear whispered confidences in the dark, who had wanted to come to see her and Christopher at Christmas; who had not come because Faye knew how much Rupert hated her familiarities.

More blame. More sadness and loss. She could not think of it and went to a rest center, hot food sending her into instant sleep on the floor, to wake creaking with stiffness, sweating from the image of Betty crushed and agonized in the hot coals of her kitchen.

I must not think of it, she said aloud; she could not think of it.

It was another beautiful dawn, sun fingering through the haze which would hang over Canterbury for days yet. She went to the cathedral first, as if to touch the talisman of its stone before searching lists again. It was quiet, and in its quietness she realized for the first time since she had come how great was the noise and confusion all around. Some fallen stone was embedded in the piled earth covering the cathedral floor, the north transept ended in hastily piled sandbags, the library was shattered, otherwise it was intact.

"A modern building," said an old canon viewing the ruins of the library with covert satisfaction while he collected scattered documents. "And everything of value long since sent away."

"Did you know my father?" asked Faye. "Mr. Haskell, he often worked in the library."

"Yes, my dear, I know him, a fine scholar. Although he has some strange theories on early medieval innings of the marsh," he added severely.

"He . . . he . . . I've been looking for him ever since the raid. You don't know—"

"He was here." He looked around vaguely, as if expecting to find true scholars still poring over manuscripts in the cloister. "When the library was hit I saw him telling the firemen to keep their hoses off the charter chests."

"Here? You saw him here?"

"Where else would he be if the library was hit?" the old man asked in mild surprise. "You couldn't just run over to the deanery for me, could you, and find a basket to put these documents in?"

Her father's name was still unlisted, and Faye spent the rest of the day questioning clergy, hope released again. He had been alive after the raid started, he had not been in the devastated southern side of the city. She found him at last in one of the dormitories of the King's School, turned into an emergency clearing station.

"He had a heart attack," said the only nurse Faye could find, a Red Cross Auxiliary, worried beyond patience by a floorful of casualties dumped on her inexperience. "He's got something draining in his leg, but the doctor said it was his heart."

"Will he get well?" His face looked like blown glass.

"How do I know? There's a lot worse than him, but he's old, isn't he?"

Sixty-eight, thought Faye. Not the right age for fighting fires and digging through rubble. She stayed the rest of the day, helping where she could, but between them she and the Red Cross girl knew little more than first aid. In the evening the dormitory was evacuated, the patients sent to a hospital in Ashford as order returned, an exhausted doctor reassuring when Faye asked his opinion.

He was probably trying to comfort her, she decided, mind detached. She had handled many casualties over the past three years and thought perhaps he had an even chance, the frail appearance of the old was deceptive. She hitched a ride to Dover, and looked back once to see Bell Harry tower clear against a twilight sky: the Germans said this raid was vengeance for an RAF attack on Cologne and there the cathedral had escaped too, with destruction all around. Blind chance, a miracle of God, or did even airmen inured to war falter sometimes when a cathedral filled their sights?

That night the Germans came to Canterbury again, and still the cathedral stood.

Chapter Twenty-two

Her father lived.

Each time she went to see him, he made an effort to seem better even when he was not. Within a month he had scribbled notes scattered over his bed, dozing over them when he thought she had gone. His determination not to add to her anxieties possibly saved his life, giving him a will to live, for he had been both shocked and worried by the atmosphere at Reydenham during his short Christmas visit.

Faye wanted to take him back there with her when he was convalescent, but he refused. "Rupert will be home on leave again soon, and will not expect his house to be full of invalids. I'm best on my own after all these years."

"You had Betty before," Faye said gently. "You can't manage alone."

His thin blue-veined hand wandered among his papers, starting a landslip to the floor. "I won't be beholden. Never have, never will. Canon Rosebery has offered me a room and he needs company. I'll go there when I'm well. I've lived all my life in Canterbury, the Close will be a fitting end."

"Is he the one who disapproves of your theory on medieval marsh innings? If so, I met him gathering up charters in a basket after the raid."

"Poor Michael has strange notions on chronology," he said pensively. "Although I venture to think that even he admits me his master on phililogical evidence."

Faye laughed. "I can see that you'll be better matched in his house than mine! You must come to Reydenham until you're stronger though, those houses in the Close are all stairs and drafts." She hesitated, and then added awkwardly, "Rupert won't be home again for a while. He thinks he really will go overseas in the autumn and have embarkation leave just before."

"It's not working out for you, is it?" He shuffled his papers together, not looking at her. "What is the trouble, or would you rather not speak of it?"

Faye shook her head. "I'd rather not speak of it." For all his courage, her father was too frail to be worried with her concerns. "It's the war, I daresay it will work out again afterward. It's got to," she added with sudden fierceness.

It must, it's got to, she repeated to herself, all the tedious, over-crowded bus journey home. When the war is over, somehow we must live together in comfort again. She found herself adding up time and guiltily stifled thought: Christopher was four years old and sole heir to Reydenham, he must grow up there and she must stay with him. Rupert's last leave had been easier than the calamities of Christmas, somehow she would unlearn all the independence the war had taught her and become the wife he wanted. Yet she had guarded herself against having another child, the calculation that pregnancy would add more years to the time she must stay unacknowledged in her mind.

Slowly, the months of 1942 flicked by, the balance evenly poised, then tipping toward victory. The Japanese drive for Australia was stopped by the Americans in the Coral Sea; Rommel held a scant afternoon's drive from the Suez Canal; then with winter came the holocaust of Stalingrad, and the German Army was seen to be mortal like the rest. At Reydenham they heard not only German bombers coming in on the dusk, but the RAF going out in their hundreds and then, at last, the Americans too, by day. Shelling became intermittent as the Germans found better uses for their ammunition and one Sunday in November church bells were rung in celebration of victory at El Alamein, the first time they had been heard since 1940, when they became the signal of invasion. The first true victory since 1940 too, except for the supreme victory of staying alive and undefeated.

Christopher was entranced by the bells, chanting their names and gabbling about triples and bob majors after a visit to the church tower, and for nearly everyone else they were a breath of normality out of the past, a conscious moment of relief that the worst was over.

Inevitably, Gabriel was the exception. "I dunno," he confided to Faye. "Them bells was the invasion warnin' when church be the one place sartin sure to have no telephone, now they ring 'em for a pack of gutted Jerries when the rest of the year Parson be preachin' peace on earth. To my mind, a salute of shotguns'd be more fittin'."

"On victory night you must fire your volley from Radigund's Hill," said Faye, smiling. "Surely another year must see it done."

"I dunno, Mrs. Rupert, there be a long road to march yet." Faye began to argue, then was stopped by inconvenient memory: five years, John had said in the spring of 1941. They had served only twenty-one months of that sentence and he had been right before. Yet surely he could not have guessed at the merciful madness which brought in Russia and America so soon? Her mind switched abruptly, she ought to have heard from John.

She went into the library and stared at a calendar, frowning. She had last heard at the beginning of April, the same day she was told of Alan's death; she ought to have heard again by now. He had been late before, when the parcel came from America; he might be anywhere and ships sank with parcels on board. She put it from her mind when a letter arrived from Rupert next day to say he was ordered overseas at last.

He came home in tearing spirits, wearing another pip as captain after three years a lieutenant, and for a few days Faye hardly dared believe how completely everything had changed. The slip was under camouflage nets while the extension was being built and most work suspended, so she need not fret about going there. It was a joy to be with Rupert as he rode every corner of the valley, rose in the dawn to walk the stubble with his shotgun, and wangled his way into the army camp at Dungeness to go sea fishing. Faye felt herself coming to life again as anxiety faded and Christopher no longer hid when his father was around: it was going to be all right.

She anticipated their rations recklessly to give him food he liked, planned expeditions which would amuse him at a dreary time of year, enlisting the help of Colonel Druitt with pheasants, Dickson with his ferrets, one of the men at the slip who had a pass to take his dinghy fishing under the cliffs. She stored up amusing things to tell him in the evening, and came to him with the gladness of relief at night. She still did not sleep well, lying wakeful with each sense stretched tight, planning like a general how to reinforce success on the morrow.

They climbed one morning to the southern edge of the valley, and looked out over gray Channel waters to France, every detail clear in rain-washed winter air. As they watched, the last of the night's bombers were coming home: these were the stragglers, dangerously exposed by daylight, instruments shot away perhaps and a hundred miles off course, welcoming the white cliffs like a blind man with sight restored. Some trailed smoke and others had undercarriages hanging loose; once Faye had seen an American Fortress with half its wing missing, still flying somehow. Fighters flicked overhead in protection, and in mid-Channel was the speck of an air-sea rescue launch, plumed shell bursts rising with deceptive gentleness in its wake. She pointed it out to Rupert, then immediately wished she hadn't, it was difficult to remember the pitfalls a casual word could open at her feet.

"One of your pals aboard?" he inquired disagreeably. Several times he had not resisted the impulse to rub at old suspicion, but Faye had brushed the moment past, her whole mind devoted to rebuilding contentment, the warmth on which content was built shriveling unnoticed under the impact of so much contriving. Now her intellect signaled the need for a gesture to divert him and she slipped her arm through his. "I don't know anyone in air-sea rescue. They're RAF and I deal only with navy repairs."

Rupert did not recognize her slippery, nervous brightness for what it was, anxiety to please without the instinctive harmony which once had let her please him unthinkingly. Instead, the falseness of her tone annoyed him afresh. "I suppose I should be thankful that at least we don't live near an airfield; those boys survive half a tour of operations if they're lucky and haven't time to waste."

I won't throw it all away, Faye thought fiercely, when everything is so much better. She squeezed his arm. "The Army will do for me."

He grunted, eyes on a Lancaster low over the sea, two engines straining to keep it in the air, two stopped altogether. "He'd do better to ditch than try for base on two engines."

She watched too, petty differences squeezed out by an unknown airman's desperate efforts to lift his battered machine over the hills. It disappeared at last, skimming the trees. "Oh God, I hope they make it."

"They should have ditched," Rupert repeated. "There are a lot of rabbits up here, I'll bring my gun up later." He began poking about among the burrows, sufficiently diverted by the bomber to be unwilling to pursue conflict any further.

Faye stared at his back, suddenly overwhelmed by the futility of it all. Everything had been going well, then one chance remark and their whole relationship crinkled like skin on boiled milk. Abruptly, she turned and stumbled away down the hill; he had not noticed her gesture of affection as he had not noticed a dozen others, he probably would not notice whether she stayed or went.

She was wrong; he came into their bedroom half an hour later, his face tight with temper. "Where the hell did you run off to?"

"I came home," she said without expression. "I didn't think you'd notice if I left."

"Well, of course I noticed! Going off without so much as—"

"Without your permission? Listen, Rupert, you've been home nine days, can you think of a single thing in all that time you have done for me?"

"Good God, Faye—"

"Don't swear at me, just think. Can you? Oh yes, I'm sorry, I forgot. You offered to get the rations in Dover, and came home with nothing because the queues were too long."

"They were damned long," he said defensively. "Right out on the pavement."

"Yes, I know. I wait in them two or three times a week."

"It's no good blaming me for the rationing system. What are you complaining of anyway? That I went to look at some rabbit burrows instead of kissing you in an icy December wind?"

"I'm tired, Rupert." She was driven beyond care, beyond any chance of holding back a torrent long since spilled within her, detachment burned up in anger, nerves splintered by strain stretching back as long as she could now remember. "I'm tired of thinking up subjects which won't annoy you, tired of planning food you don't think anything out of the ordinary, tired of welcoming you night after night and not once being handled with tenderness or asked whether perhaps I might be unwilling—"

"I have twelve days' embarkation leave and you are my wife," interrupted Rupert. "Why should you be unwilling?"

She shook her head, hands fumbling among pots on her dressing table. "I wasn't, only—"

"Well, then, what is all the fuss about?"

She sat on the bed and put her head in her hands. "I'm very

tired," she repeated, there seemed nothing else to say. She felt
empty of will, empty certainly of more words; everything which
had sustained her through years of repeated shocks, drained and
running into nothing. No more to explain, nothing to give any
more. She was defeated not by unfaithfulness or separation, but
by the wall of his incomprehension, his lack of generosity. He did
not care what she thought because it did not occur to him that he
ought to care, did not ask what she did except with suspicion, because he could not see her apart from himself. She was him or she
was nothing.

She was nothing.

She also had to stay with him until Christopher was grown. Re-
hearsed responses snapped tight on her mind again and she looked
up at him out of clear eyes. "I'm sorry, I was behaving stupidly."
She stood and kissed him lightly on the cheek. "I so much want
everything to be right for you."

Rupert stared at her, repelled. The transformation was complete: the girl who adored and owed everything to him had disappeared, her place taken by a hard-featured stranger who kissed like
Judas. He had been trying too, forced by uncertainty to rely on
the only means of expression he thought would not fail him, attempting to wipe out loss with the imprint of his body.

He loved the valley still, but so long as it was in another's care
the spell of Reydenham eluded him; his son too, however he
sought to tighten his grasp, slithered through his comprehension.

Now Faye.

He turned and left her, false kisses still on his lips.

Chapter Twenty-three

Faye was unaware of any change in herself. Once Rupert had gone, she returned to the certainty that next time it must be better. She would think of a way. Blind stone had changed under her hands into a thing of beauty; she had turned financial disaster into prosperity, asked someone she scarcely knew for a loan and been given riches without so much as a receipt. She had charmed a steamroller out of the Camber and smashed torpedo boats onto the Ludlow slip.

Certainly she would find a way to live in peace with Rupert once their life returned to its normal pattern. She would not admit despair, and instead wondered why she was locked in black depression which no amount of activity could shift.

Mrs. Ludlow noticed the change, and her father also. Both in their own ways did what they could to help.

"Faye dear, I don't want to hurt you," observed Mrs. Ludlow, in the voice of one who has every intention of doing exactly that. "But I must tell you that you have become positively *dowdy* recently."

"I need my clothing coupons for the house and for Christopher," answered Faye indifferently.

"A woman should always have pride in herself. There's no excuse for becoming hard and unfeminine, just because you choose to work like a laborer. Middle age is always such a difficult time with men," she added. "When Rupert comes home he will be disappointed if you are different from his memories of you."

Faye walked out of the room.

She went to see her father the following week. There was no petrol and she felt too tired to cycle the long, uphill miles to Canterbury; instead she had to wait in freezing February rain for buses which never arrived at the time they were expected. Canterbury was full of open spaces and thrown-back rubble, the cathedral more visible than ever before. She did not even glance at it, clothes clinging like sodden cardboard, feet icy from puddles in the churned pavement. I suppose dear Mama would say I looked like a peasant, she thought bitterly: what a pity to spoil my complexion amusing myself in the rain.

Her father had a room on the first floor of Canon Rosebery's house in the Close; he was frail but seemed well content, apparently aware of little except the tranquillity of his surroundings and scholarly discussions on medieval charters. After those two devastating nights the previous summer, the Germans had not come to Canterbury again.

He was an undemanding companion and Faye went to sleep beside his fire, waking to an uncomfortably searching scrutiny. She stood up and stretched. "What an old woman I've become to go to sleep by the fire! And what a waste of my time with you, why didn't you wake me?"

"You looked so weary, my dear. I was happy to watch you rest for once."

Faye caught sight of her reflection in a yellowed mirror and grimaced at herself. Unfeminine, Mrs. Ludlow had said. Her image looked back at her defiantly, eyes smudged deep into edged sockets, straight-ruled lines at mouth and forehead; when had she last truly looked at herself?

She saw her father standing behind her; their eyes met in the mirror and he answered her thought as if she had spoken. "It is nothing to do with the way you look, Faye. If you were happy you would be more beautiful for what you have done these last years, not less."

Faye laughed and turned to face him. "I think not, with my laborer's hands and a mind full of the best way to boil fish."

"And your heart full of—what?" he said gently.

"Oh, Father—" she began impatiently, then broke off, seeing his look of distress. It was even difficult for him to stand for any length of time. She helped him back to his chair and changed the conversation but his words still hung between them. As she kissed him goodbye, she said abruptly, "A heart which brings loss on everyone I hold in affection, as it seems to me."

He shook his head. "Only if you see it so. You have brought nothing but gain to me." Which was kind, but untrue, she reflected, considering he loved my mother, who died giving me birth. Another of the tally piled up against her life.

She let herself out of the canon's house into a cold rush of rain whisking rubbish in the gutters: the ruins continually shed scraps of other people's treasures. She shuddered and thought of two hours waiting and standing in overcrowded buses back to Dover, the uphill ride to Reydenham with wind and rain in her teeth. Rupert had landed in Morocco with the First Army and was obviously relishing active service at last, although he seemed to be doing some kind of liaison with the civil authorities. She thought of her father's words again; she would find a way to live with Rupert, but could no longer believe much happiness waited for her there. And for the rest, William and Alan were dead and John more than four months overdue. She had hoped that perhaps his message had gone astray and with some pride sent repayment of his loan enclosed in a note combining thanks with carefully worded reproach for his forgetfulness, although she did not think him forgetful. She still had not heard and the check, sent to his private address, had not been paid in. Several times she nearly telephoned the unknown Joseph, but was deterred not so much by the burden of explanation as a superstitious guilt that somehow it was his contact with her which had condemned John to death.

The deadly weariness and depression which had gripped her through the winter had lifted briefly in the snug comfort of her father's room; now it closed in again. Canterbury was unlit and treacherous, the streets ragged with fallen masonry. She had been unable to find batteries for her torch, although she carried it anyway and told herself it was in case she discovered batteries. It was also a kind of talisman, of what she did not know.

The bus depot had been bombed with the rest, the waiting room hastily boarded up, crowded and rank with wet cloth. A single bulb seemed to add to the gloom, and showed a blackboard announcing a shell warning at Dover and consequent unspecified delay to services. Oh God, she thought despairingly, what wouldn't I give to have the most enormous lamp and shine it where everyone could see, to have a heated, chauffeur-driven car to take me home, tucked up in fur rugs. When this is over, I'll have every light in the house blazing, every curtain wide, I'll never cycle or go on a bus again.

"Would you care to be driven home?" said a voice behind her. She started violently to hear her thoughts so precisely echoed, then turned, blood thinning so she nearly fell. "Steady, Faye, I'm sorry if I startled you." Her arm was held, the door opened, dank air on her face again.

"Oh, John," she said quietly. "I thought I had killed you."

"I've got a car across the road. Can you walk there?"

She nodded, then remembered he could not see her in the dark. "I've got your torch in my bag, only I couldn't find any batteries for it." It seemed funny and she laughed, kept from falling by his hand, giggling like a child.

Slowly, reality solidified around her again; she was sitting in a car, rain roaring on the roof. There was no mistake, John Castellan was faintly lined beside her in the gloom, staring through the rain-streaked windscreen, hands tight on the steering wheel. He turned when she stirred. "I had no idea my appearance would upset you so much. I owed you an apology for lateness and when I rang Reydenham they said you were here and would be catching the last bus home." It had seemed a providential opportunity to see her away from prying eyes, to exorcise feeling which was surely ridiculous after three meetings in four years; which no longer seemed ridiculous now he was with her. And would she have nearly fainted at the mere sight of him, unless—

"I thought you were dead," she repeated. She could think of nothing except that he was alive.

I thought I had killed you, she said before. He looked at her, frowning; there was something very wrong here. He switched on the engine. "If you feel able to face it, we'll go in search of cod and tinned fruit. The hotels of Canterbury looked to me as if that would be the height of their endeavor."

"No," said Faye quickly. "Not in Canterbury. "There . . . there are quite a lot of people I know here."

He did not reply, but turned the car out of the city. She watched his face in the dim reflection of the dash, all hollows and shadow, revealing nothing. The headlights were blacked out except for a narrow slit, the road treacherous in pelting rain; to all appearances he was giving full attention to his driving. After a while he pulled up and went into a pub and returned, shaking his head. After the third, he came round and opened her door. "Black-market bacon and fresh eggs, we shall do better here than most places." He kept his hand on her arm until they were inside, as if still uncertain of her balance.

The bright lights and chatter of the bar struck Faye with almost physical force, so she muttered some excuse and fled upstairs to the bathroom. She scrubbed at her face unthinkingly, the shock of cold water and rough toweling still happening to someone else; only when she fumbled open her bag and saw John's torch did delight at last tear blankness aside, releasing her free and whole again.

He was waiting at the bottom of the stairs, smiling when he saw the change in her. "I thought I had concussed you for good! I ought to have left a message at Reydenham, but since I said I was allocating fertilizer, it was a little difficult."

She laughed. "I'm glad you didn't! It was just—"

"Don't think about it now. There's a fire in the parlor, you'll feel better when you've warmed up."

"I feel marvelous now." It was true, life was flowing again, the paralysis of discouragement lifted. They had the tiny parlor to themselves, a single oak table pulled close to a freshly lit fire. I bet some more Castellan money changed hands for this, she thought, watching him by the bar, head turned, replying to something the landlord said. He was wearing an old tweed jacket and fitted without effort into the bar of a Kentish pub, although she had never visualized him as other than a man of the city.

Unconsciously, her lips curved as she watched, burdens set aside and softness restored where harsh endurance had put its mark before. Deep-hidden, her heart paused, then drove her senses into the place which had long awaited them.

She was staring into the fire when he returned, two tankards in his hands. "Rough cider; nearly up to the strength of wartime gin if I'm any judge." She felt him standing beside her but did not move, fearful of what he might see. ". . . Faye?"

She turned, each detail of him etched with the clarity of love, and smiled, feeling tears in her throat. "What happened to you?" She saw now that he was moving awkwardly and the look of his face had been no trick of the dashlight. He was bone-thin and very tired. That makes two of us, she thought grimly . . . and two of us, her heart repeated.

He sat down carefully. "I've been mountaineering." He grinned. "I'm not really the cross-country type and finished up with three cracked ribs. At least they won me a Treasury car and some petrol."

"Mountaineering?" she repeated, astonished.

"I was in unoccupied France," he explained. "There's no reason why you shouldn't know, but naturally I don't want it broadcast. It was intended to be a fairly quick trip, but the Germans took the whole lot over at the wrong moment. I came out eventually by way of the Pyrenees, but it all took a great deal longer than expected." He had in fact been in Lyon, almost as much the center of the French banking system as Paris; the probable imminence of German occupation of the remainder of France giving urgency to long-term arrangements for financing resistance. Unfortunately, the Germans had moved earlier than expected.

"You've been out there four months?" She had imagined him shot down or drowned, never rubbing shoulders with Nazis in France.

"I had to go on to Switzerland and back through France again. Fraudulent accounts take a hell of a time to concoct," he added feelingly. "After the war I'll be one banker who won't be easily swindled, I must know every trick there is for cheating the audit." And if he made a single mistake in covering his illicit payments, then it was torture, not the fraud squad, which awaited those he used.

A girl bringing in plates heaped with prewar quantities of bacon and eggs saved her from the need to reply, and gave an excuse to keep her eyes from him. She had been hungry, but the first mouthful almost choked her; she chewed doggedly, longing to get away. Unable to bear the thought of being away, alone as never before. "You don't have to eat it," he said gently. "What is the trouble, Faye?"

You are the trouble. She was horrified by how nearly she said it aloud. She shook her head. "There's no trouble. Did you get my check?"

"When I got back last week. I haven't paid it in yet."

"Why not?"

"I wanted to be sure you had not paid me off just to be rid of inconvenient memory. Guilt before solvency perhaps."

A year ago she had felt like that exactly. "No, we're . . . we're doing well now." How very well she and Rupert were doing, she thought bitterly.

"And our bargain still stands, after the war you go back to stone carving?"

There was a long silence. "I shouldn't think so," Faye said at last. "Heaven knows why it was your condition, but I don't suppose I shall be able to keep it."

"Another of my fraudulent accounts?"

She heard the edge in his voice and flushed, hands tight on the table. "I deserved that, I suppose. I ought never to have asked you for the money. Pay it in and be done, the future is not mine to promise."

She found herself confronted by a purposeful stare which most bankers in the City of London and quite a few elsewhere would have recognized. "When people default on their contracts, I like at least to know why."

"I don't want to discuss it." She could not imagine Rupert letting her anywhere near stone or chisel once he was home again; or the slip, or Reydenham, she thought drearily, and they had troubles enough without her adding to them. She saw John ease his position cautiously and added, "Don't you think we ought to go? I will be expected home soon and you must be uncomfortable in that chair."

"It is about as hard as the Pyrenees," he agreed, "and catching me in several of the same places. But that is something only time will cure, like the delay on your bus to Dover. I'll take you home in good time; meanwhile there is still a great deal I don't understand. When you saw me first, you said you thought you had killed me. Why?"

She was disconcerted by the change of subject, being unaccustomed to the interrogator's art. "I thought you were dead."

"That was not what you said."

She twisted her fingers nervously in the strap of her bag. "I've seemed a very unlucky person to know. I thought—it seemed as if everyone I was . . . fond of had some kind of fate on them." She found herself telling him of William and Alan, of the devastating shocks of the raid on Canterbury, even of her mother's death long ago. He had seemed formidable, yet once restraint was broken she did not find it strange to be telling him things she had told no one else before.

"And your husband is overseas?" Careful, very careful now. It was only speculation, but she had not mentioned him, above all not as someone on whom her affections might bring ill fortune.

"Yes, in Morocco." Her face closed again. "Please, John, take your money and let me be."

"No more six-monthly clearances?"

"No." Her lips felt stiff. "You said once that for both our sakes it was best for us to be done with each other. I did not know then what you meant. Now I do."

She heard him grunt as unwary movement caught him, then he pulled her to her feet, hands tight on her arms. "You mean that, Faye?"

She nodded. "Yes, I mean it. It won't do us any good." She put her head on his shoulder; God, she was tired.

"I came today because it seemed absurd still to be thinking of you. How wrong I was, my sweet." He cupped her face with his hands to kiss her, then drew back sharply at what he saw. "You know this is no light thing with me, Faye. When you are free I want to marry you, and you would not have nearly fainted at the sight of me unless . . ."

"Unless you were very much more than a bank balance to me?" She smiled faintly. "I haven't understood what was wrong with me these past four months: tonight I found out. It still won't do us any good."

"Your husband does not love you," he said harshly. "He never did, nor recognized more than the face of the woman he married."

"Bait," she said in the same detached voice. "I remember. I can see now why you were so angry, but he loved me once. Perhaps still loves me in his own way." In his own way, not hers. Never anything but his way, ever.

"As chattel, foreman, and pawnbroker perhaps, everything but his wife and you know it." This fury he had carried with him a long time, understanding her burdens before she did.

"We've had our good times. It doesn't matter, none of it matters. There's no point speaking of it, since I could never marry you." She thought then of Alan and the remorse she had felt; heaven knew where John might be going next. She could feel the beat of his heart through a thickness of cloth; for him, for her, she could not walk away from him now, though in the future she intended to keep what faith she could with Rupert. "I will sleep with you if you want."

The words fell clattering at their feet, fragmented heart and spirit no longer able to unfold her love with grace.

There was a fractional pause, then he laughed and dropped his hands. "Your war work? Thank you, no." He sounded as if he was rejecting a dubious claret.

She had expected passion, possibly even anger that Rupert held her still, but was annoyed by laughter. "It was not intended as a joke."

"You know, Faye, you and I have the damnedest conversations. Over the years, I have not spent long in your company and so far I've been involved in a confidence trick, an unsecured loan, a major explosion, and now a seduction. I think we might find such a pace exhausting if we had to keep it up."

"You haven't mentioned the time I was drunk," said Faye coldly. "And there is no future for us. I should like you to take me home now."

"I want to marry you, Faye. Since your present marriage . . . is not happy, don't you think I have the right to know why you have refused me? Then I will tell you why I refused you."

She hesitated, then sat down again. She supposed she must explain, but did not know how much longer she could stay across a space of table and keep from seeking his comfort. He remained standing, leaning on the back of a chair; now every line of him was focused through the prism of her love, she saw in his face so much offered for her that she did not know how to begin. He also looked wretchedly unwell.

"Tell me," he said at last. "This at least we need to have straight between us."

"It's Christopher; no, let me finish," as she saw him about to speak. "I expect you would give him a home, be a better father to him than Rupert. But he's sole heir to the Ludlows, Rupert would never let me take him away from Reydenham, and it would not be right to do so. Four hundred years have bred Ludlows and their valley together and already it is part of Chris as it is of Rupert. For all that they think of me as an underbred shopkeeper's daughter, I have conscience enough not to take my son's inheritance from him."

"Is that what they call you?" She saw the flush of temper on his face and then it was gone. "My grandfather started out sewing buttons on gentlemen's suits and my father earned his first money giving skating lessons at Hackney ice rink. What the devil does it matter?"

"It doesn't. I don't let it worry me, although it hurt at first.

Christopher matters though, and Reydenham a little, too. He is afraid of his father, John; only love of the valley holds them together, nothing else. I would not get custody of him if I left Rupert, could not fight for it when I knew how he would suffer if he had to leave Reydenham. Yet neither can I leave him behind, alone in his unhappiness."

"He is young and would eventually accept what he did not have. Better to grow up free from fear, surely, than with your soul in pawn to a pattern of earth and trees."

She shook her head. "If he was old enough to ask, it is a price he would pay willingly. You don't understand about Reydenham and the Ludlows."

"Then let me tell you why I will not take you except with intent to make you my wife, and see if you understand me any better. Any man in his senses would want you, it is madness to be talking like this across a yard of floor. But in that kind of relationship there is never time for anything except bodily love; you are that to me but so much more besides, which we could not hope to find in snatched meetings and deceit. And even that would soon be soured since I love you too well to be able to share or hide it; tonight you did not want to be seen with me in Canterbury, and I couldn't live like that. I don't enjoy falsifying accounts even in a good cause, I couldn't exist in a permanent fraud. Without the right to come when you were in trouble, perhaps father a child I must say was not mine, having to watch you split apart by strain I could not ease. You want me now, God knows I want you too, but how will you feel tomorrow, alone in your husband's house?"

She put her face in her hands. "Easier. Surely I would be healed by loving you, even if it is to be only once."

"My sweet love, don't you know already that what is done once between us is done for always? We love too much for anything else, or would if the chance was ours. I want it done for always, but you—"

"I do too, but I can't. John, I can't, why won't you understand?"

He shifted suddenly, the desperate appeal in her voice cutting at control, roughening difficult words. "A wife to your husband, and just once, or twice perhaps, with me, soft memory locked away. It isn't like that, or would not be with us. This I know, and you do not. Look at me, Faye."

She lifted her head from her hands and looked, at exhausted face and lover's mouth; at hands he would not take from the chair in case they both were lost, at curved bones stripped down to view by strain. She had not thought of it before, but of course he was a man well used to women. How else had he understood her so well if it was not by the measure of others? She was silent, numb with jealousy.

He nodded when he saw she had grasped what he could not say. "You have known one man only, and him you do not love although you may think that once you did. So I must choose for you because you can only discover the burden of once or twice between us by feeling its great weight, and you have little strength left for bearing heavier burdens. You can live with your husband, loving me. You would be destroyed by the touch of his body which was not mine, when I lay between you every night, my lips were his. You would endure, God knows you have endurance enough, but one night you would reach the end of it, and then your mind would tear and you would wake screaming in the dark." His hands were shaking, the chair could not stop them. "This at least I can spare you. We have to learn something from our lives."

She covered her face, fingers trying to block out his voice. "I have learned something too. I cannot cheat my son of what is rightfully his, nor can I leave him to grow up alone, harassed by a father who shows him very little understanding." She was whispering, but each word was shaped as if carved in stone.

A clock was ticking on the mantelpiece, the fire snapping below, from two people who grasped the extent of their bondage came not even a drawn breath. He moved at last, and came, and held her hands against his cheek. "My love, for the moment we lose. But in the losing you healed the hurt you gave. You threw your body at me as if it was a bone to keep the dog from yapping."

Her fingers curled tight on his. The kiss for gain, the urgent snatch at wants because she could have so little, vanished forever. She stood, and smiled, and kissed him, tears slipping on her cheeks. "And you picked it up and gave me myself again. It is a while since others set value on what I gave; I had forgotten how it felt."

"Bankers," he tried for lightness, finding her tears difficult to bear. "They're devils on value." And time, for a short while passed them by.

Until it knocked, insistent, telling him it was late, and he drove her home.

There was a barrier outside the town. "I forgot." Faye spoke for the first time since they had left their brief haven. "The town's restricted, you can't come any further. I'll walk from here." She fumbled for her pass.

"You still have the strangest ideas about me if you think I would throw you into the road to walk home." He wound down the window for the sentry, taking her pass and adding papers of his own. "I know better than to come to a place like Dover without whatever passes I need."

The spell was broken then, which had kept her silent, staring through the windscreen, mind shuttered. She twisted in her seat and watched her love, who would soon be gone. "Once more, John. When the war ends, let me know you have survived. Then —I would hate it if you forgot me, but put me aside. I should like to think of you happy."

She saw the long mouth twitch, shadow deepen on his face. "If it had not been for the kind of work I have been doing, I daresay I should have married again. Now—now, I think I shall love you always." He stopped the car and kissed her, once. "It is not a matter for regret, my dear, anything else being altogether beyond my power." He held her an instant, released her. "How do you usually go home from here?"

"My . . . my bicycle. I left it at the bus garage."

"You cycle up to Reydenham on a night like this?" he demanded.

She laughed shakily. "I must look horribly blotchy. Rain will turn me into my usual drowned rat."

She gave him directions for the bus garage, but once there he insisted on loading her bicycle across the boot while she hovered, not daring to protest that in Dover of all places she could not afford to be seen with him, so overwhelmingly happy at having five minutes more together that she could not think of protest.

He levered himself back into the car, swearing at his ribs,

temper chafed raw by the prospect of having to leave her to cycle the last mile to Reydenham. He felt very far from accepting defeat, being a man who normally saw difficulties in terms of eliminating them; before, he had been riled by his own stupidity in loving a woman who thought only fleetingly of him, now he was infuriated by his helplessness. He loved her more for her resolve, had surely always loved her for her valiant spirit: argument stillborn when it would achieve nothing but to distress her further, yet at that moment he was swept by rage, not love.

Then Faye said something; he did not catch her words, but heard instead the placating note in her voice. She had lived so long with those who slaked their anger at her expense.

"My gallant love," he said. "Remember, if things change—"

"No. You must not feel bound, they will not change." She was desolate, yet certain in her mind.

He pulled to the side of the road where the slope of the valley began, rain hammering, blackness complete. On such a night he had come this way before, half running in fury from demons which told him this woman could never be his. They sat a moment, knowing it was over, holding the seconds as they scampered past. "Something I thought of for no reason, sitting under a French hedge one night," he said suddenly. "That boat of yours you lost, did you ever claim for her?"

"Claim?" She stared at him, bewildered.

"War loss. You are entitled to payment, even if you won't get a fraction of what she cost. Did you register the sinking at the time?"

She nodded. "A man was killed; once everyone caught their breath, there was quite a lot of paperwork." She thought of Alf and the sad dignity of his wife. It made some things easier to bear.

"Go to the Town Hall and ask for the forms you need. It will give you a little surplus for the future." His mouth tightened. "God, money again. It is all I can give you, my love. It seems to be all I can ever give." He jerked open the door.

She heard him stumble and scrambled out hastily, he was not fit to heave bicycles about and stand soaking in a gale. "John, please go now, and don't look back." She kissed him swiftly, the only way she could bear. "For my sake as well as yours, don't ever look back." She tore the bicycle from his hold and pedaled into the dark.

He stood a long time in rain and wind, and did not notice it at all.

Chapter Twenty-four

Faye began to carve stone again.

The shaping hands and seeing eye had been stilled so long, struck aside by an unquiet mind and crowding cares. Yet now it seemed nothing could stop her, although her pressures had not eased at all. An inner stillness had returned even in the midst of such unhappiness that sometimes when morning came after a wakeful night, she did not know how to bear another day. Then she would remember stone waiting, a purpose regained when all else was lost.

If she lacked time, then she carved at night, by a single bulb in the generator shed, shadows adding excitement to her work. She had her punches and chisels still, and spent a week sharpening and cleaning them of rust; Gabriel made her a set of mallets and fallen stone copings were material enough. They split easily and resisted detail: it did not matter. Flow and rhythm came again, the seeking mind and senses tuned to shapes as yet unseen.

Sometimes she carved the whole night long, completely engrossed, astonished in the dawn by what had grown under her hands. In Canterbury she had been confined by marching pillars and precise geometry of rib and vault, now it was her own skills flowering, pouring images out of the years of turmoil which had passed. There was Alf sliding from stone smoothed so it looked like engine grease; Henry, all jutting chin and defiant bones; Cook with sagging jowls and globular eyes, indignant at serving corned beef in place of partridge.

She carved Christopher in streaked slashes so the face seemed in motion, while rooted deep in stone. "It doesn't look like me," he said, disappointed, when she yielded to his entreaties and showed him the half-finished block which was himself. "I'm not lines like that."

"It's how I see you, darling," explained Faye. "Stone is still and you are not, stone is old and you are young, with your future still to seek. It is more the long life of Reydenham than you."

But he was disappointed and wandered off to the comfort of his pony; as she said, he was seldom still. She looked at the stone again; it was her own and showed things others could not see. She had set this Christopher in a frame of curled foliage and sloped hill shapes: her son entering in on his inheritance. Only in one respect was Christopher's criticism justified; the mouth was wrong. She smiled and touched it gently, she had given this eager boy John's mouth, love flowing into stone, into the carving she dared not make and gave instead to Reydenham's heir.

She could not carve Rupert either, nor show Mrs. Ludlow the narrow, grudging rib of stone which grew her disappoving stare. Instead, one day she wandered into the church, dilapidated and sharing a parson with two others nearby. It was crudely built and must have had little grace even when new six hundred years before: the windows deep-set, pillars badly proportioned and undecorated. At this time of day a single shaft of light, blurred with dust and cobwebs, lit a blank stone corner beyond the Ludlow pew. She examined it with rising excitement, then went to see the vicar.

Each sunny afternoon after that saw her grudging every moment she could not spend in the church. The days were drawing into another autumn, to harvest and fruit picking and preserving and endless sawing of logs for winter. The expanded slip was busier than ever, most of her time was still spent there, laboring over steam, arguing quantities with the Navy, enduring endless frustrating delays over finding the equipment they needed. Shelling was intensifying too; the summer had been quiet except for two appalling days in June when one shell had killed and injured nearly fifty people and another exploded inside the post office, destroying the switchboards and killing the operators. Now, shells began coming over at any time of day or night, warnings in force for hours with nothing happening, then an unexpected salvo arriving after the all clear. The people of Dover began to hate their own guns beyond the Castle—nicknamed Winnie and Pooh—for when all seemed quiet they often opened fire and within minutes the Germans would reply, Dover town and not the guns receiving most of it. Above the torn streets the Castle was still intact, the harbor rubble-strewn but seldom badly hit. There was a shelter near the slip but shell warnings were so uncertain it was impossible to stay there until danger had passed; for it never truly passed and work could not be interrupted for days on end.

Yet in spite of it all, there was the occasional hour when she could start on the slab in the church, and with her newfound urgency of line stone sprang to life under her hands. She intended no monument, but instead a memory of William in the valley where he belonged. She had nothing planned and there was no face or form of William, only laughing lines and a splendid gull with its wings protectively curved over ships in sea below; and down in one corner a rabbit, eye closed and whiskers slanting with wicked joy.

Christopher came often to look and loved the rabbit, so when the door clicked she did not turn, calling, "Come and look! It's nearly finished!"

"It's strange," said a voice she did not recognize. "And I reckon Parson won't like rabbits in his church."

Faye looked round in surprise and saw a young woman, heavily made up, artificially bright hair lit by the sun. "Hullo. I thought it was my son, he at least likes rabbits in church."

The girl shrugged. "I thought I'd come and have a look, most of the valley thinking you crazy-like to be chipping stone all day."

"Just a minute," said Faye slowly. "It's Susan, isn't it? I remember you now." Her maid, how strange even the idea of a lady's maid seemed now. The absorption of stone was fading and she stood, brushing dust from her clothes, trying not to resent the insolence of the girl's tone. So much had changed.

"That's right. My Len's a prisoner in Italy, so Pa told me I'd best come home. The valley," she added contemptuously. "Tattling old busybodies up the back end of nowhere. Give me London, any day."

Faye said nothing, remembering Dickson had told her mournfully of Susan's baby born over a year after Len's departure. She began to gather up her tools, wishing the girl would go.

Susan showed no inclination to go, perching on the side of a pew and lighting a cigarette. "You have any news of Mr. Ludlow these days?"

"Of course," said Faye coldly. "He hopes to be back early next year." Everyone knew that sometime next year the invasion of France would be launched, and Rupert expected his headquarters to be one of those brought back to Britain as part of the massive transfer of troops now taking place.

"Nice for him. My Len now, it'll be a while before he's home, but I reckon they've both of 'em got a surprise coming. Len is quiet angry, not violent at all; what about yours?"

Faye's first reaction was disbelief, then she looked at the girl's taunting face and felt her stomach knot.

"Can't think of nothing to say? You'll have to do better than that once your man's back."

Faye finished bundling her tools together. "I don't know what you think such rudeness will gain you, Susan. You resented losing your job, I understand, but—"

She flicked ash into the aisle. "I'm not worried about no job, London's the place for me. I got temporary work as barmaid at the Hop Pocket for the moment."

"Well, I hope you don't flick ash all over the place there!" snapped Faye. "You'd best leave the door open when you leave."

"Over towards Canterbury," said Susan softly, unmoved. "Where I saw you and your fancy friend shut up together very snug in the parlor."

Faye smiled involuntarily, thinking of John. She ought to be alarmed; she was alarmed, stomach double-knotted now, yet her lips curved in remembrance of his love. "What is it you want of me?" she said levelly.

Susan looked disconcerted for a moment, then laughed. "Nothing, now. I reckon you haven't got much, even if I asked for it. I'm just warning you, as it were, so you've plenty of time to think about it before Mr. Ludlow comes home. Then I expect there'll be a few things I'll be needing to keep quiet."

"Then you're a fool. You've lived up at the manor, you know well enough there's no money to spare, even if I was willing to pay you, which I'm not."

"We'll see, won't we? You'd best ask your pal to pay up if you can't."

"He's overseas, and I'm not expecting to see him again," said Faye shortly. She could feel her hand tight on the burnished sharpness of her chisels: no circumstance or threat could induce her to ask John for money again. "Run where you will with your tales, there's nothing of which I am ashamed."

Susan stood and ground out her cigarette on the floor. "Ah,

well, we'll see, won't we? You may not be ashamed—" A smile flashed out suddenly. "I'm not ashamed of what I done either, with Len away two years. That doesn't alter the fact that neither of us wants to do too much explaining. With a kid in the cradle, I've not much choice and money might help. You have." She sauntered off down the aisle, enjoying power as much as the prospect of money. She paused at the door. "Shall I tell you something? For all he seemed such a gentleman, I always thought Mr. Ludlow had a nasty, spiteful temper not too deep down. I'll do better with Len than you will with him."

Faye picked up the cigarette end, swept dust, laid her hand once on fresh-carved stone. Thank God she had finished the grace she gave for William's life, before this dirt could touch it.

She let herself out into sun pouring light on towering storm clouds: winter was nearly here again, this endless war already run as long as the earlier one which had shadowed her childhood with its horrors. And still it was far from won.

Christopher was playing football in the road with two boys from Ridge Farm, and her heart tightened as the meaning of Susan's threat sank deeper. The little she could pay would only serve to excite greed, and while her new serenity might enable her to bring peace to her relationship with Rupert, she knew she could not long withstand exposure of her love for John. She could hide it, there was no way for her to endure it mocked and trampled.

Certainly Susan had only the evidence of her eyes, but Rupert's suspicions were so easily aroused he would believe anything she chose to say. Would want to believe, when Faye could not deny the fact of her love. Then he would heap such humiliation on her that staying would become a purgatory, and going—her thought stopped short. Dear God, how gladly she would go. But where before she had thought it wrong to take Christopher from Reydenham, it still remained a last resort; now Susan's word would make hopeless any attempt to gain custody of him. Whatever the law said, and it would not favor her, judges were male and human. If she could not deny John, then no court would believe that his scruple had kept them apart, supposing she could bear to drag him to the witness box for such a purpose. Even she only partly believed in the reasons he had given; although she did not doubt his fear and care for her, there was more to it than that, some

deep reluctance in him she could not comprehend. She still fret-
ted to remember each word he had spoken, looking for something
she had missed; the time they met in London too, he had held
himself from her then as well. A judge would not search for
reasons but simply condemn a desk-bound civilian and a faithless
wife who had betrayed her husband, fighting for his country overseas. Wars were merciless affairs, not least to wives who waited
cold and bleak at home.

She purged her fury that night with a savage travesty of Susan,
gouged deep into stone she chose because it was already weath-
ered and ugly. She took it into the yard in the early light and felt
a pang of satisfaction as she looked at it: so medicine men felt
with clay images of their enemies ready to roast on the fire. She
moved her hands apart and let it fall, kicking the splinters aside,
and suddenly she laughed.

"What a fool I am," she said aloud, and stretched, aware of
weariness she had not felt all night. Crazy-like, the valley thought
her; well, she would not satisfy them in that, either. There was
nothing to be done but wait; when the time came she would
think of a way to keep Susan quiet. There is always a way if only
you look hard enough; she thought of John again, there was no
way for them. There might not be for this.

Christmas 1943. The last of the war, people said, looking sideways to see if they were believed. Rations were shorter than ever, a
handful of dried fruit the only Christmas extra and an orange for
the children. At Reydenham they did better than most, with a
few eggs set aside from chickens they kept when others had one a
month, the occasional cut of pork though it meant they had no
regular bacon ration in exchange for pig food. For the rest, it was
a case of standing in endless queues, a tedious choice between
tinned apricots this week or sardines next; meals made up of frozen cod hacked from yard-square blocks, vegetable pies and
whale meat, which was marvelously lean but tasted of fish manure. Salt instead of sugar on stewed fruit to neutralize the acid.

There was enough; after four years it was the endless contriving,
the sheer fatigue of getting about without petrol or spares or reliable public services which unraveled resolve and splintered
tempers. Shops began to show sour pleasure in poor service; when
everyone was short, one of the few satisfactions left was seeing
others lacking more. Everybody had been crowded together for so

long, in trains and buses, with evacuees in spare rooms, in over-worked factories, and foul-smelling shelters: no holidays for four years, no changes in routine except those brought by disaster, no color, no lights on the darkest nights. Where before any extra had been a matter for common rejoicing, now many clutched it to themselves and felt resentful if they were called selfish. What had flowered as unity and comradeship was fruiting into bitter claustrophobia.

Each Sunday night, before the news, the BBC played the national anthems of all the allies: the French and Belgian brisk, most of the rest sounding depressingly defeated. It was the only time when Faye felt any sense of the Grand Alliance building for the kill, touched something of the world which stood at Dover's back. London might be spilling over with Poles and New Zealanders and Americans, East Anglia be full of Flying Fortresses and Surrey with Canadians, but in Dover it was a completely British affair still, the enemy out of sight only when their twenty-mile front line was blotted out by storms or fog. And even then, shells came at any time. There was a Norwegian MTB, some Frenchmen in Royal Navy uniform; for the rest it was Britain alone, as if it was still 1940. Welch Fusiliers dug the dead out of the shelled GPO, Northumbrians manned the town defenses, Manx boats had been and gone, Scots trawlers blew up terrifyingly often, sweeping mines right up to the harbor entrance. Gloucesters, Devons, East Sussex, Lancastrians: the British regiments came and went, but invasion was almost launched before the first Canadians appeared in East Kent, and Dover remained an intensely private place.

Toward the end of January 1944, Faye was working in the slip office when a naval officer came up the ladder, clutching a roll of plans. "Mrs. Ludlow?"

Faye nodded. "It's a rotten ladder with your hands full."

He laughed. "Better than a destroyer in a gale. How many men have you working here now?"

"Fourteen. But they're all over fifty and only half are skilled, now we've nearly doubled in size. You're not thinking of taking over at this stage, are you?" She had fought hard against a navy take-over, never complaining over unreasonable deadlines, attempting always to have work finished before schedule, and in the end the whole matter had been shelved.

"Far from it." He unrolled his plans. "We want you to turn over your production to these things."

Faye stared at the plans in astonishment. "What on earth are they?"

"I'm afraid I can't tell you. The whole dock area is being sealed off and only those with essential work will be allowed through. That means the Railway Packet Yard and you so far as civilians are concerned, so you'll have to maintain absolute secrecy about what you're making."

"I couldn't do anything else. They look like farm gates to me." She scaled off dimensions: sections and sections of braced planks knocked into rectangles. "They'll fall apart if you sneeze on them."

"Then you definitely mustn't catch cold, Mrs. Ludlow. How many could you make each week?"

"If I can persuade Henry to degrade his skill by making such things at all, about—" She paused. She had learned a great deal about boatbuilding in three years, but had no idea how to estimate for such extraordinary objects. "Two hundred, perhaps a few more."

"I'd like you to aim at doubling that, painted one coat of black or brown paint. We'll get both these MTBs towed out of here by the end of the week; the first timber will be arriving tomorrow. I'll send men to put camouflage nets over it, we don't want the Jerries to see what we're doing."

"A row of Nazis sitting on the Prince of Wales pier couldn't make sense of this lot," said Faye frankly.

"You'd be surprised. They'd know what it isn't, at any rate."

"Look like half-finished coffins to me," said Henry disgustedly when she showed him the plans. "D'you mean we've got to botch up planks for weeks on end?"

They would know what it isn't, the officer had said. "They must be foxing the Germans into thinking we're building something here," said Faye slowly. "I don't suppose we'll have to wait long to find out what."

They did not. The labor was intensely monotonous and very hard, they all hated it and the frequency of flu and lumbago keeping men from work rose alarmingly. Then, one bright February morning as she coasted down the Western Heights, Faye saw the change in the harbor. Moored side by side was a long rank of what looked like landing craft.

The next night another twenty appeared, and more each night after that, until the Admiralty harbor was crowded with dummies made from canvas stretched over the scantlings they and the Packet Yard were making. From a distance they looked good, and the men worked cheerfully again, although indignant now it was clear that the invasion would not be coming through Dover, since so much effort was being put into making it seem as if it would. The frames they made were covered with canvas in what had once been public gardens at the other end of the harbor, and launched at night. Concrete ramps were being built and lines painted everywhere to give the impression of embarkation points.

"Must fair puzzle old Jerry where them craft is coming from," remarked Henry. "Every day the Channel's clear, then in the night we scramble in twenty or thirty boats. 'E must think we've got a miracle tugboat service."

With the spring, depression was cast off. Everyone was frantically busy, and as all the conscription lists were double-checked, there was scarcely a young face to be seen out of uniform. Underage boys were drafted for salvage collections and concrete mixing, camouflage netting hung in the drill hall and housewives with the odd hour to spare were urged to make up knotting groups—a hated job, since the old canvas used for camouflage was full of dust.

Reydenham now had three times as much plowland as before the war, double the sheep, four times the pigs and poultry, and to do the work there were women and children and only two men under forty in the whole valley. One by one the young men and girls came home on leave before "the balloon went up," as everyone said. Will Pakenham from Ridge Farm, who was in the Buffs, the parson's two boys in the Guards' Armoured Division, Nanny's engineer nephew, various girls Faye did not recognize and who talked even more incomprehensible slang than the boys.

Rupert.

Chapter Twenty-five

He was splendidly bronzed and his health made everyone else look pallid. Although over forty now, he had squared and filled out with regular work and plenty of leisure under the African sun: he had been gone over a year and enjoyed every moment of it, his only regret that he had come no nearer than twenty miles from the firing line.

"A couple of ships were torpedoed in the convoy going out, though," he added, "and we were strafed a few times on the ground."

To Faye, this hankering to be under fire was incomprehensible. She loathed the noise and dust of shelling, the lurch of fear worse, not better, for the years she had endured it. Bombs were bad enough but at least raids had a beginning and an end, with luck a warning, even if the Germans were only three minutes' flying time away: shells she hated with deadly intensity and it made little difference whether they were British or German. "Don't let's think about it. You're still in one piece, and so am I; in the time we have, let's be ourselves and forget the war." She held out her hand to him, and tilted her face to be kissed, quite naturally. She had set her course and was giving Rupert what was his: she had thought it would be overwhelmingly difficult and found it quite easy. Because she loved intensely, she had more of herself to give, not less; to Christopher, for whose sake she had set aside her wants, and now to Rupert. If the driving force of her love lay elsewhere, then that was her affair and no duplicity, it was not diminished by what others took.

Only, she could not sleep, and stone lay dead in her hands again.

Rupert had no pass to enter Dover, and now D day was close, the town was completely barricaded off. No matter what his protests, Faye had to go down to the slip each day, so his week's leave had a structure which hid from her how much of an interlude it was. He complained each morning when she went, yet when she returned the pleasure of his day made him forget to be annoyed by her absence, and before supper she tried to plan something they could do together, something which Christopher did well. When she was away he always seemed to have failed to polish the car properly, or upset Rupert's fishing basket, or stuttered over a poem his grandmother set him to learn.

"He ought to be at school. You'd better see to it in time for the summer term," remarked Rupert as they returned from a picnic one evening. "You'll enjoy that, brat. It must be lonely for you in the valley." After a year away his son seemed more of a stranger than ever. He did not know what to talk to him about, except to correct bad habits which had developed in his absence. Subconsciously, he believed that Ludlows ought to excel in everything and his own failures made no difference to this feeling: the effort of molding Chris was infinitely worthwhile, but it was a burden he needed to share. It was unfair if his son came to dislike him simply because he was forced to cram a year's discipline into a week.

"School?" Faye nodded. "You'd like to go, wouldn't you, Chris? It's just that there aren't any close enough. They've opened again in Dover, but I certainly don't think the town is safe for children. I feel guilty at having kept him whenever we get shells in the valley."

Rupert shrugged. "It's quiet enough. Of course he's safe here."

"You wouldn't say so if you had been here last month!" It was exasperating the way the Germans never shelled Dover when Rupert was home. "Half a dozen shells went into the woods and it was really bad in Dover again. I wish our guns would leave the Germans alone, they were quiet enough until we started firing."

"You can't win a war by not firing at the enemy."

"You can't win a war by shooting fifty shells into Boulogne beach. All you do is get half a dozen Frenchmen and then some of us killed. They never hit each other's guns, more's the pity."

"If you talk like that in front of Christopher, then the sooner he goes to school, the better. He's been pampered in women's skirts long enough."

"He's very far from pampered. He helped with the lambing this spring and the threshing, too, and that's a horrible job."

"All grains in your face." Christopher screwed up his eyes. "I sticked at it though, didn't I, Mummy?"

"You certainly did, darling. And at riddling the potatoes."

"I'm never going to be a farmer." Christopher turned confidentially to Rupert. "It's wet and early morning, I like snug and by the fire times. But Mummy says it's my war work."

"School," said Rupert. "You need a bit more wet and early morning. I remember at my prep school, Matron made sure we washed in cold water every day of the year."

"Chris, run and see if the church is open, will you? I want to show Daddy the panel I carved for Uncle William." When he had gone, she turned to Rupert. "You aren't thinking of sending him to boarding school at six years old?"

"Do him good. If there is nothing suitable near here, he'll have to go away."

"I'll advertise and see if I can find him a tutor or something for a few months. Once we've invaded, the shelling will be over and he can go into Dover."

"No, Faye. I'm right in this. He needs to settle and be with boys his own age."

"I know," said Faye unhappily. "Only—"

"Only, nothing. The summer term must start next week. I'll ring round a few places tonight."

"Next week! He isn't six yet!"

"You're just being silly, Faye. He is six in three weeks' time, and plenty of children leave their parents for years at that age, if they're serving in India or somewhere. You were going to send him to Yorkshire far younger than this."

"To save his life, when I thought invasion was coming. This is different."

"I'm not arguing, I'm right and that's all there is to it. You run just about everything else in this valley, you're not running me."

She was silent. He was quite possibly right, it was the manner of his rightness which flaked at her guard, the feeling that he wanted his son away from her thoughts and comfort.

Christopher came scampering over the field, shouting that the church was open. "You'll like the rabbit, Daddy," he added, dragging at his hand. "And the gull's wings are huge and curled, like that." He held his arms wide, wrists limp, his body poised for flight. He was an unconsciously graceful boy, forgetful and often dreaming, and became clumsy with anxiety. Yet when his mind was absorbed elsewhere, he moved like a racehorse.

"For God's sake, you look like a ballet dancer." Rupert snatched away as if his son had touched him with lust.

Christopher scowled, kicking at tufts of grass. "I like ballet dancers."

Faye heard her laugh rattle inside her head. "What a whopper! Perhaps one day you will, but I'll give you a double sweet ration if you can tell Daddy what they are now."

Christopher rubbed his hands thoughtfully on the seat of his shorts, weighing the advantages of sweets against his father's certain fury if he was fortunate enough to pretend accurately to knowledge of these mysterious creatures he mustn't like. "No," he said regretfully at last. "One day I'll like them, though."

"You'll be sorry if you do," snapped Rupert.

"I might be sorry after I've liked them," pointed out Christopher. "I can't be sorry until I have."

Faye laughed involuntarily, but Rupert had not previously encountered his son's brand of logic, and liked it no better than the awkwardness he had condemned before. He cast them both a look of acute dislike and strode across the field to the church, to stand unspeaking before Faye's panel.

Christopher put his fingers on the rabbit, as he always did. "It's nice, isn't it, Daddy?"

"I'm no judge," said Rupert shortly. "But it is easy enough to see where your strange notions come from. Why not a plaque with his name and date, for God's sake?"

"I wanted it how William was, all laughter and light. He would have liked it." Faye looked at the rabbit, and smiled. She had not expected Rupert to like it, and found she did not care about his disapproval, only for Christopher's disappointment. It was the best thing she had done and nothing he said could change it.

Only, walking home in silence, Christopher vanished into the woods as he had done before to avoid his father, and she could not escape the bitter knowledge that they had lasted a mere five days in some kind of concord. Two days of Rupert's leave to go, and already she felt sucked dry, exhausted enough for her heart to pound as if she had been running. However would she last when he was home for good?

She had seen no more of Susan since their encounter in the church; now she was in the lane waiting for them as if by chance.

Rupert recognized her at once and inquired after Len in prison camp; he was good with the valley people and seldom forgot a face.

"I haven't heard from him in a while, since them Italians gave in. His dad thinks he's probably escaped, or else been sent to Germany. We can't all be as lucky as Mrs. Ludlow and have our husbands home before this dratted war ends." Her eyes rested on Faye with derisive malice.

Rupert laughed. "The good air of Reydenham must be a welcome change for you after London, anyway. Are you in one of the services now?"

"I've got a child to care for, Mr. Ludlow. I help out at a pub in the evenings, and like it well enough. You'd be surprised at some of the goings-on in wartime, wouldn't he, Mrs. Ludlow?"

"You may be right," said Faye carefully. "But I expect it is often a case of the onlooker seeing what she wants to see."

Susan put her hands in her pockets and jingled some loose coins there. "Oh, I don't know, there's not much wrong with my eyes. But so long as folks pays for their pleasures, that's all right with me. Nice to see you about again, Mr. Ludlow." She sauntered off, humming under her breath.

"Poor old Dickson," remarked Rupert. "The war has certainly given him a tart for a daughter. Nice figure, though."

Faye felt cold panic as he looked after Susan appreciatively. "She's a born troublemaker."

He laughed, "That sort always are, but the world would be a dull place without them."

The rest of his leave passed well enough, or she thought it did; afterwards she could remember little except the crawling length of nights spent staring at the ceiling, and sunlit days telescoped by fatigue. When he had gone, she slept as though stunned.

Within days Christopher went too, to a boarding school so deeply hidden in the flat Thanet plain behind Canterbury that it was one of the few not evacuated. Cook and Nanny and Faye had to pool every clothing coupon they possessed to equip him with all the gray flannel and different-colored socks still thought necessary for a small boy going to school, the last-minute rush to get him ready throttling regrets.

Christopher himself shifted between moods of intense anticipation and equally intense fear. He had known so few variations in his life that a complete uprooting in a matter of days assumed the proportions of heaven and hell. And when he was gone, Faye spent more and more time at the slip as an escape from the silences of Reydenham and also, as it prospered, because she was gripped by the sheer excitement of her achievement there.

Planks were still being knocked to shape, but she had her least skilled men working on them outside under nets so MTBs could be hauled up the slip again. Patrols were dangerous in the short summer nights and she did not intend to miss her share of costly patching. There were also mysterious modifications to be carried out on some of the boats, for special tasks they would do when invasion came; no one would have thought of giving the Ludlow yard such work, but she was searching for it now and wellknown enough to wheedle her way into Wellington Dock and look for possibilities herself. The slip was hers, and soon she would have to give it up. Another year perhaps and Rupert would be home for good; even if he allowed it, they would quarrel in a day if they attempted to work together.

Knowing her time was nearly done, she found the slip becoming strangely precious to her, although she never dealt lightly with anything she undertook. She had taken it over in dilapidation and bankruptcy and brought it to thriving success; no matter by what expedients or the special circumstances of war, this she had done and nothing could take it from her. And when peace came, with any luck the Navy would lose interest and be satisfied by a token payment for the extension and all the repairs and equipment she had coaxed from the engineers at Wellington Dock; then the slip could become a proper designing yard and its profits secure Reydenham's future, too. She was already scheming how to make the transition and thought she would not mind handing over to Rupert once everything was ready-packaged for success, with perils left behind.

There would be a symmetrical completeness about it which pleased her, and when it was done, she could start carving again.

May passed in a series of cloudless days and ill-spelled letters from Christopher, conveying little beyond formal information that he was well. Abruptly, work at the slip ended. The MTBs left, Wellington Dock lay silent and deserted. The harbor was packed with fragile, waterlogged dummy landing craft, time standing still as Dover became a backwater to events shaping elsewhere. Even the Germans seemed to lose interest, as if they were not deceived, and in the whole month there were only two days' shelling.

Faye set Henry to working out their requirements when they would design and build again instead of repair, the rest of the men to clearing rubbish, but there was little for her to do. Instead, she wandered through the town, truly looking at it for the first time in years. It was not destroyed, but greatly changed. There was only false traffic, to the harbor and back again to give the impression of activity; the roads were roughly patched, the shopfronts boarded. People went about their business, long queues stretching onto the pavement and tangling with sailors strolling with their girls, but there was an air of dejection which was new. Some ruins had lain uncleared for years, repairs were shoddy, twisted metal heavy with rust; above all, Dover was not used to being left aside, a decoy duck to other people's endeavors. It was stripped of men and troops and weapons, its ships made of laths, its guns out of date. All the world might look to the Channel narrows for the great invasion, Dover knew better; the blow would fall elsewhere. Their part was done.

Faye went back to Reydenham thankfully, depressed by the atmosphere of the town, when under the heaviest bombardment there had been jaunty defiance, a shared pride in the midst of terror. She listened each night to the news, everyone putting forward ideas of where the Allies would strike while she sat silent, thoughts elsewhere. The announcer sometimes spoke of partisans, quislings, or maquis resistance, and each time her brain squeezed tight with fear, not only for John's life but for the strain she had sensed in him so long as other men's lives hung on his contriving.

In June, the weather changed, a blustering Channel gale rattling creeper and ripping tiles off barn roofs. Shells fell again, jarring windows, then one night there was the drone of aircraft overhead, hour after hour, from dusk to dawn: the RAF flying precisely back and forth across the straits, dropping tinfoil which would look on enemy radar like landing craft approaching France. She could not believe it had started when she dressed in a bleak and ugly dawn, the valley blotted out, clouds driving overhead. Surely there had never been a more unpropitious day for a great seaborne invasion. There was no announcement either, but people stood in fields and roads, heads cocked and listening, hearing far downwind the distant booming rumble of guns.

By midmorning, it was official. The invasion was fairly launched, the last phase begun at last. It was Gabriel who told her of the convoy; he seldom moved from his garden, yet little happened within a ten-mile radius he did not know, the fact that this time the ten miles was out to sea making no difference. Faye climbed alone to the Western Heights three miles beyond the valley, and found crowds of people there, standing and gazing at a symbol of victory Dover understood. For the first time since Dunkirk the straits were full of shipping, column after column of ships steaming at speed, crammed with troops and guns, fussed over by escorts, a protective cover of aircraft overhead. Occasionally a shell spout rose, lazily glinting in clearing murk, one ship was hit and swerved out of line; the rest passed untouched, and passed and passed.

Hardly anyone spoke, but Faye was not the only one who felt tightness in her throat. After four long years, the Straits of Dover were back in business.

Chapter Twenty-six

It was Gabriel, also, who told her of the strange happenings in Romney Marsh. "A fly beetle, Mrs. Rupert, crashed with bangers in its stummick."

"An aircraft? They often explode when they're shot down." They had had enough crippled machines crashing around Dover for her to feel surprise that he bothered to tell her; there was the German pilot buried in Reydenham churchyard, and a still-blackened patch above Ridge Farm where a Spitfire had struck with a full load of fuel and ammunition on board.

"Different," he insisted. "As I 'eard, 'e were whistling and stuttering not like any aeryplane at all, an' blew up with a rare ole bang."

It was the first they heard of the pilotless V-1, their yattering engines soon a constant accompaniment overhead, bloated bodies stuffed with explosive. Not many fell around Dover, being aimed for London, but there were few times in the day when the foul objects were not there, hammering in knowledge that nothing could stop their lethal loads exploding. Sound also built up fiercely again. Within days, more guns began to arrive, convoys and defenses were pulled out and sent to the coast. There was no point shooting down V-1s if they crashed on houses anyway, the more open country of Kent and Sussex the inevitable alternative. So to the bugs overhead was added the massive roar of concentrated artillery, the crackling scream of fighters diving from height to obtain the necessary speed to shoot such craft down. If Dover largely escaped, Kent did not: of three thousand V-1s sent over England in two months, over half fell in the county.

London, too. Rupert was safe enough at a signals headquarters in Wiltshire, Christopher delighted to come home from the quietness of Thanet to spot doodlebugs in his holidays at Reydenham, but John . . . The news reader never gave precise locations to help the Germans with their sighting, but it was plain that central London was badly hit, and tight on the tail of the V-1s came the V-2s, rockets no one saw which blasted a quarter of a mile flat without a second of warning.

Each night Faye listened to the news with dread sunk into bone and nerve, hand scarcely held from the telephone. It would not help, with each day the same. If he lived now, by ringing she would need even more to ring again tomorrow. She lay sleepless through the endless nights and came to understand something of what he had meant, when he said there was no once or twice between them, only always: with the hope of always lost, then whatever they took made love harder to bear, not easier.

Her temper shortened with exhaustion and strain. Sometimes she caught Christopher looking at her with the same apprehension he showed to his father, and tried to grip her sliding will, to switch her mind and bring some happiness to his holidays, but it was so hard she often failed.

On a fine day toward the end of August, she took him for an all-day hike along the cliff edge. It was like a voyage of discovery for them both: Dover had been de-restricted only the day before, the cliff paths reopened even if surrounded by wire and minefields it would take years to clear. It was the first real sign that peace at last was coming close; British troops were driving almost unopposed into Belgium after heavy fighting in Normandy, the Americans spilling south and eastward over France. The V-1s were thinning at last as their launching ramps were overrun, the longer-range V-2s taking their place.

They had brought sandwiches and apples, which were plentiful but sour this year with doodlebugs exploding in Kent orchards and harvesting the whole crop a month early, and sat to enjoy them in a hollow looking out over the sea.

"Can we go over there one day?" asked Christopher presently, waving his hand at Calais and Boulogne, surf crumbling at the foot of Cap Gris-Nez, clearly in sight on this perfect day. "Daddy told me he often used to go across in fishing boats."

"Soon. They're still German now." It was hard to believe, but the war had passed by this part of the Channel coast and the French ports remained in enemy hands, the occasional shell an unpleasant surprise when the dangerous years seemed over.

"I'd like to go and see the guns. Don't you think it would be fun to see guns which have fired at us so long, Mummy?"

Faye shivered. "No. After the war I don't want to see another gun, ever. Especially not those. Let's get on with repairing the ruins they've made instead."

"Well, I'd like to see them. Jones minor at school has a German helmet his father brought back from Dieppe, and one of the big boys has got a swastika off a Dornier's tail." He jumped up and began running, arms outstretched, making a high-pitched yowl in imitation of aero engines. He had become much noisier and more boisterous since he had been at school.

Faye put her head on her drawn-up knees, hands over her ears. She wanted to shout at him to be quiet, but did not. After a while, he let down his undercarriage and made a careful three-point landing beside her, fingers whirling as he feathered his propeller. She lifted her head and laughed. "Do you play airplanes all day at your school?"

He considered it seriously. "We work on Mondays with old Baggers, or he wallops us. And Thursdays is music; I work then, although a lot of the others mess about."

As soon as he came home for the summer he had started to talk about music, banging sticks down the banisters in rhythm and asking whether he could have his own violin. Faye was pleased, but surprised: it had never occurred to her that he might be musical, and somehow he did not give that impression now.

She looked down at her fingers; she needed to know how serious he was before Rupert came home, to judge whether a battle to win him the right to try something so unlike the Ludlows would be worthwhile. "Do you miss your music here? I must try to find someone who could come—"

"Oh no!" he said blithely, preparing to take off again. "It's just that it makes me think of things. Here I've got the things themselves."

"What sort of things?"

"I don't know," he said vaguely, revving up. "All the valley. Owls and stars and climbing down the ivy while Nanny's still snoring. I got a lovely snore on an oboe once. Don't tell Nanny, will you, Mummy?" He taxied to the end of his runway and took off over some rabbit holes, which became enemy guns, so he had to jink violently.

The valley, of course the valley. At least her sacrifice was not for nothing; as she had known he would be, Christopher was already

as unconsciously part of Reydenham as so many Ludlows had
been before him. Faye put her hands over her ears again, staring
out over the Channel. With luck, Rupert would not think snoring
down an oboe or dreaming of the valley to a violin showed an
effeminate Haskell taint. The sun was glinting on the French
coast, striking sparks off the cliffs . . . "Christopher!" She started
up in sudden panic. "Down, lie down, quick!" He did not hear
her, absorbed in an emergency landing with his ailerons shot
away, and she scrambled to her feet, running, racing over the
grass, knocking him flat, body tight over his.

A second later, the explosions started. Far over by Alkham
crossroads, stitching down toward Hougham and Reydenham;
then much closer, puffs of chalk striding across from the Western
Heights, ground shaking, bursting upward, the strange clatter of
falling flints and shrapnel between each one.

It went on and on. The coast shook to the intensity of it as
every gun across the Channel fired as fast as stockpiled ammunition allowed, no pretense at aim, just a whirlwind of exploding
steel hurled across the water before the batteries should fall.
There was no cover on their cliff path, only the curved, bare hill
under brown, dust-laden sun, battered senses, the jerking, tearing
ground. Christopher lay quiet at first, excited, a little scared,
which was part of the excitement. Then a shell landed three hundred yards up the hill, tumbling chalk and tussocked grass down
the slope, and Faye had to hold him still by force, screaming
against her. Another further off, some freak of blast pelting stones
all around; a few very distant toward Folkestone, then a tremendous shock, too close for sound and impact to separate.

The barrage did not end as it always had before. Instead, the
aimless straddling ceased and a tempest of steel began to fall on
Dover itself. Reydenham was no safer than anywhere else, but
Faye had only one thought in her mind when the shells switched
from them at last: to get home, away from that hateful open cliff.
Christopher . . . he was curled beside her, hands clutched deep
into the earth, a smear of blood at nose and ears, and quivered
when she touched him.

She pulled him to his feet, but he was stupid with shock and
had to be driven every step of the way since she could not carry
him. A chalk slope, the road, another slope and path. A steep-
curving hill, two sudden roars of closer shells sending them scam-

pering for cover, too far gone for further fear. One foot before the other, deathly cold, teeth chattering with cold, surely it should not be so cold in August?

Dusk reached out to them as they stumbled down the track to Reydenham, to be met by Gabriel, scolding for the fright they had given him. "Ten shells, Mrs. Rupert, end to end down the valley. I 'eard un whistling an' dropped flat, an' un sent a shower o' muck right up over. Rare turn it did give me."

"Is anyone hurt?" Faye was steadied by the familiarity of home and Gabriel.

"Couple o' Ted Dickson's pigs, but then us knows 'im and 'is pigs. Good story for the ministry, I reckon." He winked. "T'manor's shook up and glass broke."

She did not grasp it at first, everything looked so normal, the guns silent at last. Only the windows were strangely black in the westering sun, without angled panes to reflect the light.

There was glass everywhere, the mess indescribable. Furniture and floors were covered with soot jarred from the chimneys, doors sagging, curtain poles broken, shards of glass embedded in chairs and carpets and beds.

She stood in the hall and stared around her numbly. No. Not Reydenham. Christopher must go to bed with something hot; she needed a bath and food and clean clothes more than it was possible to imagine wanting anything in normal life. It could not have happened now, when everything was nearly over. Now, when she was exhausted beyond belief.

But it had.

Christopher. He must come first. Somewhere there would be milk and blankets free from glass; hot water from the hob. From an infinite distance she began to fumble will and method together again, discovering Cook in the kitchen surrounded by strung onions dropped from the ceiling. She forced herself to think where stored blankets were kept, lighted candles since they had no current with storage jars for the generator smashed.

She held John's torch as if it was his hand in hers; after they parted he had sent her more batteries and so long as she held it she could imagine him with her, not under London rubble, nor set apart forever once peace came. She sat by Christopher until he slept and made herself a bed on the floor with what coverings she could find from chests and cupboards. Until daylight came, it was too dangerous to move about a house so trapped with glass.

She slept awhile from sheer exhaustion, then woke sweating and trembling, back on a bare hill under the muzzles of German guns. She turned as if expecting to be held and felt nothing, the endless nothing where her love should be. I will not weep, she said aloud, and felt tears wet on her face. My love, where are you now? For all my brave words, surely I cannot last a lifetime like this.

Upstairs, she heard Christopher whimper and Nanny's voice, gruff and soothing. He would probably do better with her, since she had no connection with the horrors of the afternoon. She turned again and lay staring at dim shapes of fallen plaster, a cold wind blowing across her face from the shattered windows. She had to last, there was no choice.

She slept a little toward morning, and woke feeling dazed and strange. Without consciously thinking about it, she had taken a series of decisions during the night, the most urgent being that Christopher must go. In daylight, the valley looked so peaceful it was hard to imagine danger, but if the Germans had decided to throw their remaining ammunition at Dover, then another day would not change their mind. Whatever Rupert said about Ludlows staying with their valley, no argument would sway her now. Fortunately, the telephone was dead and he would know nothing until Christopher had gone.

"How is he?" Faye found Nanny sitting beside his bed.

She put her fingers to her lips and tiptoed from the room. "Nightmares, poor lamb. He's sleeping well now."

"Can he hear properly?" She had worried in the night over the blood at his ears.

"He can hear, how well I'm not saying yet. He ought to have the doctor."

Faye bit her lip. "I know, but Dover was badly hit yesterday. I doubt whether one would come so far. I'm going down there to see whether I can get some money from the bank; when I come back I'm going to drive you and Chris as far as I can before the petrol runs out. You'd better start packing now."

"I'm too old to go sitting in fields, Mrs. Rupert." Nanny looked uncertainly at the shambles of a nursery where only Christopher's toys were usually out of place.

Faye laughed. "You'll be staying away until all those guns have been captured. A field won't do, that's why I need some money." She went down to measure how much petrol she had left, the need to be active sucking her free from shock. She had to use a stick dipped in the tank, the gauge unreliable long ago, and guessed she had about thirty miles if she used all her reserves, so drove in comfort down to Dover. She could not face cycling and was desperate to have Christopher away before shelling started again.

She hardly recognized the town.

One lethal afternoon had done more damage than all the previous four years. Whole streets were down, where before it had been blocks and single houses; Ladywell, Biggin Street, and Cannon Street were roped off and under a pall of smoke, fire fighting and rescue a nightmare of short-circuited electricity and pressureless mains.

Christopher first. She did not feel guilt at turning her back on it; this time she was looking after her own before all else, and there was not even time to see if the slip was safe.

"We'll go by Canterbury," she said to Nanny, bundling them into the car on her return. "I'll get some money there somehow, it's hopeless in Dover."

"It's quiet enough now." Nanny looked doubtfully at the sky, as if she expected to see shells poised to strike. "Don't you think it might be wiser to wait?" She had left the valley only a handful of times in all her life and was more alarmed by going than by staying in danger in the place she knew.

"You gedout an' be thankful. You'll be leaving all that there glass to we," said Gabriel, grinning. He had his shotgun over his shoulder again as if the Germans might come with their shells; he did not mind much if he died and was enjoying the return of drama to his life.

Christopher was pale and silent, clutching a rubbed bear he had abandoned when he went to school. He seemed to hear well enough, and brightened when an aircraft flashed overhead. "Look, Mummy, Thunderbolt! 'Merican, and Jones minor says it's so heavy you have to haul on *everything* when you land or it never stops! It looks heavy, doesn't it, Mummy?"

The road was full of rescue lorries and ambulances going into Dover, driving slow and difficult, Faye acutely conscious of her precious petrol burning away. When she did not reply immediately, he repeated, "Doesn't it, Mummy? Doesn't it?"

"Yes, it does." She was so relieved by the change in him she wanted to stop the car and hug him, nerves shredding again almost at once when he began to rev up his engines, bouncing on Nanny's lap. "For heaven's sake, Chris, have a little consideration! Nanny's tired and you're too heavy for bouncing like that!"

"Sorry, Nanny, I won't sit on you any longer," he said obligingly, burrowing into bundled clothes on the seat, droning under his breath. He rather thought that if he fastened his hands really hard on a suitcase handle and pulled, he would be able to land a Thunderbolt without crashing it.

"'Tis children, Mrs. Rupert. They're easy down, easy up. He'll be boasting of being shelled by the time he goes back to school." Nanny settled back with a grunt.

"Jones minor was bombed once, but I bet he's never been shelled." Christopher's face appeared over her shoulder, lips trembling as if not quite sure whether to be pleased about it. "He couldn't have been shelled, could he, Mummy?"

"For his sake, I hope not," said Faye shortly. At this rate she wouldn't get further than another ten miles.

"I expect you're the only boy in the whole school to be shelled," said Nanny comfortably. "Anyone can be bombed, you have to live near Dover to be shelled."

"Really? Only Dover, Nanny?" Dimly, Faye heard them discussing shelling with growing pride. When it's over at last, I shall remember only my fear and feel no pride at all, she thought.

She pulled up at the first bank she came to in Canterbury, and found the manager willing to cash her check, the disaster at Dover common knowledge in East Kent, although scarcely referred to on the wireless. Beauty's money; she had claimed for her loss and received settlement only the week before: she looked at the notes in her hand and thought of John again, who had thought of her, too, while being harried through France. Love was surely one of the hounds of heaven, which would not let their quarry rest.

She was tempted to leave Nanny and Christopher in Canterbury, with enough petrol left to get her halfway home, but decided against it. The Germans had come here in revenge before, and now that spite was all they had left, might come again. She left them instead at a fishing inn not far from Christopher's school, and the car, too. It had a drain of petrol left, but not enough to be worth having to abandon it beside the road home.

She stayed the night in a room looking over calm fields, with only the plop of fish to break the silence. No guns, no hateful black bugs trailing their menace across the sky, no sudden boom of a mine from the Channel across a line of hills. She had heard silence over the past five years, but never freed from foreboding about what the next minute would bring. Here, security seemed sunk into the earth, as if the war was already over.

She walked four miles before being given a lift to the main road; after that it was easy. She went the rest of the way with a team from a south London electricity company, who were going to help repair the grid at Dover. There had been more shelling, they told her, and delays already that morning because of random salvos on the road.

"What are you going back for, lady?" said one bluntly. "The more out of there until it's over, the better."

"I live there." It seemed as good an explanation as any, and she was not abandoning Reydenham now.

"If folks had let themselves be evacuated the way the government wanted, there'd be plenty alive now instead of cold mutton. Kids, too."

Faye nodded, she realized just how lucky she had been, since she had escaped the retribution which awaits those who take chances with the lives of others. Christopher had stayed at Reydenham not because of any conscious decision, but because she lacked courage to fight Rupert any longer, was too involved with the slip to take him away herself. "Do you all come from London?" she asked at length. "What is it like there now? I'm surprised you can be spared to come down here with the rockets still falling."

One of them winked. "Experienced, that's what they call us. High-tension cables shorting into the sewers, unexploded bombs in the main switchgear: you name it and we've done it. Fix Dover up in a couple of hours and be back in the smoke by tonight."

She questioned them eagerly about London, but they knew very little, immersed as everyone was in their own minute section of the war. Only the driver had been north of the river recently, and when she asked about the City, he shrugged. "It's the hell of a mess. Not too much left to flatten any more. It's east, you see, and them bloody bugs come in that way, just like the bombers in the Blitz. Around St. Paul's there's nothing left but weeds and rubbish."

Again the cold lurch of dread, mind driven from one hold to the next. Millions lived in London unharmed, the odds on life enormous: the trouble was that the heart refused to reckon in statistics.

Dover was being shelled again, and she dropped off the lorry well clear of the town and cut over the hills for Reydenham; although within range all the way, there was an illusion of safety away from the vortex of Dover's streets. She was very tired when she reached the valley at last, mellow in another dusk. Harvesting was under way, the creak of carts and drone of tractors strange when her ears had been tuned to the suck of air which was all the warning shells gave.

"It's been quieter today," said Dickson when she stopped to talk to the harvesters. "A couple o' bursts on the hill, the rest all over by Dover. I reckon them Jerries have just about shot off their stores."

"What do they hope to prove by killing another dozen here?" said Faye bitterly. "They've no hope of escape from Calais, why not surrender and let us be?"

"Ah, well, as to that, Mrs. Rupert, I daresay if it were us as 'ad lost the war, with Germany under our muzzles and shells to put in 'em, we'd be tempted to kill any of the bastards we could while we 'ad the chance. But 'tis too good a day for harvest to be wasting time crouching in 'oles. Rain be more certain than my name on a shell."

Faye thought about it, walking up the lane to the manor; would she feel tempted to kill Germans, any Germans, when it could accomplish no possible purpose? She looked around and remembered 1940, Gabriel with his shotgun and Cook disputing possession of her carving knife with Colonel Druitt. Yes, she supposed so, but it was still a damned silly time to get killed.

Reydenham looked depressing in the extreme. The windows had a curious blind stare, gouged furniture forlorn, as if awaiting the junk dealer's call. Cook had brought order to the kitchen, onions in sacks instead of hanging in plaited lines from the beams; the rest of the rooms were covered with soot and glass, and Faye could not bear to look at them.

She had not shopped for days, but Gabriel had preferred to shoot rabbits rather than clear up glass, so at least there was a hot meal waiting and once she had eaten it was possible to start thinking about what must be done.

"The ARP left rolls of linen in the church porch for the windows in the valley," offered Cook. "They say there's no glass available yet awhile."

"And not much point putting it in either, so long as it might be blown out again tomorrow," said Faye. "I'll send Gabriel down to fetch a roll in the morning."

Cook snorted, "Be lucky if you sees him back, once he slips through your fingers."

After another night camping on the floor, Faye was in no mood to be tolerant of Gabriel's shortcomings. Broken glass was everywhere: inside drawers, standing in upright slivers in the dining-room table, embedded in mattresses and cushions. She was used to the work of the slip, to tramping the valley and cycling in all weathers; but hour after hour of scrubbing soot, beating upholstery, and polishing wood seemed like labor straight from hell itself.

However careful she was, knees and hands were soon cut, her back ached, while the sheer endlessness of it defeated attempts at cheerfulness. The weather had changed again, blowing drizzle through the gaping windows, and she set Gabriel to tacking linen into the frames. "Tain't no manner of good, Mrs. Rupert," he kept repeating. "You won't see nothing with that there muck on the windows. The generator, that comes first, I reckon."

"No," said Faye obstinately. "Keep the weather out first." Once he disappeared she would never entice him back: the nearest shell had landed less than fifty yards away, and until the battery jars were replaced she did not think that Gabriel's scanty knowledge would have much effect on the generator.

"Be cold without glass in t'winter," he said with unmistakable relish. "September tomorrow."

"There'll be glass before winter." Surely, she thought, they must capture those guns within the next few days.

"They reckoned on the end of war afore winter. I don't see no end to it yet, not by a long chalk."

Faye went for more hot water, she would have boxed his ears if she had stayed, and found Cook placidly peeling potatoes. "Why aren't you cleaning the drawing room, as I asked?"

She sliced a potato precisely. "I was not engaged as a scrubbing woman, Mrs. Rupert."

"Neither was I," retorted Faye.

Cook shook her head, lips pursed. "I'm too old to be down on my knees in broken glass. My own kitchen now, that's different. I couldn't cook with onions bowling around my feet, but it's not my work to be scrubbing up soot."

"You don't think that most people are doing others' work at the moment?"

It was no good. She was too old, her feet hurt, she would not change the habits of a lifetime because of a pack of Germans with shells: she would gladly have defended her kitchen with a carving knife, but preferred to leave rather than do something she regarded as degrading. "And it's no good you dismissing me, Mrs. Rupert," she added. "Ludlows engaged me thirty years past, and I'm sure I've always given satisfaction. Mr. Rupert won't find another who cooks his game pie as he likes it."

"In that case you had better ask Mrs. Ludlow for your wages, you'll not get them from me," said Faye coldly.

"Likely enough she'll pay them, Mrs. Rupert."

"Why don't you go and see?" Mrs. Ludlow had been blown on the floor, when the shells struck but, like everyone else, had had a miraculous escape. She was still recovering from it at leisure in bed, her windows the first to be covered over, one of their few candles burning in her room.

Cook's eyes flickered, she knew that some elastic was the most would be offered. "T'wouldn't be right to bother her, like as she is."

"No, it wouldn't, would it?" said Faye deliberately. "So you are back with me again. I'll be in to help with the glass in the furniture as soon as you've got the worst off the floor." It was a victory of a sort, but it made little difference. Gabriel was willing even if he worked at his own pace; Cook dragged around the house complaining and stirred up as much dirt as she swept, serving cold and unappetizing meals because she said she had no time to produce anything better, until Mrs. Ludlow sent messages demanding that she be returned to her kitchen.

Faye gave in, she was too tired to care.

Chapter Twenty-seven

Slowly Reydenham returned to some kind of order. It was rather like living inside a yellowed parchment book, full of musty smells and faintly illuminated by tawny light. By day the linen kept out the sun, at night it was too thin to stop icy drafts blowing everywhere; the house became stuffily hot and bitterly cold in turn. At least the worst of the filth was cleared, bedding and upholstery picked clear of glass, furniture carefully pared clear of splinters.

The bombardment went on and on.

On September 1 the grid was fractured again, on the second the flour mills at Charlton were hit and blazed with a gigantic yellow glow which lit the whole sky and threw shadows from the trees at midnight: bread disappeared from the shops and lorries bringing it in from outside found distribution almost impossible with shell warnings in force up to sixteen hours a day.

On September 5 the BBC announced that Dover's ordeal was over, the guns captured at last: even as the news reader spoke, British guns firing across the Channel at German boats attempting the evacuation of Calais and Boulogne provoked a fresh cyclone of fire. Biggin Street again, Alkham valley, Charlton Green, Wellington Place, Reydenham valley. Faye lay in bed, blankets over her head, and listened to it coming nearer, the old house shaking, the sky glowing from yet another fire. Rain clattered on stretched linen, driven by a blustering up-Channel wind: it made no difference to the guns, only to people who could not face adding the icy mud of an outdoor shelter to the bleak misery of fear. At least in Dover they had caves, deep under the cliffs.

And in the morning, plaster and soot again, dusted over everything so painfully cleaned.

She had no idea what day it was, and only the harvest recalled the season. She worked outside when the rain stopped, unable to face the house again, unchanging rhythms of reaping and carting taking on fresh meaning in a shifting world. Next day, the guns stopped.

At first they could not believe it, laughing at jokes they would not normally have found amusing, counting time, thinking secretly that if they had a whole day free from shells it must mean that the guns were taken at last.

It stayed quiet all day, and then the next.

The telephone was repaired and the Navy phoned to say the Ludlow slip was gone. The slip. As with Betty's death, she could not grasp it. The years of fear and labor all for nothing; the endless contrivings which had brought tools and work and new buildings where there had been nothing but tumbledown sheds before; memories of 20017 waterlogged on the ramp, the countless other boats repaired for gallant boys to die in; the cherished hope of this one thing which would be hers, done and finished and turned to peace again. All gone. They would be paid, but it would not be the same: I mustn't think of it, she said aloud, and could not stop thinking of it. At least Henry and the rest were safe, living with most of Dover in the caves.

Her father phoned and she held the receiver outside the window so he could believe that all was peaceful again.

Rupert phoned, and was dismayed when she told him of the damage at Reydenham. "Everything is quiet now?"

"Thank God. We can hear fighting across the Channel, but they say the Canadians are into Boulogne."

"The BBC said they had the guns a week ago."

"Well, they didn't. Could you get a few days' leave?" However awkwardly they dealt together, he was not afraid and she needed his strength desperately.

"Soon, I hope, but we're very busy here. You've been marvelous, my dear, but it's over now and you can sit back at last. How has Chris taken it?"

Faye fiddled with a long gouge across the top of his desk, splintered edges rough under her fingers. "He was badly shocked the first day, so I took him and Nanny to a little place in Thanet. They'll be safe enough there."

"I thought I told you he must stay?"

"Yes, you did," she said evenly. "I didn't think I was justified in keeping him here any longer under such shelling."

"So the first Ludlow in four hundred years has left his people behind and run away."

"Rubbish!" she said irritably. "This isn't some kind of children's dare. What is the point of risking his life so he can say later that at the age of six he didn't run away?"

"I suppose you wouldn't understand it, but at least I'd expect my wife to do what she was told. There wasn't much chance of anything worse than broken glass in the valley anyway."

Faye felt helpless: statistics again. They had survived with no more than broken glass, even if glass could kill and maim. Perhaps later Christopher would resent that she had taken from him something Ludlows valued: avoidable risks for no purpose still seemed absurd to her; to accept such risks for those she loved, impossible.

After Rupert had rung off, she joined the many who phoned the exchange to ask which day it was, the only step she could think of to start restoring reality.

The lull lasted nearly a week, then they discovered that Boulogne and Calais still held, a sixteen-hour bombardment the longest yet, another the following day adding Priory Station to the staggering toll of damage. Then there was another lull, and they heard that in the north of the country the blackout was ended, although in London and the southeast the rocket attack intensified daily, and in Dover it was their fourth day without milk or bread.

On September 19, Boulogne fell to the Canadians at last. Apart from scattered shots, it was surely over at last.

Rupert did not telephone again, and Faye found herself almost wishing for a few more near-misses at Reydenham, so contrary is human nature. A week before she had been begging on her knees for it to finish, now in clear skies and blessed silence she wanted a few more shells: far enough away to be harmless, near enough to convince Rupert when he came of risks he would not grasp.

Two days later, Beryl phoned. Reydenham seemed to have become the end of the line, the backwater she had longed for and now found filled with emptiness. "Is that you, Faye? How do you like peace, then?"

Faye looked at linen-covered windows and gritty surfaces. "I like it."

"Strange, though, ain't it? Blimey, you should just see Dover! You been down 'ere lately?"

"Two weeks ago. The slip has gone, the Navy rang."

"I'll say. The 'ole seafront could be shoveled into an 'ospital bag. You thinkin' of comin' down to 'ave a look?"

Faye shivered, she did not want to see the ruins of Dover. "I suppose I'll have to; I must find someone to fix the generator and we're out of everything."

"You wouldn't take over me duty, would you? My Billy, 'e's 'ome on leave and 'e says to meet 'im in London an' we'll 'ave a rare ole ring-out together. The thing is, I'm on call Thursday to Sunday."

"It's all over, though, Beryl. You must be owed plenty of time off, and who is going to care any more?"

"That ole Jewell will," said Beryl grimly. "You remember 'ow 'e was quite nice when things was tight? Well, last week 'e was fine, but now 'e can see 'is job nearly gone, 'e's a proper bastard again. The only time 'e brightens up is when the odd shell comes over from Calais, the Jerries is 'is best friends now. I've served five years, I don't want to get kicked out in the last stretch."

"All right." She was not sorry to be away from Reydenham for a few days. "If you think he won't mind."

"On the strength, ain't you? 'Pissed off on other duty' you're still marked. It'll be okay."

It seemed strange to go back to ambulances, as if the war was set on a treadmill without end. She even enjoyed it, eased of the need to think. Meals and petrol and hours of duty were someone else's concern, the irresponsibility of well-trodden discipline a measureless relief. A few shells still came across, as if the Germans could not bear to stop until the last gun was taken, but Dover was so ruined that most simply plowed into rubble piled on every side.

The whole seafront had gone, the huddled dock streets and rows of stuccoed boardinghouses flattened. The center of the town was shattered but still recognizable, the slopes to west and east gaping like a kicked fence, the villages edging the Canterbury road almost worse hit than the town itself, cinders from the gutted flour mill blackening everything downwind. Although she was on call, Faye worked shifts with the rest, and walked down one evening to the Ludlow slip.

Barricades were pulled aside, the whole area forlorn and squalid under a gray sky. The Prince of Wales and Admiralty piers were deserted, the hulks blocking the western entry rust-streaked and looking like the seal on Dover's death.

The slip was indeed gone. A shell had struck the pier beside it and only splintered piles were left, and a handful of planks caught in barbed wire. She stared and thought again of Beauty building there, of . . . abruptly, she turned and walked away: don't look back, don't ever look back on a past which is past and must not be loosed from the padlocks of the mind.

She was woken from off-duty sleep by the familiar crashing roar. It was not possible. Everyone said there were only a few guns left in German hands: all around her people were stirring, staring at each other in disbelief. Doubt was settled almost at once, the door blown open by another salvo near enough to snap eardrums tight, the double wail of a shell warning following after.

"My God," said a rescue worker bitterly. "And they said it was bloody over."

The loudspeaker crackled. "Attention! Salvation Army hostel in Snargate Street. Two ambulances and all rescue equipment. Go!"

There was another tearing suck overhead, ground bounding to the impact, then another, followed by the deeper blast they recognized as being from the largest-caliber gun. Over the years, there were few in Dover who could not tell armor-piercing from impact, eight-inch from fifteen.

The hostel had collapsed inward, pressure squeezing an avalanche of bricks, china, trays, and bodies on the ground. The rescue squads were all very good at what must be done, they had shored up ruins, crawled down treacherous shock lines to reach the trapped so many times; they had winched concrete aside and reversed fractured water mains to build up pressure for the hoses, left the dead and cleared tottering masonry to reach the living. The only difference was, they had thought it done for the last time. There were seven killed at the hostel, and Faye lost count of the wounded; she had also lost the knack of ignoring blood and crushed flesh in the needs of the moment.

And after the hostel, another shell landed on the entry to a public shelter, fortunately without killing anyone, but concussing everyone inside. Then there was a dog howling, struggling with its own guts in the middle of Biggin Street, and after that a warden crushed when a wall collapsed.

Faye was crewing with Anne Simpson, which added to the illusion that they were in a bondage which would never end. She looked up once and smiled. "Soon I shan't believe we've invaded France at all."

"Peace before Christmas." Faye stared at a knot of people gathered around a doctor lying on rubble while he amputated a trapped leg. "We've heard that before, too."

Anne was friendly now Faye had returned to ambulances, and had never given up her claim to understand military strategy. "Not this year, now Arnhem has failed. Another winter, then the Japs. Roll on 1946."

Five years, John had said, back in 1941. It had seemed unimaginable then.

They both ducked to another pattern of explosions, this time on the far edge of town, and did not look at each other after. This last test had come so late, when they thought themselves safe. Terror was harder to hide than before, the effort of leaving shelter, of standing quietly by unsafe walls scarcely attainable any more. Yet with achievement blown to dust with the slip, Faye had an overwhelming desire to do this well. It would matter to no one but herself; others would not understand how great an effort it was simply to stay by an unprotected ambulance under shelling, but for herself, she wanted to end it well.

There is nothing so tiring as fear, and by evening she was exhausted. She had lost track of the days again, but tomorrow she was down for standby at the main casualty clearing station, the worst duty of them all. She thought it was Mr. Jewell taking his revenge for three years' absence building boats, but perhaps did him an injustice since someone had to do it. A shell warning was still in force, so she decided to go to a deep shelter under the cliff for her rest period. It seemed an enormous distance to walk, but once there, completely safe. She did not think she could face another duty without some relief from strain.

She was picking her way through the shambles of Market Square when she felt a hand under her arm and turned.

It was John.

He tightened his hold and smiled, deep into her eyes. "Keep walking, my love, since I cannot avoid giving you these shocks, and Dover is your backyard."

Light became lighter, the touch of his hands, the feel of him walking beside her and the husk of her filled with life again, ruins and fear still there but their burden slipped. They reached the har-

bor before words returned as tools to use. Sunset light lay golden
on the water, promenade and pier deserted, since those without essential work were in shelter and the harbor area flattened beyond
the need for wardens or rescue. She put up her face without
thought to be kissed; if there were eyes to see, then she did not
care. "My love, you came."

"I flew back from Canada this morning, or I would have been
here before. I did not know—" He nodded across the Channel
where Calais was clearly etched against the evening sky. "I read
yesterday about Canadian troops taking Boulogne, and the paper
mentioned the shelling here as if it did not matter at all. Quebec
is half a world away."

She laughed, nothing mattered any more. They were both alive,
and together she could not think beyond this time. "You read
about it yesterday and you are here today? I hope you had finished
whatever it was you were doing."

"No, I hadn't, it is one of those conferences full of haggling,
which go on forever. It no longer seemed important. Are there
mines on that beach?"

"Not any more. They often have to take water from the harbor
for fire fighting."

He picked his way down crumbled stonework and held out his
arms for her to follow. Sitting on sand with their backs to remains
of wall, there was only the still glint of the harbor and themselves.
Yet once there, he sat very quietly, staring out over the water,
while she watched him. He looked better than last time she had
seen him, although his face had the drawn whiteness brought by
too much work on insufficient sleep and forgotten meals. He had
had a rotten war, too, she reflected. On the wrong end of bombs
and V bugs, sitting through the night over figures and in conferences, solitary and in danger when he went abroad for purposes
she only guessed at. At length, when he showed no sign of breaking his silence, she laughed. "What are you thinking about? The
Lords of the Treasury giving you the sack for walking out on your
post in Quebec?"

"Since I have no intention of staying with the Treasury a moment longer than I must, I rather hope they will. Ten years' hard
labor this war has cost me, and I think my time is nearly done.
No, I was thinking of you. I have loved you so long, Faye, and no
amount of parting changes it. Eighteen months since we were last

a few hours together, do you really think we can go on like this?"

Bleakness was there again, waiting to close in. "It was you, not I, who said we might last apart but never together, so long as I'm not free. Please, John, leave it now; nothing has changed except we have today." She put out her hand, tentatively, not sure of his reaction. It no longer seemed important, he had also said, and came all the way from Canada because he feared for her. She remembered reading of Churchill meeting Roosevelt in Quebec, and knew enough of John Castellan by now to realize that he was unlikely to be a clerk adding up other men's figures there: yet he had come and she could offer no more than he had refused already.

His fingers closed on hers tightly, so they hurt, and drew her to him. Neither spoke. She put her head on his shoulder and most unexpectedly fell instantly asleep.

Cold woke her, and without thought she burrowed closer to him, still held by serenity which had let exhaustion claim her when rest so often passed her by. Then she felt him laugh. "My sweet, we'll freeze if we stay here any longer."

She roused at once and was astonished to find it dark. "Whatever time is it? All the way from Canada and I sleep your few precious hours away!"

"At least it gave the illusion that for once we are not hounded by time." He pulled her to her feet and held her, hands caressing, the warmth of her throat and lips under his.

She had lived so long on memory of him, on the fleeting touch of his physical presence and the promise she would see him once more, not daring to look beyond it. Suddenly it was here and now, her life kicked without warning into the moment which must last her the rest of her days. She had loved him before; in the chill wind of Dover beach without a word spoken, she was possessed by love so great the lack of him was a rake of pain in her body.

He drew back at last. "I ought to have stayed in Canada."

"No, never. When I cannot go any further on my own, I shall have something of you to help me on my way." But she knew he was right. Each step they took together made the path harder which they must travel alone.

"My darling, are you sure there is no way to free yourself?" He gripped her shoulders and felt her yearning under his hands: he could seal her wants here on wind-streaked sand, find some rest for himself and in the taking bind her so her marriage must break under the power of it. As respite from strain and so much wanting, he could surely do it.

He felt her nod, denying hope, incapable of words which were not the language of love, and thought settled again. He was no easily satisfied boy, willing to slake loss and jealousy with occasional lust, and she was already nearly broken on the anvil of conflict. Love is so many things, and once craving was leashed again, he knew that for them it could not be the rape of rightness held within the heart.

No careless easing of the flesh for them and then goodbye and back to another life again; this he would not do and she must not try to do and fail. Or goodbye for the moment, see you next week or month, but still back to another life from now to then and on again. He turned from her almost roughly, revulsion as physical as love itself: this he could not, would not, would be destroyed by doing.

Faye stared at his half-turned back, senses trembling, hearing breath cruelly drawn, such as she had only heard before from those crushed under rubble. She was so close to the core of him, and dared not speak or move for fear of the damage she might do.

He turned after a moment and climbed the wall, holding his hand for her. "Where in Dover will we find something hot to eat in the middle of the night?" Even to himself, his voice sounded odd.

She shuddered once as if to the slam and bolt of doors, then her head went back, and even in the dark he could sense her smile leaping from lip to eyes, the same blaze of delight he had first seen long ago when she spoke of carving stone. "The Army brings jellified stew and sickly tea in field kitchens when the shelling stops. Another disastrous experience to keep up the pace of your encounters with me."

He laughed, only the unsteadiness of his hand on hers revealing emotions neither dared touch again. "It sounds more alarming than the confidence trick, the loan, or a cellar in an air raid." He did not mention her offer of herself at their last meeting.

Faye fumbled in her bag. "I've got your torch somewhere. If they are going to shell anyway, a torch will make no difference." She looked at him fleetingly. "It's become a kind of symbol, I carry it with me everywhere."

"Lucky torch," he said lightly. "When does the shelling usually start?"

Hands off, thought Faye grimly, emotion strictly under wraps again. Well, we'll wait and see. "Any time," she said aloud. "We've been lucky tonight, usually they send over a few shots to keep us awake if nothing more."

The streets meandered between piled rubble and pocked, crumbling walls, direction easily lost while concentrating on roughness underfoot in a small circle of torchlight. They found an army kitchen pulled into a cleared site off Cannon Street, the food marvelously hot, but otherwise exactly fulfilling Faye's predictions.

"Why they have to put sugar in tea before they pour it, beats me," observed John. "Occupied Europe does rather better on acorn and burned-bread coffee."

They were sitting on benches in a grimy drill hall, canvas tacked over blown-out glass. Several dust-caked heavy rescue men were asleep on the floor, a policeman snoring at the end of their table, head down on a wedge of bread. Faye looked around and laughed involuntarily. "What was your last meal? Smoked salmon and *tournedos chasseur* at some banquet in Quebec?"

"Complete with four different kinds of wine," he agreed. "Whatever conferences haggle over, it is never the food which suffers. As a matter of fact, it was RAF tea and stale sandwiches over the Atlantic."

"Did you ever go back to France?" asked Faye curiously; he had spoken of acorn coffee as if it was familiar. Also, she would perhaps never have another chance to discover what it was that had happened to him in the past, which stood between them still. As her own love grew she was beginning to understand why he refused even once between them, but when he turned from her on the beach she had seen revulsion, too, and was not hurt, only distressed for him.

"Once, although it wasn't really my department. I was mostly buying raw materials around the outskirts of Europe in competition with the Germans, but I sometimes dealt with certain kinds of finance for escape routes and resistance. All over now, thank God."

"I saw you once, on your way to Belgium. Do you remember?"

He smiled, more relaxed than he had been, her tactics of oblique approach paying off. "I remember every moment I have spent with you. I went to accept transfer of Belgian assets held in neutral countries, and was still signing God knows what when the armistice came. Your concern was one of the better things to remember then."

Intent perhaps on mastering his senses, he seemed less guarded under her probing than she expected, but she would have to go carefully if she wanted to discover more. "Did you do all this through your own bank, or what? Whenever I rang they said you were seldom in, yet you were there sometimes. You can't work for your own firm and the Treasury, surely?"

"Not without some very gilt-edged accounting, or I would certainly end up in jail for corruption," he agreed, "but quite a few things are different in wartime. My father has been carrying our own business, but in Spain particularly it was often better for the Treasury not to appear involved, and Castellan's are well known there. It was government money, though."

"I remember . . . you speak Spanish, don't you? Does your name mean your family came from Castile? I've never heard it before."

He laughed. "Merchant banks are mostly run by people with peculiar names, it's an occupational disease. No, it simply means castle-keeper, a guardian of other men's goods. It's a good name for bankers." His expression tightened suddenly and Faye understood him well enough to follow his mind. It was not such a good name for a lover.

"You said this war had cost you ten years," she said hastily. "I don't suppose you double your figures by accident, but it has cost the rest of us five so far."

He hesitated and then shrugged. "There are a lot of rich Jewish interests in the City and they started financing Jewish emigration from Germany after Hitler came to power. It soon degenerated into squalid bribery and I did a good deal of it for them, since it was impossible for Jews to operate successfully in Germany. We have some Jewish blood, but Castellans have married Gentiles for a good few generations now. As I would like to do." His tone was bitter, thought of his name still rankling.

Faye looked down at the rough deal table, splotched with stains. Wherever they turned, the same landslide lay across their path.

She felt his hand close on hers. "I'm sorry. It's these damned conferences again, if you niggle away long enough there some-times you gain your point."

She nodded, looking at his hand on hers: surprisingly square and powerful for a man who spent most of his time in offices. How little she knew of him after all, except . . . except all the things which mattered lay open to her grasp. She took her hand away and fastened her mind to what he had said. "I remember how you looked when Rupert accused you of dealing with Nazis; this bribery, was it done openly, then?"

"Once I had to dine with Himmler, all very friendly, their banking sympathizer from London. Do you know, Faye, I dislike talking of it even now? It wasn't particularly dangerous, just dou-ble-crossing foulness; dealing with the kind of Nazis even their fellows despised, since those with a spark of principle wouldn't ransom Jews. It cost me my marriage in the end."

She looked up, startled. "I didn't mean to pry." Nevertheless, his voice told her that she was close to what she sought.

"No. We're trying very hard, aren't we? Only, fenced in by minefields we can't move without setting something off. But you have a right to know, since it is my heart's desire to marry you if I could. I was the exception, the Castellan who married a Jewess. I became fairly well known as a Nazi sympathizer; in most of pre-war London this would probably have meant no more than a few friendships lost, but the Jewish community is tightly bound and Miriam—my wife—was very much a part of it. Not surprisingly, feeling among them ran very high, and neither she nor I lasted well under the pressure."

"Didn't you tell her what you were doing?" demanded Faye, aghast.

"You get sucked into these things gradually. At first I didn't re-alize what it would involve; later, I knew she would not be able to resist telling people, the atmosphere became so unpleasant." He hesitated and then added, "I couldn't simply say nothing, you see, when people attacked me. I had to justify more than mere interest in Nazism to explain my visits to Germany, which became very frequent as time went on. Of course it was impossible to find reasons which wouldn't infuriate Jews, and eventually antagonize nearly everyone else, too."

"And your Jewish friends who had asked you to do it, left you to sink?"

"No. They continued to invite us everywhere, and for Miriam's sake I continued to go. It would have been better to stay at home and be damned to them. My divorce had just gone through when I came to Reydenham for dinner." He supposed it was the sympathy of the trapped for another in the same state which had first drawn him to her; the long humiliations he had undergone adding a protective edge to his anger when he saw her enduring circumstances which were not so very different. "Once it all ended with the war, Rothschilds and the rest spoke for me to their friends, I have no complaint of them. Then the Treasury picked me up, thinking my experience of fraud would be useful in wartime."

"And Miriam—your wife?" She did not know whether she was making the greatest misjudgment of her life in asking, but the whole ugly business needed to be brought to the light. And then left, forever.

He put his hands flat on the table and stared at them, every line of him expressing resistance. "Do you really want to know?" His tone made it seem as if she was asking out of prurient curiosity.

"Only if you wish to tell me," she said quietly. "I make mistakes, but I am trying to help. With this at least, even if I am powerless in other ways."

She found herself watching his hands, knuckles white as his fingers locked, then back out of sight as he looked up, expression softening again. "Yes, I know. As you said once, I had forgotten how it felt. There isn't much more to it. I was often away, and we quarreled bitterly when I was home. She found others in my place, of course. I could tell." His words came awkwardly, chopped out of bitter memory.

She nodded, she had known at once with Rupert.

"Oh, God." He shifted abruptly and looked away, recognizing personal experience when he saw it. "I should not be telling you this."

"I asked, and surely I ought to know."

His eyes flicked back to her, then down to his hidden hands again. "Although I knew, it was not long before she told me, wanting to hurt. I could scarcely blame her. Her . . . friends as well, they had their ways of telling me, too. It was a small revenge for what was happening to their kin in Germany."

"Why didn't she just walk out? You . . . you had no children?"

"No. Later, she said, when we've had a few years of enjoyment." His mouth twisted. "I suppose we had one. You are too innocent, my dear, she liked my money very well. And the part of my guilt which made me free with it. I've not many excuses, though. I tried awhile, but in the end I could not bear to touch her and went elsewhere as she had done."

And then she divorced you and was handsomely paid for her trouble, thought Faye, an earlier echo in her ears. *You would endure . . . until one night your mind would tear and you would wake screaming in the dark.*

This, he had known.

Whole blocks of his personality slid into place, which formerly had baffled her. She could see now exactly why he found it intolerable to pretend anything between them, to accept half measures or contemplate yet more of his life rotted by the treacheries of deceit. And just how unbearable it had been when she offered him exactly that.

The trap had been shut on them before, this time she heard the padlock snap.

As if in tune to her thoughts, a loudspeaker crackled into life. "Gun flashes! Gun flashes! Take cover!" A moment later the salvo landed, the wail of public warning following after.

Chapter Twenty-eight

The shells made Faye realize how she had forgotten time. In less than half an hour she was on duty at the casualty clearing station, and since she could not then leave until the end of her twelve-hour shift, John came with her. The streets were deserted, the few whose duty kept them aboveground too preoccupied to notice a different face, or speculate beyond the landing of the next shell.

Yet after a few desultory salvos the guns were silent again, no casualties came in and they were able to sleep side by side on stretchers on the floor. It is the only time I will be able to turn and feel my love beside me in the dark, thought Faye, and wanted to stay awake because of it. Instead, the slide of exhaustion waited for her again, and the ease from his presence which let her sleep free of nightmares. She woke to sunshine and silence, doctors and nurses around her also snatching what rest they could. No traffic or feet on the road outside: experience told her the warning was still in force, the people of Dover spending more hours in their caves beneath the cliffs.

She was stiff from the stretcher and shifted her position gingerly, to see John sleeping across a foot of floor. He lay on his side facing her, expressive mouth relaxed, sun picking out angles of bone, assurance softened by the beginning of stubble on his jaw. He had the look of a faded watercolor and she wondered when he had slept last. She lay watching him awhile, then slept again herself.

A series of explosions woke them both, floor jarring into bone through unyielding stretchers. He stood, grunting, and helped her to her feet. "If you weren't a casualty before, you damned well would be after a while on those stretchers." He glanced at his watch. "D'you realize we've slept nearly nine hours? It's two o'clock in the afternoon."

"You needed it." Another salvo landed high on the hill behind them.

"I daresay, but—" He pushed her violently down, the suck of air and scorch of explosion smashing breath, hammering frail flesh, whirling them down fire-streaked blankness. It was over before danger or terror could be grasped, only the slide of rubble and clatter of shrapnel remaining; then another blast turned cowering bodies into a mere stretched rack of bone and muscle again, another further over, followed by a cluster so close the shock hurled their protective blast screen of sandbags across the room. Cupboards, stretcher frames, and tables splintered around them: Faye felt a blow across her legs, but the fall of debris was as remote as if it was happening elsewhere, her senses so filled with the terror of death she could not adjust to mere pain.

She had no notion how long she lay, concrete floor grinding and shuddering into her face, mind bludgeoned, thinking only of four stories of brick held off them by a few reinforced beams. After a while she became conscious of John holding her and put her face on his arm: what would have been insupportable alone became endurable again. Just.

The bombardment went on and on, shells no longer falling in salvos but with vicious speed. As if she was there, Faye could imagine the German gunners sweating to off-load every last shell they could, as one by one their batteries fell.

Slowly, slowly, their fire eased, falling short of the clearing station and into the middle of the town again. She felt John move against her. "A last throw, surely. Fewer guns firing now than there were."

She caught his words through ringing in her head, and nodded, mouth full of dust, lungs painful. An hour, two hours more of this to live through and surely it would be over. It seemed worse to think of it like that, death stripped of everything but fear when it might come from the final barrage of four long years.

Someone plunged past, yelling about casualties, and she lay a moment longer, thinking, no, I can't. Here, burrowed in our corner, they will forget us, a short while longer to endure and we will be alive. She felt weight eased from her back, until it went she had noticed nothing; somehow, she put her hands against the ground and stood, blinking at the scene around her, senses shuttering. Brick, furniture, and sandbags were littered by blast, smashed bottles, unraveled bandages everywhere, the air opaque with dust and smoke, figures lurching in and out of sight. Shells were still slamming fiercely at a distance; ah, Dover, she thought, there will be nothing left of you, even if we survive.

She felt John holding her, lips moving, and nodded in answer to the question in his eyes; beyond feeling very strange, she has suffered no more than bruises. "And you?" He had been lying across her, and must have been worse hit than she; no wonder the fall of debris had seemed remote.

She thought of the Strand Palace cellar, he seemed to make a habit of taking blows intended for her.

He smiled crookedly and wiped sweat and dust from his face. "It was as well I didn't stay in Canada, after all." She could hear better now.

She remembered the casualties and moved stiffly to the entry, marked by an orange glow in the murk. Outside, it was no better. The sun was gone and in its place a great pall of smoke and dust, the roar of flame as a gas main burned out of control. Two ambulances were there, doctors struggling to save a life with most of their equipment gone. A nurse jerked her head at Faye. "Look in the other one and see if there's anyone who won't last to the hospital without treatment. Otherwise, they're best out of here at once."

Anne was the driver, slumped over the wheel, unmoving when Faye opened the door. She shook her gently. "Anne! Are you hurt?"

She did not reply, eyes glazed and fingers tightly gripped on the wheel. Faye hesitated a moment and then left her, she must be all right to have driven there and the injured were more urgent. Perhaps it was imagination, but the shells seemed to be coming closer again, single shots several minutes apart bouncing the earth.

John had the doors open, torch probing bodies almost unrecognizable under dust pasted with blood. "One dead. The other is bleeding too badly to be moved without attention." He stood so she could not see. "Tell the doctor, Faye, he's urgently needed here." His certainty reminded her of the long, blitzed years, the experience of sudden death in the streets shared by so many Britons.

Faye returned to Anne while the doctors patched what they could in the back. She was still rigid, staring through the windscreen, arm cold and tight, without a scratch on her. Faye shivered and put her hand in John's. "That would have been me if you hadn't come. I couldn't have lasted through another attack like this alone."

"And no disgrace if you had not." He held her tight to his body as another shell landed at the corner of the street, a line of roofs hesitating, then tipping their load of tiles into the road with a rattling crash. Although his voice was steady she could feel the tremor in his hands, the slide of sweat as he held his face to hers. "It is not the sort of thing one does for fun."

She felt calmed by the fact that he was frightened too; if he had not touched her, she would never have known, and if he could hide it, so could she.

The same nurse dodged over to them across the littered street. "You know your way to the hospital at Waldershare?" Faye nodded. "We've loaded all the stretcher cases into one ambulance but the driver is in shock; can you take it for us?"

"Yes," said Faye thankfully. Out of Dover and into the peaceful countryside beyond, with any luck it would all be over when she returned.

The nurse scowled when John came with her, muttering rudely about men being wanted in the town, but quite apart from her need for him, the journey proved a nightmare of flaring, blocked-off streets and would have been impossible without help. Twice he had to find soldiers to clear enough rubble to let them through, several times she had to back, fighting ponderous steering and worn gears: without direction she would have stuck.

The shells were spacing more widely now; she tried not to count the minutes between, since dread merely added to terror when the next one came. Her hands were slippery on the wheel, her body shaking with exhaustion and strain, muscles burning from the pounding she had received at the clearing station. John was tiring, too. As she had feared, his back was badly bruised, and as it stiffened, he no longer helped clear their track and preferred to walk alongside rather than climb in and out of the ambulance too often.

Even the familiar gradient out of the town had been shelled, a pair of cottages blazing, the road blocked again with hoses, firemen uncooperative and cursing when she tried to squeeze by. The pointless savagery of this last-minute destruction had shaken everyone's nerve. John got out again and went over to them; she could not hear what he said but saw them laugh and after a mo-

ment they went together to view the blockage, hostility evapo-
rated. Faye smiled to herself: John Castellan was a subtle and determined man, with a variety of methods for getting his way.

The glare and heat of the fire was redoubled by its confinement
in dust-laden air. The ambulance was hot to the touch, and every
now and then reverberated from a closer shell, like a ship striking
green water. For God's sake, she said aloud, how much longer?
She glanced at her watch, astonished to find it was still working.
Five o'clock. Three endless hours since they had woken to clear
sunshine and the pleasure of seeing each other there. The fire engine was moving now, John half turned away, talking; in smoke
and blistering heat the slope of shoulder and spring of back distinct to the eye of love from all others in the world.

He came over, throat and face streaked with sweat and dirt,
"Take it slowly, there's a lot of clutter still." He smiled, eyes on
hers. "The last stretch, my love, and your war will be done, except
for a few more months of pedaling that damned bicycle of yours
up and down hills in a gale."

She laughed shakily. "A cold Channel gale would be welcome
now. You look what old Gabriel would call proper swelked."

"If that means well fried at the edges and melting in the middle, then Gabriel has it exactly." He walked beside her window as
she edged the ambulance over hoses and upended drain covers,
muscles tight, nerves shredded by cries from the back: the hasty
patching which was all that had been possible in the clearing station had not lasted such an unexpected length of journey.

At last they were past, and he eased himself back inside with a
grunt of relief. "That's it then. You know your way from here?"

She nodded; even the thought of Waldershare Park was welcome, with its promise of shade and quiet green spaces. They
broke out of dust and smoke abruptly, and almost at once noise
receded too, as the hills interlocked behind them, the loose rattle
of the ambulance seeming very loud when they had not heard it
at all before.

They did not speak for the rest of the journey, and Faye stayed
half asleep behind the wheel while the injured were unloaded.

She roused when her door opened and John handed her a
steaming mug. "Sweet tea, you'll be surprised to hear."

For once, she was thankful to drink it, sugar and wetness pumping life into her body again. John drove the return journey, while

she sat drowsily watching him, cool air pouring over her face. Birds were singing in the hedgerows, the only other sound the distant hum of a tractor plowing stubble. Pilots must feel like this, Faye thought hazily, mind dislocated afresh by change. One moment fighting for their lives in a hell of noise and terror, the next back on an earth whose very normality must seem monstrous.

John pulled up just short of Dover, set about by its hills and overhung by an immense pall of brick dust, turned to pink frosting by the setting sun. Beyond again was the glitter of the sea, a stain of smoke blotting out the French coast. The guns were silent at last.

"It must be over." Faye could hear disbelief in her voice; it did not seem possible that they were no longer looking down the barrels of German guns.

"Yes, it's over. Back to Canada tomorrow." He was not thinking about guns.

Faye stared at the floor, recollection sweeping into the void where violence had been before, excluding all else. There was no more either could do for the other, peace bringing the parting which war had held at bay so long. As one siege lifted, another clamped tight, leaving them alone and beleaguered in a world without respite.

The streets were almost empty apart from the remorseless work of rescue and fire fighting, but the soldiers shifting rubble were cheerful again, only Dover people glum and silent as they looked at the ruin of their town. When they reached the ambulance depot at last, Mr. Jewell poked his head in at Faye's window. "Have you heard? The Buffs took the guns in the end." He did not even notice a stranger driving one of his ambulances.

"The Buffs? I thought it was the Canadian Army over there?"

"So they are, but it took bloody Kent to wind it all up, didn't it now?" he said with satisfaction.

Faye felt herself smiling, too. Life so seldom had the right endings. "It bloody did." They all laughed, Mr. Jewell, whom she had never seen laugh before, some filthy rescue workers, an old man who kept telling anyone who would listen that his boy was in the Buffs.

John touched her hand. "I'll go and see if my car is still intact."

"Who the hell is that?" demanded Mr. Jewell, lightness forgotten as he realized that one of his ambulances had been in un-skilled hands.

"He came down from London to help," said Faye quietly. "Anne is in hospital, so he crewed with me to Waldershare." She hoped John had not heard; she had become absurdly oversensi-tized to prevarication now she understood how vulnerable he was to that particular hurt.

She left Mr. Jewell gobbling angrily, and waited for John out-side. She did not intend ever to come near an ambulance again.

It was nearly dark and people beginning to straggle out of shel-ters and caves, large-eyed and pasty after days shut away from day-light. A loudspeaker van came rattling down the street, words a crackling blur, then sharply clear as it turned. *"The mayor has re-ceived official information that all long-range guns on the other side of the Channel have been captured."* That was all. It had been Dover's private battle all along, so perhaps it was fitting to end it with the same lack of style as a demand for rates. Everyone in the street paused, an enormous fold set in time; there were no cheers, just thankfulness so profound it could be felt.

Then they moved about their business again.

On the hill above, the ancient shape of the Castle still stood against the sky, flag bright above dust and ruin; from the harbor came the crackle of engines as the MTBs went on patrol. What-ever was destroyed, Dover still held her straits secure.

Chapter Twenty-nine

The car was dented and chipped, but otherwise serviceable, and this time John refused to let her walk the last mile to Reydenham. "Call it my final ordering of your affairs if you like, but I'm taking you to the door. I will be gone before anyone has the chance to set eyes on me."

The finality of his voice petrified her. Great God Almighty, she thought, what is to become of me without you? Before, some shadow of him always remained, a last resort she had scarcely recognized; she had not truly grasped the reality of nothing any more. "Where will you go?" she said eventually, voice jumping.

"Back to Quebec, unless they have finished; Churchill left a while ago. If they have, then Washington, I expect."

She smiled. "You don't seem to have any real fear they will sack you."

"The Treasury needs all the overseas finance experts it has got at the moment. Half the countries of the world are going to be in the hell of an economic mess when this is over, and Britain will be one of them."

He was driving one-handed, fumbling his gears. She could not tell whether he was in pain with his back or feeling as she was, scarcely able to concentrate with loss so close. She changed her position, trying to see him more clearly, unable to resist touching him. "Will you promise to see a doctor before you go?"

She saw the muscles at the corner of his jaw contract. "Don't, Faye. Keep away from me. There is so very little more either of us can bear."

She snatched back her hand, cradling it against her breast as if physically hurt. They did not speak again, and of all her many journeys to Reydenham, this was the one when time and distance slid past like black water down a race.

The manor was shuttered and unwelcoming; Faye was relieved,

John swept with fury that no one watched for her after four such days away. Still neither spoke.

He turned at last, face in shadow. "I cannot hold you, Faye, so I will say it instead. I love you in every way known to man. With any other woman I might perhaps have been able to accept what could be spared for me, will you forgive me if with you I have not the strength to endure it?"

"Oh, my dear—" Faye shook her head, she must not weep. At least she must spare him that. "I could not endure it now, either."

She saw the shadows change, mouth soften into something which was not quite a smile. "We've been so long at war, you and I. Another year will see this one done, perhaps someday we will find our own peace, too."

Faye stared at the sleeping, silent valley. There was no point thinking of it, and for his sake at least, this must truly be the end. "Promise me you'll see a doctor."

"I promise." He was smiling now, and not deceived. "Don't change the subject, Faye. You can always reach me through Castellan's; ask for my father if I'm away, you'd like him if you could meet. In any event, I shall be back there after the war, he's over seventy now and it's time some of the burden was lifted from him."

The affection in his voice told her of a tight-knit family she had never known, and she was seized by panic at what she had done to him. "John, no! I won't have it! You said yourself, this is the end; you must not be bound to offering some bolt-hole of last resort I can never use." She stumbled out of the car and slammed the door.

He could not move fast, and was still by the car when she reached the manor steps. She looked back once, she could not help it. "Goodbye, my love."

She heard the missed gear change at the corner and watched the dimmed glint of his headlights up the valley. Then he was gone.

Chapter Thirty

There were bonfires in Dover and all along the cliffs when Germany finally surrendered the following May, and again in August when the atomic bomb lifted fears of more endless years struggling in jungle against the Japanese. Gabriel got drunk and emptied his shotgun through Colonel Druitt's dining-room window; he said he intended a salute of honor, but was fined ten shillings for breach of the newborn peace just the same. There were celebration sports for the children since no one had any spare rations for a tea, thanksgiving services in the churches, and dances for returning servicemen in the hastily boarded-up Maison Dieu.

But for Dover the day the bombardment stopped remained the end of their war, the rest no more than the natural outcome of it. Reconstruction began even before peace came; the town so destroyed that builders and army clearance units had to be drafted in from outside. That last furious assault of September 1944 had cost more than a hundred killed and seriously wounded, and a further two thousand houses were made uninhabitable on top of all the previous destruction. The King came to Dover in October 1945, as he and Churchill had frequently come during the years under fire, and there was a parade of the defense services which had fought so hard and long for their town: Faye was invited but did not go, memory too raw to contemplate manning ambulances in triumph.

The long wrangle over new building began, each plan seeming worse than the one before. The old Dover they had fought for had vanished, and no one could agree on what to put in its place: so the planners chose for them and the result was a network of roads and car parks and square blocks everyone hated. Like so much of Britain, they had lost their past and found little to attract them in their future.

Yet the essence of Dover remained. Slowly, the harbor was cleared and wrecks dredged from the western entrance. The ferries returned, first in war camouflage with troops on leave, then at last the refitted *Canterbury* opened normal civilian services, sirens blowing, everything which could float flying more flags than for victory. It was a very personal day of rejoicing which no one who had not Dover in their blood could truly appreciate.

Harbor and Heights were crowded, and in the streets people stopped and tilted their heads to the siren, saying as they had before, "That's the *Canterbury*, that is!" Faye stood with Christopher and Rupert on the Prince of Wales pier, remembering the blackened, listing *Canterbury* appearing through the mist as she passed in Beauty on her way to Dunkirk: a year after the end of the war, peace had struck roots at last.

As they made their way back from the pier, she saw Henry leaning on a rail, smoking his pipe, everything about him expressing satisfaction: a sailor contemplating the kind of victory he understood. I would like to carve that, Faye thought, eyes narrowed and considering. A head would not do, somehow there must be . . . she stopped, excitement stirring as imagination struggled with images in her mind, the urge to carve again like lightning out of a clear sky. She had not touched stone since William's panel in the church, the past two years so dreadfully hard she had thought her vision lost, as so much else was lost.

"What on earth are you doing, Faye?" said Rupert irritably. "It's Henry, for heaven's sake, not some gorgon-eyed monster."

She jerked back to awareness of Rupert and Christopher waiting for her, shoulders hunched in a blustering wind. Rough weather, she thought, the look on Henry's face has come from a lifetime of storms, that must show too. She caught them up but could not concentrate on what they were saying, wondering instead whether she would be able to sketch the tilt of Henry's head while it was still fresh in her mind.

"Did you hear what Daddy said, Mummy?"

Christopher was walking backwards in front of her, and she smiled. "No, I'm afraid I didn't."

"He said he's going to start up the Ludlow slip again, and I can learn how to build boats."

"The slip?" she exclaimed, startled. "Why, he can't! There's nothing left after the shelling and two winters of gales." She looked round and saw Rupert on the beach by the pier, pacing.

"He says he will, so he will, won't he, Mummy?"

Oh God, thought Faye, heart sinking, I suppose he will. She did not trust Rupert with money and a point to prove. She could scarcely remember her desolation when the slip was destroyed, it had been so swiftly followed by the immeasurably greater desolation of John, completely gained and as completely lost within twenty-four hours. Rupert had not forgotten though, would never forget the loss of anything which was the Ludlows'; she also suspected him of hankering to show that whatever she had achieved in business, he could do far better.

Rupert swung himself lightly onto the roadway beside them. He had changed very little, the years in the Army had suited him so well. "I must go and see the Harbor Board, we'll need to build at least to the full size of the expanded slip, probably more. With the war-damage compensation and the money for Beauty, we ought to manage it easily."

"There's not much of Beauty's money left," said Faye. "We've paid the last two terms of Christopher's school fees with it, and I used some when he and Nanny stayed in Thanet."

Rupert frowned. "Which was quite unnecessary."

"I wish I'd stayed at Reydenham," said Christopher wistfully. "Billy Dickson says a shell went right through their dairy and all his dad did was to sing to his cows so their milk wouldn't curdle."

"You know perfectly well you were thankful to be out of it," said Faye sharply. Recently, Christopher had begun to say whatever he thought would please his father. She sometimes wondered whether she knew her son any longer, for whom so much was sacrificed: at school two thirds of the year, his mind curled into a tight hedgehog of protective pretenses when he was home.

"These bloody taxes," said Rupert morosely. "Capital levies, surtax, income tax; I don't know why I bother with a boatyard when the socialists only let you keep one shilling out of twenty."

Faye stayed silent. She had voted Labour the year before at a general election which saw a landslide change of power and Churchill ejected from office, but had never said so. No one ever asked me, she thought defiantly, or considered that a Ludlow might be anything but Conservative. Or a Haskell either: her father would have been deeply shocked if he knew she had voted for a party which abolished the extra vote previously enjoyed by scholars of Oxford and Cambridge. Nevertheless, she was ashamed she had never admitted to her vote.

"Do you think it is worth the risk?" she said at last. "If tax is so heavy, wouldn't it be better to keep what we have for Reydenham? So long as we're still rationed there will be plenty of subsidies for farming, and rationing looks like going on forever."

"Bloody socialists," said Rupert again. "They're only happy when everyone is queueing up together for the same miserable shares. You may be content to live like that, but I'm not."

"As the one who spends most of her time in the queues, I'm not either," said Faye lightly. "But I imagine that neither we nor the country can afford more than necessities at the moment, and Reydenham is necessity while a boatyard is not."

"You leave me to mange my own affairs since you aren't able to lift your nose out of the housekeeping purse," snapped Rupert. He resented the way she judged what he did, the core of her he could no longer touch, and assailed the slightest sign of either with quickly flaring rage. "We can't live in a siege forever."

"Oh, can't we?" she said bitterly. "There are some sieges which last a lifetime."

"I think a boatyard would be fun, Daddy," said Christopher.

She lay beside Rupert that night, staring into the dark as she so often did. Loneliness was complete; sometimes it would recede for a while with a touch or a laugh, or Christopher's clear voice calling, but always it was a square about her moving closer again. Tonight she seemed to be physically drowning in it, breath short and hard, body an unjointed puppet under Rupert's handling. She did not know whether he noticed anything amiss: he had seemed satisfied and slept peacefully now, so she supposed it was all right.

She had tried so hard, not feigning gladness when Rupert came home again and thankful to hand over Reydenham's affairs; even when he was away she had never thought of her responsibilities in the valley as more than caretaking. The slip she would have found much harder to give up, however often she told herself she would not mind. So much had happened there, so much effort spent for the achievement she had gained that she knew now it was better destroyed, the break complete.

Rupert shifted beside her and she turned to watch his face in the moonlight: she had even welcomed him to her body. She craved warmth back in her life again, an end to empty nights; cherished the hope he would somehow come to her in her trap and with the love which had once been theirs build something fresh between them.

Yet it had not happened; he had tried too, but trying had not been enough. Whatever she willed, she had less of herself to give and Rupert's efforts were directed towards repossessing everything which was his. Once he was home, it was as if he had never been away so far as Reydenham was concerned and he spilled extravagant care on the valley because there alone he was free from doubt; Christopher he dominated, then felt frustrated because the boy showed no spirit. His wife. He failed to see her giving, because of what she could not give. He wanted everything, and was offended by the self-reliant temper the war had put on her mind. He sensed the flaw of falsehood in her attitude to him, the tough and independent will with which she forced herself into the mold he wanted; it would have been better if he was less perceptive. The mold was his, but nothing else, nor ever could be, since she was not like the ideal he cherished and only came close to it by concealment, the harsh effort of it putting her further from his reach than ever.

In the hall, the clock struck three. I can't stand any more, she thought. Somewhere unknown did John lie sleepless, too? Or did he lie well-contented as she had wanted for him? As she could not bear to want for him.

She slipped from the bed and carried her clothes to the bathroom. There was still pleasure in turning on a light and opening windows wide, blackout ceremonially burned on the victory bonfire. She caught sight of herself in the mirror, crudely overlit, eyes deep in shadowed sockets. A lifetime under siege, she thought, and it is beginning to show. She looked closer and saw a fleck of gray in her hair, then laughed, watching lines smooth, eyes light so they were not shadowed any more. Don't let's make a great drama of it; I'm fed and clothed and live in a place dear to my heart, I'm lucky compared to some. Self-pity was the last and greatest destroyer of them all, and must somehow be kept at bay.

She dressed and went downstairs, John's torch in her hand. The air outside was cool, the faintest opal touch growing in the east, a yawning twitter of birds shredding silence. The generator shed was much as she had left it three years before: a pile of salvaged stone, the greased bundle of her tools in one corner, her feet slipping on chips underfoot. She chose a fallen coping, heart stirring to the feel of it. Yes, she thought, oh yes. The familiar, unfamiliar excitement took her then. She did not hear the household stirring, or notice Christopher beside her, watching.

"You haven't done that for a long time, Mummy."

She looked round, startled. He was standing very quiet and grave, hands in his pockets. Nowadays he was seldom still, fidgeting and running everywhere with unnecessary energy. "It is something I needed to do, suddenly, like that." She tapped her mallet on an empty paraffin drum and they both laughed at the boom of it.

"Yesterday, on the pier, looking at Henry?"

"How did you know?"

"I knew. You looked different then, excited, not upset even when Daddy was unkind."

"Daddy wasn't—" she began, then stopped. She had been alarmed by the mask behind which her son was hiding, she could not force deceit on him. "It was the way Henry looked," she said after a pause. "I can't describe it, I don't know whether I can show it in stone, but I need to try."

He nodded. "Like Uncle William. A laughing rabbit shows more of him than a row of letters saying he crashed in 1941."

"Hullo, there! Aren't we going to get any breakfast this morning?" Rupert came in and kissed her.

"Yes, of course." Faye rubbed stained hands guiltily. Cook had retired on her anger after clearing glass, and was not replaced; Nanny, too, had returned to her cottage muttering that Reydenham needed another baby and only children grew up spoiled. Faye now did all the work of the manor, with occasional help from women of the valley.

"My God, that old generator ought to be in a glass case!" Rupert wandered around it, rubbing his finger over the steel castings of another age.

"The man who fixed it after the shelling said we'd have to replace it next time it broke down. It was leaking paraffin and shorting onto the casing, or something. I suppose they must be very expensive now, though."

"Yes," said Rupert shortly. "And I shan't get sidetracked from the slip by an old generator. You'll have to lay your traps better than that."

"I don't think Mummy meant she wanted another generator," said Christopher clearly.

"Just what do you mean by that?"

He flushed. "Nothing."

"Then I suggest you keep a civil tongue in your head and do something more useful than scuffling your feet in the dust. Find a broom and sweep this place out while your mother gets breakfast."

Christopher went, but as so often when unsettled by Rupert's anger floundered in his confusion. He put out a hand to save himself and dislodged a pile of stacked stone. "I'm sorry," he muttered. "They . . . they weren't any you were carving, were they, Mummy?"

Faye hugged him. "No. We'll have a good clear-out together later." She glanced around. "I hadn't realized what a mess it was in."

"Well, pick them up, for God's sake," said Rupert. "Or do you expect your mother to heave stone like a navvy? You can take them down to the new wall we're building in the kitchen garden."

Christopher looked at Faye uncertainly. "Mummy keeps this stone for carving."

"So that's what you've been doing in the middle of the night." He went over and looked at the piece she had been working on. "What is it?"

Faye had never minded critical fingering of her carving before: roof bosses and fluting followed other men's vision. She found that she detested it now, when fulfillment lay unrealized in her mind. "You'll have to see it when it's finished, if it ever is. I know what I want to do, not yet whether I can do it." She stripped off the sack she had tied around her waist. "I'll go and get breakfast."

"It seems a waste of time to me, when you've more than enough to do running the manor. You can't muck about in here anyway, stone dust will fix the generator for sure." He picked up the slab, grunting with the weight. "I'll put it in the tool shed for you."

"I can't carve there, with people in and out all day," said Faye desperately. The garden was producing vegetables for sale, two men working full-time as well as Gabriel, who was in the tool shed more often than not, resting between one labor and the next.

"In that case, it will do to hold the end of the seed incubator.

For God's sake, Faye, you can't spend your time chipping swirls into old coping stones, when there is so much else to be done! There was some point to it in Canterbury, but this kind of stuff you can't even explain—"

Faye stared at the stone in his hands; perhaps it did look strange, part-shaped and tapped with guidelines. "All right, it doesn't matter." She felt cold and sick, her vision voided, no longer able to remember how Henry looked the day before.

"I'll help you rebuild the wall with all these stones, Daddy," said Christopher.

Chapter Thirty-one

"Good God!" said Rupert, rustling newspaper. "Do you remember that fellow Castellan who came here before the war?"

Faye's face did not change but her whole body tipped sensation into a well of stillness—so still was she that Rupert simply assumed surprise and puzzlement. "You must remember, he was damned rude and pelted off into a gale."

She could not ask, mouth painful with not asking.

He slapped the paper irritably. "Oh, well, it doesn't matter, but he's been appointed to the Court of the Bank of England. I suppose that once the socialists have nationalized everything, we shall get used to being run by third-rate scoundrels who fought their war from behind a Treasury desk."

Her breath caught on roughness in her throat. Her mind had leaped to disaster and she could think of nothing but fear released. When Rupert went out of the room she snatched up the paper and the paragraph stared at her, as if instinct drew her eyes directly to it. *His Majesty has approved the appointment of Mr. John Castellan to the Court of the Bank of England, with effect from 1 June 1946. Mr. Castellan, aged 42, is a partner in the merchant banking firm of J. Castellan & Son, and was attached to the Treasury during the war.*

"Is there anything you need in Dover?" Rupert came back into the room. "I've just about enough petrol for the trip, but it'll be the last this month, so you'd better come if you want much."

"No, thank you," said Faye automatically. There was not enough money to buy anything except necessities. "Rupert, what is the Court of the Bank of England?"

"The same as a board of directors, only grander. Or it was when the Bank of England counted for something more than a socialist rubber stamp. Why so interested all of a sudden?"

Her heart was beating in strange jerks, fingers trembling as she folded the paper in her lap. She wanted very much to tell him exactly why. "I voted Labour, Rupert. I expect Mr. Castellan thought that the Bank still needed to be run as well as possible, whether it was nationalized or not." One truth at least, in place of so much she could not say.

His face darkened. "You did what?"

"I voted Labour. It seemed to me that we all needed a fresh start."

"I hope you are enjoying it. A pack of maniacs passing regulations as fast as they can churn out paper, then snatching every penny we have to pay for their crackbrained schemes."

"No, I'm not enjoying it. I think it was necessary."

"Oh, really?" he said sarcastically. "I'd like to hear what you think was necessary about making general strikes legal, or taking so much tax I can't afford to re-roof old Dickson's barn."

Faye stared at the paper, John's name leaping at her again. She took a deep breath; in the six months since Rupert had come home she could not remember expressing a single opinion of her own. "I can't argue with you. I only know that to me it seemed rather splendid that Britain should choose not to sit tight on her victory, but set out to right old wrongs without stopping to count the cost. We were tired and ruined when the war ended, I was proud we didn't take the excuse to go back to a life which is past. Of course we shall make mistakes; I think it will be worth it."

"If we were ruined before, we are doubly ruined now," said Rupert grimly. "When you are bankrupt, it is not a very sensible reaction to go out and pawn the furniture so you can have another spending spree while no one is looking. One day you have to come back to an empty house."

Faye laughed, she felt freed by having spoken without guard for once. "I knew I would never win an argument with you! I just think it had to be done, pawned furniture or not."

Rupert looked down at her, not unkindly. "It is precisely that kind of reasoning which has landed us in the swamp. It is also why I have to get the slip going again: I don't believe in your way of everyone sharing out the same rotten little ration. We need to earn the extra we want, and I intend to see the Ludlows at least succeed."

Faye saw Christopher hesitating in the doorway, raised voices enough to keep him out of the room. She stood up, hands unconsciously gentle on the paper in her lap. "Come in, sweetheart! Daddy and I have been talking politics and I've been thoroughly trounced! In theory," she added, smiling at Rupert. "In practice, women don't always listen to reason."

Rupert's expression set abruptly. "Then don't think you have the right to fill the boy's head with your stupid fancies! Stop slouching, Chris. What do you want?"

Lowered guard and recent ease combined to tear self-control apart, as bondage snapped tight again. "Leave him alone! Can't he come into the room without fear?"

She saw fury break in Rupert's eyes and for a moment thought he would hit her. Then he turned and went out of the room.

"I only came to tell you a woman is at the door," said Christopher miserably. "She says Daddy offered her a job, cleaning."

Faye rubbed her face, hands trembling. She was failing. She knew she was failing, and could do nothing about it. She ought to go after Rupert and apologize for speaking so sharply in front of Christopher, to attempt yet again to bring softness back into their relationship, but she could not face it. She was making things worse for Christopher, not better, because she lacked the touch to turn intimidation aside without offense. Another woman might be able to do it, her own failure stared her in the face. Spontaneity was lost, laughter carefully watched for fear of the harm it might do, physical pleasure turned to torment because another man held her heart.

She had known she could not cheat her son of his inheritance, but what if John was right after all and the price of wretchedness simply too great to pay? "Tell me, Chris," she said slowly. "You know how hard it is to keep Reydenham these days, with taxes so high. Would it matter terribly to you if we failed?"

He twisted his toe in a worn patch of carpet, pushing an untidy end of hair out of his eyes. He looked defenseless and very young. "I suppose it's in us, isn't it? Ludlows and Reydenham, I mean. We're all so mixed up together, we'd neither be the same apart." He thought a moment and added conscientiously, "I don't mean better or worse, just not the same."

Faye glanced down at her hands, clenched bone-white on the paper. There was no escape. "It's going to be a struggle to keep it. We'll just all have to do our best."

"You mean Daddy is going to lose more money on the slip?" he said disconcertingly.

"No, I don't!" She saw him flinch, and suddenly felt quite exhausted. It was exactly what she feared; how could she keep her son from specious untruth when his world was trapped with it? She stood up. "I'd better come and see this woman about the cleaning. Who is it, do you know?"

He shook his head, but Faye recognized her instantly. It was Susan.

"Good morning, madam. Sorry to disturb you, I'm sure." Her eyes flickered from Faye to Christopher. "Mr. Ludlow said you needed some help here."

"No," said Faye instinctively. "We manage quite well with what we have." She had lived through an agony of suspense when Rupert first came home, but Len had returned from prisoner-of-war camp about the same time, and he and Susan had vanished from the valley. As weeks and then months passed, the threat of Susan had become disarmed in her mind.

Christopher was staring at her, large-eyed. More deceit, she thought bitterly, he knows I'm desperate for help. With only occasional assistance, the manor was enormously difficult to run as Rupert liked it.

"Well, now, isn't that strange? Mr. Ludlow engaged me himself, and told me to come Tuesdays and Thursdays. I shall have to talk to him again, shan't I, if you was to say anything different." Menace was scarcely cloaked.

"Why didn't you say Mr. Ludlow had already engaged you?" said Faye hastily. She needed time, then surely she would think of something. "You . . . you'd better start in the kitchen, I'll come and see you when I've cleared the breakfast."

Her mind remained obstinately blank while she cleared dishes and delayed going to see Susan. She could pay so little and Susan must know it, yet she had come for payment and would not go unsatisfied.

She had also come for pleasure. When Faye entered the kitchen she found her sitting by the range drinking tea, idly polishing a few forks. Nothing else seemed to have been done. "Cup of tea?" she asked casually, staying seated.

"No, thank you," said Faye drily. "The floor needs scrubbing, the silver was done last week."

Susan breathed on a fork and rubbed it on her sleeve. "I don't mind polishing silver. Floors is different, I reckon you're going to have to scrub them, Mrs. Ludlow."

"What are you after?" demanded Faye. "Why did you come here?"

Susan laughed. "Len's walked out on me. We gave it a go, and it didn't work out. I thought I'd come here while I looked around, since the pay would be the best hereabouts."

"How much are you asking?"

"Five bob an hour," she replied promptly. "And a few specials."

It was nearly three times the usual rate. "What do you mean by specials?"

"Well—" She looked Faye over lazily. "I rather like that scarf you're wearing, and I need half a dozen coupons for some stockings."

Faye stared at her incredulously. "Do you seriously expect me to pay you three times what you are worth, and give you my clothes as well?"

"The way I see it, you haven't much choice." She stood up and tumbled silver on the table. "I'll be back Thursday, you can tell me then which it's to be. And don't try saying I've no evidence, 'cos we're not talking about no court of law. Mr. Ludlow's not the kind of gentleman to be understanding about his wife snuggling up behind closed doors when his back's turned, and you know it. If I was you, I'd pay, or get my pal to come and bail me out if I remembered his name."

She paid.

Nothing had changed; she could not leave Christopher behind nor could she take him since Rupert would fight custody, with Susan's malice only one of many reasons why he would win. Refuge with John would simply be another, his career in ruins again as scandal raked up the past against him. He had not said, but however he was privately vindicated later, his divorce must have been a thoroughly unpleasant affair, with dirt enough for the most exacting gossip columnist.

When she could not find sufficient shillings to pay Susan at the end of a month, she would accept less, and then later Faye would find her going through her drawers, or simply miss a blouse or tin of fruit. Rationing was stricter than ever, bread added to the list, quantities of everything pared by half ounces from amounts they had thought justified only by the need for victory. Now victory had come and gone, and gone and gone, and there was no coal, no good-quality cloth, no metal to replace worn-out pans, no leather for shoes, no petrol, no tires, very little paraffin for the generator. Faye did not dare ask Rupert for more housekeeping money since she could not account for what she had, and scraping for every penny, she was unable to buy the few unrationed extras. Rupert was unused to civilian rations and grumbled at endless vegetable pies and stewed rabbit; Christopher said quite frankly that he ate better at school.

"You ought to be getting something from your boy friend," said Susan unsympathetically when Faye had to swallow her pride and plead not to pay in December, since otherwise she would have nothing left for Christmas. "It's a long time ago, I know, but he might be good for a fiver."

Faye laughed, her sense of the ridiculous aroused by her few shillings' housekeeping set in the balance against the Bank of England and Castellan wealth. She wished she could share the joke and laughed again: don't let's be too tragic about it, she told herself firmly. She seemed to have thought that rather often before.

She looked up, smiling. "I'm going to pay you half a crown an hour this month, and that is more than you'd get anywhere else for the poor work you do. You know I can't pay more, and there's no fiver coming in from anywhere." She left the room without waiting for a reply.

Susan stood looking after her, wiping her hands on a towel. "Well . . ." she said aloud. "Well, now, perhaps money isn't everything, after all."

They had quite a good Christmas. The carol singers came again and Christopher joined them, tramping around the valley and coming back flushed and giggling from too much rough cider. Mrs. Ludlow roused from her drowsing on the sofa and gave them all gifts of perished elastic which made even Rupert laugh, and Susan seemed to accept Faye's ultimatum about money.

Nevertheless, Faye felt uneasy, watching the artificial respect of Susan's manner and the greater diligence of her work. She had idled through such tasks as she pleased before and Faye had had to lie to Rupert to hide how little she did, now she realized what an excellent worker Susan could be if she chose, the task of running the manor infinitely lightened. Also, although she looked carefully through her depleted drawers, she could not find anything else missing.

That winter was the hardest in living memory. Week after week of snow and ice, industry gasping to a standstill for lack of fuel, repairs to shattered Dover stopped by arctic gales. At Reydenham they managed better than most, game forced into the open by the harsh weather and with plenty of timber in the woods for warmth even if they all grumbled over the endless chore of sawing.

When spring arrived at last, the Chancellor of the Exchequer struck again with higher taxes.

"The bastard enjoys it," said Rupert savagely. "Just look at the sneer on the swine's face."

Faye stared at Chancellor Dalton's complacent pleasure on the front page of the newspaper, feeling as if her vote made her personally responsible for renewed disaster. "They say they are going to rebuild industry with the American loan, and make the pound convertible again, so perhaps we are past the worst." She had followed the endless negotiations for an American loan during the winter, searching through Dover Public Library for explanations of financial jargon. She had no idea what part the Bank of England played in such dealings, or whether its court had more than ceremonial functions, but felt comfort in even the pretense of contact with John. She had gathered, however, that the Bank had strenuously resisted American demands for the pound to be made convertible against the dollar within a year, but their resistance had at last been swept aside. No convertibility, no loan.

"You may be a good party member, Faye, but for God's sake don't start mouthing claptrap at me. We shan't be past the worst until everyone learns to keep their noses out of other people's concerns." Rupert threw a letter across at her. "No materials at present available for rebuilding such a low-priority item as a boatyard, they say. My solicitor tells me they're just wasting time until the Planning Bill becomes law; then they can say no for good."

"Why?"

"It doesn't fit in with the new plan for Dover to have a boatyard on the seafront. Mum and the kids must be able to sit on the beach without nasty hammers making a noise. I'm not beaten yet, though."

"Can you get a loan from the bank?" She knew his efforts to get the slip started again had been expensive. How life seemed to go in circles.

His eyes narrowed. "They want Reydenham as security."

"They never asked that before!"

He shot back his chair with savage force and went over to stand by the window. "It's a second loan. I had to take one out last year. Every day it's more damned bills coming in. I owe nearly six thousand pounds in tax alone."

Faye was silent. The war-damage money had soaked away in repairs to the manor and estate, in school fees, in fees for advice on building a new slip, a new car at well over list price because they were so scarce. Reydenham was profitable, but tax rates were too high for Rupert to be able to accumulate enough capital to open the slip as well, too high even to maintain the estate properly. "Why don't we take over Ridge Farm ourselves, now it is coming vacant? We'd do better farming our own land than we would with double-taxed rent."

Rupert whirled round. "Just how often do I have to tell you to keep your interfering paws out of my affairs? You may have looked after it awhile, but Reydenham is mine! I'll not mortgage it to any damned bank, and I'll not have you perpetually asking why we don't do this or that!"

"I wanted to help," said Faye quietly. She detested his overbearing manner which worsened with every setback he suffered, yet was too well aware of the humiliation in which it was rooted not to feel sympathy for him. He needed to succeed in all he did, if only to compensate for her success during the war; only she knew that she would have failed too, but for Castellan money.

She was relieved to hear him laughing later, and surprised enough to come up from stacking firewood in the cellar to find its cause. He did not often laugh nowadays. The cellar steps were stone and her soft shoes made no sound: from the entry she saw Rupert with Susan in his arms. His back was turned to her, but Susan saw her at once, and smiled, and drew his face down to hers again.

Faye was so astonished she could not move. If anger had broken first she would have torn them apart with all the force of her own unslaked longing, but it did not. She stood transfixed and then Susan's deliberate defiance drove through consciousness with a single stroke, cleaving thought from mind, will from intent. The sensation was as physical as snapped bone, and wiped out everything except the urge to hide in the dark.

But short of death, life has no ends.

She did not know long she sat on the cellar steps, head on her knees. She heard Christopher calling in the end, and went up and cooked the lunch. He was making a model airplane, so she admired it; Rupert had lost his coat, and she found it for him. Somehow she ate, and sat, and spoke and stood: they did not seem to find her manner strange. Perhaps no one really looked at her any more.

She stood at the window afterwards and saw Rupert striding down the valley road. Dickson's farm lay that way, and Susan, gone before Faye came up from the cellar. Watching him, she was not sure. When he returned, she knew.

He was relaxed and smiling, teasing Christopher instead of finding fault, and when he kissed her the dregs of a different passion rested in his touch. She muttered some excuse and fled to the kitchen, and stood leaning against the wall, forehead on cold tiles. She ought to be angry, she would feel better if thought was stripped clear by rage, instead there was little left but weariness.

She went over to the stove and her hands did all the things they had to do. She heard a voice speaking, and listened, surprised. In silence again, she realized it was her own: she thought back laboriously to discover what she had said, the first fresh stir of will dredging through recollection. She had spoken aloud the reassurance she had used so often: don't make a great drama of it, you know it has happened before. It happens to millions of women every day, if not always before their eyes.

It happens to men, too.

She stared out at the slope of the valley she loved so well, brilliantly green with the heat of another year. She had not been unfaithful with her body, but she had wanted to be; and was unfaithful still with all the strength of mind and heart.

Chapter Thirty-two

She set herself to endure it.

She could not leave, so she must stay: it was as easy and as impossible as that. The trouble was, she had no weapons left to fight for Rupert. If she still loved him she would have used every wile she possessed to win him back; if he had ever truly loved her she would have outfaced Susan and thrown her out of the house. Both paths were blocked: there could be no corruption worse than coldly using herself to entice Rupert when another man held all she had to give, and with scarcely a shadow of affection left between them, the months of blackmail would give further credit to any accusation Susan cared to make. And there was no way to bear the touch of others on her love.

Rupert seemed to notice nothing different in her manner, but sometimes she wondered. He was easier to live with, and Faye thought wryly that Susan probably suited him very well for a while. She loathed the nights when he made love to her still and never slept afterwards, only long familiarity between them somehow making it endurable.

Susan was everywhere. She took pleasure in working wherever Faye was, in asking for instructions and not quite touching Rupert under her eyes. She could not often leave the manor; when she did, Susan followed. Into the garden offering help, up to Mrs. Ludlow's room carrying carefully laid tea trays, eyes sparkling with uncomplicated delight in her triumph.

Everyone said what a splendid worker she was, how lucky Faye had been to find such a treasure.

It was a beautiful summer; day after day of cloudless blue, yet being Reydenham, there was always underlying coolness from the Channel a couple of miles away across the hills. The harvest promised to be the best for years, the valley rich with beasts and crops and contentment. Faye loved to climb the hill behind the manor and sit looking out over the sweep of it, conflict briefly stilled. This remained. This and a thousand villages and valleys like it, this and a million streets like those in Dover. People might talk of crisis, and she read of it every day, but this was solid and showed no crack at all.

She came more and more often to find a measure of peace, to gather strength to face another day: nothing else changed, except that she struggled towards a measure of acceptance.

She was sitting there one evening late in July when she heard the hum of a car change to a direct drone as it took the turn for the valley, saw the flash of sun on a windscreen; Rupert still drove as if the road were as much his as the manor. She watched him vanish from sight into the stable yard, even from so far the snap and snarl of the engine suggested exasperation.

She went down slowly, enjoying the freshness of evening after heat, refusing to think. Rupert pounced on her in the hall. "The answer is no! After all these months!"

"The slip?" She felt a lurch of relief.

"Of course, the slip! They even had the effrontery to offer me another site beyond the western arm."

"You're not going to take it?" The old site was bad enough, some new and probably unsuitable one would be infinitely worse. The tenants at Reydenham were prospering, why must he persist in regarding the slip as some kind of crusade against socialism, when with their finances it made no possible commercial sense?

"No, I'm not," he said shortly. "Why should I? I do things my way or I don't do them at all. Anyway—" He hesitated and for the first time Faye saw a kind of appeal in his eyes. "The swine have won. You've seen the paper today?"

She nodded, mystified. There was a major sterling crisis, and as always, she had followed intently such detail as she understood. According to the conditions of the American loan, the pound had been made convertible into dollars ten days previously, and ever since, as British officials had feared, the remaining strength of sterling was being destroyed by the rush to change pounds into dollars while the chance lasted. If the Americans had hoped to change British policies by exposing sterling to market forces, then they had failed in their intent; if the British thought to evade the consequences of those policies by a loan of comforting size, then they were mistaken, too, for it was already swept away in the flood.

Rupert poured whisky and gulped it thirstily. "Interest rates are going up. I saw the bank manager. He was devilish polite of course, all pinstripe and glasses on the end of his nose, but he wants our overdraft paid off. Any outstanding loan will cost more, too."

"Can we pay it off?"

"No, of course we can't," he said irritably.

She wondered what to say: anything she suggested usually provoked him into doing the opposite, but tonight perhaps was different. "What about the rents? Wouldn't the bank wait until they come in at the end of September?"

"I expect they might, there's not much else they could do in the time. But every penny of rent for the half-year wouldn't cover what we need, and what do we live on meanwhile?"

"For heaven's sake," she said, startled. "However big is this overdraft?"

He shrugged. "About nine thousand. I had to pay another tax bill in July. We owe the hell of a lot elsewhere, too, and God knows how much more tax in January again."

"But—" Nine thousand, it wasn't possible. Reydenham was doing well, and there were tax concessions for agriculture. "Rupert, are you sure it is as much as that?"

"Well, of course I'm sure!" He poured more whisky. "We've had a lot of expenses lately."

He had certainly spent freely after his return from the Army, lavishing the care of love on the valley, anxious to bring it back to pre-war standards of repair. Even so . . . "You'll get higher rent for all the improvements this year," she said after a pause. "Couldn't you negotiate phased repayment with the bank and perhaps ask the tenants to pay quarterly for a year or two?" There was little she did not know about repaying debts.

"Training for the bank yourself, by the sound of it. Shut up, Faye. We can't live with nothing coming in for years."

She bit her lip and went over to the window, mostly to hide confusion at how accidentally close his gibe had come; she was too well used to brusque rejection to feel more than passing anger at rudeness he neither intended nor noticed in himself.

For this time Reydenham itself was threatened, the one great love of his life ruined and lost to the Ludlows forever through his actions. How would he ever survive if it should happen, when his mind and spirit would be castrated by such loss? Surely, it must not, could not happen.

Dinner was a silent meal, made no better by a slow dimming of the lights: Gabriel sometimes forgot to switch the generator on during the day to charge the batteries. "Bloody thing," said Rupert morosely. "We could get them to connect us to the mains if we could pay nine hundred pounds. The valley needs it."

"Rupert, where has all the money gone?" She would offer no more suggestions, but surely he ought to tell her why disaster had come so close. Even Susan could not have helped herself to more than a hundred pounds.

He looked at her in yellow light, and laughed. He seldom drank much, but had been drinking steadily through the meal. "I intended to get all the permits I needed for the slip before the Planning Bill became law, have everything ready to start construction at once." He shrugged. "With no materials to buy without God knows how many licenses and pieces of paper, you must pay for these things. Then there are solicitors and designers: I even had a couple of fellows drawing up plans for a Beauty the Second."

Without a slip to put her on or an order in sight. Her lips framed the words but no sound came. Bribery, too. "Don't you think someone might have wondered a little when all those materials turned up just when you wanted them?"

"They would have accepted it once it was done. Ludlows have been around Dover a long time." Generations of men who had had their way without question were in his tone.

He went out to switch on the generator and she was left staring at the polish of Reydenham dining room. She thought now that they had been very lucky. He might have paid a few minor crooks to obtain materials, the refusal of permission to build was evidence enough that he had done no more than arouse suspicion. With thousands of houses to rebuild and repair in Dover, there would have been no mercy for anyone who tried to bleed off supplies for his own purposes. Rupert had never thought scruple relevant where Reydenham was concerned; success at the slip had become his challenge to a changed world he detested and imperceptibly scruple had been eroded there, too, as success eluded his grasp.

He came in again, his mood strangely changed from despair she had felt in him before. He seemed almost feverish, pacing the same stretch of carpet, steps unsteady with whisky, hands waving as he thought aloud. "Timber to sell. Furniture. Those old pictures. My mother must come downstairs and live in the drawing room."

Faye looked up from the shirt she was mending. "Your mother move down here?"

"We'll use the library. Then we can sell that Chinese furniture out of her room, and some of the stuff from the drawing room. It's meant to be valuable."

Someone else pawning the furniture to pay for a spending spree, thought Faye ruefully. She was relieved to find determination had sparked in him again, but was bewildered by his attitude during the following days, though he seldom spoke; only whisky had loosened his intentions that first night.

Normally a courteous if not a particularly fond son, he overrode his mother's tears with an indifference which amounted to brutality, carrying her downstairs himself when she refused to leave her room. He worked like a man possessed all day, and slept as if stunned at night. He did not often notice Susan any more; when he did, he took her hastily, almost without bothering to hide it. Faye watched him with a kind of horrified pity, no longer hurt since he held no part of her love, and the years of trial had made her more understanding than before. Even if she could, she would not have left him now; it would have seemed like leaving the country in 1940.

The days slid by, breathlessly hot. Harvest was under way by the beginning of August, the valley crinkling with dryness. Christopher came home from school, alarmed and upset when the great beeches along the valley rim began to be felled. "Not the beeches, Daddy! They're as old as Reydenham, the valley will look like Dover after the shelling without them. Please, not the beeches."

Rupert winced. "It won't be all of them. Some need to come down, anyway. I'm going to replant."

"It is all of them! Come and see, they've got crosses on nearly every one!"

Rupert smiled, a secret smile of real pleasure which surprised Faye. "Leave it, Chris. They're taking the worst ones first."

Christopher appealed to her when he was gone, but she could offer no comfort. "We have to find a great deal of money in a short time. It is trees and furniture, or Reydenham itself."

"The valley won't be Reydenham without the beeches," he muttered.

She agreed with him, heart aching as trees came crashing down which had been old when Napoleon was defeated. She changed the subject instead. "Come and see your grandmother, Chris. She's had to lose most of her furniture, after all." She found it hard to forgive Rupert's harshness toward his mother, although now she was out of her room he went every evening to sit beside her in a gesture of apology.

Christopher came, unwillingly. Mrs. Ludlow had aged greatly, and was not an enlivening companion for a boy of nine. "I'm glad Daddy sold that horrid furniture. He can sell all mine, too, if it will save the beeches."

"He'll probably need to," said Faye drily. "Have some pity for others, Chris. Your father loves the valley even more than you do."

Christopher kicked at some books parceled ready for sale. "Jones minor asked me to stay and go airplane spotting with him. Can I go tomorrow? I don't want to stay here and watch."

Faye nodded: Rupert would have to stay and watch.

Yet he seemed more cheerful every day, with a jaunty arrogance she had never seen in him before. The library and their bedroom were left untouched, but he seemed to find pleasure in clearing the rest, or sometimes just piling more and more into the drawing room, as if in recompense for his treatment of his mother. He laughed openly at the spreading national disaster headlined in the papers each day: the pound plunging to destruction, Britain's reserves draining away in an unstoppable hemorrhage, the government pitched out of holiday torpor like a mown anthill. "Bloody socialists," he said with satisfaction. "At least they're ruined as well as us."

"Since they're likely to bring the country down with them, it seems something of a luxury to rejoice in it," said Faye tartly. So many had not died, nor entered with such great hope on peace, for their ancient heritage to be heedlessly brought under the auctioneers' hammer. Reydenham and Britain both: for Reydenham was Britain, and the sickness was here too.

"So it is 'they' now, is it, Faye? Don't forget this is your precious outfit, not mine."

"And don't forget the ruin of Reydenham is your precious effort, not mine!" she flashed, goaded.

He laughed, good humor undisturbed. "In the end, Ludlows don't get beaten. Britain doesn't either. Both will outlast socialists and pawnbrokers alike, you'll see."

She stared at him, disconcerted afresh by this unknown Rupert. She would not have been surprised if he had hit her, yet he seemed more carefree than she had ever known him. He had a long, naturally inexpressive face, only the bright, intolerant blue of his eyes betraying both temper and pride. He was still unlined, hair untouched by gray, his body compact for his years: his step remained light and there was a new eagerness about him she could not place.

She climbed to the beech woods in breathless heat, and could not help thinking that London must be an inferno for scurrying politicians and harassed bankers alike. In the middle of financial crisis the whole Indian subcontinent had been granted its independence almost unnoticed, another door closed on Britain's past, another mighty shift of ground beneath the nation's feet. It seemed threateningly symbolic to see Reydenham's beeches lying on the ground, leaves wilting, to walk among those still standing and hear the chink of axes clear in dead air. She spent a long time examining markings, pausing sometimes over the odd pattern of felling, then sat with her back to an ancient trunk and thought over what she had seen. All the trees were marked, which was not surprising since Rupert had obtained a license to clear fell and replant. Yet they were being felled selectively; what had been done so far would not show in a year or two once the mess was cleared.

She walked home in a thoughtful frame of mind, other incidents she had hardly noticed fitting a pattern she could not grasp, but which was still a pattern. She went to the generator shed and stared at drums of paint stacked there: when she had protested that the valley could wait another year for its buildings to be repainted, Rupert had just laughed and said paint was important. She wandered into the kitchen and stood absently by the table: it was when he went to the generator shed the night he told her of disaster that Rupert's mood had changed. Since then, he had had experts up to look at the generator and electricity men to estimate for bringing in the mains, regardless of the nine hundred pounds it would cost. He had been delighted when Christopher left to stay with Jones minor—not just pleased, but complacent, as if his departure fitted . . . what? On impulse, she went up to Mrs. Ludlow's empty rooms; they were closed and stifling hot. She stared about her, opening cupboards and doors, unsure of what she was looking for, certain now there was something to find. A trapped bee was droning against the glass and she opened the window, coolness touching her face, the first real wind for weeks freshening up-Channel. She leaned out gratefully, a summer storm would be welcome after such long heat.

Mrs. Ludlow's old rooms were part of the original weatherboarded farmhouse, already old when prosperous Ludlows had extended and faced the rest with brick and stone. She looked out over garden and sheds: nothing there. Gabriel was still in the greenhouse, the other men gone home, and as she watched, Rupert drove into the stable yard. He looked up and waved when he saw her, unworried, nothing to hide. Unworried. She thought about him carefully again: he was not hiding worry or refusing to consider disaster, he was no longer worried at all. Yet Reydenham . . . for Reydenham he ought to be beside himself with desperate fear.

He kissed her casually when she went downstairs and she smelled Susan's powder on his hands: he wasn't worrying about that, either. She was suddenly utterly sickened by it all, anger and hurt so long in the past she was surprised by the strength of her own recoil.

It is over, she thought, I have fought and lost. I don't even understand him any longer and now I can't bear him to touch me, ever again. It is over.

"Can I have a drink?" she said aloud, voice cool and steady.

He looked surprised. "We haven't got much."

"You always seem to find some when you want it." She went into the library and he followed reluctantly. She found a drain of whisky in the desk cupboard, divided it meticulously, and handed him a glass.

He grinned. "Neat?"

She nodded. "I need it. Rupert, I can't live with you any longer; I think I've probably been wrong to try for so long."

"You're going? That's impossible, you can't go. You're my wife."

"I thought so, too. Not any longer, though."

"Why?" He seemed genuinely surprised. "We've been married ten years now."

She looked down at her glass. "How many would you say had been happy?"

"Good God, how would I know? I never did know what you were thinking. They have been good enough years to me."

"Have they, Rupert? Why do you need to make love to Susan if you are so well satisfied with me?"

He shrugged; he did not seem particularly interested, in fact he gave the impression of thinking of something else so strongly that he scarcely understood what she was saying. "I wondered whether you knew."

She stared at him, completely nonplussed. "Of course I knew. And all the times you came home on leave with the skills of other women in your touch. I should think wives nearly always do; they may choose not to notice."

Rupert looked away, hands fidgeting over account books on the desk; she would not have known he was listening but for a certain tightness about his head and shoulders.

When he said nothing, she added, "For Christopher's sake, and perhaps a little for yours at the moment, I will stay here if we live apart. I can't go on as your wife any longer." She felt enormous relief and heartbreak, both. Her sentence possibly was not done, yet at least there would be some reprieve for the spirit.

He went over to the window and leaned out, eyes on the weathercock. "A westerly at last, thank God." He turned, face dark against the glare. "Yes, stay. It would look odd if you went now."

She set down her drink, untasted. "Is that all you can say?"

"I think so. We'll talk about it again another time." He laughed with genuine amusement. "Nothing we say today is going to make much odds."

She was prepared for fury or contempt, perhaps for him to blame their failure on her coldness. She never dreamed that he simply would not give any time to thinking about her at all. She had thought he could no longer hurt her, and found she was mistaken: his indifference turned the years of trying and empty longing into a ludicrous farce he had not even noticed.

And Reydenham might still be lost as well.

She lay awake most of the night, alone in a cold bed, and heard

Rupert moving about the house. Perhaps he was more disturbed than she had thought, for usually he was a tranquil sleeper.

The wind rose all night, rattling windows and bringing winter creaks to the old house, trees roaring outside. It did not rain, and the dawn was full of golden dust haze; despite herself, Faye felt her senses rouse under the shock of so much beauty: sheep like blown glass, the countless shading of greens, smoke from a dozen waking fires driven into coiling strangeness up the valley.

She felt rather than heard the explosion, and paused, half dressed. She heard Rupert's door open and called to him, "What do you think that was?"

"Why the hell are you up so early?" He looked surprisingly angry and forgot her room was no longer his to enter when he pleased.

"I couldn't sleep; nor did you from what I heard," she said shortly.

"I—" He cocked his head, listening. "What the devil is going on?" He went out and slammed the door.

Faye finished dressing, hearing nothing above wind in the trees outside. The door had stuck tight, as it always did when slammed, and took a while to open. When she succeeded at last, she was assailed by smoke. Smoke! She paused a moment, heart beating, then heard a sucking crackle followed immediately by much thicker smoke. She ran down the passage, calling, smoke so dense she could not call again. Stop and think. Where was the fire? It seemed everywhere, smoke coiling sluggishly in corners, rolling down passages and stairs. A strange, ripping boom somewhere in the distance, like the one she had heard before, and for the first time, a sense of heat.

No, please, not Reydenham.

She ran back to the stairs, desperate for air and a chance to judge what was happening. Familiar, carved banister rail under her hand; the hall, not quite so full of smoke as upstairs but hot, and crackling with the sound of flames. She hesitated by the front door, remembering civil defense drills: fires should be starved of air. Telephone, too. Rupert had probably rung, but two calls were better than none and Reydenham was six miles and several hills from the nearest fire station.

She shut the library door and lifted the receiver. The line was dead. Her mind cleared abruptly: the fire was somewhere at the back of the house and the wires went out that way. She climbed out of the window and ran round to the stable yard; through the arch she could see the generator shed throwing flames thirty feet into the air, brilliant yellow and exploding with stored paint and paraffin. Gouts of blazing liquid had been hurled at the back of the house and into the trees around, dry weatherboarding well alight, trees shedding puffs of burning foliage on the roof. The heat was enormous and she saw men standing helpless, extinguisher jets falling short of the fire.

Rupert was there, and he noticed her only when she shook his arm. "Have you sent for the fire brigade?"

He stared at her, face streaked with oily smuts, eyes savagely, exultantly blue. "The telephone is dead."

She swung round and ran to the garage, backing the car out in clumsy jerks, thumping a wing on stone as she went. Someone up the valley had probably seen the fire and rung by now, but she must make sure. Dickson's farm was the nearest: they were all out in the yard, staring, Dickson himself piling extinguishers and milking pails into a trailer.

Faye pulled up with a slither. "Have you rung the fire brigade?"

"Haven't you?"

She did not stop to explain about the melted wire, pushing indoors to the telephone she remembered under the stairs, something niggling at the back of her mind as she did so. She lifted the receiver and jiggled the hook, it seemed an endless time before the operator answered. "I'm speaking from Reydenham, there's a fire at the manor here. It's bad, you'll need several engines."

"Reydenham Manor," repeated the operator patiently. "Where is that, please?"

She explained, aching with urgency. "Hurry, please hurry! The whole back of the house is alight!"

"Hop in the trailer," said Dickson gruffly when she came out again. "I'm going down with all the buckets I can find. You, too, Susan lass, they'll need as much help as we can bring."

So Faye found herself sharing the trailer with the woman who had finally split her marriage apart, and did not think of it at all.

Approaching up the lane, the extent of the fire could be seen. The stable block was burning now, and part of the rear wall of the house, flames snapping with paint and driven by the wind.

Dickson left his tractor well away and they ran through the

house; it was obvious that nothing could be done in the great heat outside.

The house was savagely hot too, paneling cracking but not yet alight. They formed a bucket chain and soaked the doors and floors nearest to the fire but their efforts did little good. Once the tank in the roof was empty there was no more water, the supply normally being pumped up once a day; joists were grinding ominously overhead as support from the rear wall was lost, paneling smoking when they heard the first fire bell.

Dickson jerked his head. "Thank God. There's not much more us can do."

"Water." Faye stared at the useless taps. "Where is the nearest water for them? They'll never get near the well." It was alongside the generator shed.

After the long drought ponds and streams were little more than mud. "If they've brought enough pipe, there's the gravity feed up the hill," said Dickson after a pause. "I'll go and show 'em." This was an old dam which fed cattle troughs down the valley.

Faye followed him into the drive; the rear of the manor was burning along its whole length now; if they had not brought enough pipe, there would soon be nothing left to save, fire tenders would never carry sufficient water for such a blaze.

The fire engines spewed gravel as they turned, firemen spilling out and running, water exploding like shellfire from red-hot wood and brick.

Faye suddenly thought of Mrs. Ludlow, blood lurching in alarm. She pushed past figures she could not see in the smoke and stumbled into unexpected blackness in the drawing room, curtains still drawn. The bed. Sheets, an unstrung shape like old rags to the touch. She was heavier than Faye expected, and as much as she could manage to lift outside. She set her down on trampled grass and flopped beside her, head on her knees, utterly spent.

She was roused by ambulance men, and was thankful to find she did not know them. "No, not me. I'm all right." She knelt beside her mother-in-law.

"Don't worry, we'll look after her." The men were brusque but kind, not wanting amateur help and offering a thermos of tea.

She drank thirstily, amusement touching life with normality again. Another crisis soothed with tea.

She went in search of Rupert, and found him standing near the generator shed, watching firemen struggling up the hill with their hoses. Black smoke drove down the length of the valley, the fire now hot and red, the deadly yellow roar of burning paint and paraffin silenced at last. She stood a moment, watching him: he was very still, hands linked behind his back. He was not smiling but his head was cocked in a way she knew, as if he wished he could.

She came up behind him. "You'd better try not to look so pleased."

He swung round, startled, then relaxed, his hand going around her shoulders in the first gesture of spontaneous affection for months. "God, what a mess."

"It would have been worse if the firemen had not been here so quickly."

"They were bloody quick." He did not sound particularly pleased. "It is still the hell of a mess, though."

"What happened?"

"Gabriel started the generator as he always does first thing, and the whole lot went up in flames. The fuel tank caught, and then the paint, those were the explosions you heard. There was nothing anyone could do."

"A pity you stored the paint there," she said drily. "Is Gabriel all right?"

He grinned. "He had his whiskers singed. He'll be stood beer on the story for the rest of his life."

She pulled away from him. She did not know how he had done it, but this fire was his and Gabriel could have been killed.

Reydenham, too. Outbuildings and half the stables were charred and stinking, center section of roof tumbled; the back of the manor a fungoid growth of spilled bricks and folded, blackened timbering, the thickest beams standing out like bones in a rotted corpse. This was Christopher's heritage which she had thought to save for him.

She turned away, nauseated by the ugliness and ruin of it all.

Then turned back, knowing what had teased her mind about the telephone. The wire ran from the house to the stable block, ten paces clear of the generator shed. As the house caught, it would have melted; it should have lasted until it did. Rupert had wanted even more destroyed.

She saw Dickson and thanked him for his help, and asked him

to tell Rupert that she would be on the hill if he should want her.

He nodded. "Aye, 'tis a mortal sad day for us all, Mrs. Rupert, and not something to stay and look upon. You'll be best away and up on the hill."

"From the front you'd hardly know." She stared at untouched brick, only singed creeper and burst glass showed any change.

"You're welcome to stay with us awhile," he said awkwardly.

She thanked him again, and said she did not know what they would do. She could not think any more, instead she climbed the hill and lay staring at wind-driven clouds through fronded grass, the manor hidden from sight below.

Chapter Thirty-three

Rupert came at last and stood watching her, smiling faintly. "What do you propose to do, my wife, with all the facts your busy little mind has been gathering?"

She sat up, feeling chilled and sick. Everything about her smelled of smoke, her mouth as day as ash. "I'd like to go to the police and tell them everything."

"But you won't?" He sat beside her, hands idly sifting grass.

She rubbed at her face; she wanted a bath, food, and to be away. She felt quite unprepared for anything else, whereas Rupert . . . She looked at him closely; he was still intent on his purposes. She wondered suddenly what he would do if she said she would go to the police. "No, I won't," she agreed wearily, at last. "If Gabriel or your mother had been harmed—"

"I brought her down from the back," he interrupted. "I thought you'd worked that out. And the best furniture, saying I was going to sell it."

She was swept with anger. "You had no right to risk Gabriel's life. For that alone, you deserve to go to prison."

"What we deserve and what we get are often two very different things," he said carelessly. "As an insurance company is about to discover."

"You think it was worth it? Reydenham ruined so if you can't have it, no one else will? Not even your son."

"No, of course not, what do you think I am? Chris will have it all right. I'd have liked a little more burned, but the insurance should still be enough to clear our debts." He laughed aloud. "No more beeches felled. The manor isn't Reydenham, you know; it's a part, no more. This way the valley will be saved."

"Ludlows don't run away or become absentee landlords; or so you always told me. Where will Chris live when he inherits what is left, with the house burned and all the insurance used to pay your debts?"

He lay back and closed his eyes, lips still smiling. "He'll live in the manor when he is grown. I'll grant a fourteen-year full repairing lease, rent free, to some fat profiteer anxious to show he's a country gentleman with no expenses spared. And you can let that tender conscience of yours rest, too, for I'm well punished with exile from my home. Justice all round, you see." He opened his eyes. "It was worth it to beat them all for once. You do see the joke, don't you, Faye? The new Planning Act will force any tenant to restore it how it was. Socialist laws will give me my own again."

"How did you do it?" she said slowly. "You seem very sure no one will suspect anything wrong."

"Except you. And you understand me rather too well, don't you, Faye?" He glanced at her swiftly and then away again, the whiff of menace back in his tone. "You know how the generator starts on petrol and switches to paraffin? I loosened the joint below the petrol tank and bent the pipe so it would drip over the exhaust all night. The maintenance fellow I had up the other day will witness there was a gasket blown, he had one on order for me. Shortages again. My God, how I enjoyed making these damned regulations work my way for once. They'll never prove a thing, and the generator is buckled in every direction now."

The pride and lust of possession; this was what it could do to the mind of man. She had long understood the place Reydenham held in Rupert's life, perhaps she ought also to understand the logic of what he had now done: how many through the ages had burned and killed, preferring to destroy rather than see another's hand on what was theirs? She thought then of petrol dripping all night, of Gabriel unsuspectingly switching the engine on, the sheet of flame as the exhaust warmed. A few seconds' delay had sufficed for him to get clear; he could just as easily have stayed to wipe something clean.

She ought not to let Rupert go free.

On the other hand . . . Christopher would be the victim if she told, and all the years of denial go for nothing. Rupert had lost Reydenham for most of his lifetime, and no court could give him a harder sentence.

Justice.

"What will you do once the claim is settled?"

He frowned. "Go somewhere away from civil servants shoveling out paper. Kenya, perhaps. You're leaving too, aren't you? You must see now that it would have looked devilish odd if you had rushed off the night before a fire. I've been waiting days for a wind to do the job for me."

"Yes, I'm going. I suppose the price of my silence is plenty of written evidence about you and Susan." Then there would be no grounds for him to contest her custody of Christopher, and Susan would probably have sufficient hopes of the future to keep quiet while the divorce went through, but it did not sound pretty put like that. She felt much as Reydenham looked from the filth of it all.

He sighed and closed his eyes again. She realized he accepted her silence now he could see a purpose to it: before he had not been sure. She wondered again how safe she had been on this empty hillside above the sheltered peace of Reydenham valley. Men kill as well as burn to keep possessions safe, and in this one thing she could no longer gauge Rupert's mind at all.

Don't look back. Don't let's make a tragedy of it. If her stomach had not been empty she would have vomited with the sludge of betrayal in which she had drifted so long. She knew now exactly how John had felt before.

John.

Rupert was sleeping when she stood up at last: flat on his back, lips smiling. She watched him awhile; without the disconcerting blue of his eyes it was hard to believe this monstrous thing he had done, in which she was now joined by her complicity.

She set off down the hill, Channel air salt on her face.

The firemen still had a hose connected, and she took a bucket of water upstairs with her: it was stale and cold but at least cleaned off the worst of the grime. She packed a case hastily, wanting to be away before Rupert roused; after seven years of rationing and one of Susan's pilfering, she had little left worth taking with her. There was two pounds in the housekeeping and her own checkbook she had kept hidden since paying John back his money; twenty pounds in her account a last reserve she had never touched and now all she possessed. She took the car, too, and smiled to think of Rupert cycling to Dover instead of using all their petrol about his affairs. Yesterday she had known her marriage ended but still felt pity for him; today pity was slaughtered by his callous disregard for Gabriel.

She left their last bottle of brandy at Gabriel's cottage, the old man himself was spending the night in hospital. Then she drove up the winding valley road, rich pasture scenting the air, Dickson lifting his hand as he went to milk his cows. Past Ridge Farm and Stone Cross Farm, past the dip where unarmed soldiers had once planned to trap German tanks in oil; into yellow-tinged coppice shuffling in dry wind, past scarred beech; change down for the corner where Ludlows always stopped to view their valley. She did not stop, and a moment later the valley was gone, in its place the Western Heights and unfolding dip where Dover lay, harbor rattling with cranes and salvage ships, the town patched and rising afresh from its ruins.

She called at the hospital to see Mrs. Ludlow, and found her staring and plucking at the sheets, breath wheezing. "It's the smoke," said a nurse sympathetically. "I daresay she'll be better in a day or two, but she's not too clear in her mind at the moment."

"Just as well." Faye looked down at her, pity stirring afresh. She would never live in her home again, and the less she knew of it all, the better. Faye thought vaguely that she ought to go to Christopher, but could not face it; perhaps he might return to Reydenham eventually, but for a boy his age such a distant future would be unimaginable. After today she knew he was better away, with a chance to grow up as himself and set a balance into the relationship of Ludlows with their valley, but he would not yet see it like that. Also, she could not think what to tell him about his father.

She stayed the night in Canterbury, seeing her father and telephoning Jones minor's parents (whom she never thought of in any other way), asking them to keep Christopher a few days longer and hide the local papers from him. By then, she would surely be able to think and plan again.

She told her father as little as she could, then later walked across the twilight close and into the cathedral. There was scaffolding everywhere, and honey stone brightly spotted where it had been inserted into shrapnel pocks, stained glass growing in the windows as it was sorted out of crates long hidden in Welsh caves. High in Bell Harry tower they were picking out fronds of vaulting with finicking care: repair was not enough, it must be finer than before.

Soon, no one would know how once this space of light and air had stood, surrounded by flame; how at each thinning of smoke hearts had stopped, waiting for it to fall. She touched stone and smiled, thinking of Reydenham. As she left the valley earlier, she had decided never to return; now she could imagine that one day she might go down through trees again, and stop, and see it restored and better than before. As a place of beauty which she loved, and no more: perhaps it would not be quite so hard to tell Christopher now.

She moved slowly around the cathedral's familiar flags; instinct had brought her here, where so much early shaping of her life was done, which she had left in eagerness to be finished with safe havens. Now she was back, much battered by the storm.

She fingered a block of half-dressed stone: she had not held punch or chisel in more than a year. It is what you were surely made to do, John had once said, and pledged her to it instead of interest on his money. She could make a fresh start here, and usually there would be content. No storms, and the joy of captive skills released, thirsting for light and still to fruit.

I love you in every way known to man, he had also said.

Nearly three years since she refused to hold him bound, and for all the bitter weave of past hurts and unslipped bondage which had kept them apart, she did not doubt that he was a man of strong emotions, so strong he had not dared touch her at their parting. If she had lived through a desperate ten years, so too had he, and more besides; she had known then that he ought not to be left to face more strain alone. If she would soon be free, probably he by now was not.

She went out into the cloister, shadow-dark and jumbled with fallen and rotten stone. No repair here yet and the shattered library still to rebuild; it was quiet and very empty, although full of stone. She stared about her: one day her hands would shape and cut in ways which, as yet, she only dimly discerned.

I wonder, she said aloud, and laughed, not thinking of stone at all.

Kent looked very lovely as she drove next day through orchards heavy with fruit, the sky cloudless again. She felt rested and content to travel slowly. Specters of want and crisis stalked through the newspapers, they left no mark here; Rupert might go searching the earth for a life which was gone, but in the end it was here still, roots deeply sunk against its shock of circumstance. She had no sense of urgency; she was coming home after long voyaging, or too much time had been counted against her to make it possible. There was nothing more she could do about it.

She had never driven in London before and drew up by a telephone box near the Elephant and Castle, solid heat thrown in her face when she got out of the car.

"Castellan's," a girl's voice answered her ring, and she wondered whether it was the same one.

"Is Mr. Joseph Castellan there?" Usually she disliked ringing strangers, this time she did not even think about it. It would be ironic, though, if this once Joseph was not there.

"Who is calling, please?"

She gave her name and added: "He doesn't know me and may not want to be disturbed, but Mr. John Castellan asked me to ring his father if he was out." News vendors were shouting outside, their placards scored with black crisis lines: another hundred million pounds of Britain's reserves had vanished in a week; if the Americans insisted on the pound staying convertible, soon there would be nothing left. It was a fair guess that a director of the Bank of England would not be in his own office today.

She put a handful of pennies in the slot, and waited.

His voice was a surprise when it came: a young man's voice, lifting slightly at the end of his words as if in salute to a huckstering past. "Mrs. Ludlow? Joseph Castellan here, what made you think I might not be willing to speak to you? If you are who I think you are, then I am delighted to hear from you."

She laughed involuntarily. You would like my father, John had said. "I think I might be. Could I possibly see you away from the office? I won't keep you long."

"Where are you now?"

"In a phone box near the Elephant and Castle. I didn't mean this instant," she added hastily. "I expect you're busy. I could come to the City this evening."

"I think we might improve on the Elephant and Castle. Would you be able to meet me in an hour at the Voyagers' Club in Hanover Square? It is going bankrupt and was prosecuted for serving goat meat a month ago, so we should be undisturbed." A somewhat different reception from the one the Ludlows had given her, she reflected as she replaced the receiver, remembering the icy cross-questioning she had faced the first time Rupert took her to Reydenham.

She recognized him the moment he came through the door, although physically he was not very like John, his white hair thick above the sculptured bones of an Old Testament prophet. He was taller than his son, too; wide shoulders and vigorous carriage telling of past strength. Rather it was the swift judgment she recognized, the sense of force well held within himself. Kindness, too. In the years without John, there had been no one else who instinctively thought of her needs first.

He took her hand. "You did well to get in here at all. I forgot to tell you that they grudge entry to the ladies and only let them in by the cellar steps. I apologize for asking you to such a burial chamber of a place." He glanced around. "They must have cooked the cats, too, since I was last here. What would you like to do? Risk something to eat, or stay with adulterated gin and pickled onions in the bar?"

"I don't want anything," said Faye awkwardly. "At least—"

He smiled. "A meal, I think, and talk later. We shall do better together when we are at least slightly acquainted. Stay here a minute while I go and threaten the chef."

Faye had expected that he would demand some explanation from her for hauling him out of his office in the middle of what must be a very trying day for bankers; instead, he encouraged her to talk about anything except herself, made her laugh with his caustic comments, and showed no sign of haste at all. It was obvious that John had mentioned her in some way, probably when he was frequently out of the country at the end of the war, yet he would not have said much. However close they were, she could not visualize men like the Castellans discussing their intimate affairs for entertainment.

"I think you required some assistance from me," he remarked eventually. "I shall be happy to serve you in any way I can."

She stared at him, and then smiled. "Tell me, Mr. Castellan, do you usually take complete strangers out to lunch when they ring you at inconvenient times in the office?"

He laughed. "When I have high hopes of them, yes."

She wondered where to begin, urgency driving again now, with her love across the table in the set of his head and shape of his hands. If John was not free, she must go and he must never know she had come.

"Would it be easier if I told you that my son loves you still, and has waited very long for you?" he said gently. "I am deeply thankful you have come."

There was no joy like it, neither shock nor surprise, instead each nerve alight with happiness, each lack assuaged. "I love him, too," she said simply. "I could not come before."

Two hours later she was installed in a hotel overlooking the Thames. She looked at her watch and calculated carefully: this time yesterday she had been sitting beside Mrs. Ludlow in hospital. Joseph had left her, promising to send John when he emerged from crisis talks at the Bank, in which she gathered he had been enmeshed on and off for much of the summer. She looked around at painted paneling and expensive furniture, reflecting wryly that she would have to become used to being well organized by the Castellans. She had been certain before, now she was touched by unexpected panic: she had come yet again to a different life and this time to a man she had not seen in three years. To a man who had not seen her in three years, when she knew herself very much changed.

John would have altered, too. Joseph was both fond and proud of his son, he was also sufficiently anxious about him to be profoundly relieved by her arrival.

Yet she and John had been driven together by pressures beyond their control, there was no way of telling whether their balance was exact enough to hold of its own strength: and if it was not, then each had the power to hurt the other beyond bearing.

When he came into the room, she saw at once that her fears had been shadows.

He stayed by the door, hands on the wood behind. She had stood at his step, heart pounding, and they stared at each other across sunlight streaming through open windows. "My love, you came." His voice was thick.

"Your father told you why?"

He nodded. "More or less. I expect there is more to it, which only you and I would understand."

She was silent, the tide of happiness lapping through chinked armor. She had told Joseph as little as she could, as John had done to smooth her way if she needed help. It had been enough, the rest they alone understood. "I'm not free yet," she said baldly, at last.

"No." Still, he had not moved.

One more thing remained to be said, which her lips could not easily frame even if she no longer believed it necessary. Yet it must be said. "John, I—" She broke off, wishing he would help her a little. Then she stiffened; if it must be done, let it be done simply and without shuffling. "I nearly didn't come. Minds and bodies change in three years, and I more than most perhaps. I did not know what we might have together any more."

"Why do you think I am waiting here, except this must not be forced?" He was different; mouth tight where it had softened always for her, lined face thrown into harshness by the merciless sun. "I nearly did not come either. I found I disliked facing you with myself, and feared our chance had come too late."

Her lips curved. "And has it?"

He shifted suddenly, uncontrollably, and looked away. "Not for me, when you look at me like that. When I loved you it was for always. I told you before."

She realized then that he would not make the first move, and understood, too, why Joseph was anxious about his son. John had held himself free for her, but the burden of it showed very clearly: as a man of position who could not afford gossip, he had undoubtedly been forced by stress and loneliness into the kind of dealings with women he most detested in himself. He had come to her before, this time only she could cross the final gulf between them.

She went over and laid her hands on his shoulders. "No further alone, my love. It is surely not too late for us."

He moved at last and held her, lightly still, tripped pulses beating in his touch. "My dear . . . my dear . . . your last chance. I shall not ask again. You are sure?"

"I am sure." Words soft in a dry throat, then no more need for words at all.

Much later, laughter returned and smaller pleasures they had never known. Time running for them instead of inexorably against; thought flicking unrestrained to a future they must still wait for, yet a future together at last; the long relief of overstretched guard relaxed and speaking the first nonsense which came to mind.

"Convertibility ended; personal and national all in one day," observed John once, and kissed her on the promise in his tone. "I think I'm going to find it hard to regard the sterling crisis with due seriousness tomorrow."

She laughed. There was no lack of constancy in him for her to fear, and great need for love to bring its gifts of lightness and grace into their lives again. "You look the part of crisis well enough. The battalions of the pound sterling marching out to war." He had come straight from some emergency meeting; black jacket and stiff collar stiflingly unsuitable in oppressive heat. Unsuitable too, for holding a woman curled on your knees.

"Beaten battalions of the pound sterling, I'm afraid," he said ruefully. "These past weeks have been an expensive way of proving that nowadays our commitments far outweigh any resources we may scrape up. As if we did not know it already." He laughed, tense lines easing as she watched. "It's lucky that love has no dealings with such foolishness, since I am committed so far beyond measure there is no reckoning it at all."

"Dear heart, who cares for reckoning now?" And as they kissed, she thought how much there was no one could ever reckon.

The flames of Reydenham, which also burned their prison down; the long and bitter war they both had fought and sometimes lost, which was now so unexpectedly won; her vision of stone changed by her skills set against certainty there was no other way ahead but, for them both, together. The crisis panic of the moment when put in the balance of sunlit Kentish fields, the settled contentment of a people who had lived very long in peace together.

No storm lasts forever, and afterward comes the harvest.